EVERYMAN, *I will go with thee,*

and be thy guide,

In thy most need to go by thy side

American Short Stories
of the
Nineteenth Century

INTRODUCTION BY
JOHN COURNOS

DENT: LONDON
EVERYMAN'S LIBRARY
DUTTON: NEW YORK

NO. 840

INTRODUCTION

NOWHERE, with the possible exception of France and Russia, has the art of the short story flourished more abundantly than in the United States. Qualitatively and quantitatively, the shorter forms of fiction have, during the nineteenth century, shown such exuberant development that even if other literary forms were to be left out of the reckoning, this country would still have a place on the map scarcely to be ignored by students of literary geography. A glance at the crowded map presents an astonishing number of distinguished names: Washington Irving, Nathaniel Hawthorne, Edgar Allan Poe, Herman Melville, Fitz-James O'Brien, Thomas Bailey Aldrich, Bret Harte, Henry James, Mark Twain, William Dean Howells, Sarah Orne Jewett, Frank Stockton, Ambrose Bierce, Mary E. Wilkins, Kate Chopin, Richard Harding Davis, Stephen Crane, Jack London, and last but not least, O. Henry. Still more numerous are the names inscribed in smaller letters, and by no means to be ignored. Many a "minor" artist pleads for remembrance in that he or she has written one or two stories worthy of the name of "masterpiece." Altogether, the cumulation and the variety offered are prodigious; moreover, the achievement has enjoyed a continuity and may, therefore, with justification, demand the attention of the historian. Many histories and handbooks have indeed been written; and the American short story has not been without its influence on the literature of other lands. Writers of such diverse gifts as Poe and O. Henry have countless admirers abroad; the author of "The Murders in the Rue Morgue" has left his mark on French literature, the author of "The Four Million" is read almost as widely in Russia as he is in his native country.

Various theories have been advanced to explain this pre-eminence of the American short story; the most interesting of these by the writers themselves. It has been vaguely asserted that the American temperament, evolved out of a preoccupation with concrete, practical matters, and a tendency to rush and hurry, demands its literature terse and to the point.

An analysis of the main components should prove of some value in determining the most decisive factor in shaping the American short story.

There is, first of all, humour. Humour in itself is not a quality peculiar to any nation; and while American humour undoubtedly has a quality of its own and therefore a factor not to be ignored it can scarcely be said to be the whole factor. The anecdotal factor may be even more cursorily dismissed, and on the same grounds. The use of dialect, i.e. the localisation of the American scene, must be considered, but no more than any component which does not affect the basic mood and structure of a tale told well. We get nearer to the secret when we examine the democratic element, which, incidentally, embraces the nature of humour, of the anecdote, and of the forms of speech. We get nearer to it still in the matter of precision, when we scrutinise the journalese factor, of which the author of "The Luck of Roaring Camp" so glowingly speaks. The whole secret is here, and everything else is secondary. From the beginning a great democratic community, America has found her voice in the periodicals and the public press; and it is to these that, with the exceptions which prove the rule, the whole development of the American short story may be traced. Implications follow, interesting alike to the literary student and the student of social and political economy. Indeed, a whole book may be written on the subject of the American short story and economics, and fascinating reading it would make. Mr. Fred Lewis Pattee, Professor of American Literature in the Pennsylvania State College, has already, if vaguely, touched upon it in his "Development of the American Short Story"; but he is far too interested in the critical aspect of things to grasp more fully the significance of the dominant tendency. One thing, however, is made clear: in a democracy the people dictate the sort of literature they will have. In no other country has the law of supply and demand affected the literary art as it has in the United States. No stricture on the law is implied; it must be admitted that in the nineteenth century it has produced some admirable results, though latterly its effect has been to foster, in the widespread magazine press, an inferior product which has come to be known as the "formula story," a story written according to one and the same design, optimistic in character, with the ending inevitably happy at all costs.

Three great writers of the short story stand out, unaffected by economics. They are Hawthorne, Melville, and Henry James. Hawthorne's recognition came late, Melville's posthumously, and James during most of his life remained a writers' writer. It was the more sensational element in "The Scarlet Letter" which first gave Hawthorne his public; Melville's dæmonism and metaphysics could not appeal to a democratic public at any time; as for James, he had his private income, and he had no need to make a plea for public support; he went on writing about sophisticated people for sophisticated people, and to this day his public is limited. These three men alone, among the great American fiction writers, wrote what they wanted and how they wanted. To these might be added some lesser figures like Mary E. Wilkins, Sarah Orne Jewett, etc. The form of the others was more or less dictated by public conditions and private circumstances in which the authors found themselves placed. And, oddly enough, in many instances the results have been extremely felicitous. It would be ungrateful of us to cavil at what these authors might have done in circumstances unaffected by the law of supply and demand. For we come upon what appears like a contradiction here: the law would seem to have made good writers as well as poor ones, who would have been poor in any case. It has done more than that: it has created the shorter form by forcing writers to adopt it in preference to the longer.

What Poe might have done had he received the anticipated fortune from his foster-father, Mr. Allan, is altogether problematical. He was, indeed, destined for quite another career than that of literature. But when the blow fell, only one outlet for his talents remained, and he became a writer. His difficulties arose in that for him literature was poetry, and poetry "not a pursuit, but a passion." His poetry could scarcely provide a living, and there was a market for prose; which meant that one must write for the annuals and the ladies' books so popular in his day. Short pieces were in demand, and so Poe wrote short pieces. To that extent, the influence was good, since it made a short story writer of Poe and left us some superb tales to read and treasure. But Poe's own misfortune was that he did not, or could not, comply with the particular demands made by his country and his time. A great publishing firm of his day refused to publish his tales unless he would "lower himself a little to the ordinary comprehension of the generality." It has been plausibly asserted that Poe's satires came out of his bitterness, due to his failure to market his work. Hard is the lot of the man who refused to bow to Demos where Demos rules.

A luckier fate awaited Fitz-James O'Brien, "soldier of fortune and literary adventurer," whose name has been often coupled with Poe's in that in his short stories he had shown the ability to make "copy" of new discoveries and scientific theories. "The two men," says Mr. Pattee, "undoubtedly were alike in one thing: both wrote tales with journalistic intent." But a lighter touch, the touch so vociferously demanded by editors of American periodicals had won the day for the author of "The Diamond Lens." With a product less perfect, he had more "efficiently" than Poe responded to the wants of the periodicals and the public who read them; but he had not even then all the necessary ingredients. If his manner had a measure of rightness, his materials were not all what they should be. Bret Harte was among the first to supply the lack and to answer the demand of the American public in a way it had not been answered before. The publication of "The Luck of Roaring Camp" in the new California magazine, *The Overland Monthly*, in 1868, provided a real national sensation. The fact to be noted is that the author of the story was the editor of the magazine; in short, a journalist; moreover, a journalist who had worked up through all the departments to the editor's chair. Demos was pleased and heaped rewards on his head. Not that his good fortune was not justified. Within limitations, Bret Harte enriched the art of the short story, and in many examples of his craft attained admirable levels.

An even greater success was achieved by Thomas Bailey Aldrich when his wellnigh flawless short story, "Marjorie Daw," appeared in the *Atlantic Monthly* in 1873; but the effect of his success (economical as well as artistic) was to awaken an ambition to write a long novel. His longer pieces never quite reached the perfection of his short stories. This only shows that successful economics may work both ways: a man who has made money may do what he pleases, and what he pleases to do may not be as good as circumstances dictated him to do. One need only add that Aldrich, like Bret Harte, was an editor.

But even practised journalists may not deviate from the formula, flexible up to a point, of a short story required by the law of supply and demand; as Ambrose Bierce—"Bitter Bierce" he was called in his native San Francisco—found to his sorrow. He was what is commonly known in the United States as a "columnist," and edited a column called "Prattle" in the *Examiner*, of which a contemporary said that it was "the most wickedly clever, the most audaciously personal, and the most eagerly devoured column of causerie that probably ever was printed in this country." Attracted to the short story form, he achieved his first success in England with some satiric fables collected under the title of "Cobwebs From an Empty Skull," but when later in San Francisco he wrote some magnificent, if gruesome tales, magazines and publishers alike would have none of them.

In spite of all exceptions, such as Hawthorne, James, Melville, Mary E. Wilkins, who wrote "masterpieces" without regard to the immediate demands of the public; or such wayward authors as Poe and Bierce, rejected because they were too individual to please the many; merit, and often high merit, was not to be denied to the successful men, the entertainers of the vast public. Nevertheless, time has worked its revenges; and the American short story, which has arisen from journalism and economics threatens to end in journalism and economics. That is to say, the writing of short stories has become such a profitable affair that the market is being glutted with an article so palpably journalese that the question of artistic merit does not even enter into it. Signs of this were not wanting even a generation ago. A novelist of merit like Frank Norris could assert in 1902 that the writer of fiction must be like the writer of news for the daily paper, in closest touch with the great democratic mass called "the American people." He should, with closest precision, study what the people want, for "in the last analysis the people are always right." Jack London, who in 1900 and 1901 had come to the fore with such strong tales as "The Son of the Wolf" and "The God of His Fathers," could at the beginning of his career give voice to the demands of his time in these words:

Make it concrete, to the point, with snap and go and life, crisp and crackling and interesting. . . . Be terse in style, vigorous of phrase, apt, concretely apt, in similitude. Avoid platitudes and common-places. Get the atmosphere, the colour, strong colour, lots of it. . . . Seize upon things salient, eliminate the rest and you have the pictures. Paint those pictures in words. Then put a snapper at the end, so if they are crowded for space they can cut off your contents anywhere, re-attach the snapper, and the story will still retain form.

The last sentence, in particular, deserves to be read carefully. What would Maupassant have thought of it? Or Chekhov? Did not the latter, too, write for a great democratic people, democratic in spite of the Tsar? Yet Jack London came near being a great writer, honoured abroad as well as at home; but evidence appears to exist of a confession made by him to the effect that if he had had his freedom—freedom, we suppose, from the mob, the press, economics—he would have written quite differently. The reader may draw his own conclusion.

American journalists who, in their different ways, were also fine short story writers include such names as Stephen Crane, Richard Harding Davis, and O. Henry. The last-named contri-buted his short stories to the Sunday edition of a New York newspaper; these stories are as good as anything which is journalistic can be, yet retain a good measure of authentic narrative art. The ingredients will not always bear looking into; but the stories are nearly always amusing, which, after all, was the chief intent of the author.

This volume is not only a collection of American short stories. It is also, by its deliberate sequence, a history of the development of the short story in the United States. I wish to express especial indebtedness to Mr. Edward J. O'Brien and Mr. R. N. Linscott, to whose co-operation this volume owes not a little of its representative quality.

JOHN COURNOS.

CONTENTS

PETER RUGG, THE MISSING MAN[1]

By WILLIAM AUSTIN (1778–1841)

From Jonathan Dunwell of New York to
Mr. Herman Krauff

SIR,—Agreeably to my promise, I now relate to you all the particulars of the lost man and child which I have been able to collect. It is entirely owing to the humane interest you seemed to take in the report, that I have pursued the inquiry to the following result.

You may remember that business called me to Boston in the summer of 1820. I sailed in the packet to Providence, and when I arrived there I learned that every seat in the stage was engaged. I was thus obliged either to wait a few hours or accept a seat with the driver, who civilly offered me that accommodation. Accordingly, I took my seat by his side, and soon found him intelligent and communicative. When we had travelled about ten miles, the horses suddenly threw their ears on their necks, as flat as a hare's. Said the driver, "Have you a surtout with you?"

"No," said I; "why do you ask?"

"You will want one soon," said he. "Do you observe the ears of all the horses?"

"Yes; and was just about to ask the reason."

---

[1] "The tale was first printed in Buckingham's *New England Galaxy*, 10 Sept., 1824. . . . The original story purports to belong to the year 1820, and the scene of a later continuation is laid in the year 1825, both these being reprinted in *The Boston Book* for 1841."—Thomas Wentworth Higginson, "A Precursor of Hawthorne," in *The Independent*, 29 March, 1888. Republished in *The Literary Papers of William Austin* (Little, Brown & Co., 1890), edited by James Walker Austin; and as a separate volume (John W. Luce & Co., 1910), with an introduction by Thomas Wentworth Higginson.

"They see the storm-breeder, and we shall see him soon."

At this moment there was not a cloud visible in the firmament. Soon after, a small speck appeared in the road.

"There," said my companion, "comes the storm-breeder. He always leaves a Scotch mist behind him. By many a wet jacket do I remember him. I suppose the poor fellow suffers much himself—much more than is known to the world."

Presently a man with a child beside him, with a large black horse, and a weather-beaten chair, once built for a chaise-body, passed in great haste, apparently at the rate of twelve miles an hour. He seemed to grasp the reins of his horse with firmness, and appeared to anticipate his speed. He seemed dejected, and looked anxiously at the passengers, particularly at the stage-driver and myself. In a moment after he passed us, the horses' ears were up, and bent themselves forward so that they nearly met.

"Who is that man?" said I; "he seems in great trouble."

"Nobody knows who he is, but his person and the child are familiar to me. I have met him more than a hundred times, and have been so often asked the way to Boston by that man, even when he was travelling directly from that town, that of late I have refused any communication with him; and that is the reason he gave me such a fixed look."

"But does he never stop anywhere?"

"I have never known him to stop anywhere longer than to inquire the way to Boston; and let him be where he may, he will tell you he cannot stay a moment, for he must reach Boston that night."

We were now ascending a high hill in Walpole; and as we had a fair view of the heavens, I was rather disposed to jeer the driver for thinking of his surtout, as not a cloud as big as a marble could be discerned.

"Do you look," said he, "in the direction whence the man came; that is the place to look. The storm never meets him; it follows him."

We presently approached another hill; and when at the height, the driver pointed out in an eastern direction a little black speck about as big as a hat. "There," said he, "is the seed-storm. We may possibly reach Polley's before it reaches us, but the wanderer and his child will go to Providence through rain, thunder, and lightning."

And now the horses, as though taught by instinct, hastened with increased speed. The little black cloud came on rolling over the turnpike, and doubled and trebled itself in all directions. The appearance of this cloud attracted the notice of all the passengers, for after it had spread itself to a great bulk it suddenly became more limited in circumference, grew more compact, dark, and consolidated. And now the successive flashes of chain lightning caused the whole cloud to appear like a sort of irregular network, and displayed a thousand fantastic images. The driver bespoke my attention to a remarkable configuration in the cloud. He said every flash of lightning near its centre discovered to him, distinctly, the form of a man sitting in an open carriage drawn by a black horse. But in truth I saw no such thing; the man's fancy was doubtless at fault. It is a very common thing for the imagination to paint for the senses, both in the visible and invisible world.

In the meantime the distant thunder gave notice of a shower at hand; and just as we reached Polley's tavern the rain poured down in torrents. It was soon over, the cloud passing in the direction of the turnpike toward Providence. In a few moments after, a respectable-looking man in a chaise stopped at the door. The man and child in the chair having excited some little sympathy among the passengers, the gentleman was asked if he had observed them. He said he had met them; that the man seemed bewildered, and inquired the way to Boston; that he was driving at great speed, as though he expected to outstrip the tempest; that the moment he had passed him, a thunderclap broke directly over the man's head, and seemed to envelop both man and child, horse and carriage. "I stopped," said the gentleman, "supposing the lightning had struck him; but the horse only seemed to loom up and increase his speed; and as well as I could judge, he travelled just as fast as the thunder-cloud."

While this man was speaking, a pedlar with a cart of tin merchandise came up, all dripping; and on being questioned, he said he had met that man and carriage, within a fortnight, in four different states; that at each time he had inquired the way to Boston; and that a thunder-shower like the present had each time deluged his wagon and his wares, setting his tin pots, etc. afloat, so that he had determined to get a marine insurance for the future. But that which excited his surprise most was the strange conduct of his horse, for long before he could distinguish the man in the chair his own horse stood still in the road, and flung back his ears. "In short," said the pedlar, "I wish never to see that man and horse again; they do not look to me as though they belonged to this world."

This was all I could learn at that time; and the occurrence soon after would have become with me "like one of those things which had never happened," had I not, as I stood recently on the door-step of Bennett's hotel in Hartford, heard a man say, "There goes Peter Rugg and his child! He looks wet and weary, and farther from Boston than ever." I was satisfied it was the same man I had seen more than three years before; for whoever has once seen Peter Rugg can never after be deceived as to his identity.

"Peter Rugg!" said I; "and who is Peter Rugg?"

"That," said the stranger, "is more than anyone can tell exactly. He is a famous traveller, held in light esteem by all innholders, for he never stops to eat, drink, or sleep. I wonder why the government does not employ him to carry the mail."

"Ay," said a bystander, "that is a thought bright only on one side; how long would it take in that case to send a letter to Boston? for Peter has already, to my knowledge, been more than twenty years travelling to that place."

"But," said I, "does the man never stop anywhere; does he never converse with anyone? I saw the same man more than three years since, near Providence, and I heard a strange story about him. Pray, sir, give me some account of this man."

"Sir," said the stranger, "those who know the most respecting that man say the least. I have heard it asserted that Heaven sometimes sets a mark on a man, either for judgment or a trial. Under which Peter Rugg now labours, I cannot say; therefore I am rather inclined to pity than to judge."

"You speak like a humane man," said I; "and if you have known him so long, I pray you will give me some account of him. Has his appearance much altered in that time?"

"Why, yes. He looks as though he never ate, drank, or slept; and his child looks older than himself, and he looks like time broken off from eternity, and anxious to gain a resting-place."

"And how does his horse look?" said I.

"As for his horse, he looks fatter and gayer, and shows more animation and courage than he did twenty years ago. The last time Rugg spoke to me he inquired how far it was to Boston. I told him just one hundred miles.

"'Why,' said he, 'how can you deceive me so? It is cruel to mislead a traveller. I have lost my way; pray direct me the nearest way to Boston.'

"I repeated, it was one hundred miles.

"'How can you say so?' said he; 'I was told last evening it was but fifty, and I have travelled all night.'

"'But,' said I, 'you are now travelling from Boston. You must turn back.'

"'Alas,' said he, 'it is all turn back! Boston shifts with the wind, and plays all around the compass. One man tells me it is to the east, another to the west; and the guide-posts too, they all point the wrong way.'

"'But will you not stop and rest?' said I; 'you seem wet and weary.'

"'Yes,' said he, 'it has been foul weather since I left home.'

"'Stop, then, and refresh yourself.'

"'I must not stop; I must reach home to-night, if possible: though I think you must be mistaken in the distance to Boston.'

"He then gave the reins to his horse, which he restrained with difficulty, and disappeared in a moment. A few days afterward I met the man a little this side of Claremont, winding around the hills in Unity, at the rate, I believe, of twelve miles an hour."

"Is Peter Rugg his real name, or has he accidentally gained that name?"

"I know not, but presume he will not deny his name; you can ask him—for see, he has turned his horse, and is passing this way."

In a moment a dark-coloured, high-spirited horse approached, and would have passed without stopping, but I had resolved to speak to Peter Rugg, or whoever the man might be. Accordingly I stepped into the street; and as the horse approached, I made a feint of stopping him. The man immediately reined in his horse. "Sir," said I, "may I be so bold as to inquire if you are not Mr. Rugg? for I think I have seen you before."

"My name is Peter Rugg," said he. "I have unfortunately lost my way; I am wet and weary, and will take it kindly of you to direct me to Boston."

"You live in Boston, do you; and in what street?"

"In Middle Street."

"When did you leave Boston?"

"I cannot tell precisely; it seems a considerable time."

"But how did you and your child become so wet? It has not rained here to-day."

"It has just rained a heavy shower up the river. But I shall not reach Boston to-night if I tarry. Would you advise me to take the old road or the turnpike?"

"Why, the old road is one hundred and seventeen miles, and the turnpike is ninety-seven."

"How can you say so? You impose on me; it is

wrong to trifle with a traveller; you know it is but forty miles from Newburyport to Boston."

"But this is not Newburyport; this is Hartford."

"Do not deceive me, sir.   Is not this town Newburyport, and the river that I have been following the Merrimack?"

"No, sir; this is Hartford, and the river, the Connecticut."

He wrung his hands and looked incredulous.   "Have the rivers, too, changed their courses, as the cities have changed places?   But see! the clouds are gathering in the south, and we shall have a rainy night.   Ah, that fatal oath!"

He would tarry no longer; his impatient horse leaped off, his hind flanks rising like wings; he seemed to devour all before him, and to scorn all behind.

I had now, as I thought, discovered a clue to the history of Peter Rugg; and I determined, the next time my business called me to Boston, to make a further inquiry.   Soon after, I was enabled to collect the following particulars from Mrs. Croft, an aged lady in Middle Street, who has resided in Boston during the last twenty years.   Her narration is this:

Just at twilight last summer a person stopped at the door of the late Mrs. Rugg.   Mrs. Croft on coming to the door perceived a stranger, with a child by his side, in an old weather-beaten carriage, with a black horse. The stranger asked for Mrs. Rugg, and was informed that Mrs. Rugg had died at a good old age, more than twenty years before that time.

The stranger replied, "How can you deceive me so? Do ask Mrs. Rugg to step to the door."

"Sir, I assure you Mrs. Rugg has not lived here these twenty years; no one lives here but myself, and my name is Betsy Croft."

The stranger paused, looked up and down the street, and said, "Though the paint is rather faded, this looks like my house."

"Yes," said the child, "that is the stone before the door that I used to sit on to eat my bread-and-milk."

"But," said the stranger, "it seems to be on the wrong side of the street. Indeed, everything here seems to be misplaced. The streets are all changed, the people are all changed, the town seems changed, and what is strangest of all, Catherine Rugg has deserted her husband and child. Pray," continued the stranger, "has John Foy come home from sea? He went a long voyage; he is my kinsman. If I could see him, he could give me some account of Mrs. Rugg."

"Sir," said Mrs. Croft, "I never heard of John Foy. Where did he live?"

"Just above here, in Orange-tree Lane."

"There is no such place in this neighbourhood."

"What do you tell me! Are the streets gone? Orange-tree Lane is at the head of Hanover Street, near Pemberton's Hill."

"There is no such lane now."

"Madam, you cannot be serious! But you doubtless know my brother, William Rugg. He lives in Royal Exchange Lane, near King Street."

"I know of no such lane; and I am sure there is no such street as King Street in this town."

"No such street as King Street! Why, woman, you mock me! You may as well tell me there is no King George. However, madam, you see I am wet and weary, I must find a resting-place. I will go to Hart's tavern, near the market."

"Which market, sir? for you seem perplexed; we have several markets."

"You know there is but one market near the town dock."

"Oh, the old market; but no such person has kept there these twenty years."

Here the stranger seemed disconcerted, and uttered to himself quite audibly: "Strange mistake; how much this looks like the town of Boston! It certainly has a great resemblance to it; but I perceive my mistake now. Some other Mrs. Rugg, some other Middle Street. Then," said he, "madam, can you direct me to Boston?"

"Why, this is Boston, the city of Boston; I know of no other Boston."

"City of Boston it may be; but it is not the Boston where I live. I recollect now, I came over a bridge instead of a ferry. Pray, what bridge is that I just came over?"

"It is Charles River bridge."

"I perceive my mistake; there is a ferry between Boston and Charlestown; there is no bridge. Ah, I perceive my mistake. If I were in Boston my horse would carry me directly to my own door. But my horse shows by his impatience that he is in a strange place. Absurd, that I should have mistaken this place for the old town of Boston! It is a much finer city than the town of Boston. It has been built long since Boston. I fancy Boston must lie at a distance from this city, as the good woman seems ignorant of it."

At these words his horse began to chafe, and strike the pavement with his forefeet. The stranger seemed a little bewildered, and said, "No home to-night"; and giving the reins to his horse, passed up the street, and she saw no more of him.

It was evident that the generation to which Peter Rugg belonged had passed away.

This was all the account of Peter Rugg I could obtain from Mrs. Croft; but she directed me to an elderly man, Mr. James Felt, who lived near her, and who had kept a record of the principal occurrences for the last fifty years. At my request she sent for him; and after I had related to him the object of my inquiry, Mr. Felt told me he had known Rugg in his youth, and that his disappearance had caused some surprise; but as it sometimes happens that men run away—sometimes to be rid of others, and sometimes to be rid of themselves —and Rugg took his child with him, and his own horse and chair, and as it did not appear that any creditors made a stir, the occurrence soon mingled itself in the stream of oblivion; and Rugg and his child, horse, and chair were soon forgotten.

"It is true," said Mr. Felt, "sundry stories grew out

of Rugg's affair, whether true or false I cannot tell; but stranger things have happened in my day, without even a newspaper notice."

"Sir," said I, "Peter Rugg is now living. I have lately seen Peter Rugg and his child, horse, and chair; therefore I pray you to relate to me all you know or ever heard of him."

"Why, my friend," said James Felt, "that Peter Rugg is now a living man, I will not deny; but that you have seen Peter Rugg and his child, is impossible, if you mean a small child; for Jenny Rugg, if living, must be at least—let me see—Boston massacre, 1770— Jenny Rugg, was about ten years old. Why, sir, Jenny Rugg, if living, must be more than sixty years of age. That Peter Rugg is living, is highly probable, as he was only ten years older than myself, and I was only eighty last March; and I am as likely to live twenty years longer as any man."

Here I perceived that Mr. Felt was in his dotage, and I despaired of gaining any intelligence from him on which I could depend.

I took my leave of Mrs. Croft, and proceeded to my lodgings at the Marlborough Hotel.

"If Peter Rugg," thought I, "has been travelling since the Boston massacre, there is no reason why he should not travel to the end of time. If the present generation know little of him, the next will know less, and Peter and his child will have no hold on this world."

In the course of the evening, I related my adventure in Middle Street.

"Ha!" said one of the company, smiling, "do you really think you have seen Peter Rugg? I have heard my grandfather speak of him, as though he seriously believed his own story."

"Sir," said I, "pray let us compare your grandfather's story of Mr. Rugg with my own."

"Peter Rugg, sir—if my grandfather was worthy of credit—once lived in Middle Street, in this city. He was a man in comfortable circumstances, had a wife and one daughter, and was generally esteemed for his sober life and manners. But unhappily, his temper, at times, was altogether ungovernable, and then his language was terrible. In these fits of passion, if a door stood in his way, he would never do less than kick a panel through. He would sometimes throw his heels over his head, and come down on his feet, uttering oaths in a circle; and thus in a rage, he was the first who performed a somersault, and did what others have since learned to do for merriment and money. Once Rugg was seen to bite a tenpenny nail in halves. In those days everybody, both men and boys, wore wigs; and Peter, at these moments of violent passion, would become so profane that his wig would rise up from his head. Some said it was on account of his terrible language; others accounted for it in a more philosophical way, and said it was caused by the expansion of his scalp, as violent passion, we know, will swell the veins and expand the head. While these fits were on him, Rugg had no respect for heaven or earth. Except this infirmity, all agreed that Rugg was a good sort of a man; for when his fits were over, nobody was so ready to commend a placid temper as Peter.

"One morning, late in autumn, Rugg, in his own chair, with a fine large bay horse, took his daughter and proceeded to Concord. On his return a violent storm overtook him. At dark he stopped in Menotomy, now West Cambridge, at the door of a Mr. Cutter, a friend of his, who urged him to tarry the night. On Rugg's declining to stop, Mr. Cutter urged him vehemently. 'Why, Mr. Rugg,' said Cutter, 'the storm is overwhelming you. The night is exceedingly dark. Your little daughter will perish. You are in an open chair, and the tempest is increasing.' '*Let the storm increase*,' said Rugg, with a fearful oath, '*I will see home to-night, in spite of the last tempest, or may I never see home!*' At these words he gave his whip to his high-spirited horse and disappeared in a moment. But Peter Rugg did not reach home that night, nor the next; nor, when he became a missing man, could he ever be traced beyond Mr. Cutter's, in Menotomy.

"For a long time after, on every dark and stormy night the wife of Peter Rugg would fancy she heard the crack of a whip, and the fleet tread of a horse, and the rattling of a carriage passing her door. The neighbours, too, heard the same noises, and some said they knew it was Rugg's horse; the tread on the pavement was perfectly familiar to them. This occurred so repeatedly that at length the neighbours watched with lanterns, and saw the real Peter Rugg, with his own horse and chair and the child sitting beside him, pass directly before his own door, his head turned towards his house, and himself making every effort to stop his horse, but in vain.

"The next day the friends of Mrs. Rugg exerted themselves to find her husband and child. They inquired at every public-house and stable in town; but it did not appear that Rugg made any stay in Boston. No one, after Rugg had passed his own door, could give any account of him, though it was asserted by some that the clatter of Rugg's horse and carriage over the pavements shook the houses on both sides of the streets. And this is credible, if indeed Rugg's horse and carriage did pass on that night; for at this day, in many of the streets, a loaded truck or team in passing will shake the houses like an earthquake. However, Rugg's neighbours never afterward watched. Some of them treated it all as a delusion, and thought no more of it. Others of a different opinion shook their heads and said nothing.

"Thus Rugg and his child, horse, and chair were soon forgotten; and probably many in the neighbourhood never heard a word on the subject.

"There was indeed a rumour that Rugg was seen afterward in Connecticut, between Suffield and Hartford, passing through the country at headlong speed. This gave occasion to Rugg's friends to make further inquiry; but the more they inquired, the more they were baffled. If they heard of Rugg one day in Connecticut, the next they heard of him winding round the hills in New Hampshire; and soon after a man in a chair, with a small child, exactly answering the description of Peter Rugg, would be seen in Rhode Island inquiring the way to Boston.

"But that which chiefly gave a colour of mystery to the story of Peter Rugg was the affair at Charlestown bridge. The toll-gatherer asserted that sometimes, on the darkest and most stormy nights, when no object could be discerned, about the time Rugg was missing, a horse and wheel-carriage, with a noise equal to a troop, would at midnight, in utter contempt of the rates of toll, pass over the bridge. This occurred so frequently that the toll-gatherer resolved to attempt a discovery. Soon after, at the usual time, apparently the same horse and carriage approached the bridge from Charlestown square. The toll-gatherer, prepared, took his stand as near the middle of the bridge as he dared, with a large three-legged stool in his hand; as the appearance passed, he threw the stool at the horse, but heard nothing except the noise of the stool skipping across the bridge. The toll-gatherer on the next day asserted that the stool went directly through the body of the horse, and he persisted in that belief ever after. Whether Rugg, or whoever the person was, ever passed the bridge again, the toll-gatherer would never tell; and when questioned, seemed anxious to waive the subject. And thus Peter Rugg and his child, horse, and carriage, remain a mystery to this day."

This, sir, is all that I could learn of Peter Rugg in Boston.

FURTHER ACCOUNT OF PETER RUGG

By Jonathan Dunwell

IN the autumn of 1825 I attended the races at Richmond in Virginia. As two new horses of great promise were run, the race-ground was never better attended, nor was expectation ever more deeply excited. The partisans of Dart and Lightning, the two racehorses, were equally anxious and equally dubious of the result. To an indifferent spectator, it was impossible to perceive any difference. They were equally beautiful to behold, alike in colour and height, and as they stood side by side they measured from heel to forefeet within half an inch of each other. The eyes of each were full, prominent, and resolute; and when at times they regarded each other, they assumed a lofty demeanour, seemed to shorten their necks, project their eyes, and rest their bodies equally on their four hoofs. They certainly showed signs of intelligence, and displayed a courtesy to each other unusual even with statesmen.

It was now nearly twelve o'clock, the hour of expectation, doubt, and anxiety. The riders mounted their horses; and so trim, light, and airy they sat on the animals as to seem a part of them. The spectators, many deep in a solid column, had taken their places, and as many thousand breathing statues were there as spectators. All eyes were turned to Dart and Lightning and their two fairy riders. There was nothing to disturb this calm except a busy woodpecker on a neighbouring tree. The signal was given, and Dart and Lightning answered it with ready intelligence. At first they proceed at a slow trot, then they quicken to a canter, and then a gallop; presently they sweep the plain. Both horses lay themselves flat on the ground, their riders bending forward and resting their chins between their horses' ears. Had not the ground been perfectly level, had there been any undulation, the least rise and fall, the spectator would now and then have lost sight of both horses and riders.

While these horses, side by side, thus appeared, flying without wings, flat as a hare, and neither gaining on the other, all eyes were diverted to a new spectacle. Directly in the rear of Dart and Lightning, a majestic black horse of unusual size, drawing an old weather-beaten chair, strode over the plain; and although he appeared to make no effort, for he maintained a steady trot, before Dart and Lightning approached the goal the black horse and chair had overtaken the racers, who, on perceiving this new competitor pass them, threw back their ears, and suddenly stopped in their course. Thus neither Dart nor Lightning carried away the purse.

The spectators now were exceedingly curious to learn whence came the black horse and chair. With many it was the opinion that nobody was in the vehicle. Indeed, this began to be the prevalent opinion; for those at a short distance, so fleet was the black horse, could not easily discern who, if anybody, was in the carriage. But both the riders, very near to whom the black horse passed, agreed in this particular—that a sad-looking man and a little girl were in the chair. When they stated this I was satisfied that the man was Peter Rugg. But what caused no little surprise, John Spring, one of the riders (he who rode Lightning), asserted that no earthly horse without breaking his trot could, in a carriage, outstrip his racehorse, and he persisted, with some passion, that it was not a horse—or, he was sure it was not a horse, but a large black ox. "What a great black ox can do," said John, "I cannot pretend to say; but no racehorse, not even flying Childers, could out-trot Lightning in a fair race."

This opinion of John Spring excited no little merriment, for it was obvious to everyone that it was a powerful black horse that interrupted the race; but John Spring, jealous of Lightning's reputation as a horse, would rather have it thought that any other beast, even an ox, had been the victor. However, the "horse-laugh" at John Spring's expense was soon suppressed; for as soon as Dart and Lightning began to breathe more freely, it was observed that both of them walked deliberately to the track of the race-ground, and putting their heads to the earth, suddenly raised them again and began to snort. They repeated this till John Spring said, "These horses have discovered something strange; they suspect foul play. Let me go and talk with Lightning."

He went up to Lightning and took hold of his mane; and Lightning put his nose toward the ground and smelt of the earth without touching it, then reared his head very high, and snorted so loudly that the sound echoed from the next hill. Dart did the same. John Spring stooped down to examine the spot where Lightning had smelled. In a moment he raised himself up, and the countenance of the man was changed. His strength failed him, and he sidled against Lightning.

At length John Spring recovered from his stupor, and exclaimed, "It was an ox! I told you it was an ox. No real horse ever yet beat Lightning."

And, now, on a close inspection of the black horse's tracks in the path, it was evident to everyone that the forefeet of the black horse were cloven. Notwithstanding these appearances, to me it was evident that the strange horse was in reality a horse. Yet when the people left the race-ground, I presume one-half of all those present would have testified that a large black ox had distanced two of the fleetest coursers that ever trod the Virginia turf. So uncertain are all things called historical facts.

While I was proceeding to my lodgings, pondering on the events of the day, a stranger rode up to me, and accosted me thus: "I think your name is Dunwell, sir."

"Yes, sir," I replied.

"Did I not see you a year or two since in Boston, at the Marlborough Hotel?"

"Very likely, sir, for I was there."

"And you heard a story about one Peter Rugg?"

"I recollect it all," said I.

"The account you heard in Boston must be true, for here he was to-day. The man has found his way to

Virginia, and for aught that appears, has been to
Cape Horn. I have seen him before to-day, but never
saw him travel with such fearful velocity. Pray, sir,
where does Peter Rugg spend his winters, for I have
seen him only in summer, and always in foul weather
except this time?"

I replied, "No one knows where Peter Rugg spends his
winters; where or when he eats, drinks, sleeps, or lodges.
He seems to have an indistinct idea of day and night,
time and space, storm and sunshine. His only object
is Boston. It appears to me that Rugg's horse has some
control of the chair; and that Rugg himself is, in some
sort, under the control of his horse."

I then inquired of the stranger where he first saw the
man and horse.

"Why, sir," said he, "in the summer of 1824, I
travelled to the North for my health; and soon after
I saw you at the Marlborough Hotel I returned homeward to Virginia, and, if my memory is correct, I saw
this man and horse in every state between here and
Massachusetts. Sometimes he would meet me, but
oftener overtake me. He never spoke but once, and
that once was in Delaware. On his approach he checked
his horse with some difficulty. A more beautiful horse
I never saw; his hide was as fair and rotund and glossy
as the skin of a Congo beauty. When Rugg's horse
approached mine he reined in his neck, bent his ears
forward until they met, and looked my horse full in
the face. My horse immediately withered into half a
horse, his hide curling up like a piece of burnt leather;
spellbound, he was fixed to the earth as though a nail
had been driven through each hoof.

"'Sir,' said Rugg, 'perhaps you are travelling to
Boston; and if so, I should be happy to accompany
you, for I have lost my way, and I must reach home
to-night. See how sleepy this little girl looks; poor
thing, she is a picture of patience.'

"'Sir,' said I, 'it is impossible for you to reach home
to-night, for you are in Concord, in the county of
Sussex, in the state of Delaware.'

"'What do you mean,' said he, 'by state of Delaware? If I were in Concord, that is only twenty miles from Boston, and my horse Lightfoot could carry me to Charlestown ferry in less than two hours. You mistake, sir; you are a stranger here; this town is nothing like Concord. I am well acquainted with Concord. I went to Concord when I left Boston.'

"'But,' said I, 'you are in Concord, in the state of Delaware.'

"'What do you mean by state?' said Rugg.

"'Why, one of the United States.'

"'States'! said he, in a low voice; 'the man is a wag, and would persuade me I am in Holland.' Then, raising his voice, he said, 'You seem, sir, to be a gentleman, and I entreat you to mislead me not; tell me, quickly, for pity's sake, the right road to Boston, for you see my horse will swallow his bits; he has eaten nothing since I left Concord.'

"'Sir,' said I, 'this town is Concord—Concord in Delaware, not Concord in Massachusetts; and you are now five hundred miles from Boston.'

"Rugg looked at me for a moment, more in sorrow than resentment, and then repeated, 'Five hundred miles! Unhappy man, who would have thought him deranged; but nothing in this world is so deceitful as appearances. Five hundred miles! This beats Connecticut River.'

"What he meant by Connecticut River, I know not; his horse broke away, and Rugg disappeared in a moment."

I explained to the stranger the meaning of Rugg's expression, "Connecticut River," and the incident respecting him that occurred at Hartford, as I stood on the door-stone of Mr. Bennett's excellent hotel. We both agreed that the man we had seen that day was the true Peter Rugg.

Soon after, I saw Rugg again, at the toll-gate on the turnpike between Alexandria and Middleburgh. While I was paying the toll, I observed to the toll-gatherer that the drought was more severe in his vicinity than farther south.

"Yes," said he, "the drought is excessive; but if I had not heard yesterday, by a traveller, that the man with the black horse was seen in Kentucky a day or two since, I should be sure of a shower in a few minutes."

I looked all around the horizon, and could not discern a cloud that could hold a pint of water.

"Look, sir," said the toll-gatherer, "you perceive to the eastward, just above that hill, a small black cloud not bigger than a blackberry, and while I am speaking it is doubling and trebling itself, and rolling up the turnpike steadily, as if its sole design was to deluge some object."

"True," said I, "I do perceive it; but what connection is there between a thunder-cloud and a man and horse?"

"More than you imagine, or I can tell you; but stop a moment, sir, I may need your assistance. I know that cloud; I have seen it several times before, and can testify to its identity. You will soon see a man and black horse under it."

While he was speaking, true enough, we began to hear the distant thunder, and soon the chain-lightning performed all the figures of a country-dance. About a mile distant we saw the man and black horse under the cloud; but before he arrived at the toll-gate, the thunder-cloud had spent itself, and not even a sprinkle fell near us.

As the man, whom I instantly knew to be Rugg, attempted to pass, the toll-gatherer swung the gate across the road, seized Rugg's horse by the reins, and demanded two dollars.

Feeling some little regard for Rugg, I interfered, and began to question the toll-gatherer, and requested him not to be wroth with the man. The toll-gatherer replied that he had just cause, for the man had run his toll ten times, and moreover that the horse had discharged a cannon-ball at him, to the great danger of his life; that the man had always before approached so rapidly that he was too quick for the rusty hinges of the toll-gate; "but now I will have full satisfaction."

Rugg looked wistfully at me, and said, "I entreat

you, sir, to delay me not; I have found at length the direct road to Boston, and shall not reach home before night if you detain me. You see I am dripping wet, and ought to change my clothes."

The toll-gatherer then demanded why he had run his toll so many times.

"Toll! Why," said Rugg, "do you demand toll? There is no toll to pay on the king's highway."

"King's highway! Do you not perceive this is a turnpike?"

"Turnpike! there are no turnpikes in Massachusetts."

"That may be, but we have several in Virginia."

"Virginia! Do you pretend I am in Virginia?"

Rugg then, appealing to me, asked how far it was to Boston.

Said I, "Mr. Rugg, I perceive you are bewildered, and am sorry to see you so far from home; you are, indeed, in Virginia."

"You know me, then, sir, it seems; and you say I am in Virginia. Give me leave to tell you, sir, you are the most impudent man alive; for I was never forty miles from Boston, and I never saw a Virginian in my life. This beats Delaware!"

"Your toll, sir, your toll!"

"I will not pay you a penny," said Rugg; "you are both of you highway robbers. There are no turnpikes in this country. Take toll on the king's highway! Robbers take toll on the king's highway!" Then in a low tone, he said, "Here is evidently a conspiracy against me; alas, I shall never see Boston! The highways refuse me a passage, the rivers change their courses, and there is no faith in the compass."

But Rugg's horse had no idea of stopping more than one minute; for in the midst of this altercation, the horse, whose nose was resting on the upper bar of the turnpike-gate, seized it between his teeth, lifted it gently off its staples, and trotted off with it. The toll-gatherer, confounded, strained his eyes after his gate.

"Let him go," said I, "the horse will soon drop your gate, and you will get it again."

I then questioned the toll-gatherer respecting his knowledge of this man; and he related the following particulars:

"The first time," said he, "that man ever passed this toll-gate was in the year 1806, at the moment of the great eclipse. I thought the horse was frightened at the sudden darkness, and concluded he had run away with the man. But within a few days after, the same man and horse repassed with equal speed, without the least respect to the toll-gate or to me, except by a vacant stare. Some few years afterward, during the late war, I saw the same man approaching again, and I resolved to check his career. Accordingly I stepped into the middle of the road, and stretched wide both my arms, and cried, 'Stop, sir, on your peril!' At this the man said, 'Now, Lightfoot, confound the robber!' At the same time he gave the whip liberally to the flank of his horse, which bounded off with such force that it appeared to me two such horses, give them a place to stand, would overcome any check man could devise. An ammunition wagon which had just passed on to Baltimore had dropped an eighteen-pounder in the road; this unlucky ball lay in the way of the horse's heels, and the beast, with the sagacity of a demon, clinched it with one of his heels and hurled it behind him. I feel dizzy in relating the fact, but so nearly did the ball pass my head, that the wind thereof blew off my hat; and the ball embedded itself in that gate-post, as you may see if you will cast your eye on the post. I have permitted it to remain there in memory of the occurrence—as the people of Boston, I am told, preserve the eighteen-pounder which is now to be seen half embedded in Brattle Street church."

I then took leave of the toll-gatherer, and promised him if I saw or heard of his gate I would send him notice.

A strong inclination had possessed me to arrest Rugg and search his pockets, thinking great discoveries might be made in the examination; but what I saw and heard that day convinced me that no human force could

detain Peter Rugg against his consent. I therefore
determined if I ever saw Rugg again to treat him in
the gentlest manner.

In pursuing my way to New York, I entered on the
turnpike in Trenton; and when I arrived at New Bruns-
wick, I perceived the road was newly macadamised.
The small stones had just been laid thereon.   As I
passed this piece of road, I observed that, at regular
distances of about eight feet, the stones were entirely
displaced from spots as large as the circumference of a
half-bushel measure.   This singular appearance induced
me to inquire the cause of it at the turnpike-gate.

"Sir," said the toll-gatherer, "I wonder not at the
question, but I am unable to give you a satisfactory
answer.   Indeed, sir, I believe I am bewitched, and that
the turnpike is under a spell of enchantment; for what
appeared to me last night cannot be a real transaction,
otherwise a turnpike-gate is a useless thing."

"I do not believe in witchcraft or enchantment,"
said I; "and if you will relate circumstantially what
happened last night, I will endeavour to account for it
by natural means."

"You may recollect the night was uncommonly dark.
Well, sir, just after I had closed the gate for the night,
down the turnpike, as far as my eye could reach, I beheld
what at first appeared to be two armies engaged.   The
report of the musketry, and the flashes of their firelocks,
were incessant and continuous.   As this strange spectacle
approached me with the fury of a tornado, the noise
increased; and the appearance rolled on in one compact
body over the surface of the ground.   The most splendid
fireworks rose out of the earth and encircled this moving
spectacle.   The divers tints of the rainbow, the most
brilliant dyes that the sun lays in the lap of spring,
added to the whole family of gems, could not display
a more beautiful, radiant, and dazzling spectacle than
accompanied the black horse.   You would have thought
all the stars of heaven had met in merriment on the
turnpike.   In the midst of this luminous configuration
sat a man, distinctly to be seen, in a miserable-looking

chair, drawn by a black horse. The turnpike-gate ought, by the laws of nature and the laws of the state, to have made a wreck of the whole, and have dissolved the enchantment; but no, the horse without an effort passed over the gate, and drew the man and chair horizontally after him without touching the bar. This was what I call enchantment. What think you, sir?"

"My friend," said I, "you have grossly magnified a natural occurrence. The man was Peter Rugg, on his way to Boston. It is true, his horse travelled with unequalled speed, but as he reared high his forefeet, he could not help displacing the thousand small stones on which he trod, which flying in all directions struck one another, and resounded and scintillated. The top bar of your gate is not more than two feet from the ground, and Rugg's horse at every vault could easily lift the carriage over that gate."

This satisfied Mr. McDoubt, and I was pleased at that occurrence; for otherwise Mr. McDoubt, who is a worthy man, late from the Highlands, might have added to his calendar of superstitions. Having thus disenchanted the macadamised road and the turnpike-gate, and also Mr. McDoubt, I pursued my journey homeward to New York.

Little did I expect to see or hear anything further of Mr. Rugg, for he was now more than twelve hours in advance of me. I could hear nothing of him on my way to Elizabethtown, and therefore concluded that during the past night he had turned off from the turnpike and pursued a westerly direction; but just before I arrived at Powles's Hook, I observed a considerable collection of passengers in the ferry-boat, all standing motionless, and steadily looking at the same object. One of the ferry-men, Mr. Hardy, who knew me well, observing my approach delayed a minute, in order to afford me a passage, and coming up, said, "Mr. Dunwell, we have a curiosity on board that would puzzle Dr. Mitchell."

"Some strange fish, I suppose, has found its way into the Hudson?"

"No," said he, "it is a man who looks as if he had lain hidden in the ark, and had just now ventured out. He has a little girl with him, the counterpart of himself, and the finest horse you ever saw, harnessed to the queerest-looking carriage that ever was made."

"Ah, Mr. Hardy," said I, "you have, indeed, hooked a prize; no one before you could ever detain Peter Rugg long enough to examine him."

"Do you know the man?" said Mr. Hardy.

"No, nobody knows him, but everybody has seen him. Detain him as long as possible; delay the boat under any pretence, cut the gear of the horse, do anything to detain him."

As I entered the ferry-boat, I was struck at the spectacle before me. There, indeed, sat Peter Rugg and Jenny Rugg in the chair, and there stood the black horse, all as quiet as lambs, surrounded by more than fifty men and women, who seemed to have lost all their senses but one. Not a motion, not a breath, not a rustle. They were all eye. Rugg appeared to them to be a man not of this world; and they appeared to Rugg a strange generation of men. Rugg spoke not, and they spoke not; nor was I disposed to disturb the calm, satisfied to reconnoitre Rugg in a state of rest. Presently, Rugg observed in a low voice, addressed to nobody, "A new contrivance, horses instead of oars; Boston folks are full of notions."

It was plain that Rugg was of Dutch extraction. He had on three pairs of small clothes, called in former days of simplicity breeches, not much the worse for wear; but time had proved the fabric, and shrunk one more than another, so that they showed at the knees their different qualities and colours. His several waist-coats, the flaps of which rested on his knees, made him appear rather corpulent. His capacious drab coat would supply the stuff for half a dozen modern ones; the sleeves were like meal bags, in the cuffs of which you might nurse a child to sleep. His hat, probably once black, now of a tan colour, was neither round nor crooked, but in shape much like the one President

Monroe wore on his late tour. This dress gave the rotund face of Rugg an antiquated dignity. The man, though deeply sunburned, did not appear to be more than thirty years of age. He had lost his sad and anxious look, was quite composed, and seemed happy. The chair in which Rugg sat was very capacious, evidently made for service, and calculated to last for ages; the timber would supply material for three modern carriages. This chair, like a Nantucket coach, would answer for everything that ever went on wheels. The horse, too, was an object of curiosity; his majestic height, his natural mane and tail, gave him a commanding appearance, and his large open nostrils indicated inexhaustible wind. It was apparent that the hoofs of his forefeet had been split, probably on some newly macadamised road, and were now growing together again; so that John Spring was not altogether in the wrong.

How long this dumb scene would otherwise have continued I cannot tell. Rugg discovered no sign of impatience. But Rugg's horse having been quiet more than five minutes, had no idea of standing idle; he began to whinny, and in a moment after, with his right forefoot he started a plank. Said Rugg, "My horse is impatient, he sees the North End. You must be quick, or he will be ungovernable."

At these words, the horse raised his left forefoot; and when he laid it down every inch of the ferry-boat trembled. Two men immediately seized Rugg's horse by the nostrils. The horse nodded, and both of them were in the Hudson. While we were fishing up the men, the horse was perfectly quiet.

"Fret not the horse," said Rugg, "and he will do no harm. He is only anxious, like myself, to arrive at yonder beautiful shore; he sees the North Church, and smells his own stable."

"Sir," said I to Rugg, practising a little deception, "pray tell me, for I am a stranger here, what river is this, and what city is that opposite, for you seem to be an inhabitant of it?"

"This river, sir, is called Mystic River, and this is Winnisimmet ferry—we have retained the Indian names —and that town is Boston. You must, indeed, be a stranger in these parts, not to know that yonder is Boston, the capital of the New England provinces."

"Pray, sir, how long have you been absent from Boston?"

"Why, that I cannot exactly tell. I lately went with this little girl of mine to Concord, to see my friends; and I am ashamed to tell you, in returning lost the way, and have been travelling ever since. No one would direct me right. It is cruel to mislead a traveller. My horse, Lightfoot, has boxed the compass; and it seems to me he has boxed it back again. But, sir, you perceive my horse is uneasy; Lightfoot, as yet, has only given a hint and a nod. I cannot be answerable for his heels."

At these words Lightfoot reared his long tail, and snapped it as you would a whiplash. The Hudson reverberated with the sound. Instantly the six horses began to move the boat. The Hudson was a sea of glass, smooth as oil, not a ripple. The horses, from a smart trot, soon pressed into a gallop; water now ran over the gunwale; the ferry-boat was soon buried in an ocean of foam, and the noise of the spray was like the roaring of many waters. When we arrived at New York, you might see the beautiful white wake of the ferry-boat across the Hudson.

Though Rugg refused to pay toll at turnpikes, when Mr. Hardy reached his hand for the ferriage, Rugg readily put his hand into one of his many pockets, took out a piece of silver, and handed it to Hardy.

"What is this?" said Mr. Hardy.

"It is thirty shillings," said Rugg.

"It might once have been thirty shillings, old tenor," said Mr. Hardy, "but it is not at present."

"The money is good English coin," said Rugg; "my grandfather brought a bag of them from England, and had them hot from the mint."

Hearing this, I approached near to Rugg, and asked permission to see the coin. It was a half-crown, coined by the English Parliament, dated in the year 1649. On one side, "The Commonwealth of England," and St. George's cross encircled with a wreath of laurel. On the other, "God with us," and a harp and St. George's cross united. I winked at Mr. Hardy, and pronounced it good current money; and said loudly, "I will not permit the gentleman to be imposed on, for I will exchange the money myself."

On this, Rugg spoke: "Please to give me your name, sir."

"My name is Dunwell, sir," I replied.

"Mr. Dunwell," said Rugg, "you are the only honest man I have seen since I left Boston. As you are a stranger here, my house is your home; Dame Rugg will be happy to see her husband's friend. Step into my chair, sir, there is room enough; move a little, Jenny, for the gentleman, and we will be in Middle Street in a minute."

Accordingly I took a seat by Peter Rugg.

"Were you never in Boston before?" said Rugg.

"No," said I.

"Well, you will now see the queen of New England, a town second only to Philadelphia, in all North America."

"You forget New York," said I.

"Poh, New York is nothing; though I never was there. I am told you might put all New York in our mill-pond. No, sir, New York, I assure you, is but a sorry affair; no more to be compared with Boston than a wigwam with a palace."

As Rugg's horse turned into Pearl Street, I looked Rugg as fully in the face as good manners would allow, and said, "Sir, if this is Boston, I acknowledge New York is not worthy to be one of its suburbs."

Before we had proceeded far in Pearl Street, Rugg's countenance changed: his nerves began to twitch; his eyes trembled in their sockets; he was evidently bewildered. "What is the matter, Mr. Rugg? you seem disturbed."

"This surpasses all human comprehension; if you know, sir, where we are, I beseech you to tell me."

"If this place," I replied, "is not Boston, it must be New York."

"No, sir, it is not Boston; nor can it be New York. How could I be in New York, which is nearly two hundred miles from Boston?"

By this time we had passed into Broadway, and then Rugg, in truth, discovered a chaotic mind. "There is no such place as this in North America. This is all the effect of enchantment; this is a grand delusion, nothing real. Here is seemingly a great city, magnificent houses, shops and goods, men and women innumerable, and as busy as in real life, all sprung up in one night from the wilderness; or what is more probable, some tremendous convulsion of nature has thrown London or Amsterdam on the shores of New England. Or, possibly, I may be dreaming, though the night seems rather long; but before now I have sailed in one night to Amsterdam, bought goods of Vandogger, and returned to Boston before morning."

At this moment a hue-and-cry was heard, "Stop the madmen, they will endanger the lives of thousands!" In vain hundreds attempted to stop Rugg's horse. Lightfoot interfered with nothing; his course was straight as a shooting-star. But on my part, fearful that before night I should find myself behind the Alleghanies, I addressed Mr. Rugg in a tone of entreaty, and requested him to restrain the horse and permit me to alight.

"My friend," said he, "we shall be in Boston before dark, and Dame Rugg will be most exceeding glad to see us."

"Mr. Rugg," said I, "you must excuse me. Pray look to the west; see that thunder-cloud swelling with rage, as if in pursuit of us."

"Ah!" said Rugg, "it is in vain to attempt to escape. I know that cloud; it is collecting new wrath to spend on my head." Then checking his horse, he permitted me to descend, saying, "Farewell, Mr. Dunwell, I shall be happy to see you in Boston; I live in Middle Street."

It is uncertain in what direction Mr. Rugg pursued

his course, after he disappeared in Broadway; but one thing is sufficiently known to everybody—that in the course of two months after he was seen in New York, he found his way most opportunely to Boston.

It seems the estate of Peter Rugg had recently fallen to the Commonwealth of Massachusetts for want of heirs; and the Legislature had ordered the solicitor-general to advertise and sell it at public auction. Happening to be in Boston at the time, and observing his advertisement, which described a considerable extent of land, I felt a kindly curiosity to see the spot where Rugg once lived. Taking the advertisement in my hand, I wandered a little way down Middle Street, and without asking a question of anyone, when I came to a certain spot I said to myself, "This is Rugg's estate; I will proceed no farther. This must be the spot; it is a counterpart of Peter Rugg." The premises, indeed, looked as if they had fulfilled a sad prophecy. Fronting on Middle Street, they extended in the rear to Ann Street, and embraced about half an acre of land. It was not uncommon in former times to have half an acre for a house-lot; for an acre of land then, in many parts of Boston, was not more valuable than a foot in some places at present. The old mansion-house had become a powder-post, and been blown away. One other building, uninhabited, stood ominous, courting dilapidation. The street had been so much raised that the bedchamber had descended to the kitchen and was level with the street. The house seemed conscious of its fate; and as though tired of standing there, the front was fast retreating from the rear, and waiting the next south wind to project itself into the street. If the most wary animals had sought a place of refuge, here they would have rendezvoused. Here, under the ridge-pole, the crow would have perched in security; and in the recesses below, you might have caught the fox and the weasel asleep. "The hand of destiny," said I, "has pressed heavy on this spot; still heavier on the former owners. Strange that so large a lot of land as this should want an heir! Yet Peter Rugg,

*B 84ᶜ

at this day, might pass by his own door-stone, and ask, 'Who once lived here?'"

The auctioneer, appointed by the solicitor to sell this estate, was a man of eloquence, as many of the auctioneers of Boston are. The occasion seemed to warrant, and his duty urged, him to make a display. He addressed his audience as follows:

"The estate, gentlemen, which we offer you this day, was once the property of a family now extinct. For that reason it has escheated to the Commonweath. Lest any one of you should be deterred from bidding on so large an estate as this for fear of a disputed title, I am authorised by the solicitor-general to proclaim that the purchaser shall have the best of all titles—a warranty-deed from the Commonwealth. I state this, gentlemen, because I know there is an idle rumour in this vicinity, that one Peter Rugg, the original owner of this estate, is still living. This rumour, gentlemen, has no foundation, and can have no foundation in the nature of things. It originated about two years since, from the incredible story of one Jonathan Dunwell, of New York. Mrs. Croft, indeed, whose husband I see present, and whose mouth waters for this estate, has countenanced this fiction. But, gentlemen, was it ever known that any estate, especially an estate of this value, lay unclaimed for nearly half a century, if any heir, ever so remote, were existing? For, gentlemen, all agree that old Peter Rugg, if living, would be at least one hundred years of age. It is said that he and his daughter, with a horse and chaise, were missed more than half a century ago; and because they never returned home, forsooth, they must be now living, and will some day come and claim this great estate. Such logic, gentlemen, never led to a good investment. Let not this idle story cross the noble purpose of consigning these ruins to the genius of architecture. If such a contingency could check the spirit of enterprise, farewell to all mercantile excitement. Your surplus money, instead of refreshing your sleep with the golden dreams of new sources of speculation, would turn to the nightmare. A man's money, if not employed, serves only to disturb his rest. Look, then, to the prospect before you. Here is half an acre of land — more than twenty thousand square feet — a corner lot, with wonderful capabilities; none of your contracted lots of forty feet by fifty, where, in dog-days, you can breathe only through your scuttles. On the contrary, an architect cannot contemplate this lot of land without rapture, for here is room enough for his genius to shame the temple of Solomon. Then the prospect — how commanding! To the east, so near to the Atlantic that Neptune, freighted with the select treasures of the whole earth, can knock at your door with his trident. From the west, the produce of the river of Paradise—the Connecticut—will soon, by the blessings of steam, railways, and canals, pass under your windows; and thus, on this spot, Neptune shall marry Ceres, and Pomona from Roxbury, and Flora from Cambridge, shall dance at the wedding.

"Gentlemen of science, men of taste, ye of the literary emporium—for I perceive many of you present —to you this is holy ground. If the spot on which in times past a hero left only the print of a footstep is now sacred, of what price is the birthplace of one who all the world knows was born in Middle Street, directly opposite to this lot; and who, if his birthplace were not well known, would now be claimed by more than seven cities! To you, then, the value of these premises must be inestimable. For ere long there will arise in full view of the edifice to be erected here, a monument, the wonder and veneration of the world. A column shall spring to the clouds; and on that column will be engraven one word which will convey all that is wise in intellect, useful in science, good in morals, prudent in counsel, and benevolent in principle—a name of one who, when living, was the patron of the poor, the delight of the cottage, and the admiration of kings; now dead, worth the whole seven wise men of Greece. Need I tell you his name? He fixed the thunder and guided the lightning.

"Men of the North End! Need I appeal to your patriotism, in order to enhance the value of this lot? The earth affords no such scenery as this; there, around that corner, lived James Otis; here, Samuel Adams; there, Joseph Warren; and around that other corner, Josiah Quincy. Here was the birthplace of Freedom; here Liberty was born, and nursed, and grew to manhood. Here man was newly created. Here is the nursery of American Independence—I am too modest —here began the emancipation of the world; a thousand generations hence millions of men will cross the Atlantic just to look at the North End of Boston. Your fathers —what do I say!—yourselves—yes, this moment, I behold several attending this auction who lent a hand to rock the cradle of Independence.

"Men of speculation—ye who are deaf to everything except the sound of money—you, I know, will give me both of your ears when I tell you the city of Boston must have a piece of this estate in order to widen Ann Street. Do you hear me—do you all hear me? I say the city must have a large piece of this land in order to widen Ann Street. What a chance! The city scorns to take a man's land for nothing. If it seizes your property, it is generous beyond the dreams of avarice. The only oppression is, you are in danger of being smothered under a load of wealth. Witness the old lady who lately died of a broken heart when the mayor paid her for a piece of her kitchen-garden. All the faculty agreed that the sight of the treasure, which the mayor incautiously paid her in dazzling dollars, warm from the mint, sped joyfully all the blood of her body into her heart, and rent it with raptures. Therefore, let him who purchases this estate fear his good fortune, and not Peter Rugg. Bid, then, liberally, and do not let the name of Rugg damp your ardour. How much will you give per foot for this estate?"

Thus spoke the auctioneer, and gracefully waved his ivory hammer. From fifty to seventy-five cents per foot were offered in a few moments. The bidding laboured from seventy-five to ninety. At length one dollar was offered. The auctioneer seemed satisfied; and looking at his watch, said he would knock off the estate in five minutes, if no one offered more.

There was a deep silence during this short period. While the hammer was suspended, a strange rumbling noise was heard, which arrested the attention of everyone. Presently, it was like the sound of many shipwrights driving home the bolts of a seventy-four. As the sound approached nearer, some exclaimed, "The buildings in the new market are falling in promiscuous ruins." Others said, "No, it is an earthquake; we perceive the earth tremble." Others said, "Not so; the sound proceeds from Hanover Street, and approaches nearer"; and this proved true, for presently Peter Rugg was in the midst of us.

"Alas, Jenny," said Peter, "I am ruined; our house has been burned, and here are all our neighbours around the ruins. Heaven grant your mother, Dame Rugg, is safe."

"They don't look like our neighbours," said Jenny; "but sure enough our house is burned, and nothing left but the door-stone and an old cedar post. Do ask where mother is."

In the meantime more than a thousand men had surrounded Rugg and his horse and chair. Yet neither Rugg personally, nor his horse and carriage, attracted more attention than the auctioneer. The confident look and searching eyes of Rugg carried more conviction to everyone present that the estate was his than could any parchment or paper with signature and seal. The impression which the auctioneer had just made on the company was effaced in a moment; and although the latter words of the auctioneer were, "Fear not Peter Rugg," the moment the auctioneer met the eye of Rugg his occupation was gone; his arm fell down to his hips, his late lively hammer hung heavy in his hand, and the auction was forgotten. The black horse, too, gave his evidence. He knew his journey was ended; for he stretched himself into a horse and a half, rested his head over the cedar post, and whinnied thrice, causing his harness to tremble from headstall to crupper.

Rugg then stood upright in his chair, and asked with some authority, "Who has demolished my house in my absence, for I see no signs of a conflagration? I demand by what accident this has happened, and wherefore this collection of strange people has assembled before my door-step. I thought I knew every man in Boston, but you appear to me a new generation of men. Yet I am familiar with many of the countenances here present, and I can call some of you by name; but in truth I do not recollect that before this moment I ever saw any one of you. There, I am certain, is a Winslow, and here a Sargent; there stands a Sewall, and next to him a Dudley. Will none of you speak to me—or is this all a delusion? I see, indeed, many forms of men, and no want of eyes, but of motion, speech, and hearing, you seem to be destitute. Strange! Will no one inform me who has demolished my house?"

Then spake a voice from the crowd, but whence it came I could not discern: "There is nothing strange here but yourself, Mr. Rugg. Time, which destroys and renews all things, has dilapidated your house, and placed us here. You have suffered many years under an illusion. The tempest which you profanely defied at Menotomy has at length subsided; but you will never see home, for your house and wife and neighbours have all disappeared. Your estate, indeed, remains, but no home. You were cut off from the last age, and you can never be fitted to the present. Your home is gone, and you can never have another home in this world."

RIP VAN WINKLE[1]

A POSTHUMOUS WRITING OF DIEDRICH KNICKERBOCKER

By WASHINGTON IRVING (1783–1859)

> By Woden, God of Saxons,
> From whence comes Wensday, that is Wodensday,
> Truth is a thing that ever I will keep
> Unto thylke day in which I creep into
> My sepulchre.   CARTWRIGHT.

The following tale was found among the papers of the late Diedrich Knickerbocker, an old gentleman of New York, who was very curious in the Dutch history of the province, and the manners of the descendants from its primitive settlers. His historical researches, however, did not lie so much among books as among men; for the former are lamentably scanty on his favourite topics; whereas he found the old burghers, and still more their wives, rich in that legendary lore so invaluable to true history. Whenever, therefore, he happened upon a genuine Dutch family, snugly shut up in its low-roofed farmhouse, under a spreading sycamore, he looked upon it as a little clasped volume of black-letter, and studied it with the zeal of a bookworm.

The result of these researches was a history of the province during the reign of the Dutch governors, which he published some years since. There have been various opinions as to the literary character of his work, and, to tell the truth, it is not a whit better than it should be. Its chief merit is its scrupulous accuracy, which indeed was a little questioned on its first appearance, but has since been completely established; and it is now admitted into all historical collections as a book of unquestionable authority.

The old gentleman died shortly after the publication of his work; and now that he is dead and gone, it cannot do

---

[1] "Rip Van Winkle" was first published in *The Sketch-Book of Geoffrey Crayon, Gent* (1819–20), by Washington Irving, May 1819.

much harm to his memory to say that his time might have been much better employed in weightier labours. He, however, was apt to ride his hobby in his own way; and, though it did now and then kick up the dust a little in the eyes of his neighbours, and grieve the spirit of some friends, for whom he felt the truest deference and affection, yet his errors and follies are remembered "more in sorrow than in anger," and it begins to be suspected that he never intended to injure or offend. But however his memory may be appreciated by critics, it is still held dear by many folk whose good opinion is well worth having; particularly by certain biscuit-bakers, who have gone so far as to imprint his likeness on their New Year cakes; and have thus given him a chance for immortality, almost equal to the being stamped on a Waterloo medal, or a Queen Anne's farthing.

WHOEVER has made a voyage up the Hudson, must remember the Catskill Mountains. They are a dismembered branch of the great Appalachian family, and are seen away to the west of the river, swelling up to a noble height, and lording it over the surrounding country. Every change of season, every change of weather, indeed every hour of the day, produces some change in the magical hues and shapes of these mountains; and they are regarded by all the good wives, far and near, as perfect barometers. When the weather is fair and settled, they are clothed in blue and purple, and print their bold outlines on the clear evening sky; but sometimes, when the rest of the landscape is cloudless, they will gather a hood of grey vapours about their summits, which, in the last rays of the setting sun, will glow and light up like a crown of glory.

At the foot of these fairy mountains the voyager may have descried the light smoke curling up from a village whose shingle roofs gleam among the trees, just where the blue tints of the upland melt away into the fresh green of the nearer landscape. It is a little village of great antiquity, having been founded by some of the Dutch colonists, in the early times of the province, just about the beginning of the government of the good Peter Stuyvesant (may he rest in peace!), and there were some of the houses of the original settlers standing within a few years, built of small yellow bricks brought from Holland, having latticed windows and gabled fronts, surmounted with weathercocks.

In that same village, and in one of these very houses (which, to tell the precise truth, was sadly time-worn and weather-beaten), there lived many years since, while the country was yet a province of Great Britain, a simple, good-natured fellow, of the name of Rip Van Winkle. He was a descendant of the Van Winkles who figured so gallantly in the chivalrous days of Peter Stuyvesant, and accompanied him to the siege of Fort Christina. He inherited, however, but little of the martial character of his ancestors. I have observed that he was a simple, good-natured man; he was, moreover, a kind neighbour, and an obedient, hen-pecked husband. Indeed, to the latter circumstance might be owing that meekness of spirit which gained him such universal popularity; for those men are most apt to be obsequious and conciliating abroad who are under the discipline of shrews at home. Their tempers, doubtless, are rendered pliant and malleable in the fiery furnace of domestic tribulation, and a cur-tain lecture is worth all the sermons in the world for teaching the virtues of patience and long-suffering. A termagant wife may, therefore, in some respects, be considered a tolerable blessing; and if so, Rip Van Winkle was thrice blessed.

Certain it is, that he was a great favourite among all the good wives of the village, who, as usual with the amiable sex, took his part in all family squabbles, and never failed, whenever they talked those matters over in their evening gossipings, to lay all the blame on Dame Van Winkle. The children of the village, too, would shout with joy whenever he approached. He assisted at their sports, made their playthings, taught them to fly kites and shoot marbles, and told them long stories of ghosts, witches, and Indians. Whenever he went dodging about the village, he was surrounded by a troop of them hanging on his skirts, clambering on his back, and playing a thousand tricks on him with impunity; and not a dog would bark at him throughout the neighbourhood.

The great error in Rip's composition was an insuperable aversion to all kinds of profitable labour. It could not be from the want of assiduity or perseverance; for he would sit on a wet rock, with a rod as long and heavy as a Tartar's lance, and fish all day without a murmur, even though he should not be encouraged by a single nibble. He would carry a fowling-piece on his shoulder for hours together, trudging through woods and swamps, and up hill and down dale, to shoot a few squirrels or wild pigeons. He would never refuse to assist a neighbour, even in the roughest toil, and was a foremost man at all country frolics for husking Indian corn or building stone fences. The women of the village, too, used to employ him to run their errands, and to do such little odd jobs as their less obliging husbands would not do for them—in a word, Rip was ready to attend to anybody's business but his own; but as to doing family duty, and keeping his farm in order, he found it impossible.

In fact, he declared it was of no use to work on his farm; it was the most pestilent little piece of ground in the whole country; everything about it went wrong, and would go wrong in spite of him. His fences were continually falling to pieces; his cow would either go astray, or get among the cabbages; weeds were sure to grow quicker in his fields than anywhere else; the rain always made a point of setting in just as he had some out-of-door work to do; so that though his patrimonial estate had dwindled away under his management, acre by acre, until there was little more left than a mere patch of Indian corn and potatoes, yet it was the worst-conditioned farm in the neighbourhood.

His children, too, were as ragged and wild as if they belonged to nobody. His son Rip, an urchin begotten in his own likeness, promised to inherit the habits, with the old clothes of his father. He was generally seen trooping like a colt at his mother's heels, equipped in a pair of his father's cast-off galligaskins, which he had much ado to hold up with one hand, as a fine lady does her train in bad weather.

Rip Van Winkle, however, was one of those happy mortals, of foolish, well-oiled dispositions, who take the world easy, eat white bread or brown, whichever can be got with least thought or trouble, and would rather starve on a penny than work for a pound. If left to himself, he would have whistled life away in perfect contentment; but his wife kept continually dinning in his ears about his idleness, his carelessness, and the ruin he was bringing on his family.

Morning, noon, and night, her tongue was incessantly going, and everything he said or did was sure to produce a torrent of household eloquence. Rip had but one way of replying to all lectures of the kind, and that, by frequent use, had grown into a habit. He shrugged his shoulders, shook his head, cast up his eyes, but said nothing. This, however, always provoked a fresh volley from his wife, so that he was fain to draw off his forces, and take to the outside of the house—the only side which, in truth, belongs to a henpecked husband.

Rip's sole domestic adherent was his dog Wolf, who was as much henpecked as his master; for Dame Van Winkle regarded them as companions in idleness, and even looked upon Wolf with an evil eye as the cause of his master's going so often astray. True it is, in all points of spirit befitting an honourable dog, he was as courageous an animal as ever scoured the woods— but what courage can withstand the ever-during and all-besetting terrors of a woman's tongue? The moment Wolf entered the house, his crest fell, his tail drooped to the ground, or curled between his legs, he sneaked about with a gallows air, casting many a sidelong glance at Dame Van Winkle, and at the least flourish of a broom-stick or ladle he would fly to the door with yelping precipitation.

Times grew worse and worse with Rip Van Winkle, as years of matrimony rolled on: a tart temper never mellows with age, and a sharp tongue is the only edged tool that grows keener with constant use. For a long while he used to console himself, when driven from home, by frequenting a kind of perpetual club of the sages, philosophers, and other idle personages of the village, which held its sessions on a bench before a small inn, designated by a rubicund portrait of His Majesty George the Third.	Here they used to sit in the shade, of a long lazy summer's day, talking listlessly over village gossip, or telling endless sleepy stories about nothing.	But it would have been worth any statesman's money to have heard the profound discussions that sometimes took place, when by chance an old newspaper fell into their hands, from some passing traveller. How solemnly they would listen to the contents, as drawled out by Derrick Van Bummel, the schoolmaster, a dapper, learned little man, who was not to be daunted by the most gigantic word in the dictionary; and how sagely they would deliberate upon public events some months after they had taken place.

The opinions of this junto were completely controlled by Nicholas Vedder, a patriarch of the village, and landlord of the inn, at the door of which he took his seat from morning till night, just moving sufficiently to avoid the sun, and keep in the shade of a large tree; so that the neighbours could tell the hour by his movements as accurately as by a sundial.	It is true, he was rarely heard to speak, but smoked his pipe incessantly. His adherents, however (for every great man has his adherents), perfectly understood him, and knew how to gather his opinions.	When anything that was read or related displeased him, he was observed to smoke his pipe vehemently, and to send forth short, frequent, and angry puffs; but when pleased, he would inhale the smoke slowly and tranquilly, and emit it in light and placid clouds, and sometimes taking the pipe from his mouth and letting the fragrant vapour curl about his nose, would gravely nod his head in token of perfect approbation.

From even this stronghold the unlucky Rip was at length routed by his termagant wife, who would suddenly break in upon the tranquillity of the assemblage, and call the members all to naught; nor was that august personage, Nicholas Vedder himself, sacred from the daring tongue of this terrible virago, who charged him outright with encouraging her husband in habits of idleness.

Poor Rip was at last reduced almost to despair, and his only alternative to escape from the labour of the farm and clamour of his wife was to take gun in hand, and stroll away into the woods. Here he would sometimes seat himself at the foot of a tree, and share the contents of his wallet with Wolf, with whom he sympathised as a fellow-sufferer in persecution. "Poor Wolf," he would say, "thy mistress leads thee a dog's life of it; but never mind, my lad, whilst I live thou shalt never want a friend to stand by thee!" Wolf would wag his tail, look wistfully in his master's face; and if dogs can feel pity, I verily believe he reciprocated the sentiment with all his heart.

In a long ramble of the kind, on a fine autumnal day, Rip had unconsciously scrambled to one of the highest parts of the Catskill Mountains. He was after his favourite sport of squirrel-shooting, and the still solitudes had echoed and re-echoed with the reports of his gun. Panting and fatigued, he threw himself, late in the afternoon, on a green knoll covered with mountain herbage, that crowned the brow of a precipice. From an opening between the trees, he could overlook all the lower country for many a mile of rich woodland. He saw at a distance the lordly Hudson, far, far below him, moving on its silent but majestic course, with the reflection of a purple cloud, or the sail of a lagging bark, here and there sleeping on its glassy bosom, and it last losing itself in the blue highlands.

On the other side he looked down into a deep mountain glen, wild, lonely, and shagged, the bottom filled with fragments from the impending cliffs, and scarcely lighted by the reflected rays of the setting sun. For some time Rip lay musing on this scene; evening was gradually advancing; the mountains began to throw their long blue shadows over the valleys; he saw that it would be dark long before he could reach the village; and he heaved a heavy sigh when he thought of encountering the terrors of Dame Van Winkle.

As he was about to descend he heard a voice from a distance hallooing, "Rip Van Winkle! Rip Van Winkle!" He looked round, but could see nothing but a crow winging its solitary flight across the mountain. He thought his fancy must have deceived him, and turned again to descend, when he heard the same cry ring through the still evening air, "Rip Van Winkle! Rip Van Winkle!"—at the same time Wolf bristled up his back and, giving a low growl, skulked to his master's side, looking fearfully down into the glen. Rip now felt a vague apprehension stealing over him: he looked anxiously in the same direction, and perceived a strange figure slowly toiling up the rocks, and bending under the weight of something he carried on his back. He was surprised to see any human being in this lonely and unfrequented place, but supposing it to be some-one of the neighbourhood in need of his assistance, he hastened down to yield it.

On nearer approach, he was still more surprised at the singularity of the stranger's appearance. He was a short, square-built old fellow, with thick bushy hair, and a grizzled beard. His dress was of the antique Dutch fashion — a cloth jerkin strapped round the waist—several pair of breeches, the outer one of ample volume, decorated with rows of buttons down the sides, and bunches at the knees. He bore on his shoulder a stout keg, that seemed full of liquor, and made signs for Rip to approach and assist him with the load. Though rather shy and distrustful of this new acquaintance, Rip complied with his usual alacrity, and mutually relieving one another, they clambered up a narrow gully, apparently the dry bed of a mountain torrent. As they ascended, Rip every now and then heard long rolling peals, like distant thunder, that seemed to issue out of a deep ravine or rather cleft between lofty rocks, towards which their rugged path conducted. He paused for an instant, but supposing it to be the muttering of one of those transient thunder-showers which often take place in mountain heights, he proceeded. Passing through the ravine, they came to a hollow, like a small amphitheatre, surrounded by perpendicular precipices, over the brinks of which impending trees shot their branches, so that you only caught glimpses of the azure sky, and the bright evening cloud. During the whole time Rip and his companion had laboured on in silence; for though the former marvelled greatly what could be the object of carrying a keg of liquor up this wild mountain, yet there was something strange and incomprehensible about the unknown that inspired awe, and checked familiarity.

On entering the amphitheatre, new objects of wonder presented themselves. On a level spot in the centre was a company of odd-looking personages playing at ninepins. They were dressed in a quaint outlandish fashion: some wore short doublets, others jerkins, with long knives in their belts, and most of them had enormous breeches, of similar style with that of the guide's. Their visages, too, were peculiar; one had a large beard, broad face, and small piggish eyes: the face of another seemed to consist entirely of nose, and was surmounted by a white sugar-loaf hat, set off with a little red cock's tail. They all had beards, of various shapes and colours. There was one who seemed to be the commander. He was a stout old gentleman, with a weather-beaten countenance; he wore a laced doublet, broad belt and hanger, high-crowned hat and feather, red stockings, and high-heeled shoes with roses in them. The whole group reminded Rip of the figures in an old Flemish painting, in the parlour of Dominie Van Shaick, the village parson, and which had been brought over from Holland at the time of the settlement.

What seemed particularly odd to Rip was that, though these folks were evidently amusing themselves, yet they maintained the gravest faces, the most mysterious silence, and were, withal, the most melancholy party of pleasure he had ever witnessed. Nothing interrupted the stillness of the scene but the noise of the balls, which, whenever they were rolled, echoed along the mountains like rumbling peals of thunder.

As Rip and his companion approached them, they suddenly desisted from their play, and stared at him with such fixed, statue-like gaze, and such strange, uncouth, lack-lustre countenances, that his heart turned within him, and his knees smote together. His companion now emptied the contents of the keg into large flagons, and made signs to him to wait upon the company. He obeyed with fear and trembling; they quaffed the liquor in profound silence, and then returned to their game.

By degrees Rip's awe and apprehension subsided. He even ventured, when no eye was fixed upon him, to taste the beverage, which he found had much of the flavour of excellent Hollands. He was naturally a thirsty soul, and was soon tempted to repeat the draught. One taste provoked another, and he reiterated his visits to the flagon so often that at length his senses were overpowered, his eyes swam in his head, his head gradually declined, and he fell into a deep sleep.

On waking, he found himself on the green knoll whence he had first seen the old man of the glen. He rubbed his eyes—it was a bright, sunny morning. The birds were hopping and twittering among the bushes, and the eagle was wheeling aloft, and breasting the pure mountain breeze. "Surely," thought Rip, "I have not slept here all night." He recalled the occurrences before he fell asleep. The strange man with the keg of liquor— the mountain ravine—the wild retreat among the rocks —the woebegone party at ninepins—the flagon—"Oh! that flagon! that wicked flagon!" thought Rip—"what excuse shall I make to Dame Van Winkle?"

He looked round for his gun, but in place of the clean, well-oiled fowling-piece, he found an old firelock lying by him, the barrel encrusted with rust, the lock falling off, and the stock worm-eaten. He now suspected that the grave roisterers of the mountain had put a trick upon him, and, having dosed him with liquor, had robbed him of his gun. Wolf, too, had disappeared, but he might have strayed away after a squirrel or partridge. He whistled after him, and shouted his name, but all in vain; the echoes repeated his whistle and shout, but no dog was to be seen.

He determined to revisit the scene of the last evening's gambol, and if he met with any of the party to demand his dog and gun. As he rose to walk, he found himself stiff in the joints, and wanting in his usual activity. "These mountain beds do not agree with me," thought Rip, "and if this frolic should lay me up with a fit of the rheumatism, I shall have a blessed time with Dame Van Winkle!" With some difficulty he got down into the glen; he found the gully up which he and his companion had ascended the preceding evening; but to his astonishment a mountain stream was now foaming down it, leaping from rock to rock, and filling the glen with babbling murmurs. He, however, made shift to scramble up its sides, working his toilsome way through thickets of birch, sassafras, and witch-hazel; and sometimes tripped up or entangled by the wild grape-vines that twisted their coils or tendrils from tree to tree, and spread a kind of network in his path.

At length he reached to where the ravine had opened through the cliffs to the amphitheatre; but no traces of such opening remained. The rocks presented a high, impenetrable wall, over which the torrent came tumbling in a sheet of feathery foam, and fell into a broad, deep basin, black from the shadows of the surrounding forest. Here, then, poor Rip was brought to a stand. He again called and whistled after his dog; he was only answered by the cawing of a flock of idle crows, sporting high in air about a dry tree that overhung a sunny precipice; and who, secure in their elevation, seemed to look down and scoff at the poor man's perplexities. What was to be done? The morning was passing away, and Rip felt famished for want of his breakfast. He grieved to give up his dog and gun; he dreaded to meet his wife; but it would not do to starve among the mountains. He shook his head, shouldered the rusty firelock, and with a heart full of trouble and anxiety turned his steps homeward.

As he approached the village he met a number of people, but none whom he knew, which somewhat surprised him, for he had thought himself acquainted with everyone in the country round. Their dress, too, was of a different fashion from that to which he was accustomed. They all stared at him with equal marks of surprise, and whenever they cast their eyes upon him, invariably stroked their chins. The constant recurrence of this gesture induced Rip, involuntarily, to do the same, when, to his astonishment, he found his beard had grown a foot long!

He had now entered the skirts of the village. A troop of strange children ran at his heels, hooting after him, and pointing at his grey beard. The dogs, too, not one of which he recognised for an old acquaintance, barked at him as he passed. The very village was altered: it was larger and more populous. There were rows of houses which he had never seen before, and those which had been his familiar haunts had disappeared. Strange names were over the doors—strange faces at the windows—everything was strange. His mind now misgave him; he began to doubt whether both he and the world around him were not bewitched. Surely this was his native village, which he had left but the day before. There stood the Catskill Mountains—there ran the silver Hudson at a distance—there was every hill and dale precisely as it had always been—Rip was sorely perplexed—"That flagon last night," thought he, "has addled my poor head sadly!"

It was with some difficulty that he found the way to his own house, which he approached with silent awe, expecting every moment to hear the shrill voice of Dame Van Winkle. He found the house gone to decay—the roof fallen in, the windows shattered, and the doors off the hinges. A half-starved dog, that looked like Wolf, was skulking about it. Rip called him by name, but the cur snarled, showed his teeth, and passed on. This was an unkind cut indeed. "My very dog," sighed poor Rip, "has forgotten me!"

He entered the house, which, to tell the truth, Dame

Van Winkle had always kept in neat order. It was empty, forlorn, and apparently abandoned. This desolateness overcame all his connubial fears—he called loudly to his wife and children—the lonely chambers rang for a moment with his voice, and then all again was silence.

He now hurried forth, and hastened to his old resort, the village inn—but it too was gone. A large rickety wooden building stood in its place, with great gaping windows, some of them broken, and mended with old hats and petticoats, and over the door was painted, "The Union Hotel, by Jonathan Doolittle." Instead of the great tree that used to shelter the quiet little Dutch inn of yore, there now was reared a tall naked pole, with something on the top that looked like a red nightcap, and from it was fluttering a flag, on which was a singular assemblage of stars and stripes—all this was strange and incomprehensible. He recognised on the sign, however, the ruby face of King George, under which he had smoked so many a peaceful pipe, but even this was singularly metamorphosed. The red coat was changed for one of blue and buff, a sword was held in the hand instead of a sceptre, the head was decorated with a cocked hat, and underneath was painted in large characters, "General Washington."

There was as usual a crowd of folk about the door, but none that Rip recollected. The very character of the people seemed changed. There was a busy, bustling, disputatious tone about it, instead of the accustomed phlegm and drowsy tranquillity. He looked in vain for the sage Nicholas Vedder, with his broad face, double chin, and fair, long pipe, uttering clouds of tobacco smoke, instead of idle speeches; or Van Bummel, the schoolmaster, doling forth the contents of an ancient newspaper. In place of these, a lean, bilious-looking fellow, with his pockets full of handbills, was haranguing vehemently about rights of citizens—election—members of Congress—liberty—Bunker Hill—heroes of '76—and other words which were a perfect Babylonish jargon to the bewildered Van Winkle.

The appearance of Rip, with his long, grizzled beard, his rusty firelock, his uncouth dress, and an army of women and children at his heels, soon attracted the attention of the tavern politicians. They crowded round him, eyeing him from head to foot, with great curiosity. The orator bustled up to him, and drawing him partly aside, inquired "on which side he voted." Rip stared in vacant stupidity. Another short but busy little fellow pulled him by the arm, and rising on tiptoe, inquired in his ear "whether he was Federal or Democrat." Rip was equally at a loss to comprehend the question; when a knowing, self-important old gentleman, in a sharp cocked hat, made his way through the crowd, putting them to the right and left with his elbows as he passed, and planting himself before Van Winkle, with one arm akimbo, the other resting on his cane, his keen eyes and sharp hat penetrating, as it were, into his very soul, demanded in an austere tone, "what brought him to the election with a gun on his shoulder, and a mob at his heels, and whether he meant to breed a riot in the village?"

"Alas! gentlemen," cried Rip, somewhat dismayed, "I am a poor, quiet man, a native of the place, and a loyal subject of the king, God bless him!"

Here a general shout burst from the bystanders— "A Tory! a Tory! a spy! a refugee! hustle him! away with him!"

It was with great difficulty that the self-important man in the cocked hat restored order; and having assumed a tenfold austerity of brow, demanded again of the unknown culprit what he came there for, and whom he was seeking. The poor man humbly assured him that he meant no harm, but merely came there in search of some of his neighbours, who used to keep about the tavern.

"Well—who are they? Name them."

Rip bethought himself a moment, and inquired, "Where's Nicholas Vedder?"

There was a silence for a little while, when an old man replied, in a thin, piping voice, "Nicholas Vedder?

Why, he is dead and gone these eighteen years! There was a wooden tombstone in the churchyard that used to tell all about him, but that's rotten and gone too."

"Where's Brom Dutcher?"

"Oh, he went off to the army in the beginning of the war; some say he was killed at the storming of Stony Point—others say he was drowned in a squall, at the foot of Anthony's Nose. I don't know—he never came back again."

"Where's Van Bummel, the schoolmaster?"

"He went off to the wars, too; was a great militia general, and is now in Congress."

Rip's heart died away, at hearing of these sad changes in his home and friends, and finding himself thus alone in the world. Every answer puzzled him, too, by treating of such enormous lapses of time, and of matters which he could not understand: war—Congress—Stony Point—he had no courage to ask after any more friends, but cried out in despair, "Does nobody here know Rip Van Winkle?"

"Oh, Rip Van Winkle!" exclaimed two or three. "Oh, to be sure! that's Rip Van Winkle yonder, leaning against the tree."

Rip looked, and beheld a precise counterpart of himself as he went up the mountain; apparently as lazy and certainly as ragged. The poor fellow was now completely confounded. He doubted his own identity, and whether he was himself or another man. In the midst of his bewilderment, the man in the cocked hat demanded who he was, and what was his name?

"God knows," exclaimed he, at his wits' end; "I'm not myself—I'm somebody else—that's me yonder—no—that's somebody else, got into my shoes—I was myself last night, but I fell asleep on the mountain, and they've changed my gun, and everything's changed, and I'm changed, and I can't tell what's my name, or who I am!"

The bystanders began now to look at each other, nod, wink significantly and tap their fingers against their foreheads. There was a whisper, also, about securing the gun, and keeping the old fellow from doing mischief; at the very suggestion of which the self-important man with the cocked hat retired with some precipitation. At this critical moment a fresh, comely woman pressed through the throng to get a peep at the grey-bearded man. She had a chubby child in her arms, which, frightened at his looks, began to cry. "Hush, Rip," cried she, "hush, you little fool; the old man won't hurt you." The name of the child, the air of the mother, the tone of her voice, all awakened a train of recollections in his mind.

"What is your name, my good woman?" asked he.

"Judith Gardenier."

"And your father's name?"

"Ah, poor man, Rip Van Winkle was his name; but it's twenty years since he went away from home with his gun, and never has been heard of since—his dog came home without him; but whether he shot himself, or was carried away by the Indians, nobody can tell. I was then but a little girl."

Rip had but one question more to ask; but he put it with a faltering voice:

"Where's your mother?"

Oh, she too had died but a short time since: she broke a blood-vessel in a fit of passion at a New England pedlar.

There was a drop of comfort, at least, in this intelligence. The honest man could contain himself no longer. He caught his daughter and her child in his arms. "I am your father!" cried he—"young Rip Van Winkle once—old Rip Van Winkle now! Does nobody know poor Rip Van Winkle?"

All stood amazed, until an old woman, tottering out from among the crowd, put her hand to her brow, and peering under it in his face for a moment, exclaimed, "Sure enough! it is Rip Van Winkle—it is himself. Welcome home again, old neighbour. Why, where have you been these twenty long years?"

Rip's story was soon told, for the whole twenty years had been to him but as one night. The neighbours

stared when they heard it; some were seen to wink at
each other, and put their tongues in their cheeks; and
the self-important man in the cocked hat, who, when
the alarm was over, had returned to the field, screwed
down the corners of his mouth, and shook his head—
upon which there was a general shaking of the head
throughout the assemblage.

It was determined, however, to take the opinion of
old Peter Vanderdonk, who was seen slowly advancing
up the road. He was a descendant of the historian of
that name, who wrote one of the earliest accounts of
the province. Peter was the most ancient inhabitant
of the village, and well versed in all the wonderful
events and traditions of the neighbourhood. He
recollected Rip at once, and corroborated his story in
the most satisfactory manner. He assured the company that it was a fact, handed down from his ancestor
the historian, that the Kaatskill Mountains had always
been haunted by strange beings. That it was affirmed
that the great Hendrick Hudson, the first discoverer
of the river and country, kept a kind of vigil there every
twenty years, with his crew of the *Half Moon*, being
permitted in this way to revisit the scenes of his enterprise, and keep a guardian eye upon the river and the
great city called by his name. That his father had once
seen them in their old Dutch dresses playing at ninepins in a hollow of the mountain; and that he himself
had heard, one summer afternoon, the sound of their
balls, like distant peals of thunder.

To make a long story short, the company broke up,
and returned to the more important concerns of the
election. Rip's daughter took him home to live with
her, she had a snug, well-furnished house, and a stout,
cheery farmer for a husband, whom Rip recollected
for one of the urchins that used to climb upon his back.
As to Rip's son and heir, who was the ditto of himself,
seen leaning against the tree, he was employed to work
on the farm, but evinced an hereditary disposition to
attend to anything else but his business.

Rip now resumed his old walks and habits; he soon

found many of his former cronies, though all rather the worse for the wear and tear of time; and preferred making friends among the rising generation, with whom he soon grew into great favour.

Having nothing to do at home, and being arrived at that happy age when a man can be idle with impunity, he took his place once more on the bench, at the inn door, and was reverenced as one of the patriarchs of the village, and a chronicle of the old times "before the war." It was some time before he could get into the regular track of gossip, or could be made to comprehend the strange events that had taken place during his torpor. How that there had been a Revolutionary War—that the country had thrown off the yoke of old England—and that, instead of being a subject of His Majesty George the Third, he was now a free citizen of the United States. Rip, in fact, was no politician; the changes of states and empires made but little impression on him; but there was one species of despotism under which he had long groaned, and that was—petticoat government. Happily, that was at an end; he had got his neck out of the yoke of matrimony, and could go in and out whenever he pleased, without dreading the tyranny of Dame Van Winkle. Whenever her name was mentioned, however, he shook his head, shrugged his shoulders, and cast up his eyes; which might pass either for an expression of resignation to his fate, or joy at his deliverance.

He used to tell his story to every stranger that arrived at Mr. Doolittle's hotel. He was observed, at first, to vary on some points every time he told it, which was doubtless owing to his having so recently awakened. It at last settled down precisely to the tale I have related, and not a man, woman, or child in the neighbourhood but knew it by heart. Some always pretended to doubt the reality of it, and insisted that Rip had been out of his head, and that this was one point on which he always remained flighty. The old Dutch inhabitants, however, almost universally gave it full credit. Even to this day, they never hear a thunder-storm of a summer

afternoon about the Kaatskill, but they say Hendrick
Hudson and his crew are at their game of ninepins;
and it is a common wish of all henpecked husbands in
the neighbourhood, when life hangs heavy on their hands,
that they might have a quieting draught out of Rip
Van Winkle's flagon.

NOTE.—The foregoing tale, one would suspect, had been
suggested to Mr. Knickerbocker by a little German superstition about the Emperor Frederick der Rothbart and the
Kypphaüser Mountain; the subjoined note, however, which
he had appended to the tale, shows that it is an absolute
fact, narrated with his usual fidelity:

"The story of Rip Van Winkle may seem incredible to
many, but nevertheless I give it my full belief, for I know
the vicinity of our old Dutch settlements to have been
very subject to marvellous events and appearances. Indeed,
I have heard many stranger stories than this, in the villages
along the Hudson, all of which were too well authenticated
to admit of a doubt. I have even talked with Rip Van
Winkle myself, who, when last I saw him, was a very
venerable old man, and so perfectly rational and consistent
on every other point, that I think no conscientious person
could refuse to take this into the bargain; nay, I have
seen a certificate on the subject taken before a country
justice, and signed with a cross, in the justice's own handwriting. The story, therefore, is beyond the possibility
of a doubt.   D. K."

THE TELL-TALE HEART [1]

By EDGAR ALLAN POE (1809–49)

TRUE!—nervous,—very, very dreadfully nervous I had been and am! but why *will* you say that I am mad? The disease had sharpened my senses—not destroyed—not dulled them. Above all was the sense of hearing acute. I heard all things in the heaven and in the earth. I heard many things in hell. How, then, am I mad? Hearken! and observe how healthily — how calmly I can tell you the whole story.

It is impossible to tell how first the idea entered my brain; but once conceived, it haunted me day and night. Object there was none. Passion there was none. I loved the old man. He had never wronged me. He had never given me insult. For his gold I had no desire. I think it was his eye! Yes, it was this! One of his eyes resembled that of a vulture—a pale blue eye, with a film over it. Whenever it fell upon me, my blood ran cold; and so by degrees—very gradually—I made up my mind to take the life of the old man, and thus rid myself of the eye forever.

Now this is the point. You fancy me mad. Madmen know nothing. But you should have seen *me*. You should have seen how wisely I proceeded—with what caution—with what foresight—with what dissimulation I went to work!

I was never kinder to the old man than during the whole week before I killed him. And every night, about midnight, I turned the latch of his door and opened it —oh, so gently! And then, when I had made an opening sufficient for my head, I put in a dark-lantern, all closed, closed, so that no light shone out, and then I thrust in my head. Oh, you would have laughed to see how cunningly I thrust it in! I moved it slowly—

[1] First appeared in the *Pioneer*, in 1843.

very, very slowly, so that I might not disturb the old
man's sleep. It took me an hour to place my whole
head within the opening so far that I could see him
as he lay upon his bed. Ha!—would a madman have
been so wise as this? And then, when my head was
well in the room, I undid the lantern cautiously—oh,
so cautiously—cautiously (for the hinges creaked)—
I undid it just so much that a single thin ray fell upon
the vulture eye. And this I did for seven long nights
—every night just at midnight—but I found the eye
always closed; and so it was impossible to do the work;
for it was not the old man who vexed me, but his Evil
Eye. And every morning, when the day broke, I went
boldly into the chamber, and spoke courageously to
him, calling him by name in a hearty tone, and inquiring
how he had passed the night. So you see he would
have been a very profound old man, indeed, to suspect
that every night, just at twelve, I looked in upon him
while he slept.

Upon the eighth night I was more than usually
cautious in opening the door. A watch's minute-hand
moves more quickly than did mine. Never before that
night had I *felt* the extent of my own powers—of my
sagacity. I could scarcely contain my feelings of
triumph. To think that there I was, opening the door,
little by little, and he not even to dream of my secret
deeds or thoughts. I fairly chuckled at the idea; and
perhaps he heard me; for he moved on the bed suddenly
as if startled. Now you may think that I drew back—
but no. His room was as black as pitch with the thick
darkness (for the shutters were close fastened, through
fear of robbers), and so I knew that he could not see the
opening of the door, and I kept pushing it on steadily,
steadily.

I had my head in, and was about to open the lantern,
when my thumb slipped upon the tin fastening, and the
old man sprang up in bed, crying out, "Who's there?"

I kept quite still and said nothing. For a whole hour
I did not move a muscle, and in the meantime I did not
hear him lie down. He was still sitting up in the bed

listening; — just as I have done, night after night, hearkening to the death-watches in the wall.

Presently I heard a slight groan, and I knew it was the groan of mortal terror. It was not a groan of pain or grief—oh no!—it was the low stifled sound that arises from the bottom of the soul when overcharged with awe. I knew the sound well. Many a night, just at midnight, when all the world slept, it has welled up from my own bosom, deepening, with its dreadful echo, the terrors that distracted me. I say I knew it well. I knew what the old man felt, and pitied him, although I chuckled at heart. I knew that he had been lying awake ever since the first slight noise, when he had turned in the bed. His fears had been ever since growing upon him. He had been trying to fancy them causeless, but could not. He had been saying to himself, "It is nothing but the wind in the chimney—it is only a mouse crossing the floor," or "it is merely a cricket which has made a single chirp." Yes, he had been trying to comfort himself with these suppositions; but he had found all in vain. *All in vain;* because Death, in approaching him, had stalked with his black shadow before him, and enveloped the victim. And it was the mournful influence of the unperceived shadow that caused him to feel—although he neither saw nor heard —to *feel* the presence of my head within the room.

When I had waited a long time, very patiently, without hearing him lie down, I resolved to open a little —a very, very little crevice in the lantern. So I opened it—you cannot imagine how stealthily, stealthily— until, at length, a single dim ray, like the thread of the spider, shot from out the crevice and full upon the vulture eye.

It was open—wide, wide open—and I grew furious as I gazed upon it. I saw it with perfect distinctness —all a dull blue, with a hideous veil over it that chilled the very marrow in my bones; but I could see nothing else of the old man's face or person: for I had directed the ray, as if by instinct, precisely upon the damned spot.

And now—have I not told you that what you mistake

for madness is but over-acuteness of the senses?—now, I say, there came to my ears a low, dull, quick sound, such as a watch makes when enveloped in cotton. I knew *that* sound well too. It was the beating of the old man's heart. It increased my fury, as the beating of a drum stimulates the soldier into courage.

But even yet I refrained and kept still. I scarcely breathed. I held the lantern motionless. I tried how steadily I could maintain the ray upon the eye. Meantime the hellish tattoo of the heart increased. It grew quicker and quicker, and louder and louder every instant. The old man's terror *must* have been extreme! It grew louder, I say, louder every moment!—do you mark me well? I have told you that I am nervous: so I am. And now at the dead hour of night, amid the dreadful silence of that old house, so strange a noise as this excited me to uncontrollable terror. Yet, for some minutes longer I refrained and stood still. But the beating grew louder, louder! I thought the heart must burst. And now a new anxiety seized me—the sound would be heard by a neighbour! The old man's hour had come! With a loud yell, I threw open the lantern and leaped into the room. He shrieked once—once only. In an instant I dragged him to the floor, and pulled the heavy bed over him. I then smiled gaily, to find the deed so far done. But, for many minutes, the heart beat on with a muffled sound. This, however, did not vex me; it would not be heard through the wall. At length it ceased. The old man was dead. I removed the bed and examined the corpse. Yes, he was stone, stone dead. I placed my hand upon the heart and held it there many minutes. There was no pulsation. He was stone dead. His eye would trouble me no more.

If still you think me mad, you will think so no longer when I describe the wise precautions I took for the concealment of the body. The night waned, and I worked hastily, but in silence. First of all I dismembered the corpse. I cut off the head and the arms and the legs.

I then took up three planks from the flooring of the chamber, and deposited all between the scantlings. I then replaced the boards so cleverly, so cunningly, that no human eye—not even *his*—could have detected anything wrong. There was nothing to wash out—no stain of any kind—no blood-spot whatever. I had been too wary for that. A tub had caught all—ha! ha!

When I had made an end of these labours, it was four o'clock—still dark as midnight. As the bell sounded the hour, there came a knocking at the street door. I went down to open it with a light heart—for what had I *now* to fear? There entered three men, who introduced themselves, with perfect suavity, as officers of the police. A shriek had been heard by a neighbour during the night: suspicion of foul play had been aroused; information had been lodged at the police office, and they (the officers) had been deputed to search the premises.

I smiled—for *what* had I to fear? I bade the gentlemen welcome. The shriek, I said, was my own in a dream. The old man, I mentioned, was absent in the country. I took my visitors all over the house. I bade them search—search *well*. I led them, at length, to *his* chamber. I showed them his treasures, secure, undisturbed. In the enthusiasm of my confidence, I brought chairs into the room, and desired them *here* to rest from their fatigues, while I myself, in the wild audacity of my perfect triumph, placed my own seat upon the very spot beneath which reposed the corpse of the victim.

The officers were satisfied. My *manner* had convinced them. I was singularly at ease. They sat, and while I answered cheerily, they chatted familiar things. But, ere long, I felt myself getting pale and wished them gone. My head ached, and I fancied a ringing in my ears: but still they sat and still chatted. The ringing became more distinct:—it continued and became more distinct: I talked more freely to get rid of the feeling: but it continued and gained definitiveness—until, at length, I found that the noise was *not* within my ears.

No doubt I now grew *very* pale—but I talked more

fluently, and with a heightened voice. Yet the sound increased—and what could I do? It was *a low, dull, quick sound—much such a sound as a watch makes when enveloped in cotton*. I gasped for breath—and yet the officers heard it not. I talked more quickly—more vehemently; but the noise steadily increased. Why *would* they not be gone? I paced the floor to and fro with heavy strides, as if excited to fury by the observation of the men—but the noise steadily increased. Oh, God! what *could* I do? I foamed—I raved—I swore! I swung the chair upon which I had been sitting, and grated it upon the boards, but the noise arose over all and continually increased. It grew louder—louder—*louder* !—And still the men chatted pleasantly, and smiled. Was it possible they heard not? Almighty God!—no, no! They heard!—they suspected!—they *knew* !—they were making a *mockery* of my horror!—this I thought, and this I think. But anything was better than this agony! Anything was more tolerable than this derision! I could bear those hypocritical smiles no longer! I felt that I must scream or die! —and now—again!—hark! louder! louder! louder! *louder* !—

"Villains!" I shrieked, "dissemble no more! I admit the deed!—tear up the planks!—here, here!—it is the beating of his hideous heart!"

ETHAN BRAND [1]

A CHAPTER FROM AN ABORTIVE ROMANCE

By NATHANIEL HAWTHORNE (1804–64)

BARTRAM the lime-burner, a rough, heavy-looking man, begrimed with charcoal, sat watching his kiln, at night-fall, while his little son played at building houses with the scattered fragments of marble, when, on the hillside below them, they heard a roar of laughter, not mirthful, but slow, and even solemn, like a wind shaking the boughs of the forest.

"Father, what is that?" asked the little boy, leaving his play, and pressing betwixt his father's knees.

"Oh, some drunken man, I suppose," answered the lime-burner; "some merry fellow from the bar-room in the village, who dared not laugh loud enough within doors lest he should blow the roof of the house off.   So here he is, shaking his jolly sides at the foot of Graylock."

"But, father," said the child, more sensitive than the obtuse, middle-aged clown, "he does not laugh like a man that is glad.   So the noise frightens me!"

"Don't be a fool, child!" cried his father gruffly. "You will never make a man, I do believe; there is too much of your mother in you.   I have known the rustling of a leaf startle you.   Hark!   Here comes the merry fellow now.   You shall see that there is no harm in him."

Bartram and his little son, while they were talking thus, sat watching the same lime-kiln that had been the scene of Ethan Brand's solitary and meditative life, before he began his search for the Unpardonable Sin. Many years, as we have seen, had now elapsed, since that

[1] Written in 1848: published in Holden's *Dollar Magazine* in 1851.

portentous night when the IDEA was first developed. The kiln, however, on the mountain-side stood unimpaired, and was in nothing changed since he had thrown his dark thoughts into the intense glow of its furnace, and melted them, as it were, into the one thought that took possession of his life. It was a rude, round, towerlike structure, about twenty feet high, heavily built of rough stones, and with a hillock of earth heaped about the larger part of its circumference; so that the blocks and fragments of marble might be drawn by cart-loads, and thrown in at the top. There was an opening at the bottom of the tower, like an oven-mouth, but large enough to admit a man in a stooping posture, and provided with a massive iron door. With the smoke and jets of flame issuing from the chinks and crevices of this door, which seemed to give admittance into the hillside, it resembled nothing so much as the private entrance to the infernal regions, which the shepherds of the Delectable Mountains were accustomed to show to pilgrims.

There are many such lime-kilns in that tract of country, for the purpose of burning the white marble which composes a large part of the substance of the hills. Some of them, built years ago, and long deserted, with weeds growing in the vacant round of the interior, which is open to the sky, and grass and wild flowers rooting themselves into the chinks of the stones, look already like relics of antiquity, and may yet be overspread with the lichens of centuries to come. Others, where the lime-burner still feeds his daily and night-long fire, afford points of interest to the wanderer among the hills, who seats himself on a log of wood or a fragment of marble, to hold a chat with the solitary man. It is a lonesome, and, when the character is inclined to thought, may be an intensely thoughtful, occupation; as it proved in the case of Ethan Brand, who had mused to such strange purpose, in days gone by, while the fire in this very kiln was burning.

The man who now watched the fire was of a different order, and troubled himself with no thoughts save the very few that were requisite to his business. At frequent intervals he flung back the clashing weight of the iron door, and, turning his face from the insufferable glare, thrust in huge logs of oak, or stirred the immense brands with a long pole. Within the furnace were seen the curling and riotous flames, and the burning marble, almost molten with the intensity of heat; while without, the reflection of the fire quivered on the dark intricacy of the surrounding forest, and showed in the foreground a bright and ruddy little picture of the hut, the spring beside its door, the athletic and coal-begrimed figure of the lime-burner, and the half-frightened child, shrinking into the protection of his father's shadow. And when again the iron door was closed, then reappeared the tender light of the half-full moon, which vainly strove to trace out the indistinct shapes of the neighbouring mountains; and, in the upper sky, there was a flitting congregation of clouds, still faintly tinged with the rosy sunset, though thus far down into the valley the sunshine had vanished long and long ago.

The little boy now crept still closer to his father, as footsteps were heard ascending the hillside, and a human form thrust aside the bushes that clustered beneath the trees.

"Halloo! what is it?" cried the lime-burner, vexed at his son's timidity, yet half infected by it. "Come forward, and show yourself, like a man, or I'll fling this chunk of marble at your head!"

"You offer me a rough welcome," said a gloomy voice, as the unknown man drew nigh. "Yet I neither claim nor desire a kinder one, even at my own fireside."

To obtain a distincter view, Bartram threw open the iron door of the kiln, whence immediately issued a gush of fierce light, that smote full upon the stranger's face and figure. To a careless eye there appeared nothing very remarkable in his aspect, which was that of a man in a coarse, brown, country-made suit of clothes, tall and thin, with the staff and heavy shoes of a wayfarer. As he advanced, he fixed his eyes—which were very bright—intently upon the brightness of the furnace, as if he beheld, or expected to behold, some object worthy of note within it.

"Good evening, stranger," said the lime-burner; "whence come you, so late in the day?"

"I come from my search," answered the wayfarer; "for, at last, it is finished."

"Drunk!—or crazy!" muttered Bartram to himself. "I shall have trouble with the fellow. The sooner I drive him away, the better."

The little boy, all in a tremble, whispered to his father, and begged him to shut the door of the kiln, so that there might not be so much light; for that there was something in the man's face which he was afraid to look at, yet could not look away from. And, indeed, even the lime-burner's dull and torpid sense began to be impressed by an indescribable something in that thin, rugged, thoughtful visage, with the grizzled hair hanging wildly about it, and those deeply sunken eyes, which gleamed like fires within the entrance of a mysterious cavern. But, as he closed the door, the stranger turned towards him, and spoke in a quiet, familiar way that made Bartram feel as if he were a sane and sensible man, after all.

"Your task draws to an end, I see," said he. "This marble has already been burning three days. A few hours more will convert the stone to lime."

"Why, who are you?" exclaimed the lime-burner. "You seem as well acquainted with my business as I am myself."

"And well I may be," said the stranger; "for I followed the same craft many a long year, and here, too, on this very spot. But you are a new-comer in these parts. Did you never hear of Ethan Brand?"

"The man that went in search of the Unpardonable Sin?" asked Bartram, with a laugh.

"The same," answered the stranger. "He has found what he sought, and therefore he comes back again."

"What! then you are Ethan Brand himself?" cried the lime-burner, in amazement. "I am a new-comer here, as you say, and they call it eighteen years since you left the foot of Graylock. But, I can tell you, the good folks still talk about Ethan Brand, in the village yonder, and what a strange errand took him away from his lime-kiln. Well, and so you have found the Unpardonable Sin?"

"Even so!" said the stranger calmly.

"If the question is a fair one," proceeded Bartram, "where might it be?"

Ethan Brand laid his finger on his own heart.

"Here!" replied he.

And then, without mirth in his countenance, but as if moved by an involuntary recognition of the infinite absurdity of seeking throughout the world for what was the closest of all things to himself, and looking into every heart, save his own, for what was hidden in no other breast, he broke into a laugh of scorn. It was the same slow, heavy laugh that had almost appalled the lime-burner when it heralded the wayfarer's approach.

The solitary mountain-side was made dismal by it. Laughter, when out of place, mistimed, or bursting forth from a disordered state of feeling, may be the most terrible modulation of the human voice. The laughter of one asleep, even if it be a little child—the madman's laugh—the wild, screaming laugh of a born idiot—are sounds that we sometimes tremble to hear, and would always willingly forget. Poets have imagined no utterance of fiends or hobgoblins so fearfully appropriate as a laugh. And even the obtuse lime-burner felt his nerves shaken, as this strange man looked inward at his own heart, and burst into laughter that rolled away into the night, and was indistinctly reverberated among the hills.

"Joe," said he to his little son, "scamper down to the tavern in the village, and tell the jolly fellows there that Ethan Brand has come back, and that he has found the Unpardonable Sin!"

The boy darted away on his errand, to which Ethan Brand made no objection, nor seemed hardly to notice it. He sat on a log of wood, looking steadfastly at the iron door of the kiln. When the child was out of sight, and

his swift and light footsteps ceased to be heard treading
first on the fallen leaves and then on the rocky mountain path, the lime-burner began to regret his departure.
He felt that the little fellow's presence had been a
barrier between his guest and himself, and that he must
now deal, heart to heart, with a man who, on his own
confession, had committed the one only crime for which
Heaven could afford no mercy. That crime, in its
indistinct blackness, seemed to overshadow him. The
lime-burner's own sins rose up within him, and made
his memory riotous with a throng of evil shapes that
asserted their kindred with the Master Sin, whatever
it might be, which it was within the scope of man's
corrupted nature to conceive and cherish. They were
all of one family; they went to and fro between his
breast and Ethan Brand's, and carried dark greetings
from one to the other.

Then Bartram remembered the stories which had
grown traditionary in reference to this strange man,
who had come upon him like a shadow of the night,
and was making himself at home in his old place, after
so long absence that the dead people, dead and buried
for years, would have had more right to be at home, in
any familiar spot, than he. Ethan Brand, it was said,
had conversed with Satan himself in the lurid blaze of
this very kiln. The legend had been matter of mirth
heretofore, but looked grisly now. According to this
tale, before Ethan Brand departed on his search, he
had been accustomed to evoke a fiend from the hot
furnace of the lime-kiln, night after night, in order to
confer with him about the Unpardonable Sin; the man
and the fiend each labouring to frame the image of some
mode of guilt which could neither be atoned for nor
forgiven. And, with the first gleam of light upon the
mountain-top, the fiend crept in at the iron door, there
to abide the intensest element of fire, until again summoned forth to share in the dreadful task of extending
man's possible guilt beyond the scope of Heaven's else
infinite mercy.

While the lime-burner was struggling with the horror

of these thoughts, Ethan Brand rose from the log, and flung open the door of the kiln. The action was in such accordance with the idea in Bartram's mind, that he almost expected to see the Evil One issue forth, red-hot from the raging furnace.

"Hold! hold!" cried he, with a tremulous attempt to laugh; for he was ashamed of his fears, although they overmastered him. "Don't, for mercy's sake, bring out your Devil now!"

"Man!" sternly replied Ethan Brand, "what need have I of the Devil? I have left him behind me, on my track. It is with such half-way sinners as you that he busies himself. Fear not, because I open the door. I do but act by old custom, and am going to trim your fire, like a lime-burner, as I was once."

He stirred the vast coals, thrust in more wood, and bent forward to gaze into the hollow prison-house of the fire, regardless of the fierce glow that reddened upon his face. The lime-burner sat watching him, and half suspected his strange guest of a purpose, if not to evoke a fiend, at least to plunge bodily into the flames, and thus vanish from the sight of man. Ethan Brand, however, drew quietly back, and closed the door of the kiln.

"I have looked," said he, "into many a human heart that was seven times hotter with sinful passions than yonder furnace is with fire. But I found not there what I sought. No, not the Unpardonable Sin!"

"What is the Unpardonable Sin?" asked the lime-burner; and then he shrank farther from his companion, trembling lest his question should be answered.

"It is a sin that grew within my own breast," replied Ethan Brand, standing erect, with a pride that distinguishes all enthusiasts of his stamp. "A sin that grew nowhere else! The sin of an intellect that triumphed over the sense of brotherhood with man and reverence for God, and sacrificed everything to its own mighty claims! the only sin that deserves a recompense of immortal agony! Freely, were it to do again, would I incur the guilt. Unshrinkingly I accept the retribution!"

"The man's head is turned," muttered the lime-burner to himself. "He may be a sinner, like the rest of us—nothing more likely—but, I'll be sworn, he is a madman too."

Nevertheless, he felt uncomfortable at his situation, alone with Ethan Brand on the wild mountain-side, and was right glad to hear the rough murmur of tongues, and the footsteps of what seemed a pretty numerous party, stumbling over the stones and rustling through the underbrush. Soon appeared the whole lazy regiment that was wont to infest the village tavern, comprehending three or four individuals who had drunk flip beside the bar-room fire through all the winters, and smoked their pipes beneath the stoop through all the summers, since Ethan Brand's departure. Laughing boisterously, and mingling all their voices together in unceremonious talk, they now burst into the moonshine and narrow streaks of firelight that illuminated the open space before the lime-kiln. Bartram set the door ajar again, flooding the spot with light, that the whole company might get a fair view of Ethan Brand, and he of them.

There, among other old acquaintances, was a once ubiquitous man, now almost extinct, but whom we were formerly sure to encounter at the hotel of every thriving village throughout the country. It was the stage-agent. The present specimen of the genus was a wilted and smoke-dried man, wrinkled and red-nosed, in a smartly cut, brown, bob-tailed coat, with brass buttons, who, for a length of time unknown, had kept his desk and corner in the bar-room, and was still puffing what seemed to be the same cigar that he had lighted twenty years before. He had great fame as a dry joker, though, perhaps, less on account of any intrinsic humour than from a certain flavour of brandy toddy and tobacco smoke, which impregnated all his ideas and expressions, as well as his person. Another well-remembered though strangely altered face was that of Lawyer Giles, as people still called him in courtesy; an elderly ragamuffin, in his soiled shirt-sleeves and tow-cloth trousers. This poor fellow had been an attorney, in what he called his better days, a sharp practitioner, and in great vogue among the village litigants; but flip, and sling, and toddy, and cocktails, imbibed at all hours, morning, noon, and night, had caused him to slide from intellectual to various kinds and degrees of bodily labour, till, at last, to adopt his own phrase, he slid into a soap vat. In other words, Giles was now a soap-boiler, in a small way. He had come to be but the fragment of a human being, a part of one foot having been chopped off by an axe, and an entire hand torn away by the devilish grip of a steam-engine. Yet, though the corporeal hand was gone, a spiritual member remained; for, stretching forth the stump, Giles steadfastly averred that he felt an invisible thumb and fingers with as vivid a sensation as before the real ones were amputated. A maimed and miserable wretch he was; but one, nevertheless, whom the world could not trample on, and had no right to scorn, either in this or any previous stage of his misfortunes, since he had still kept up the courage and spirit of a man, asked nothing in charity, and with his one hand—and that the left one—fought a stern battle against want and hostile circumstances.

Among the throng, too, came another personage, who, with certain points of similarity to Lawyer Giles, had many more of difference. It was the village doctor; a man of some fifty years, whom, at an earlier period of his life, we introduced as paying a professional visit to Ethan Brand during the latter's supposed insanity. He was now a purple-visaged, rude, and brutal, yet half-gentlemanly figure, with something wild, ruined, and desperate in his talk, and in all the details of his gesture and manners. Brandy possessed this man like an evil spirit, and made him as surly and savage as a wild beast, and as miserable as a lost soul; but there was supposed to be in him such wonderful skill, such native gifts of healing, beyond any which medical science could impart, that society caught hold of him, and would not let him sink out of its reach. So, swaying to and fro upon his horse, and grumbling thick accents at the bedside, he visited all the sick-chambers for miles about among the mountain towns, and sometimes raised a dying man, as it were, by miracle, or quite as often, no doubt, sent his patient to a grave that was dug many a year too soon. The doctor had an everlasting pipe in his mouth, and, as somebody said, in allusion to his habit of swearing, it was always alight with hell-fire.

These three worthies pressed forward, and greeted Ethan Brand each after his own fashion, earnestly inviting him to partake of the contents of a certain black bottle, in which, as they averred, he would find something far better worth seeking for than the Unpardonable Sin. No mind, which has wrought itself by intense and solitary meditation into a high state of enthusiasm, can endure the kind of contact with low and vulgar modes of thought and feeling to which Ethan Brand was now subjected. It made him doubt—and, strange to say, it was a painful doubt—whether he had indeed found the Unpardonable Sin and found it within himself. The whole question on which he had exhausted life, and more than life, looked like a delusion.

"Leave me," he said bitterly, "ye brute beasts, that have made yourselves so, shrivelling up your souls with fiery liquors! I have done with you. Years and years ago, I groped into your hearts, and found nothing there for my purpose. Get ye gone!"

"Why, you uncivil scoundrel," cried the fierce doctor, "is that the way you respond to the kindness of your best friends? Then let me tell you the truth. You have no more found the Unpardonable Sin than yonder boy Joe has. You are but a crazy fellow—I told you so twenty years ago—neither better nor worse than a crazy fellow, and a fit companion of old Humphrey, here!"

He pointed to an old man, shabbily dressed, with long white hair, thin visage, and unsteady eyes. For some years past this aged person had been wandering about among the hills, inquiring of all travellers whom he met for his daughter. The girl, it seemed, had gone off with a company of circus performers; and occasionally tidings of her came to the village, and fine stories were told of her glittering appearance as she rode on horseback in the ring, or performed marvellous feats on the tight-rope.

The white-haired father now approached Ethan Brand, and gazed unsteadily into his face.

"They tell me you have been all over the earth," said he, wringing his hands with earnestness. "You must have seen my daughter, for she makes a grand figure in the world, and everybody goes to see her. Did she send any word to her old father, or say when she was coming back?"

Ethan Brand's eye quailed beneath the old man's. That daughter, from whom he so earnestly desired a word of greeting, was the Esther of our tale, the very girl whom, with such cold and remorseless purpose, Ethan Brand had made the subject of a psychological experiment, and wasted, absorbed, and perhaps annihilated her soul, in the process.

"Yes," murmured he, turning away from the hoary wanderer; "it is no delusion. There is an Unpardonable Sin!"

While these things were passing, a merry scene was going forward in the area of cheerful light, beside the spring and before the door of the hut. A number of the youth of the village, young men and girls, had hurried up the hillside, impelled by curiosity to see Ethan Brand, the hero of so many a legend familiar to their childhood. Finding nothing, however, very remarkable in his aspect—nothing but a sunburnt wayfarer, in plain garb and dusty shoes, who sat looking into the fire, as if he fancied pictures among the coals—these young people speedily grew tired of observing him. As it happened, there was other amusement at hand. An old German Jew, travelling with a diorama on his back, was passing down the mountain road towards the village just as the party turned aside from it, and, in hopes of eking out the profits of the day, the showman had kept them company to the lime-kiln.

"Come, old Dutchman," cried one of the young men,

"let us see your pictures, if you can swear they are worth looking at!"

"Oh yes, Captain," answered the Jew—whether as a matter of courtesy or craft, he styled everybody Captain —"I shall show you, indeed, some very superb pictures!"

So, placing his box in a proper position, he invited the young men and girls to look through the glass orifices of the machine, and proceeded to exhibit a series of the most outrageous scratchings and daubings, as specimens of the fine arts, that ever an itinerant showman had the face to impose upon his circle of spectators. The pictures were worn out, moreover, tattered, full of cracks and wrinkles, dingy with tobacco smoke, and otherwise in a most pitiable condition. Some purported to be cities, public edifices, and ruined castles in Europe; others represented Napoleon's battles and Nelson's sea fights; and in the midst of these would be seen a gigantic, brown, hairy hand—which might have been mistaken for the Hand of Destiny, though, in truth, it was only the showman's—pointing its forefinger to various scenes of the conflict, while its owner gave historical illustrations. When, with much merriment at its abominable deficiency of merit, the exhibition was concluded, the German bade little Joe put his head into the box. Viewed through the magnifying glasses, the boy's round, rosy visage assumed the strangest imaginable aspect of an immense Titanic child, the mouth grinning broadly, and the eyes and every other feature overflowing with fun at the joke. Suddenly, however, that merry face turned pale, and its expression changed to horror, for this easily impressed and excitable child had become sensible that the eye of Ethan Brand was fixed upon him through the glass.

"You make the little man to be afraid, Captain," said the German Jew, turning up the dark and strong outline of his visage, from his stooping posture. "But look again, and, by chance, I shall cause you to see somewhat that is very fine, upon my word!"

Ethan Brand gazed into the box for an instant, and then starting back, looked fixedly at the German. What had he seen? Nothing, apparently; for a curious youth, who had peeped in almost at the same moment, beheld only a vacant space of canvas.

"I remember you now," muttered Ethan Brand to the showman.

"Ah, Captain," whispered the Jew of Nuremberg, with a dark smile, "I find it to be a heavy matter in my show-box—this Unpardonable Sin! By my faith, Captain, it has wearied my shoulders, this long day, to carry it over the mountain."

"Peace," answered Ethan Brand sternly, "or get thee into the furnace yonder!"

The Jew's exhibition had scarcely concluded, when a great, elderly dog—who seemed to be his own master, as no person in the company laid claim to him—saw fit to render himself the object of public notice. Hitherto, he had shown himself a very quiet, well-disposed old dog, going round from one to another, and, by way of being sociable, offering his rough head to be patted by any kindly hand that would take so much trouble. But now, all of a sudden, this grave and venerable quadruped, of his own mere motion, and without the slightest suggestion from anybody else, began to run round after his tail, which, to heighten the absurdity of the proceeding, was a great deal shorter than it should have been. Never was seen such headlong eagerness in pursuit of an object that could not possibly be attained; never was heard such a tremendous outbreak of growling, snarling, barking, and snapping—as if one end of the ridiculous brute's body were at deadly and most unforgivable enmity with the other. Faster and faster, round about went the cur; and faster and still faster fled the unapproachable brevity of his tail; and louder and fiercer grew his yells of rage and animosity; until, utterly exhausted, and as far from the goal as ever, the foolish old dog ceased his performance as suddenly as he had begun it. The next moment he was as mild, quiet, sensible, and respectable in his deportment, as when he first scraped acquaintance with the company.

As may be supposed, the exhibition was greeted with

universal laughter, clapping of hands, and shouts of encore, to which the canine performer responded by wagging all that there was to wag of his tail, but appeared totally unable to repeat his very successful effort to amuse the spectators.

Meanwhile, Ethan Brand had resumed his seat upon the log, and moved, it might be, by a perception of some remote analogy between his own case and that of this self-pursuing cur, he broke into the awful laugh, which, more than any other token, expressed the condition of his inward being. From that moment, the merriment of the party was at an end; they stood aghast, dreading lest the inauspicious sound should be reverberated around the horizon, and that mountain would thunder it to mountain, and so the horror be prolonged upon their ears. Then, whispering one to another that it was late—that the moon was almost down—that the August night was growing chill—they hurried homewards, leaving the lime-burner and little Joe to deal as they might with their unwelcome guest. Save for these three human beings, the open space on the hillside was a solitude, set in a vast gloom of forest. Beyond that darksome verge, the firelight glimmered on the stately trunks and almost black foliage of pines, intermixed with the lighter verdure of sapling oaks, maples, and poplars, while here and there lay the gigantic corpses of dead trees, decaying on the leaf-strewn soil. And it seemed to little Joe—a timorous and imaginative child —that the silent forest was holding its breath, until some fearful thing should happen.

Ethan Brand thrust more wood into the fire, and closed the door of the kiln; then looking over his shoulder at the lime-burner and his son, he bade, rather than advised, them to retire to rest.

"For myself, I cannot sleep," said he. "I have matters that it concerns me to meditate upon. I will watch the fire, as I used to do in the old time."

"And call the Devil out of the furnace to keep you company, I suppose," muttered Bartram, who had been making intimate acquaintance with the black bottle above mentioned. "But watch, if you like, and call as many devils as you like! For my part, I shall be all the better for a snooze. Come, Joe!"

As the boy followed his father into the hut, he looked back at the wayfarer, and the tears came into his eyes, for his tender spirit had an intuition of the bleak and terrible loneliness in which this man had enveloped himself.

When they had gone, Ethan Brand sat listening to the crackling of the kindled wood, and looking at the little spirts of fire that issued through the chinks of the door. These trifles, however, once so familiar, had but the slightest hold of his attention, while deep within his mind he was reviewing the gradual but marvellous change that had been wrought upon him by the search to which he had devoted himself. He remembered how the night dew had fallen upon him—how the dark forest had whispered to him—how the stars had gleamed upon him—a simple and loving man, watching his fire in the years gone by, and ever musing as it burned. He remembered with what tenderness, with what love and sympathy for mankind, and what pity for human guilt and woe, he had first begun to contemplate those ideas which afterwards became the inspiration of his life; with what reverence he had then looked into the heart of man, viewing it as a temple originally divine, and, however desecrated, still to be held sacred by a brother; with what awful fear he had deprecated the success of his pursuit, and prayed that the Unpardonable Sin might never be revealed to him. Then ensued that vast intellectual development, which, in its progress, disturbed the counterpoise between his mind and heart. The Idea that possessed his life had operated as a means of education; it had gone on cultivating his powers to the highest point of which they were susceptible; it had raised him from the level of an unlettered labourer to stand on a starlit eminence, whither the philosophers of the earth, laden with the lore of universities, might vainly strive to clamber after him. So much for the intellect! But where was the heart? That, indeed, had withered

—had contracted—had hardened—had perished! It had ceased to partake of the universal throb. He had lost his hold of the magnetic chain of humanity. He was no longer a brother-man, opening the chambers of the dungeons of our common nature by the key of holy sympathy, which gave him a right to share in all its secrets; he was now a cold observer, looking on mankind as the subject of his experiment, and, at length, converting man and woman to be his puppets, and pulling the wires that moved them to such degrees of crime as were demanded for his study.

Thus Ethan Brand became a fiend. He began to be so from the moment that his moral nature had ceased to keep the pace of improvement with his intellect. And now, as his highest effort and inevitable development—as the bright and gorgeous flower, and rich, delicious fruit of his life's labour—he had produced the Unpardonable Sin!

"What more have I to seek? what more to achieve?" said Ethan Brand to himself. "My task is done, and well done!"

Starting from the log with a certain alacrity in his gait and ascending the hillock of earth that was raised against the stone circumference of the lime-kiln, he thus reached the top of the structure. It was a space of perhaps ten feet across, from edge to edge, presenting a view of the upper surface of the immense mass of broken marble with which the kiln was heaped. All these innumerable blocks and fragments of marble were red-hot and vividly on fire, sending up great spouts of blue flame, which quivered aloft and danced madly, as within a magic circle, and sank and rose again, with continual and multitudinous activity. As the lonely man bent forward over this terrible body of fire, the blasting heat smote up against his person with a breath that, it might be supposed, would have scorched and shrivelled him up in a moment.

Ethan Brand stood erect, and raised his arms on high. The blue flames played upon his face, and imparted the wild and ghastly light which alone could have suited its expression; it was that of a fiend on the verge of plunging into his gulf of intensest torment.

"O Mother Earth," cried he, "who art no more my Mother, and into whose bosom this frame shall never be resolved! O mankind, whose brotherhood I have cast off, and trampled thy great heart beneath my feet! O stars of heaven, that shone on me of old, as if to light me onward and upward!—farewell all, and forever. Come, deadly element of Fire—henceforth my familiar frame! Embrace me, as I do thee!"

That night the sound of a fearful peal of laughter rolled heavily through the sleep of the lime-burner and his little son; dim shapes of horror and anguish haunted their dreams, and seemed still present in the rude hovel when they opened their eyes to the daylight.

"Up, boy, up!" cried the lime-burner, staring about him. "Thank Heaven, the night is gone, at last; and rather than pass such another, I would watch my lime-kiln, wide awake, for a twelvemonth. This Ethan Brand, with his humbug of an Unpardonable Sin, has done me no such mighty favour, in taking my place!"

He issued from the hut, followed by little Joe, who kept fast hold of his father's hand. The early sunshine was already pouring its gold upon the mountain-tops; and though the valleys were still in shadow, they smiled cheerfully in the promise of the bright day that was hastening onward. The village, completely shut in by hills, which swelled away gently about it, looked as if it had rested peacefully in the hollow of the great hand of Providence. Every dwelling was distinctly visible; the little spires of the two churches pointed upwards, and caught a fore-glimmering of brightness from the sun-gilt skies upon their gilded weathercocks. The tavern was astir, and the figure of the old, smoke-dried stage-agent, cigar in mouth, was seen beneath the stoop. Old Graylock was glorified with a golden cloud upon his head. Scattered likewise over the breasts of the surrounding mountains, there were heaps of hoary mist, in fantastic shapes, some of them far down into the valley, others high up towards the summits, and still others, of the same family of mist or cloud, hovering in the gold radiance of the upper atmosphere. Stepping from one to another of the clouds that rested on the hills, and thence to the loftier brotherhood that sailed in air, it seemed almost as if a mortal man might thus ascend into the heavenly regions. Earth was so mingled with sky that it was a day-dream to look at it.

To supply that charm of the familiar and homely, which Nature so readily adopts into a scene like this, the stage-coach was rattling down the mountain road, and the driver sounded his horn, while echo caught up the notes, and intertwined them into a rich and varied and elaborate harmony, of which the original performer could lay claim to little share. The great hills played a concert among themselves, each contributing a strain of airy sweetness.

Little Joe's face brightened at once.

"Dear father," cried he, skipping cheerily to and fro, "that strange man is gone, and the sky and the mountains all seem glad of it!"

"Yes," growled the lime-burner, with an oath, "but he has let the fire go down, and no thanks to him if five hundred bushels of lime are not spoiled. If I catch the fellow hereabouts again, I shall feel like tossing him into the furnace!"

With his long pole in his hand, he ascended to the top of the kiln. After a moment's pause, he called to his son:

"Come up here, Joe!"

So little Joe ran up the hillock, and stood by his father's side. The marble was all burnt into perfect, snow-white lime. But on its surface, in the midst of the circle—snow-white, too, and thoroughly converted into lime—lay a human skeleton, in the attitude of a person who, after long toil, lies down to long repose. Within the ribs—strange to say—was the shape of a human heart.

"Was the fellow's heart made of marble?" cried Bartram, in some perplexity at this phenomenon.

"At any rate, it is burnt into what looks like special good lime; and, taking all the bones together, my kiln is half a bushel the richer for him."

So saying, the rude lime-burner lifted his pole, and, letting it fall upon the skeleton, the relics of Ethan Brand were crumbled into fragments.

THE "TOWN-HO'S" STORY [1]

By HERMAN MELVILLE (1819–91)

THE Cape of Good Hope, and all the watery region round about there, is much like some noted four corners of a great highway, where you meet more travellers than in any other part.

It was not very long after speaking the *Goney* that another homeward-bound whaleman, the *Town-Ho*,[2] was encountered. She was manned almost wholly by Polynesians. In the short gam that ensued she gave us strong news of Moby Dick. To some the general interest in the White Whale was now widely heightened by a circumstance of the *Town-Ho's* story, which seemed obscurely to involve with the whale a certain wondrous, inverted visitation of one of those so-called judgments of God which at times are said to overtake some men. This latter circumstance, with its own particular accompaniments, forming what may be called the secret part of the tragedy about to be narrated, never reached the ears of Captain Ahab or his mates. For that secret part of the story was unknown to the captain of the *Town-Ho* himself. It was the private property of three confederate white seamen of that ship, one of whom, it seems, communicated it to Tashtego with Romish injunctions of secrecy, but the following night Tashtego rambled in his sleep, and revealed so much of it in that way that when he was awakened he could not well withhold the rest. Nevertheless, so potent an influence

[1] From *Harper's Magazine*, October 1851. Republished as chapter liv of *Moby Dick; or, The Whale* (1851), by Herman Melville.

[2] The ancient whale-cry upon first sighting a whale from the masthead, still used by whalemen in hunting the famous Gallipagos terrapin.

did this thing have on those seamen in the *Pequod* who came to the full knowledge of it, and by such a strange delicacy, to call it so, were they governed in this matter, that they kept the secret among themselves so that it never transpired abaft the *Pequod's* mainmast. Interweaving in its proper place this darker thread with the story as publicly narrated on the ship, the whole of this strange affair I now proceed to put on lasting record.

For my humour's sake, I shall preserve the style in which I once narrated it at Lima, to a lounging circle of my Spanish friends, one saint's eve, smoking upon the thick-gilt tiled piazza of the Golden Inn. Of those fine cavaliers, the young dons, Pedro and Sebastian, were on the closer terms with me; and hence the interluding questions they occasionally put, and which are duly answered at the time.

"Some two years prior to my first learning the events which I am about rehearsing to you, gentlemen, the *Town-Ho*, sperm whaler of Nantucket, was cruising in your Pacific here, not very many days' sail eastward from the eaves of this good Golden Inn. She was somewhere to the northward of the line. One morning upon handling the pumps, according to daily usage, it was observed that she made more water in her hold than common. They supposed a sword-fish had stabbed her, gentlemen. But the captain, having some unusual reason for believing that rare good luck awaited him in those latitudes, and therefore being very averse to quit them, and the leak not being then considered at all dangerous, though, indeed, they could not find it after searching the hold as low down as was possible in rather heavy weather, the ship still continued her cruisings, the mariners working at the pumps at wide and easy intervals; but no good luck came; more days went by, and not only was the leak yet undiscovered, but it sensibly increased. So much so that, now taking some alarm, the captain, making all sail, stood away for the nearest harbour among the islands, there to have his hull hove out and repaired.

"Though no small passage was before her, yet, if the

commonest chance favoured, he did not at all fear that his ship would founder by the way, because his pumps were of the best, and being periodically relieved at them, those six-and-thirty men of his could easily keep the ship free; never mind if the leak should double on her. In truth, well-nigh the whole of this passage being attended by very prosperous breezes, the *Town-Ho* had all but certainly arrived in perfect safety at her port without the occurrence of the least fatality, had it not been for the brutal overbearing of Radney, the mate, a Vineyarder, and the bitterly provoked vengeance of Steelkilt, a Lakeman and desperado from Buffalo.

"'Lakeman!—Buffalo! Pray, what is a Lakeman, and where is Buffalo?' said Don Sebastian, rising in his swinging mat of grass.

"On the eastern shore of our Lake Erie, don; but—I crave your courtesy—maybe, you shall soon hear further of all that. Now, gentlemen, in square-sail brigs and three-masted ships, well-nigh as large and stout as any that ever sailed out of your old Callao to far Manila, this Lakeman, in the landlocked heart of our America, had yet been nurtured by all those agrarian freebooting impressions popularly connected with the open ocean. For in their interflowing aggregate those grand freshwater seas of ours—Erie, and Ontario, and Huron, and Superior, and Michigan—possess an ocean-like expansiveness, with many of the ocean's noblest traits; with many of its rimmed varieties of races and of climes. They contain round archipelagoes of romantic isles, even as the Polynesian waters do; in large part, are shored by two great contrasting nations, as the Atlantic is; they furnish long maritime approaches to our numerous territorial colonies from the East, dotted all round their banks; here and there are frowned upon by batteries, and by the goatlike craggy guns of lofty Mackinaw; they have heard the fleet thunderings of naval victories; at intervals, they yield their beaches to wild barbarians, whose red, painted faces flash from out their peltry wigwams; for leagues and leagues are flanked by ancient and unentered forests, where the gaunt pines stand like serried lines of kings in Gothic genealogies; those same woods harbouring wild Afric beasts of prey, and silken creatures whose exported furs give robes to Tartar emperors; they mirror the paved capitals of Buffalo and Cleveland, as well as Winnebago villages; they float alike the full-rigged merchant ship, the armed cruiser of the state, the steamer, and the beech canoe; they are swept by Borean and dismasting blasts as direful as any that lash the salted wave; they know what shipwrecks are, for out of sight of land, however inland, they have drowned full many a midnight ship with all its shrieking crew. Thus, gentlemen, though an inlander, Steelkilt was wild-ocean born, and wild-ocean nurtured; as much of an audacious mariner as any. And for Radney, though in his infancy he may have laid him down on the lone Nantucket beach, to nurse at his maternal sea; though in after life he had long followed our austere Atlantic and your contemplative Pacific; yet was he quite as vengeful and full of social quarrel as the backwoods seaman, fresh from the latitudes of buckhorn-handled bowie-knives. Yet was this Nantucketer a man with some good-hearted traits; and this Lakeman, a mariner who, though a sort of devil indeed, might yet by inflexible firmness, only tempered by that common decency of human recognition which is the meanest slave's right; thus treated, this Steelkilt had long been retained harmless and docile. At all events, he had proved so thus far; but Radney was doomed and made mad, and Steelkilt—but, gentlemen, you shall hear.

"It was not more than a day or two at the farthest after pointing her prow for her island haven that the *Town-Ho's* leak seemed again increasing, but only so as to require an hour or more at the pumps every day. You must know that in a settled and civilised ocean like our Atlantic, for example, some skippers think little of pumping their whole way across it; though of a still, sleepy night, should the officer of the deck happen to forget his duty in that respect, the probability would be that he and his shipmates would never again remember it, on account of all hands gently subsiding to the bottom. Nor in the solitary and savage seas far from you to the westward, gentlemen, is it altogether unusual for ships to keep clanging at their pump-handles in full chorus even for a voyage of considerable length; that is, if it lie along a tolerably accessible coast, or if any other reasonable retreat is afforded them. It is only when a leaky vessel is in some very out-of-the-way part of those waters, some really landless latitude, that her captain begins to feel a little anxious.

"Much this way had it been with the *Town-Ho*; so when her leak was found gaining once more, there was in truth some small concern manifested by several of her company; especially by Radney the mate. He commanded the upper sails to be well hoisted, sheeted home anew, and every way expanded to the breeze. Now this Radney, I suppose, was as little of a coward, and as little inclined to any sort of nervous apprehensiveness touching his own person, as any fearless, unthinking creature on land or on sea that you can conveniently imagine, gentlemen. Therefore when he betrayed this solicitude about the safety of the ship, some of the seamen declared that it was only on account of his being a part owner in her. So when they were working that evening at the pumps, there was on this head no small gamesomeness slyly going on among them, as they stood with their feet continually overflowed by the rippling clear water; clear as any mountain spring, gentlemen—that bubbling from the pumps ran across the deck and poured itself out in steady spouts at the lee scupper-holes.

"Now, as you well know, it is not seldom the case in this conventional world of ours, watery or otherwise, that when a person placed in command over his fellow-men finds one of them to be very significantly his superior in general pride of manhood, straightway against that man he conceives an unconquerable dislike and bitterness; and if he have a chance he will pull down and pulverise that subaltern's tower, and make a little heap of dust of it. Be this conceit of mine as it may, gentlemen, at all events Steelkilt was a tall and noble animal with a head like a Roman, and a flowing golden beard like the tasselled housings of your last viceroy's snorting charger; and a brain, and a heart, and a soul in him, gentlemen, which had made Steelkilt Charlemagne, had he been born son to Charlemagne's father. But Radney, the mate, was ugly as a mule; yet as hardy, as stubborn, as malicious. He did not love Steelkilt, and Steelkilt knew it.

"Espying the mate drawing near as he was toiling at the pump with the rest the Lakeman affected not to notice him, but unawed went on with his gay banterings.

"'Ay, ay, my merry lads, it's a lively leak this; hold a cannikin, one of ye, and let's have a taste. By the Lord, it's worth bottling! I tell ye what, men, old Rad's investment must go for it! he had best cut away his part of the hull and tow it home. The fact is, boys, that sword-fish only began the job; he's come back again with a gang of ship-carpenters, saw-fish, and file-fish, and what not; and the whole posse of 'em are now hard at work cutting and slashing at the bottom; making improvements, I suppose. If old Rad were here now, I'd tell him to jump overboard and scatter 'em. They're playing the devil with his estate, I can tell him. But he's a simple old soul—Rad, and a beauty, too. Boys, they say the rest of his property is invested in looking-glasses. I wonder if he'd give a poor devil like me the model of his nose.'

"'Damn your eyes! what's that pump stopping for?' roared Radney, pretending not to have heard the sailors' talk. 'Thunder away at it!'

"'Ay, ay, sir,' said Steelkilt, merry as a cricket. 'Lively, boys, lively, now!' And with that the pump clanged like fifty fire-engines; the men tossed their hats off to it, and ere long that peculiar gasping of the lungs was heard which denotes the fullest tension of life's utmost energies.

"Quitting the pump at last, with the rest of his band, the Lakeman went forward all panting, and sat himself down on the windlass; his face fiery red, his eyes bloodshot, and wiping the profuse sweat from his brow Now what cozening fiend it was, gentlemen, that possessed Radney to meddle with such a man in that corporeally exasperated state, I know not; but so it happened. Intolerably striding along the deck, the mate commanded him to get a broom and sweep down the planks, and also a shovel, and remove some offensive matters consequent upon allowing a pig to run at large.

"Now, gentlemen, sweeping a ship's deck at sea is a piece of household work which in all times but raging gales is regularly attended to every evening; it has been known to be done in the case of ships actually foundering at the time. Such, gentlemen, is the inflexibility of sea-usages and the instinctive love of neatness in seamen; some of whom would not willingly drown without first washing their faces. But in all vessels this broom business is the prescriptive province of the boys, if boys there be aboard. Besides, it was the stronger men in the *Town-Ho* that had been divided into gangs, taking turns at the pumps; and being the most athletic seaman of them all, Steelkilt had been regularly assigned captain of one of the gangs; consequently he should have been freed from any trivial business not connected with truly nautical duties, such being the case with his comrades. I mention all these particulars so that you may understand exactly how this affair stood between the two men.

"But there was more than this: the order about the shovel was almost as plainly meant to sting and insult Steelkilt as though Radney had spat in his face. Any man who has gone sailor in a whale-ship will understand this; and all this and doubtless much more the Lakeman fully comprehended when the mate uttered his command. But as he sat still for a moment, and as he steadfastly looked into the mate's malignant eye and perceived the stacks of powder-casks heaped up in him and the slow match silently burning along toward them; as he instinctively saw all this, that strange forbearance and unwillingness to stir up the deeper passionateness in any already ireful being—a repugnance most felt, when felt at all, by really valiant men even when aggrieved—this nameless phantom feeling, gentlemen, stole over Steelkilt.

"Therefore, in his ordinary tone, only a little broken by the bodily exhaustion he was temporarily in, he answered him, saying that sweeping the deck was not his business, and he would not do it. And then, without at all alluding to the shovel, he pointed to three lads as the customary sweepers; who, not being billeted at the pumps, had done little or nothing all day. To this Radney replied with an oath, in a most domineering and outrageous manner unconditionally reiterating his command; meanwhile advancing upon the still seated Lakeman, with an uplifted cooper's club hammer which he had snatched from a cask near by.

"Heated and irritated as he was by his spasmodic toil at the pumps, for all his first nameless feeling of forbearance, the sweating Steelkilt could but ill brook this bearing in the mate; but somehow still smothering the conflagration within him, without speaking he remained doggedly rooted to his seat, till at last the incensed Radney shook the hammer within a few inches of his face, furiously commanding him to do his bidding.

"Steelkilt rose, and slowly retreating round the windlass, steadily followed by the mate with his menacing hammer, deliberately repeated his intention not to obey. Seeing, however, that his forbearance had not the slightest effect, by an awful and unspeakable intimation with his twisted hand he warned off the foolish and infatuated man; but it was to no purpose. And in this way the two went once slowly round the windlass; when, resolved at last no longer to retreat, bethinking him that he had now forborne as much as comported with his humour, the Lakeman paused on the hatches and thus spoke to the officer:

"'Mr. Radney, I will not obey you. Take that hammer away, or look to yourself.' But the predestinated mate coming still closer to him, where the Lakeman stood fixed, now shook the heavy hammer within an inch of his teeth; meanwhile repeating a string of insufferable maledictions. Retreating not the thousandth part of an inch; stabbing him in the eye with the unflinching poniard of his glance, Steelkilt, clenching his right hand behind him and creepingly drawing it back, told his persecutor that if the hammer but grazed his cheek he (Steelkilt) would murder him. But, gentlemen, the fool had been branded for the slaughter by the gods. Immediately the hammer touched the cheek; the next instant the lower jaw of the mate was stove in his head; he fell on the hatch spouting blood like a whale.

"Ere the cry could go aft Steelkilt was shaking one of the backstays leading far aloft to where two of his comrades were standing their mastheads. They were both Canallers.

"'Canallers!' cried Don Pedro. 'We have seen many whale-ships in our harbours, but never heard of your Canallers. Pardon: who and what are they?'

"'Canallers, don, are the boatmen belonging to our Grand Erie Canal. You must have heard of it.'

"'Nay, señor; hereabouts in this dull, warm, most lazy, and hereditary land, we know but little of your vigorous North.'

"Ay? Well, then, don, refill my cup. Your chicha's very fine; and, ere proceeding further, I will tell you what our Canallers are; for such information may throw sidelight upon my story.

"For three hundred and sixty miles, gentlemen, through the entire breadth of the state of New York; through numerous populous cities and most thriving villages; through long, dismal, uninhabited swamps, and affluent, cultivated fields, unrivalled for fertility; by billiard-room and bar-room; through the holy-of-holies of great forests; on Roman arches over Indian rivers; through sun and shade; by happy hearts or broken; through all the wide contrasting scenery of those noble Mohawk counties; and especially by rows of snow-white chapels, whose spires stand almost like milestones, flows one continual stream of Venetianly corrupt and often lawless life. There's your true Ashantee, gentlemen; there howl your pagans; where you ever find them, next door to you; under the long-flung shadow, and the snug patronising lee of churches. For by some curious fatality, as it is often noted of your metropolitan freebooters that they ever encamp around the halls of justice, so sinners, gentlemen, most abound in holiest vicinities.

"'Is that a friar passing?' said Don Pedro, looking downward into the crowded plaza, with humorous concern.

"'Well for our northern friend, Dame Isabella's Inquisition wanes in Lima,' laughed Don Sebastian. 'Proceed, señor.'

"'A moment! Pardon!' cried another of the company. 'In the name of all us Limeese, I but desire to express to you, sir sailor, that we have by no means overlooked your delicacy in not substituting present Lima for distant Venice in your corrupt comparison. Oh! do not bow and look surprised; you know the proverb all along this coast, "Corrupt as Lima." It but bears out your saying, too; churches more plentiful than billiard-tables, and forever open — and "Corrupt as Lima." So, too, Venice; I have been there; the holy city of the blessed evangelist, St. Mark! St. Dominic, purge it! Your cup! Thanks: here I refill; now, you pour out again.'

"Freely depicted in his own vocation, gentlemen, the Canaller would make a fine dramatic hero, so abundantly and picturesquely wicked is he. Like Mark Antony, for days and days along his green-turfed, flowery Nile, he indolently floats, openly toying with his red-cheeked Cleopatra, ripening his apricot thigh upon the sunny deck. But ashore, all this effeminacy is dashed. The brigandish guise which the Canaller so proudly sports; his slouched and gaily-ribboned hat, betoken his grand features. A terror to the smiling innocence of the villages through which he floats; his swart visage and bold swagger are not unshunned in cities. Once a vagabond on his own canal, I have received good turns from one of those Canallers; I thank him heartily; would fain be not ungrateful; but it is often one of the prime redeeming qualities of your man of violence, that at times he has as stiff an arm to back a poor stranger in a strait, as to plunder a wealthy one.   In sum, gentlemen, what the wildness of this canal life is, is emphatically evinced by this: that our wild whale-fishery contains so many of its most finished graduates, and that scarce any race of mankind, except Sydney men, are so much distrusted by our whaling captains.   Nor does it at all diminish the curiousness of this matter that, to many thousands of our rural boys and young men born along its line, the probationary life of the Grand Canal furnishes the sole transition between quietly reaping in a Christian corn-field and recklessly ploughing the waters of the most barbaric seas.

"'I see!   I see!' impetuously exclaimed Don Pedro, spilling his chicha upon his silvery ruffles.   'No need to travel!   The world's one Lima.   I had thought, now, that at your temperate North the generations were cold and holy as the hills.   But the story.'

"I left off, gentlemen, where the Lakeman shook the backstay.   Hardly had he done so, when he was surrounded by the three junior mates and the four harpooners, who all crowded him to the deck.   But sliding down the ropes like baleful comets, the two Canallers rushed into the uproar, and sought to drag their man out of it toward the forecastle.   Others of the sailors joined with them in this attempt, and a twisted turmoil ensued; while standing out of harm's way, the valiant captain danced up and down with a whale-pike, calling upon his officers to manhandle that atrocious scoundrel, and smoke him along to the quarter-deck.   At intervals, he ran close up to the revolving border of the confusion, and prying into the heart of it with his pike, sought to prick out the object of his resentment.   But Steelkilt and his desperadoes were too much for them all; they succeeded in gaining the forecastle deck, where, hastily slewing about three or four large casks in a line with the windlass, these sea-Parisians entrenched themselves behind the barricade.

"'Come out of that, ye pirates!' roared the captain,

now menacing them with a pistol in each hand, just brought to him by the steward. 'Come out of that, ye cutthroats.'

"Steelkilt leaped on the barricade, and striding up and down there, defied the worst the pistols could do; but gave the captain to understand distinctly that his (Steelkilt's) death would be the signal for a murderous mutiny on the part of all hands. Fearing in his heart lest this might prove but too true, the captain a little desisted, but still commanded the insurgents instantly to return to their duty.

"'Will you promise not to touch us, if we do?' demanded their ringleader.

"'Turn to! turn to! I make no promise; to your duty! Do you want to sink the ship, by knocking off at a time like this? Turn to!' and he once more raised a pistol.

"'Sink the ship?' cried Steelkilt. 'Ay, let her sink. Not a man of us turns to, unless you swear not to raise a rope-yarn against us. What say ye, men?' turning to his comrades. A fierce cheer was their response.

"The Lakeman now patrolled the barricade, all the while keeping his eye on the captain, and jerking out such sentences as these: 'It's not our fault; we didn't want it; I told him to take his hammer away; it was boys' business: he might have known me before this; I told him not to prick the buffalo; I believe I have broken a finger here against his cursed jaw; ain't those mincing knives down in the forecastle there, men? Look to those handspikes, my hearties. Captain, by God, look to yourself; say the word; don't be a fool; forget it all; we are ready to turn to; treat us decently, and we're your men; but we won't be flogged.'

"'Turn to! I make no promises: turn to, I say!'

"'Look ye, now,' cried the Lakeman, flinging out his arm toward him, 'there are a few of us here (and I am one of them) who have shipped for the cruise, d'ye see; now as you well know, sir, we can claim our discharge as soon as the anchor is down; so we don't want a row; it's not our interest; we want to be peaceable; we are ready to work but we won't be flogged.'

"'Turn to!' roared the captain.

"Steelkilt glanced round him a moment, and then said: "I tell you what it is now, captain, rather than kill ye, and be hung for such a shabby rascal, we won't lift a hand against ye unless ye attack us; but till you say the word about not flogging us, we don't do a hand's turn.'

"'Down into the forecastle then, down with ye, I'll keep ye there till ye're sick of it. Down ye go.'

"'Shall we?' cried the ringleader to his men. Most of them were against it; but at length, in obedience to Steelkilt, they preceded him down into their dark den, growlingly disappearing like bears into a cave.

"As the Lakeman's bare head was just level with the planks, the captain and his posse leaped the barricade and, rapidly drawing over the slide of the scuttle, planted their group of hands upon it, and loudly called for the steward to bring the heavy brass padlock belonging to the companion-way. Then opening the slide a little the captain whispered something down the crack, closed it, and turned the key upon them—ten in number —leaving on deck some twenty or more, who thus far had remained neutral.

"All night a wideawake watch was kept by all the officers, forward and aft, especially about the forecastle scuttle and fore hatchway; at which last place it was feared the insurgents might emerge, after breaking through the bulkhead below. But the hours of darkness passed in peace; the men who still remained at their duty turning hard at the pumps, whose clinking and clanking at intervals through the dreary night dismally resounded through the ship.

"At sunrise the captain went forward, and knocking on the deck summoned the prisoners to work; but with a yell they refused. Water was then lowered down to them, and a couple of handfuls of biscuit were tossed after it; when again turning the key upon them and pocketing it, the captain returned to the quarter-deck.

Twice every day for three days this was repeated; but
on the fourth morning a confused wrangling, and then a
scuffling was heard, as the customary summons was delivered; and suddenly four men burst up from the forecastle, saying they were ready to turn to.   The fetid
closeness of the air, and a famishing diet, united perhaps
to some fears of ultimate retribution, had constrained
them to surrender at discretion.   Emboldened by this,
the captain reiterated his demand to the rest, but Steelkilt shouted up to him a terrific hint to stop his babbling
and betake himself where he belonged.   On the fifth
morning three others of the mutineers bolted up into
the air from the desperate arms below that sought to
restrain them.   Only three were left.

"'Better turn to, now?' said the captain with a heartless jeer.

"'Shut us up again, will ye!' cried Steelkilt.

"'Oh! certainly,' said the captain, and the key
clicked.

"It was at this point, gentlemen, that enraged by the
defection of seven of his former associates, and stung
by the mocking voice that had last hailed him, and
maddened by his long entombment in a place as black
as the bowels of despair; it was then that Steelkilt
proposed to the two Canallers, thus far apparently of
one mind with him, to burst out of their hole at the next
summoning of the garrison; and armed with their keen
mincing knives (long, crescentic, heavy implements
with a handle at each end) run amuck from the bow-
sprit to the taffrail; and if by any devilishness of desperation possible, seize the ship.   For himself, he would
do this, he said, whether they joined him or not.   That
was the last night he should spend in that den.   But
the scheme met with no opposition on the part of the
other two; they swore they were ready for that, or
for any other mad thing, for anything, in short, but a
surrender.   And what was more, they each insisted
upon being the first man on deck, when the time to
make the rush should come.   But to this their leader
as fiercely objected, reserving that priority for himself;

particularly as his two comrades would not yield, the one to the other, in the matter; and both of them could not be first, for the ladder would but admit one man at a time. And here, gentlemen, the foul play of these miscreants must come out.

"Upon hearing the frantic project of their leader, each in his own separate soul had suddenly lighted, it would seem, upon the same piece of treachery, namely: to be foremost in breaking out, in order to be the first of the three, though the last of the ten, to surrender; and thereby secure whatever small chance of pardon such conduct might merit. But when Steelkilt made known his determination still to lead them to the last, they in some way, by some subtle chemistry of villainy, mixed their before secret treacheries together; and when their leader fell into a doze, verbally opened their souls to each other in three sentences; and bound the sleeper with cords, and gagged him with cords; and shrieked out for the captain at midnight.

"Thinking murder at hand, and smelling in the dark for the blood, he and all his armed mates and harpooners rushed for the forecastle. In a few minutes the scuttle was opened, and, bound hand and foot, the still struggling ringleader was shoved up into the air by his perfidious allies, who at once claimed the honour of securing a man who had been fully ripe for murder. But all three were collared, and dragged along the deck like dead cattle; and, side by side, were seized up into the mizzen rigging, like three quarters of meat, and there they hung till morning. 'Damn ye,' cried the captain, pacing to and fro before them, 'the vultures would not touch ye, ye villains!'

"At sunrise he summoned all hands; and separating those who had rebelled from those who had taken no part in the mutiny, he told the former that he had a good mind to flog them all around—thought, upon the whole, he would do so—he ought to—justice demanded it; but, for the present, considering their timely surrender, he would let them go with a reprimand, which he accordingly administered in the vernacular.

"'But as for you, ye carrion rogues,' turning to the three men in the rigging—'for you, I mean to mince ye up for the try-pots'; and, seizing a rope, he applied it with all his might to the backs of the two traitors, till they yelled no more, but lifelessly hung their heads sideways, as the two crucified thieves are drawn.

"'My wrist is sprained with ye!' he cried, at last; 'but there is still rope enough left for you, my fine bantam, that wouldn't give up.   Take that gag from his mouth, and let us hear what he can say for himself.'

"For a moment the exhausted mutineer made a tremulous motion of his cramped jaws, and then painfully twisting round his head, said, in a sort of hiss, 'What I say is this—and mind it well—if you flog me, I murder you!'

"'Say ye so? then see how ye frighten me'—and the captain drew off with the rope to strike.

"'Best not,' hissed the Lakeman.

"'But I must'—and the rope was once more drawn back for the stroke.

"Steelkilt here hissed out something, inaudible to all but the captain; who, to the amazement of all hands, started back, paced the deck rapidly two or three times, and then suddenly throwing down his rope, said, 'I won't do it—let him go—cut him down: d'ye hear?'

"But as the junior mates were hurrying to execute the order, a pale man, with a bandaged head, arrested them—Radney, the chief mate.   Ever since the blow, he had lain in his berth; but that morning hearing the tumult on the deck, he had crept out, and thus far had watched the whole scene.   Such was the state of his mouth, that he could hardly speak; but mumbling something about *his* being willing and able to do what the captain dared not attempt, he snatched the rope and advanced to his pinioned foe.

"'You are a coward!' hissed the Lakeman.

"'So I am, but take that.'   The mate was in the very act of striking, when another hiss stayed his uplifted arm.   He paused: and then pausing no more, made good his word, spite of Steelkilt's threat, whatever that

might have been.   The three men were then cut down,
all hands were turned to, and, sullenly worked by the
moody seamen, the iron pumps clanged as before.

" Just after dark that day, when one watch had retired
below, a clamour was heard in the forecastle; and the
two trembling traitors running up, besieged the cabin-
door, saying they durst not consort with the crew.
Entreaties, cuffs, and kicks could not drive them back,
so at their own instance they were put down in the
ship's run for salvation.   Still, no sign of mutiny reappeared among the rest.   On the contrary, it seemed
that, mainly at Steelkilt's instigation, they had resolved
to maintain the strictest peacefulness, obey all orders
to the last, and, when the ship reached port, desert her
in a body.   But in order to ensure the speediest end to
the voyage, they all agreed to another thing—namely,
not to sing out for whales, in case any should be discovered.   For, spite of her leak, and spite of all her
other perils, the *Town-Ho* still maintained her mastheads,
and her captain was just as willing to lower for a fish
that moment, as on the day his craft first struck the
cruising-ground, and Radney the mate was quite as ready
to change his berth for a boat, and with his bandaged
mouth seek to gag in death the vital jaw of the whale.

"But though the Lakeman had induced the seamen
to adopt this sort of passiveness in their conduct, he
kept his own counsel (at least till all was over) concerning his own proper and private revenge upon the
man who had stung him in the ventricles of his heart.
He was in Radney the chief mate's watch; and as if the
infatuated man sought to run more than half-way to
meet his doom, after the scene at the rigging, he insisted,
against the express counsel of the captain, upon resuming
the head of his watch at night.   Upon this, and one or
two other circumstances, Steelkilt systematically built
the plan of his revenge.

"During the night Radney had an unseamanlike way
of sitting on the bulwarks of the quarter-deck, and
leaning his arm upon the gunwale of the boat which was
hoisted up there, a little above the ship's side.   In this

attitude, it was well known, he sometimes dozed.   There
was a considerable vacancy between the boat and the
ship, and down between this was the sea.   Steelkilt
calculated his time, and found that his next trick at
the helm would come round at two o'clock, in the morning of the third day from that in which he had been
betrayed.   At his leisure, he employed the interval in
braiding something very carefully in his watches below.

"'What are you making there?' said a shipmate.

"'What do you think? what does it look like?'

"'Like a lanyard for your bag; but it's an odd one,
seems to me.'

"'Yes, rather oddish,' said the Lakeman, holding it
at arm's length before him; 'but I think it will answer.
Shipmate, I haven't enough twine—have you any?'

"But there was none in the forecastle.

"'Then I must get some from old Rad'; and he rose
to go aft.

"'You don't mean to go a-begging to *him*!' said a
sailor.

"'Why not?   Do you think he won't do me a turn,
when it's to help himself in the end, shipmate?' and
going to the mate, he looked at him quietly, and asked
him for some twine to mend his hammock.   It was
given him—neither twine nor lanyard was seen again;
but the next night an iron ball, closely netted, partly
rolled from the pocket of the Lakeman's monkey-
jacket, as he was tucking the coat into his hammock
for a pillow.   Twenty-four hours after, his trick at the
silent helm—nigh to the man who was apt to doze over
the grave always ready dug to the seaman's hand—
that fatal hour was then to come; and in the fore-
ordaining soul of Steelkilt the mate was already stark
and stretched as a corpse, with his forehead crushed in.

"But, gentlemen, a fool saved the would-be murderer
from the bloody deed he had planned.   Yet complete
revenge he had, and without being the avenger.   For
by a mysterious fatality Heaven itself seemed to step
in to take out of his hands into its own the damning
thing he would have done.

"It was just between daybreak and sunrise of the morning of the second day, when they were washing down the decks, that a stupid Teneriffe man, drawing water in the main-chains, all at once shouted out, 'There she rolls! there she rolls! Jesu! what a whale!' It was Moby Dick.

"'Moby Dick!' cried Don Sebastian; 'St. Dominic! Sir sailor, but do whales have christenings? Whom call you Moby Dick?'

"A very white, and famous, and most deadly immortal monster, don; but that would be too long a story.

"'How? how?' cried all the young Spaniards, crowding.

"Nay, dons, dons—nay, nay! I cannot rehearse that now. Let me get more into the air, sirs.

"'The chicha! the chicha!' cried Don Pedro; 'our vigorous friend looks faint; fill up his empty glass!'

"No need, gentlemen; one moment, and I proceed. Now, gentlemen, so suddenly perceiving the snowy whale within fifty yards of the ship—forgetful of the compact among the crew—in the excitement of the moment, the Teneriffe man had instinctively and involuntarily lifted his voice for the monster, though for some little time past it had been plainly beheld from the three sullen mastheads. All was now a frenzy. 'The White Whale—the White Whale!' was the cry from captain, mates, and harpooners, who, undeterred by fearful rumours, were all anxious to capture so famous and precious a fish; while the dogged crew eyed askance, and with curses, the appalling beauty of the vast milky mass, that lit up by a horizontal spangling sun, shifted and glistened like a living opal in the blue morning sea. Gentlemen, a strange fatality pervades the whole career of these events, as if verily mapped out before the world itself was charted. The mutineer was the bowsman of the mate, and when fast to a fish, it was his duty to sit next him, while Radney stood up with his lance in the prow, and haul in or slacken the line, at the word of command. Moreover, when the four boats were lowered, the mate's got the start; and none howled more fiercely with delight than did Steel-kilt, as he strained at his oar. After a stiff pull their harpooner got fast, and spear in hand, Radney sprang to the bow. He was always a furious man, it seems, in a boat. And now his bandaged cry was, to beach him on the whale's topmost back. Nothing loath, his bowsman hauled him up and up, through a blinding foam that blent two whitenesses together; till of a sudden the boat struck as against a sunken ledge, and keeling over, spilled out the standing mate. That instant, as he fell on the whale's slippery back, the boat righted, and was dashed aside by the swell, while Radney was tossed over into the sea, on the other flank of the whale. He struck out through the spray, and, for an instant, was dimly seen through that veil, wildly seeking to remove himself from the eye of Moby Dick. But the whale rushed round in a sudden maelstrom; seized the swimmer between his jaws; and rearing high up with him, plunged headlong again, and went down.

"Meantime, at the first tap of the boat's bottom, the Lakeman had slackened the line, so as to drop astern from the whirlpool; calmly looking on, he thought his own thoughts. But a sudden, terrific, downward jerking of the boat quickly brought his knife to the line. He cut it; and the whale was free. But, at some distance, Moby Dick rose again, with some tatters of Radney's red woollen shirt, caught in the teeth that had destroyed him. All four boats gave chase again; but the whale eluded them, and, finally, wholly disappeared.

"In good time the *Town-Ho* reached her port—a savage, solitary place where no civilised creature resided. There, headed by the Lakeman, all but five or six of the foremast-men deliberately deserted among the palms; eventually, as it turned out, seizing a large double war-canoe of the savages, and setting sail for some other harbour.

"The ship's company being reduced to but a handful, the captain called upon the islanders to assist him in the laborious business of heaving down the ship to stop

the leak. But to such unresting vigilance over their
dangerous allies was this small band of whites neces-
sitated, both by night and by day, and so extreme was
the hard work they underwent that, upon the vessel
being ready again for sea, they were in such a weakened
condition that the captain durst not put off with them
in so heavy a vessel. After taking counsel with his
officers, he anchored the ship as far off shore as possible;
loaded and ran out his two cannon from the bows;
stacked his muskets on the poop; and warning the
islanders not to approach the ship at their peril, took
one man with him, and setting the sail of his best
whale-boat, steered straight before the wind for Tahiti,
five hundred miles distant, to procure a reinforcement
to his crew.

"On the fourth day of the sail, a large canoe was
descried, which seemed to have touched at a low isle
of corals. He steered away from it; but the savage
craft bore down on him; and soon the voice of Steelkilt hailed him to heave to, or he would run him under
water. The captain presented a pistol. With one foot
on each prow of the yoked war-canoes, the Lakeman
laughed him to scorn; assuring him that if the pistol
so much as clicked in the lock, he would bury him in
bubbles and foam.

"'What do you want of me?' cried the captain.

"'Where are you bound? and for what are you
bound?' demanded Steelkilt; 'no lies.'

"'I am bound to Tahiti for more men.'

"'Very good. Let me board you a moment — I
come in peace.' With that he leaped from the canoe,
swam to the boat; and climbing the gunwale, stood
face to face with the captain.

"'Cross your arm, sir; throw back your head. Now,
repeat after me, "As soon as Steelkilt leaves me, I swear
to beach this boat on yonder island, and remain there
six days. If I do not, may lightnings strike me!"'

"'A pretty scholar,' laughed the Lakeman. 'Adios,
señor!' and leaping into the sea, he swam back to his
comrades.

"Watching the boat till it was fairly beached, and drawn up to the roots of the cocoanut trees, Steelkilt made sail again, and in due time arrived at Tahiti, his own place of destination. There, luck befriended him; two ships were about to sail for France, and were providentially in want of precisely that number of men which the sailor headed. They embarked; and so forever got the start of their former captain, had he been at all minded to work them legal retribution.

"Some ten days after the French ships sailed the whale-boat arrived, and the captain was forced to enlist some of the more civilised Tahitians, who had been somewhat used to the sea. Chartering a small native schooner he returned with them to his vessel; and finding all right there, again resumed his cruisings.

"Where Steelkilt now is, gentlemen, none know; but upon the island of Nantucket the widow of Radney still turns to the sea which refuses to give up its dead; still in dreams sees the awful white whale that destroyed him. . . .

"'Are you through?' said Don Sebastian quietly.

"I am, don.

"'Then I entreat you, tell me if to the best of your own convictions, this your story is, in substance, really true? It is so passing wonderful! Did you get it from an unquestionable source? Bear with me if I seem to press.'

"'Also bear with all of us, sir sailor; for we all join in Don Sebastian's suit,' cried the company, with exceeding interest.

"Is there a copy of the Holy Evangelists in the Golden Inn, gentlemen?

"'Nay,' said Don Sebastian; 'but I know a worthy priest near by, who will quickly procure one for me. I go for it; but are you well advised? This may grow too serious.'

"Will you be so good as to bring the priest also, don?

"'Though there are no *autos-da-fé* in Lima now,' said one of the company to another, 'I fear our sailor

friend runs risk of the archiepiscopacy. Let us with-
draw more out of the moonlight. I see no need of this.'

"Excuse me for running after you, Don Sebastian;
but may I also beg that you will be particular in procur-
ing the largest-sized Evangelists you can. . . .

"'This is the priest; he brings you the Evangelists,'
said Don Sebastian gravely, returning with a tall and
solemn figure.

"Let me remove my hat. Now, venerable priest,
further into the light, and hold the Holy Book before me
that I may touch it.

"So help me Heaven, and on my honour, the story
I have told ye, gentlemen, is, in substance and its great
items, true. I know it to be true; it happened on this
ball; I trod the ship; I knew the crew; I have seen and
talked with Steelkilt since the death of Radney."

THE DIAMOND LENS [1]

By Fitz-James O'Brien (1828–62)

I.   THE BENDING OF THE TWIG

From a very early period of my life the entire bent of my inclinations had been towards microscopic investigations.   When I was not more than ten years old a distant relative of our family, hoping to astonish my inexperience, constructed a simple microscope for me, by drilling in a disk of copper a small hole, in which a drop of pure water was sustained by capillary attraction. This very primitive apparatus, magnifying some fifty diameters, presented, it is true, only indistinct and imperfect forms, but still sufficiently wonderful to work up my imagination to a preternatural state of excitement.

Seeing me so interested in this rude instrument, my cousin explained to me all that he knew about the principles of the microscope, related to me a few of the wonders which had been accomplished through its agency, and ended by promising to send me one regularly constructed, immediately on his return to the city.   I counted the days, the hours, the minutes, that intervened between that promise and his departure.

Meantime I was not idle.   Every transparent substance that bore the remotest semblance to a lens I eagerly seized upon and employed in vain attempts to realise that instrument, the theory of whose construction I as yet only vaguely comprehended.   All panes of glass containing those oblate spheroidal knots familiarly known as "bull's-eyes" were ruthlessly destroyed, in

[1] "The Diamond Lens" was first published in *The Atlantic Monthly*, January 1858.   It was republished in *The Poems and Stories of Fitz-James O'Brien* (1881), and in *The Diamond Lens, with Other Stories* (1885), by Fitz-James O'Brien, both edited by William Winter.   A more recent edition, edited by Edward J. O'Brien, has been published by A. & C. Boni.

the hope of obtaining lenses of marvellous power. I even went so far as to extract the crystalline humour from the eyes of fishes and animals, and endeavoured to press it into the microscopic service. I plead guilty to having stolen the glasses from my Aunt Agatha's spectacles, with a dim idea of grinding them into lenses of wondrous magnifying properties—in which attempt it is scarcely necessary to say that I totally failed.

At last the promised instrument came. It was of that order known as Field's simple microscope, and had cost perhaps about fifteen dollars. As far as educational purposes went, a better apparatus could not have been selected. Accompanying it was a small treatise on the microscope—its history, uses, and discoveries. I comprehended then for the first time the *Arabian Nights' Entertainments*. The dull veil of ordinary existence that hung across the world seemed suddenly to roll away, and to lay bare a land of enchantments. I felt towards my companions as the seer might feel towards the ordinary masses of men. I held conversations with Nature in a tongue which they could not understand. I was in daily communication with living wonders, such as they never imagined in their wildest visions. I penetrated beyond the external portal of things, and roamed through the sanctuaries. Where they beheld only a drop of rain slowly rolling down the window-glass, I saw a universe of beings animated with all the passions common to physical life, and convulsing their minute sphere with struggles as fierce and protracted as those of men. In the common spots of mould, which my mother, good housekeeper that she was, fiercely scooped away from her jam-pots, there abode for me, under the name of mildew, enchanted gardens, filled with dells and avenues of the densest foliage and most astonishing verdure, while from the fantastic boughs of these microscopic forests hung strange fruits glittering with green and silver and gold.

It was no scientific thirst that at this time filled my mind. It was the pure enjoyment of a poet to whom a world of wonders has been disclosed. I talked of my solitary pleasures to none. Alone with my microscope, I dimmed my sight, day after day and night after night poring over the marvels which it unfolded to me. I was like one who, having discovered the ancient Eden still existing in all its primitive glory, should resolve to enjoy it in solitude, and never betray to mortal the secret of its locality. The rod of my life was bent at this moment. I destined myself to be a microscopist.

Of course, like every novice, I fancied myself a discoverer. I was ignorant at the time of the thousands of acute intellects engaged in the same pursuit as myself, and with the advantages of instruments a thousand times more powerful than mine. The names of Leeuwenhoek, Williamson, Spencer, Ehrenberg, Schultz, Dujardin, Schact, and Schleiden were then entirely unknown to me, or if known, I was ignorant of their patient and wonderful researches. In every fresh specimen of cryptogamia which I placed beneath my instrument I believed that I discovered wonders of which the world was as yet ignorant. I remember well the thrill of delight and admiration that shot through me the first time that I discovered the common wheel animalcule (*Rotifera vulgaris*) expanding and contracting its flexible spokes, and seemingly rotating through the water. Alas! as I grew older, and obtained some works treating of my favourite study, I found that I was only on the threshold of a science to the investigation of which some of the greatest men of the age were devoting their lives and intellects.

As I grew up, my parents, who saw but little likelihood of anything practical resulting from the examination of bits of moss and drops of water through a brass tube and a piece of glass, were anxious that I should choose a profession. It was their desire that I should enter the counting-house of my uncle, Ethan Blake, a prosperous merchant, who carried on business in New York. This suggestion I decisively combated. I had no taste for trade; I should only make a failure; in short, I refused to become a merchant.

But it was necessary for me to select some pursuit.

My parents were staid New England people, who insisted on the necessity of labour; and therefore, although, thanks to the bequest of my poor Aunt Agatha, I should, on coming of age, inherit a small fortune sufficient to place me above want, it was decided that, instead of waiting for this, I should act the nobler part, and employ the intervening years in rendering myself independent.

After much cogitation I complied with the wishes of my family, and selected a profession. I determined to study medicine at the New York Academy. This disposition of my future suited me. A removal from my relatives would enable me to dispose of my time as I pleased, without fear of detection. As long as I paid my academy fees, I might shirk attending the lectures, if I chose; and as I never had the remotest intention of standing an examination, there was no danger of my being "plucked." Besides, a metropolis was the place for me. There I could obtain excellent instruments, the newest publications, intimacy with men of pursuits kindred to my own—in short, all things necessary to ensure a profitable devotion of my life to my beloved science. I had an abundance of money, few desires that were not bounded by my illuminating mirror on one side and my object-glass on the other; what, therefore, was to prevent my becoming an illustrious investigator of the veiled worlds? It was with the most buoyant hopes that I left my New England home and established myself in New York.

II. THE LONGING OF A MAN OF SCIENCE

My first step, of course, was to find suitable apartments. These I obtained, after a couple of days' search, in Fourth Avenue; a very pretty second-floor unfurnished, containing sitting-room, bedroom, and a smaller apartment which I intended to fit up as a laboratory. I furnished my lodgings simply, but rather elegantly, and then devoted all my energies to the adornment of the temple of my worship. I visited Pike, the celebrated optician, and passed in review his splendid collection of microscopes—Field's Compound, Higham's, Spencer's, Nachet's Binocular (that founded on the principles of the stereoscope), and at length fixed upon that form known as Spencer's Trunnion Microscope, as combining the greatest number of improvements with an almost perfect freedom from tremor. Along with this I pur-chased every possible accessory — draw-tubes, micro-meters, a camera-lucida, lever-stage, achromatic con-densers, white cloud illuminators, prisms, parabolic condensers, polarising apparatus, forceps, aquatic boxes, fishing-tubes, with a host of other articles, all of which would have been useful in the hands of an experienced microscopist, but, as I afterwards discovered, were not of the slightest present value to me. It takes years of practice to know how to use a complicated microscope. The optician looked suspiciously at me as I made these wholesale purchases. He evidently was uncertain whether to set me down as some scientific celebrity or a madman. I think he inclined to the latter belief. I suppose I was mad. Every great genius is mad upon the subject in which he is greatest. The unsuccessful madman is disgraced, and called a lunatic.

Mad or not, I set myself to work with a zeal which few scientific students have ever equalled. I had every-thing to learn relative to the delicate study upon which I had embarked—a study involving the most earnest patience, the most rigid analytic powers, the steadiest hand, the most untiring eye, the most refined and subtile manipulation.

For a long time half my apparatus lay inactively on the shelves of my laboratory, which was now most amply furnished with every possible contrivance for facilitating my investigations. The fact was that I did not know how to use some of my scientific acces-sories—never having been taught microscopics—and those whose use I understood theoretically were of little avail, until by practice I could attain the necessary delicacy of handling. Still, such was the fury of my ambition, such the untiring perseverance of my experiments, that, difficult of credit as it may be, in the course of one year I became theoretically and practically an accomplished microscopist.

During this period of my labours, in which I submitted specimens of every substance that came under my observation to the action of my lenses, I became a discoverer—in a small way, it is true, for I was very young, but still a discoverer. It was I who destroyed Ehrenberg's theory that the *Volvox globator* was an animal, and proved that his "monads" with stomachs and eyes were merely phases of the formation of a vegetable cell, and were, when they reached their mature state, incapable of the act of conjugation, or any true generative act, without which no organism rising to any stage of life higher than vegetable can be said to be complete. It was I who resolved the singular problem of rotation in the cells and hairs of plants into ciliary attraction, in spite of the assertions of Mr. Wenham and others that my explanation was the result of an optical illusion.

But notwithstanding these discoveries, laboriously and painfully made as they were, I felt horribly dissatisfied. At every step I found myself stopped by the imperfections of my instruments. Like all active microscopists, I gave my imagination full play. Indeed, it is a common complaint against many such, that they supply the defects of their instruments with the creations of their brains. I imagined depths beyond depths in nature which the limited power of my lenses prohibited me from exploring. I lay awake at night constructing imaginary microscopes of immeasurable power, with which I seemed to pierce through all the envelopes of matter down to its original atom. How I cursed those imperfect mediums which necessity through ignorance compelled me to use! How I longed to discover the secret of some perfect lens whose magnifying power should be limited only by the resolvability of the object, and which at the same time should be free from spherical and chromatic aberrations, in short from all the obstacles over which the poor microscopist finds himself continually stumbling! I felt convinced that the simple microscope, composed of a single lens of such vast yet perfect power, was possible of construction. To attempt to bring the compound microscope up to such a pitch would have been commencing at the wrong end; this latter being simply a partially successful endeavour to remedy those very defects of the simple instrument which, if conquered, would leave nothing to be desired.

It was in this mood of mind that I became a constructive microscopist. After another year passed in this new pursuit, experimenting on every imaginable substance — glass, gems, flints, crystals, artificial crystals formed of the alloy of various vitreous materials — in short, having constructed as many varieties of lenses as Argus had eyes, I found myself precisely where I started, with nothing gained save an extensive knowledge of glass-making. I was almost dead with despair. My parents were surprised at my apparent want of progress in my medical studies (I had not attended one lecture since my arrival in the city), and the expenses of my mad pursuit had been so great as to embarrass me very seriously.

I was in this frame of mind one day, experimenting in my laboratory on a small diamond—that stone, from its great refracting power, having always occupied my attention more than any other—when a young Frenchman, who lived on the floor above me, and who was in the habit of occasionally visiting me, entered the room.

I think that Jules Simon was a Jew. He had many traits of the Hebrew character: a love of jewellery, of dress, and of good living. There was something mysterious about him. He always had something to sell, and yet went into excellent society. When I say sell, I should perhaps have said peddle; for his operations were generally confined to the disposal of single articles —a picture, for instance, or a rare carving in ivory, or a pair of duelling-pistols, or the dress of a Mexican caballero. When I was first furnishing my rooms he paid me a visit, which ended in my purchasing an

antique silver lamp, which he assured me was a Cellini
—it was handsome enough even for that—and some
other knick-knacks for my sitting-room. Why Simon
should pursue this petty trade I never could imagine.
He apparently had plenty of money, and had the entrée
of the best houses in the city—taking care, however,
I suppose, to drive no bargains within the enchanted
circle of the Upper Ten. I came at length to the
conclusion that this peddling was but a mask to cover
some greater object, and even went so far as to believe
my young acquaintance to be implicated in the slave-
trade. That, however, was none of my affair.

On the present occasion Simon entered my room in
a state of considerable excitement.

"Ah! *mon ami!*" he cried, before I could even offer
him the ordinary salutation, "it has occurred to me to
be the witness of the most astonishing thing in the world.
I promenade myself to the house of Madame—How does
the little animal—*le renard*—name himself in the Latin?"

"Vulpes," I answered.

"Ah! yes—Vulpes. I promenade myself to the house
of Madame Vulpes."

"The spirit medium?"

"Yes, the great medium. Great heavens! what a
woman! I write on a slip of paper many of questions
concerning affairs the most secret—affairs that conceal
themselves in the abysses of my heart the most profound; and behold! by example! what occurs? This
devil of a woman makes me replies the most truthful
to all of them. She talks to me of things that I do not
love to talk of to myself. What am I to think? I am
fixed to the earth!"

"Am I to understand you, Monsieur Simon, that this
Mrs. Vulpes replied to questions secretly written by
you, which questions related to events known only
to yourself?"

"Ah! more than that, more than that," he answered,
with an air of some alarm. "She related to me things—
But," he added, after a pause, and suddenly changing
his manner, "why occupy ourselves with these follies?

It was all the biology, without doubt. It goes without saying that it has not my credence. But why are we here, *mon ami*? It has occurred to me to discover the most beautiful thing as you can imagine—a vase with green lizards on it, composed by the great Bernard Palissy. It is in my apartment; let us mount. I go to show it to you."

I followed Simon mechanically; but my thoughts were far from Palissy and his enamelled ware, although I, like him, was seeking in the dark after a great discovery. This casual mention of the spiritualist, Madame Vulpes, set me on a new track. What if this spiritualism should be really a great fact? What if, through communication with subtiler organisms than my own, I could reach at a single bound the goal which perhaps a life of agonising mental toil would never enable me to attain?

While purchasing the Palissy vase from my friend Simon I was mentally arranging a visit to Madame Vulpes.

III. THE SPIRIT OF LEEUWENHOEK

Two evenings after this, thanks to an arrangement by letter and the promise of an ample fee, I found Madame Vulpes awaiting me at her residence alone. She was a coarse-featured woman, with a keen and rather cruel dark eye, and an exceedingly sensual expression about her mouth and under-jaw. She received me in perfect silence, in an apartment on the ground floor, very sparely furnished. In the centre of the room, close to where Mrs. Vulpes sat, there was a common round mahogany table. If I had come for the purpose of sweeping her chimney, the woman could not have looked more indifferent to my appearance. There was no attempt to inspire the visitor with any awe. Everything bore a simple and practical aspect. The intercourse with the spiritual world was evidently as familiar an occupation with Mrs. Vulpes as eating her dinner or riding in an omnibus.

"You come for a communication, Mr. Linley?" said the medium, in a dry, businesslike tone of voice.

"By appointment—yes."

"What sort of communication do you want? A written one?"

"Yes—I wish for a written one."

"From any particular spirit?"

"Yes."

"Have you ever known this spirit on this earth?"

"Never. He died long before I was born. I wish merely to obtain from him some information which he ought to be able to give better than any other."

"Will you seat yourself at the table, Mr. Linley," said the medium, "and place your hands upon it?"

I obeyed—Mrs. Vulpes being seated opposite me, with her hands also on the table. We remained thus for about a minute and a half, when a violent succession of raps came on the table, on the back of my chair, on the floor immediately under my feet, and even on the window-panes. Mrs. Vulpes smiled composedly.

"They are very strong to-night," she remarked. "You are fortunate." She then continued, "Will the spirits communicate with this gentleman?"

Vigorous affirmative.

"Will the particular spirit he desires to speak with communicate?"

A very confused rapping followed this question.

"I know what they mean," said Mrs. Vulpes, addressing herself to me; "they wish you to write down the name of the particular spirit that you desire to converse with. Is that so?" she added, speaking to her invisible guests.

That it was so was evident from the numerous affirmatory responses. While this was going on, I tore a slip from my pocket-book, and scribbled a name under the table.

"Will this spirit communicate in writing with this gentleman?" asked the medium once more.

After a moment's pause her hand seemed to be seized with a violent tremor, shaking so forcibly that the table vibrated. She said that a spirit had seized her hand and would write. I handed her some sheets of paper that were on the table, and a pencil. The latter she held loosely in her hand, which presently began to move over the paper with a singular and seemingly involuntary motion. After a few moments had elapsed she handed me the paper, on which I found written, in a large, uncultivated hand, the words, "He is not here, but has been sent for." A pause of a minute or so now ensued, during which Mrs. Vulpes remained perfectly silent, but the raps continued at regular intervals. When the short period I mention had elapsed, the hand of the medium was again seized with its convulsive tremor, and she wrote, under this strange influence, a few words on the paper, which she handed to me. They were as follows:

I am here. Question me.

LEEUWENHOEK.

I was astounded. The name was identical with that I had written beneath the table, and carefully kept concealed. Neither was it at all probable that an uncultivated woman like Mrs. Vulpes should know even the name of the great father of microscopics. It may have been biology; but this theory was soon doomed to be destroyed. I wrote on my slip—still concealing it from Mrs. Vulpes—a series of questions, which, to avoid tediousness, I shall place with the responses in the order in which they occurred.

I. Can the microscope be brought to perfection?

Spirit. Yes.

I. Am I destined to accomplish this great task?

Spirit. You are.

I. I wish to know how to proceed to attain this end. For the love which you bear to science, help me!

Spirit. A diamond of one hundred and forty carats, submitted to electromagnetic currents for a long period, will experience a rearrangement of its atoms *inter se*, and from that stone you will form the universal lens.

I. Will great discoveries result from the use of such a lens?

Spirit. So great, that all that has gone before is as nothing.

I. But the refractive power of the diamond is so immense that the image will be formed within the lens. How is that difficulty to be surmounted?

Spirit. Pierce the lens through its axis, and the difficulty is obviated. The image will be formed in the pierced space, which will itself serve as a tube to look through. Now I am called. Good night!

I cannot at all describe the effect that these extraordinary communications had upon me. I felt completely bewildered. No biological theory could account for the *discovery* of the lens. The medium might, by means of biological *rapport* with my mind, have gone so far as to read my questions, and reply to them coherently. But biology could not enable her to discover that magnetic currents would so alter the crystals of the diamond as to remedy its previous defects, and admit of its being polished into a perfect lens. Some such theory may have passed through my head, it is true; but if so, I had forgotten it. In my excited condition of mind there was no course left but to become a convert, and it was in a state of the most painful nervous exaltation that I left the medium's house that evening. She accompanied me to the door, hoping that I was satisfied. The raps followed us as we went through the hall, sounding on the balusters, the flooring, and even the lintels of the door. I hastily expressed my satisfaction, and escaped hurriedly into the cool night air. I walked home with but one thought possessing me—how to obtain a diamond of the immense size required. My entire means multiplied a hundred times over would have been inadequate to its purchase. Besides, such stones are rare, and become historical. I could find such only in the regalia of Eastern or European monarchs.

IV.   THE EYE OF MORNING

There was a light in Simon's room as I entered my
house.   A vague impulse urged me to visit him.   As
I opened the door of his sitting-room unannounced he
was bending, with his back toward me, over a Carcel
lamp, apparently engaged in minutely examining some
object which he held in his hands.   As I entered he
started suddenly, thrust his hand into his breast pocket,
and turned to me with a face crimson with confusion.

"What!" I cried, "poring over the miniature of some
fair lady?   Well, don't blush so much; I won't ask to
see it."

Simon laughed awkwardly enough, but made none
of the negative protestations usual on such occasions.
He asked me to take a seat.

"Simon," said I, "I have just come from Madame
Vulpes."

This time Simon turned as white as a sheet, and
seemed stupefied, as if a sudden electric shock had
smitten him.   He babbled some incoherent words, and
went hastily to a small closet where he usually kept
his liquors.   Although astonished at his emotion, I was
too preoccupied with my own idea to pay much attention
to anything else.

"You say truly when you call Madame Vulpes a devil
of a woman," I continued.   "Simon, she told me
wonderful things to-night, or rather was the means of
telling me wonderful things.   Ah! if I could only get
a diamond that weighed one hundred and forty carats!"

Scarcely had the sigh with which I uttered this desire
died upon my lips, when Simon, with the aspect of a
wild beast, glared at me savagely, and rushing to the
mantelpiece, where some foreign weapons hung on the
wall, caught up a Malay creese, and brandished it
furiously before him.

"No!" he cried in French, into which he always broke
when excited.   "No! you shall not have it!   You are
perfidious!   You have consulted with that demon, and

desire my treasure! But I will die first! Me! I am brave! You cannot make me fear!"

All this, uttered in a loud voice trembling with excitement, astounded me. I saw at a glance that I had accidentally trodden upon the edges of Simon's secret, whatever it was. It was necessary to reassure him.

"My dear Simon," I said, "I am entirely at a loss to know what you mean. I went to Madame Vulpes to consult with her on a scientific problem, to the solution of which I discovered that a diamond of the size I just mentioned was necessary. You were never alluded to during the evening, nor, so far as I was concerned, even thought of. What can be the meaning of this outburst? If you happen to have a set of valuable diamonds in your possession, you need fear nothing from me. The diamond which I require you could not possess; or if you did possess it, you would not be living here."

Something in my tone must have completely reassured him; for his expression immediately changed to a sort of constrained merriment, combined, however, with a certain suspicious attention to my movements. He laughed, and said that I must bear with him; that he was at certain moments subject to a species of vertigo, which betrayed itself in incoherent speeches, and that the attacks passed off as rapidly as they came. He put his weapon aside while making this explanation, and endeavoured, with some success, to assume a more cheerful air.

All this did not impose on me in the least. I was too much accustomed to analytical labours to be baffled by so flimsy a veil. I determined to probe the mystery to the bottom.

"Simon," I said gaily, "let us forget all this over a bottle of Burgundy. I have a case of Lausseure's Clos Vougeot downstairs, fragrant with the odours and ruddy with the sunlight of the Côte d'Or. Let us have up a couple of bottles. What say you?"

"With all my heart," answered Simon smilingly.

I produced the wine and we seated ourselves to drink.

It was of a famous vintage, that of 1848, a year when war and wine throve together—and its pure but powerful juice seemed to impart renewed vitality to the system. By the time we had half finished the second bottle Simon's head, which I knew was a weak one, had begun to yield, while I remained calm as ever, only that every draught seemed to send a flush of vigour through my limbs. Simon's utterance became more and more indistinct. He took to singing French chansons of a not very moral tendency. I rose suddenly from the table just at the conclusion of one of those incoherent verses, and fixing my eyes on him with a quiet smile, said:

"Simon, I have deceived you. I learned your secret this evening. You may as well be frank with me. Mrs. Vulpes, or rather, one of her spirits, told me all."

He started with horror. His intoxication seemed for the moment to fade away, and he made a movement towards the weapon that he had a short time before laid down. I stopped him with my hand.

"Monster!" he cried passionately, "I am ruined! What shall I do? You shall never have it! I swear by my mother!"

"I don't want it," I said; "rest secure, but be frank with me. Tell me all about it."

The drunkenness began to return. He protested with maudlin earnestness that I was entirely mistaken— that I was intoxicated; then asked me to swear eternal secrecy, and promised to disclose the mystery to me. I pledged myself, of course, to all. With an uneasy look in his eyes, and hands unsteady with drink and nervousness, he drew a small case from his breast and opened it. Heavens! How the mild lamp-light was shivered into a thousand prismatic arrows, as it fell upon a vast rose-diamond that glittered in the case! I was no judge of diamonds, but I saw at a glance that this was a gem of rare size and purity. I looked at Simon with wonder, and—must I confess it?—with envy. How could he have obtained this treasure? In reply to my questions, I could just gather from his drunken statements (of which, I fancy, half the incoherence was affected) that he had been superintending a gang of slaves engaged in diamond-washing in Brazil; that he had seen one of them secrete a diamond, but, instead of informing his employers, had quietly watched the negro until he saw him bury his treasure; that he had dug it up, and fled with it, but that as yet he was afraid to attempt to dispose of it publicly—so valuable a gem being almost certain to attract too much attention to its owner's antecedents—and he had not been able to discover any of those obscure channels by which such matters are conveyed away safely. He added that, in accordance with Oriental practice, he had named his diamond by the fanciful title of The Eye of Morning.

While Simon was relating this to me, I regarded the great diamond attentively. Never had I beheld anything so beautiful. All the glories of light, ever imagined or described, seemed to pulsate in its crystalline chambers. Its weight, as I learned from Simon, was exactly one hundred and forty carats. Here was an amazing coincidence. The hand of Destiny seemed in it. On the very evening when the spirit of Leeuwenhoek communicates to me the great secret of the microscope, the priceless means which he directs me to employ start up within my easy reach! I determined, with the most perfect deliberation, to possess myself of Simon's diamond.

I sat opposite him while he nodded over his glass, and calmly revolved the whole affair. I did not for an instant contemplate so foolish an act as a common theft, which would of course be discovered, or at least necessitate flight and concealment, all of which must interfere with my scientific plans. There was but one step to be taken—to kill Simon. After all, what was the life of a little peddling Jew in comparison with the interests of science? Human beings are taken every day from the condemned prisons to be experimented on by surgeons. This man, Simon, was by his own confession a criminal, a robber, and I believed on my soul a murderer. He deserved death quite as much as any felon condemned by the laws; why should I not, like government, contrive that his punishment should contribute to the progress of human knowledge?

The means for accomplishing everything I desired lay within my reach. There stood upon the mantelpiece a bottle half full of French laudanum. Simon was so occupied with his diamond, which I had just restored to him, that it was an affair of no difficulty to drug his glass. In a quarter of an hour he was in a profound sleep.

I now opened his waistcoat, took the diamond from the inner pocket in which he had placed it, and removed him to the bed, on which I laid him so that his feet hung down over the edge. I had possessed myself of the Malay creese, which I held in my right hand, while with the other I discovered as accurately as I could by pulsation the exact locality of the heart. It was essential that all the aspects of his death should lead to the surmise of self-murder. I calculated the exact angle at which it was probable that the weapon, if levelled by Simon's own hand, would enter his breast; then with one powerful blow I thrust it up to the hilt in the very spot which I desired to penetrate. A convulsive thrill ran through Simon's limbs. I heard a smothered sound issue from his throat, precisely like the bursting of a large air-bubble, sent up by a diver, when it reaches the surface of the water; he turned half round on his side, and as if to assist my plans more effectually, his right hand, moved by some mere spasmodic impulse, clasped the handle of the creese, which it remained holding with extraordinary muscular tenacity. Beyond this there was no apparent struggle. The laudanum, I presume, paralysed the usual nervous action. He must have died instantaneously.

There was yet something to be done. To make it certain that all suspicion of the act should be diverted from any inhabitant of the house to Simon himself, it was necessary that the door should be found in the morning *locked on the inside*. How to do this, and afterwards escape myself? Not by the window; that was a physical impossibility. Besides, I was determined that the windows *also* should be found bolted. The solution was simple enough. I descended softly to my own room for a peculiar instrument which I had used for holding small slippery substances, such as minute spheres of glass, etc. This instrument was nothing more than a long slender hand-vice, with a very powerful grip and a considerable leverage, which last was accidentally owing to the shape of the handle. Nothing was simpler than, when the key was in the lock, to seize the end of its stem in this vice, through the keyhole, from the outside, and so lock the door. Previously, however, to doing this, I burned a number of papers on Simon's hearth. Suicides almost always burn papers before they destroy themselves. I also emptied some more laudanum into Simon's glass—having first removed from it all traces of wine—cleaned the other wine-glass and brought the bottles away with me. If traces of two persons drinking had been found in the room, the question naturally would have arisen, Who was the second? Besides, the wine-bottles might have been identified as belonging to me. The laudanum I poured out to account for its presence in his stomach, in case of a post-mortem examination. The theory naturally would be that he first intended to poison himself, but, after swallowing a little of the drug, was either disgusted with its taste, or changed his mind from other motives, and chose the dagger. These arrangements made, I walked out, leaving the gas burning, locked the door with my vice, and went to bed.

Simon's death was not discovered until nearly three in the afternoon. The servant, astonished at seeing the gas burning—the light streaming on the dark landing from under the door—peeped through the keyhole and saw Simon on the bed. She gave the alarm. The door was burst open, and the neighbourhood was in a fever of excitement.

Everyone in the house was arrested, myself included. There was an inquest; but no clue to his death, beyond that of suicide, could be obtained. Curiously enough,

he had made several speeches to his friends the preceding week that seemed to point to self-destruction.
One gentleman swore that Simon had said in his presence that "he was tired of life." His landlord affirmed
that Simon, when paying him his last month's rent,
remarked that "he would not pay him rent much
longer." All the other evidence corresponded — the
door locked inside, the position of the corpse, the burnt
papers. As I anticipated, no one knew of the possession of the diamond by Simon, so that no motive was
suggested for his murder. The jury, after a prolonged
examination, brought in the usual verdict, and the
neighbourhood once more settled down into its
accustomed quiet.

V. ANIMULA

The three months succeeding Simon's catastrophe I
devoted night and day to my diamond lens. I had
constructed a vast galvanic battery, composed of nearly
two thousand pairs of plates—a higher power I dared
not use, lest the diamond should be calcined. By means
of this enormous engine I was enabled to send a powerful
current of electricity continually through my great
diamond, which it seemed to me gained in lustre every
day. At the expiration of a month I commenced the
grinding and polishing of the lens, a work of intense
toil and exquisite delicacy. The great density of the
stone, and the care required to be taken with the
curvatures of the surfaces of the lens, rendered the
labour the severest and most harassing that I had yet
undergone.

At last the eventful moment came; the lens was
completed. I stood trembling on the threshold of new
worlds. I had the realisation of Alexander's famous
wish before me. The lens lay on the table, ready to
be placed upon its platform. My hand fairly shook as
I enveloped a drop of water with a thin coating of oil
of turpentine, preparatory to its examination—a process

necessary in order to prevent the rapid evaporation of the water. I now placed the drop on a thin slip of glass under the lens and, throwing upon it, by the combined aid of a prism and a mirror, a powerful stream of light, I approached my eye to the minute hole drilled through the axis of the lens. For an instant I saw nothing save what seemed to be an illuminated chaos, a vast luminous abyss. A pure white light, cloudless and serene, and seemingly limitless as space itself, was my first impression. Gently, and with the greatest care, I depressed the lens a few hairs' breadths. The wondrous illumination still continued, but as the lens approached the object a scene of indescribable beauty was unfolded to my view.

I seemed to gaze upon a vast space, the limits of which extended far beyond my vision. An atmosphere of magical luminousness permeated the entire field of view. I was amazed to see no trace of animalculous life. Not a living thing, apparently, inhabited that dazzling expanse. I comprehended instantly that, by the wondrous power of my lens, I had penetrated beyond the grosser particles of aqueous matter, beyond the realms of Infusoria and Protozoa, down to the original gaseous globule, into whose luminous interior I was gazing, as into an almost boundless dome filled with a supernatural radiance.

It was, however, no brilliant void into which I looked. On every side I beheld beautiful inorganic forms, of unknown texture, and coloured with the most enchanting hues. These forms presented the appearance of what might be called, for want of a more specific definition, foliated clouds of the highest rarity; that is, they undulated and broke into vegetable formations, and were tinged with splendours compared with which the gilding of our autumn woodlands is as dross compared with gold. Far away into the illimitable distance stretched long avenues of these gaseous forests, dimly transparent, and painted with prismatic hues of unimaginable brilliancy. The pendent branches waved along the fluid glades until every vista seemed to break through half-lucent ranks of many-coloured, drooping silken pennons. What seemed to be either fruits or flowers, pied with a thousand hues lustrous and ever varying, bubbled from the crowns of this fairy foliage. No hills, no lakes, no rivers, no forms animate or inanimate were to be seen, save those vast auroral copses that floated serenely in the luminous stillness, with leaves and fruits and flowers gleaming with unknown fires, unrealisable by mere imagination.

How strange, I thought, that this sphere should be thus condemned to solitude! I had hoped, at least, to discover some new form of animal life—perhaps of a lower class than any with which we are at present acquainted—but still, some living organism. I find my newly discovered world, if I may so speak, a beautiful chromatic desert.

While I was speculating on the singular arrangements of the internal economy of nature, with which she so frequently splinters into atoms our most compact theories, I thought I beheld a form moving slowly through the glades of one of the prismatic forests. I looked more attentively, and found that I was not mistaken. Words cannot depict the anxiety with which I awaited the nearer approach of this mysterious object. Was it merely some inanimate substance, held in suspense in the attenuated atmosphere of the globule? Or was it an animal endowed with vitality and motion? It approached, flitting beyond the gauzy, coloured veils of cloud foliage, for seconds dimly revealed, then vanishing. At last the violet pennons that trailed nearest to me vibrated; they were gently pushed aside, and the form floated out into the broad light.

It was a female human shape. When I say "human," I mean it possessed the outlines of humanity—but there the analogy ends. Its adorable beauty lifted it illimitable heights beyond the loveliest daughter of Adam.

I cannot, I dare not, attempt to inventory the charms of this divine revelation of perfect beauty. Those eyes of mystic violet, dewy and serene, evade my words. Her long lustrous hair following her glorious head in a golden wake, like the track sown in heaven by a falling star, seems to quench my most burning phrases with its splendours. If all the bees of Hybla nestled upon my lips, they would still sing but hoarsely the wondrous harmonies of outline that enclosed her form.

She swept out from between the rainbow-curtains of the cloud-trees into the broad sea of light that lay beyond. Her motions were those of some graceful naiad, cleaving, by a mere effort of her will, the clear, unruffled waters that fill the chambers of the sea. She floated forth with the serene grace of a frail bubble ascending through the still atmosphere of a June day. The perfect roundness of her limbs formed suave and enchanting curves. It was like listening to the most spiritual symphony of Beethoven, the divine, to watch the harmonious flow of lines. This, indeed, was a pleasure cheaply purchased at any price. What cared I, if I had waded to the portal of this wonder through another's blood? I would have given my own to enjoy one such moment of intoxication and delight.

Breathless with gazing on this lovely wonder, and forgetful for an instant of everything save her presence, I withdrew my eye from the microscope eagerly—alas! As my gaze fell on the thin slide that lay beneath my instrument, the bright light from mirror and from prism sparkled on a colourless drop of water! There, in that tiny bead of dew, this beautiful being was forever imprisoned. The planet Neptune was not more distant from me than she. I hastened once more to apply my eye to the microscope.

Animula (let me now call her by that dear name which I subsequently bestowed on her) had changed her position. She had again approached the wondrous forest, and was gazing earnestly upwards. Presently one of the trees—as I must call them—unfolded a long ciliary process, with which it seized one of the gleaming fruits that glittered on its summit, and sweeping slowly down, held it within reach of Animula. The sylph took it in her delicate hand, and began to eat. My attention was so entirely absorbed by her that I could not apply myself to the task of determining whether this singular plant was or was not instinct with volition.

I watched her, as she made her repast, with the most profound attention. The suppleness of her motions sent a thrill of delight through my frame; my heart beat madly as she turned her beautiful eyes in the direction of the spot in which I stood. What would I not have given to have had the power to precipitate myself into that luminous ocean, and float with her through those groves of purple and gold! While I was thus breathlessly following her every movement, she suddenly started, seemed to listen for a moment, and then cleaving the brilliant ether in which she was floating, like a flash of light, pierced through the opaline forest, and disappeared.

Instantly a series of the most singular sensations attacked me. It seemed as if I had suddenly gone blind. The luminous sphere was still before me, but my daylight had vanished. What caused this sudden disappearance? Had she a lover, or a husband? Yes, that was the solution! Some signal from a happy fellow-being had vibrated through the avenues of the forest, and she had obeyed the summons.

The agony of my sensations, as I arrived at this conclusion, startled me. I tried to reject the conviction that my reason forced upon me. I battled against the fatal conclusion—but in vain. It was so. I had no escape from it. I loved an animalcule!

It is true, that, thanks to the marvellous power of my microscope, she appeared of human proportions. Instead of presenting the revolting aspect of the coarser creatures, that live and struggle and die in the more easily resolvable portions of the water-drop, she was fair and delicate and of surpassing beauty. But of what account was all that? Every time that my eye was withdrawn from the instrument, it fell on a miserable drop of water, within which, I must be content to know, dwelt all that could make my life lovely.

Could she but see me once! Could I for one moment

pierce the mystical walls that so inexorably rose to separate us, and whisper all that filled my soul, I might consent to be satisfied for the rest of my life with the knowledge of her remote sympathy. It would be something to have established even the faintest personal link to bind us together—to know that at times, when roaming through those enchanted glades, she might think of the wonderful stranger who had broken the monotony of her life with his presence, and left a gentle memory in her heart!

But it could not be. No invention of which human intellect was capable could break down the barriers that nature had erected. I might feast my soul upon her wondrous beauty, yet she must always remain ignorant of the adoring eyes that day and night gazed upon her, and, even when closed, beheld her in dreams. With a bitter cry of anguish I fled from the room, and, flinging myself on my bed, sobbed myself to sleep like a child.

VI. THE SPILLING OF THE CUP

I arose the next morning almost at daybreak, and rushed to my microscope. I trembled as I sought the luminous world in miniature that contained my all. Animula was there. I had left the gas-lamp, surrounded by its moderators, burning, when I went to bed the night before. I found the sylph bathing, as it were, with an expression of pleasure animating her features, in the brilliant light which surrounded her. She tossed her lustrous golden hair over her shoulders with innocent coquetry. She lay at full length in the transparent medium, in which she supported herself with ease, and gambolled with the enchanting grace that the Nymph Salmacis might have exhibited when she sought to conquer the modest Hermaphroditus. I tried an experiment to satisfy myself if her powers of reflection were developed. I lessened the lamp-light considerably.

By the dim light that remained I could see an expression of pain flit across her face. She looked upward suddenly, and her brows contracted. I flooded the stage of the microscope again with a full stream of light, and her whole expression changed. She sprang forward like some substance deprived of all weight. Her eyes sparkled, and her lips moved. Ah! if science had only the means of conducting and reduplicating sounds, as it does the rays of light, what carols of happiness would then have entranced my ears! What jubilant hymns to Adonais would have thrilled the illumined air!

I now comprehended how it was that the Count de Gabalis peopled his mystic world with sylphs—beautiful beings whose breath of life was lambent fire, and who sported forever in regions of purest ether and purest light. The Rosicrucian had anticipated the wonder that I had practically realised.

How long this worship of my strange divinity went on thus I scarcely know. I lost all note of time. All day from early dawn, and far into the night, I was to be found peering through that wonderful lens. I saw no one, went nowhere, and scarce allowed myself sufficient time for my meals. My whole life was absorbed in contemplation as rapt as that of any of the Romish saints. Every hour that I gazed upon the divine form strengthened my passion—a passion that was always overshadowed by the maddening conviction that, although I could gaze on her at will, she never, never could behold me!

At length I grew so pale and emaciated, from want of rest, and continual brooding over my insane love and its cruel conditions, that I determined to make some effort to wean myself from it. "Come," I said, "this is at best but a fantasy. Your imagination has bestowed on Animula charms which in reality she does not possess. Seclusion from female society has produced this morbid condition of mind. Compare her with the beautiful women of your own world, and this false enchantment will vanish."

I looked over the newspapers by chance. There I beheld the advertisement of a celebrated danseuse who appeared nightly at Niblo's. The Signorina Caradolce had the reputation of being the most beautiful as well as the most graceful woman in the world. I instantly dressed and went to the theatre.

The curtain drew up. The usual semicircle of fairies in white muslin were standing on the right toe around the enamelled flower-bank, of green canvas, on which the belated prince was sleeping. Suddenly a flute is heard. The fairies start. The trees open, the fairies all stand on the left toe, and the queen enters. It was the signorina. She bounded forward amid thunders of applause, and lighting on one foot remained poised in air. Heavens! Was this the great enchantress that had drawn monarchs at her chariot-wheels? Those heavy muscular limbs, those thick ankles, those cavernous eyes, that stereotyped smile, those crudely-painted cheeks! Where were the vermeil blooms, the liquid, expressive eyes, the harmonious limbs of Animula?

The signorina danced. What gross, discordant movements! The play of her limbs was all false and artificial. Her bounds were painful athletic efforts; her poses were angular and distressed the eye. I could bear it no longer; with an exclamation of disgust that drew every eye upon me, I rose from my seat in the very middle of the signorina's *pas de fascination*, and abruptly quitted the house.

I hastened home to feast my eyes once more on the lovely form of my sylph. I felt that henceforth to combat this passion would be impossible. I applied my eyes to the lens. Animula was there—but what could have happened? Some terrible change seemed to have taken place during my absence. Some secret grief seemed to cloud the lovely features of her I gazed upon. Her face had grown thin and haggard; her limbs trailed heavily; the wondrous lustre of her golden hair had faded. She was ill! ill, and I could not assist her! I believe at that moment I would have gladly forfeited all claims to my human birthright, if I could only have been dwarfed to the size of an animalcule, and permitted to console her from whom fate had forever divided me.

I racked my brain for the solution of this mystery. What was it that afflicted the sylph? She seemed to suffer intense pain. Her features contracted, and she even writhed, as if with some internal agony. The wondrous forests appeared also to have lost half their beauty. Their hues were dim and in some places faded away altogether. I watched Animula for hours with a breaking heart, and she seemed absolutely to wither away under my very eye. Suddenly I remembered that I had not looked at the water-drop for several days. In fact, I hated to see it; for it reminded me of the natural barrier between Animula and myself. I hurriedly looked down on the stage of the microscope. The slide was still there—but, great heavens! the water-drop had vanished! The awful truth burst upon me; it had evaporated, until it had become so minute as to be invisible to the naked eye; I had been gazing on its last atom, the one that contained Animula—and she was dying!

I rushed again to the front of the lens, and looked through. Alas! the last agony had seized her. The rainbow-hued forests had all melted away, and Animula lay struggling feebly in what seemed to be a spot of dim light. Ah! the sight was horrible: the limbs once so round and lovely shrivelling up into nothings; the eyes —those eyes that shone like heaven—being quenched into black dust; the lustrous golden hair now lank and discoloured. The last throe came. I beheld that final struggle of the blackening form—and I fainted.

When I awoke out of a trance of many hours, I found myself lying amid the wreck of my instrument, myself as shattered in mind and body as it. I crawled feebly to my bed, from which I did not rise for months.

They say now that I am mad; but they are mistaken. I am poor, for I have neither the heart nor the will to work; all my money is spent, and I live on charity. Young men's associations that love a joke invite me to lecture on optics before them, for which they pay me, and laugh at me while I lecture. "Linley, the mad microscopist," is the name I go by. I suppose that I talk incoherently while I lecture. Who could talk sense when his brain is haunted by such ghastly memories, while ever and anon among the shapes of death I behold the radiant form of my lost Animula!

THE LUCK OF ROARING CAMP [1]

By BRET HARTE (1839–1902)

THERE was commotion in Roaring Camp. It could not have been a fight, for in 1850 that was not novel enough to have called together the entire settlement. The ditches and claims were not only deserted, but "Tuttle's grocery" had contributed its gamblers, who, it will be remembered, calmly continued their game the day that French Pete and Kanaka Joe shot each other to death over the bar in the front room. The whole camp was collected before a rude cabin on the outer edge of the clearing. Conversation was carried on in a low tone, but the name of a woman was frequently repeated. It was a name familiar enough in the camp—"Cherokee Sal."

Perhaps the less said of her the better. She was a coarse and, it is to be feared, a very sinful woman. But at that time she was the only woman in Roaring Camp, and was just then lying in sore extremity, when she most needed the ministration of her own sex. Dissolute, abandoned, and irreclaimable, she was yet suffering a martyrdom hard enough to bear even when veiled by sympathising womanhood, but now terrible in her loneliness. The primal curse had come to her in that original isolation which must have made the punishment of the first transgression so dreadful. It was, perhaps, part of the expiation of her sin that, at a moment when she most lacked her sex's intuitive tenderness and care, she met only the half-contemptuous faces of her masculine associates. Yet a few of the spectators

[1] Reprinted by permission from *The Luck of Roaring Camp and Other Stories* by Bret Harte. Copyright by Houghton Mifflin Co.

were, I think, touched by her sufferings. Sandy Tipton thought it was "rough on Sal," and, in the contemplation of her condition, for a moment rose superior to the fact that he had an ace and two bowers in his sleeve.

It will be seen also that the situation was novel. Deaths were by no means uncommon in Roaring Camp, but a birth was a new thing. People had been dismissed the camp effectively, finally, and with no possibility of return; but this was the first time that anybody had been introduced *ab initio*. Hence the excitement.

"You go in there, Stumpy," said a prominent citizen known as "Kentuck," addressing one of the loungers. "Go in there, and see what you kin do. You've had experience in them things."

Perhaps there was a fitness in the selection. Stumpy, in other climes, had been the putative head of two families; in fact, it was owing to some legal informality in these proceedings that Roaring Camp — a city of refuge — was indebted to his company. The crowd approved the choice, and Stumpy was wise enough to bow to the majority. The door closed on the extempore surgeon and midwife, and Roaring Camp sat down outside, smoked its pipe, and awaited the issue.

The assemblage numbered about a hundred men. One or two of these were actual fugitives from justice, some were criminal, and all were reckless. Physically they exhibited no indication of their past lives and character. The greatest scamp had a Raphael face, with a profusion of blond hair; Oakhurst, a gambler, had the melancholy air and intellectual abstraction of a Hamlet; the coolest and most courageous man was scarcely over five feet in height, with a soft voice and an embarrassed, timid manner. The term "roughs" applied to them was a distinction rather than a definition. Perhaps in the minor details of fingers, toes, ears, etc., the camp may have been deficient, but these slight omissions did not detract from their aggregate force. The strongest man had but three fingers on his right hand; the best shot had but one eye.

Such was the physical aspect of the men that were

dispersed around the cabin. The camp lay in a triangular valley between two hills and a river. The only
outlet was a steep trail over the summit of a hill that
faced the cabin, now illuminated by the rising moon.
The suffering woman might have seen it from the rude
bunk whereon she lay—seen it winding like a silver
thread until it was lost in the stars above.

A fire of withered pine boughs added sociability to
the gathering. By degrees the natural levity of Roaring
Camp returned. Bets were freely offered and taken
regarding the result. Three to five that "Sal would
get through with it"; even that the child would survive;
side bets as to the sex and complexion of the coming
stranger. In the midst of an excited discussion an
exclamation came from those nearest the door, and the
camp stopped to listen. Above the swaying and moaning of the pines, the swift rush of the river, and the
crackling of the fire rose a sharp, querulous cry—a
cry unlike anything heard before in the camp. The
pines stopped moaning, the river ceased to rush, and the
fire to crackle. It seemed as if Nature had stopped to
listen too.

The camp rose to its feet as one man! It was proposed
to explode a barrel of gunpowder; but in consideration
of the situation of the mother, better counsels prevailed,
and only a few revolvers were discharged; for whether
owing to the rude surgery of the camp, or some other
reason, Cherokee Sal was sinking fast. Within an hour
she had climbed, as it were, that rugged road that led
to the stars, and so passed out of Roaring Camp, its
sin and shame, forever. I do not think that the
announcement disturbed them much, except in speculation as to the fate of the child. "Can he live now?"
was asked of Stumpy. The answer was doubtful. The
only other being of Cherokee Sal's sex and maternal
condition in the settlement was an ass. There was
some conjecture as to fitness, but the experiment was
tried. It was less problematical than the ancient
treatment of Romulus and Remus, and apparently as
successful.

When these details were completed, which exhausted another hour, the door was opened, and the anxious crowd of men, who had already formed themselves into a queue, entered in single file. Beside the low bunk or shelf, on which the figure of the mother was starkly outlined below the blankets, stood a pine table. On this a candle-box was placed, and within it, swathed in staring red flannel, lay the last arrival at Roaring Camp. Beside the candle-box was placed a hat. Its use was soon indicated. "Gentlemen," said Stumpy, with a singular mixture of authority and *ex-officio* complacency—"gentlemen will please pass in at the front door, round the table, and out at the back door. Them as wishes to contribute anything toward the orphan will find a hat handy." The first man entered with his hat on; he uncovered, however, as he looked about him, and so unconsciously set an example to the next. In such communities good and bad actions are catching. As the procession filed in, comments were audible—criticisms addressed perhaps rather to Stumpy in the character of showman: "Is that him?" "Mighty small specimen"; "Hasn't more'n got the colour"; "Ain't bigger nor a derringer." The contributions were as characteristic: a silver tobacco-box; a doubloon; a navy revolver, silver-mounted; a gold specimen; a very beautifully embroidered lady's handkerchief (from Oakhurst the gambler); a diamond breastpin; a diamond ring (suggested by the pin, with the remark from the giver that he "saw that pin and went two diamonds better"); a slung-shot; a Bible (contributor not detected); a golden spur; a silver teaspoon (the initials, I regret to say, were not the giver's); a pair of surgeon's shears; a lancet; a Bank of England note for five pounds; and about two hundred dollars in loose gold and silver coin. During these proceedings Stumpy maintained a silence as impassive as the dead on his left, a gravity as inscrutable as that of the newly born on his right. Only one incident occurred to break the monotony of the curious procession. As Kentuck bent over the candle-box half curiously, the child turned. and, in a spasm of pain, caught at his groping finger, and held it fast for a moment. Kentuck looked foolish and embarrassed. Something like a blush tried to assert itself in his weather-beaten cheek. "The d——d little cuss!" he said, as he extricated his finger, with perhaps more tenderness and care than he might have been deemed capable of showing. He held that finger a little apart from its fellows as he went out, and examined it curiously. The examination provoked the same original remark in regard to the child. In fact, he seemed to enjoy repeating it. "He rastled with my finger," he remarked to Tipton, holding up the member, "the d——d little cuss!"

It was four o'clock before the camp sought repose. A light burnt in the cabin where the watchers sat, for Stumpy did not go to bed that night. Nor did Kentuck. He drank quite freely, and related with great gusto his experience, invariably ending with his characteristic condemnation of the new-comer. It seemed to relieve him of any unjust implication of sentiment, and Kentuck had the weaknesses of the nobler sex. When everybody else had gone to bed, he walked down to the river and whistled reflectingly. Then he walked up the gulch past the cabin, still whistling with demonstrative unconcern. At a large redwood tree he paused and retraced his steps, and again passed the cabin. Half-way down to the river's bank he again paused, and then returned and knocked at the door. It was opened by Stumpy. "How goes it?" said Kentuck, looking past Stumpy toward the candle-box. "All serene!" replied Stumpy. "Anything up?" "Nothing." There was a pause — an embarrassing one — Stumpy still holding the door. Then Kentuck had recourse to his finger, which he held up to Stumpy. "Rastled with it —the d——d little cuss," he said, and retired.

The next day Cherokee Sal had such rude sepulture as Roaring Camp afforded. After her body had been committed to the hillside, there was a formal meeting of the camp to discuss what should be done with her infant. A resolution to adopt it was unanimous and enthusiastic. But an animated discussion in regard to the manner and feasibility of providing for its wants at once sprang up. It was remarkable that the argument partook of none of those fierce personalities with which discussions were usually conducted at Roaring Camp. Tipton proposed that they should send the child to Red Dog—a distance of forty miles—where female attention could be procured. But the unlucky suggestion met with fierce and unanimous opposition. It was evident that no plan which entailed parting from their new acquisition would for a moment be entertained. "Besides," said Tom Ryder, "them fellows at Red Dog would swap it, and ring in somebody else on us." A disbelief in the honesty of other camps prevailed at Roaring Camp, as in other places.

The introduction of a female nurse in the camp also met with objection. It was argued that no decent woman could be prevailed on to accept Roaring Camp as her home, and the speaker urged that "they didn't want any more of the other kind." This unkind allusion to the defunct mother, harsh as it may seem, was the first spasm of propriety—the first symptom of the camp's regeneration. Stumpy advanced nothing. Perhaps he felt a certain delicacy in interfering with the selection of a possible successor in office. But when questioned, he averred stoutly that he and "Jinny"— the mammal before alluded to—could manage to rear the child. There was something original, independent, and heroic about the plan that pleased the camp. Stumpy was retained. Certain articles were sent for to Sacramento. "Mind," said the treasurer, as he pressed a bag of gold-dust into the expressman's hand, "the best that can be got—lace, you know, and filigree-work and frills—d——n the cost!"

Strange to say, the child thrived. Perhaps the invigorating climate of the mountain camp was compensation for material deficiencies. Nature took the foundling to her broader breast. In that rare atmosphere of the Sierra foothills—that air pungent with balsamic odour, that ethereal cordial at once bracing and exhilarating—he may have found food and nourishment, or a subtle chemistry that transmuted ass's milk to lime and phosphorus. Stumpy inclined to the belief that it was the latter and good nursing. "Me and that ass," he would say, "has been father and mother to him! Don't you," he would add, apostrophising the helpless bundle before him, "never go back on us."

By the time he was a month old the necessity of giving him a name became apparent. He had generally been known as "The Kid," "Stumpy's Boy," "The Coyote" (an allusion to his vocal powers), and even by Kentuck's endearing diminutive of "The d——d little cuss." But these were felt to be vague and unsatisfactory, and were at last dismissed under another influence. Gamblers and adventurers are generally superstitious, and Oakhurst one day declared that the baby had brought "the luck" to Roaring Camp. It was certain that of late they had been successful. "Luck" was the name agreed upon, with the prefix of Tommy for greater convenience. No allusion was made to the mother, and the father was unknown. "It's better," said the philosophical Oakhurst, "to take a fresh deal all round. Call him Luck, and start him fair." A day was accordingly set apart for the christening. What was meant by this ceremony the reader may imagine who has already gathered some idea of the reckless irreverence of Roaring Camp. The master of ceremonies was one "Boston," a noted wag, and the occasion seemed to promise the greatest facetiousness. This ingenious satirist had spent two days in preparing a burlesque of the Church service, with pointed local allusions. The choir was properly trained, and Sandy Tipton was to stand godfather. But after the procession had marched to the grove with music and banners, and the child had been deposited before a mock altar, Stumpy stepped before the expectant crowd. "It ain't my style to spoil fun, boys," said the little man, stoutly eyeing the faces around him, "but it strikes me that this thing ain't exactly on the squar. It's playin' it pretty low down on this yer baby to ring in fun on him that he ain't goin' to understand. And ef there's goin' to be any godfathers round, I'd like to see who's got any better rights than me." A silence followed Stumpy's speech. To the credit of all humorists be it said that the first man to acknowledge its justice was the satirist thus stopped of his fun. "But," said Stumpy, quickly following up his advantage, "we're here for a christening, and we'll have it. I proclaim you Thomas Luck, according to the laws of the United States and the State of California, so help me God." It was the first time that the name of the Deity had been otherwise uttered than profanely in the camp. The form of christening was perhaps even more ludicrous than the satirist had conceived; but strangely enough, nobody saw it and nobody laughed. "Tommy" was christened as seriously as he would have been under a Christian roof, and cried and was comforted in as orthodox fashion.

And so the work of regeneration began in Roaring Camp. Almost imperceptibly a change came over the settlement. The cabin assigned to "Tommy Luck"— or "The Luck," as he was more frequently called—first showed signs of improvement. It was kept scrupulously clean and whitewashed. Then it was boarded, clothed, and papered. The rosewood cradle, packed eighty miles by mule, had, in Stumpy's way of putting it, "sorter killed the rest of the furniture." So the rehabilitation of the cabin became a necessity. The men who were in the habit of lounging in at Stumpy's to see "how 'The Luck' got on" seemed to appreciate the change, and in self-defence the rival establishment of "Tuttle's grocery" bestirred itself and imported a carpet and mirrors. The reflections of the latter on the appearance of Roaring Camp tended to produce stricter habits of personal cleanliness. Again, Stumpy imposed a kind of quarantine upon those who aspired to the honour and privilege of holding The Luck. It was a cruel mortification to Kentuck—who, in the carelessness of a large nature and the habits of frontier life, had begun to regard all garments as a second cuticle, which, like a snake's, only sloughed off through decay—to be debarred this privilege from certain prudential reasons. Yet such was the subtle influence of innovation that he thereafter appeared regularly every afternoon in a clean shirt and face still shining from his ablutions. Nor were moral and social sanitary laws neglected. "Tommy," who was supposed to spend his whole existence in a persistent attempt to repose, must not be disturbed by noise. The shouting and yelling, which had gained the camp its infelicitous title, were not permitted within hearing distance of Stumpy's. The men conversed in whispers or smoked with Indian gravity. Profanity was tacitly given up in these sacred precincts, and throughout the camp a popular form of expletive, known as "D——n the luck!" and "Curse the luck!" was abandoned, as having a new personal bearing. Vocal music was not interdicted, being supposed to have a soothing, tranquillising quality; and one song, sung by "Man-o'-War Jack," an English sailor from Her Majesty's Australian colonies, was quite popular as a lullaby. It was a lugubrious recital of the exploits of "the *Arethusa*, Seventy-Four," in a muffled minor, ending with a prolonged dying fall at the burden of each verse, "On b-oo-o-ard of the *Arethusa*." It was a fine sight to see Jack holding The Luck, rocking from side to side as if with the motion of a ship, and crooning forth this naval ditty. Either through the peculiar rocking of Jack or the length of his song—it contained ninety stanzas, and was continued with conscientious deliberation to the bitter end—the lullaby generally had the desired effect. At such times the men would lie at full length under the trees in the soft summer twilight, smoking their pipes and drinking in the melodious utterances. An indistinct idea that this was pastoral happiness pervaded the camp. "This 'ere kind o' think," said the Cockney Simmons, meditatively reclining on his elbow, "is 'evingly." It reminded him of Greenwich.

On the long summer days The Luck was usually carried to the gulch from whence the golden store of Roaring Camp was taken. There, on a blanket spread over pine boughs, he would lie while the men were working in the ditches below. Latterly there was a rude attempt to decorate this bower with flowers and sweet - smelling shrubs, and generally someone would bring him a cluster of wild honeysuckles, azaleas, or the painted blossoms of Las Mariposas. The men had suddenly awakened to the fact that there were beauty and significance in these trifles, which they had so long trodden carelessly beneath their feet. A flake of glittering mica, a fragment of variegated quartz, a bright pebble from the bed of the creek, became beautiful to eyes thus cleared and strengthened, and were invariably put aside for The Luck. It was wonderful how many treasures the woods and hillsides yielded that "would do for Tommy." Surrounded by playthings such as never child out of fairyland had before, it is to be hoped that Tommy was content. He appeared to be serenely happy, albeit there was an infantine gravity about him, a contemplative light in his round grey eyes, that sometimes worried Stumpy. He was always tractable and quiet, and it is recorded that once, having crept beyond his "corral"—a hedge of tessellated pine boughs, which surrounded his bed—he dropped over the bank on his head in the soft earth, and remained with his mottled legs in the air in that position for at least five minutes with unflinching gravity. He was extricated without a murmur. I hesitate to record the many other instances of his sagacity, which rest, unfortunately, upon the statements of prejudiced friends. Some of them were not without a tinge of superstition. "I crep' up the bank just now," said Kentuck one day, in a breathless state of excitement, "and dern my skin if he wasn't a-talkin' to a jaybird as was a-sittin' on his lap. There they was, just as free and sociable as anything you please, a-jawin' at each other just like two cherrybums." Howbeit, whether creeping over the pine boughs or lying lazily on his back blinking at the leaves above him, to him the birds sang, the squirrels chattered, and the flowers bloomed. Nature was his nurse and playfellow. For him she would let slip between the leaves golden shafts of sunlight that fell just within his grasp; she would send wandering breezes to visit him with the balm of bay and resinous gum; to him the tall redwoods nodded familiarly and sleepily, the bumble-bees buzzed, and the rooks cawed a slumbrous accompaniment.

Such was the golden summer of Roaring Camp. They were "flush times," and the luck was with them. The claims had yielded enormously. The camp was jealous of its privileges and looked suspiciously on strangers. No encouragement was given to immigration, and, to make their seclusion more perfect, the land on either side of the mountain wall that surrounded the camp they duly pre-empted. This, and a reputation for singular proficiency with the revolver, kept the reserve of Roaring Camp inviolate. The expressman—their only connecting link with the surrounding world—sometimes told wonderful stories of the camp. He would say, "They've a street up there in 'Roaring' that would lay over any street in Red Dog. They've got vines and flowers round their houses, and they wash themselves twice a day. But they're mighty rough on strangers, and they worship an Ingin baby."

With the prosperity of the camp came a desire for further improvement. It was proposed to build a hotel in the following spring, and to invite one or two decent families to reside there for the sake of The Luck, who might perhaps profit by female companionship. The sacrifice that this concession to the sex cost these men, who were fiercely sceptical in regard to its general virtue and usefulness, can only be accounted for by their affection for Tommy. A few still held out. But the resolve could not be carried into effect for three months, and the minority meekly yielded in the hope that something might turn up to prevent it. And it did.

The winter of 1851 will long be remembered in the foothills. The snow lay deep on the Sierras, and every mountain creek became a river, and every river a lake. Each gorge and gulch was transformed into a tumultuous watercourse that descended the hillsides, tearing down giant trees and scattering its drift and debris along the plain. Red Dog had been twice under water, and Roaring Camp had been forewarned. "Water put the gold into them gulches," said Stumpy. "It's been here once and will be here again!" And that night the North Fork suddenly leaped over its banks and swept up the triangular valley of Roaring Camp.

In the confusion of rushing water, crashing trees, and crackling timber, and the darkness which seemed to flow with the water and blot out the fair valley, but little could be done to collect the scattered camp. When the morning broke, the cabin of Stumpy, nearest the river-bank, was gone. Higher up the gulch they found the body of its unlucky owner; but the pride, the hope, the joy, The Luck, of Roaring Camp had disappeared. They were returning with sad hearts when a shout from the bank recalled them.

It was a relief-boat from down the river. They had picked up, they said, a man and an infant, nearly exhausted, about two miles below. Did anybody know them, and did they belong here?

It needed but a glance to show them Kentuck lying there, cruelly crushed and bruised, but still holding The Luck of Roaring Camp in his arms. As they bent over the strangely assorted pair, they saw that the child was cold and pulseless. "He is dead," said one. Kentuck opened his eyes. "Dead?" he repeated feebly. "Yes, my man, and you are dying, too." A smile lit the eyes of the expiring Kentuck. "Dying!" he repeated; "he's a-takin' me with him. Tell the boys I've got The Luck with me now"; and the strong man, clinging to the frail babe as a drowning man is said to cling to a straw, drifted away into the shadowy river that flows forever to the unknown sea.

MARJORIE DAW [1]

By Thomas Bailey Aldrich (1836–1907)

I. DR. DILLON TO EDWARD DELANEY, ESQ., AT THE PINES, NEAR RYE, N.H.

8 August, 1872.

MY DEAR SIR,—I am happy to assure you that your anxiety is without reason. Flemming will be confined to the sofa for three or four weeks, and will have to be careful at first how he uses his leg. A fracture of this kind is always a tedious affair. Fortunately the bone was very skilfully set by the surgeon who chanced to be in the drug-store where Flemming was brought after his fall, and I apprehend no permanent inconvenience from the accident. *Flemming is doing perfectly well physically;* but I must confess that the irritable and morbid state of mind into which he has fallen causes me a great deal of uneasiness. He is the last man in the world who ought to break his leg. You know how impetuous our friend is ordinarily, what a soul of restlessness and energy, never content unless he is rushing at some object, like a sportive bull at a red shawl; but amiable withal. He is no longer amiable. His temper has become something frightful. Miss Fanny Flemming came up from Newport, where the family are staying for the summer, to nurse him; but he packed her off the next morning in tears. He has a complete set of Balzac's works, twenty-seven volumes, piled up near his sofa, one of which he threatens to throw at Watkins whenever that exemplary servingman appears with his meals. Yesterday I very innocently brought Flemming a small basket of lemons.

You know it was a strip of lemon-peel on the curbstone that caused our friend's mischance. Well, he no sooner set his eyes upon those lemons than he fell into such a rage as I cannot adequately describe. This is only one of his moods, and the least distressing. At other times he sits with bowed head regarding his splintered limb, silent, sullen, despairing. When this fit is on him—and it sometimes lasts all day—nothing can distract his melancholy. He refuses to eat, does not even read the newspapers; books, except as projectiles for Watkins, have no charms for him. His state is truly pitiable.

Now, if he were a poor man, with a family depending on his daily labour, this irritability and despondency would be natural enough. But in a young fellow of twenty-four, with plenty of money and seemingly not a care in the world, the thing is monstrous. If he continues to give way to his vagaries in this manner, he will end by bringing on an inflammation of the fibula. It was the fibula he broke. I am at my wits' end to know what to prescribe for him. I have anæsthetics and lotions, to make people sleep and to soothe pain; but I've no medicine that will make a man have a little common sense. That is beyond my skill, but may be it is not beyond yours. You are Flemming's intimate friend, his *fidus Achates*. Write to him, write to him frequently, distract his mind, cheer him up, and prevent him from becoming a confirmed case of melancholia. Perhaps he has some important plans disarranged by his present confinement. If he has you will know, and will know how to advise him judiciously. I trust your father finds the change beneficial? I am, my dear sir, with great respect, etc.

II. EDWARD DELANEY TO JOHN FLEMMING, WEST 38TH
STREET, NEW YORK

9 August, 1872.

MY DEAR JACK,—I had a line from Dillon this morning and was rejoiced to learn that your hurt is not so bad as reported. Like a certain personage, you are not so black and blue as you are painted. Dillon will put you on your pins again in two or three weeks, if you will only have patience and follow his counsels. Did you get my note of last Wednesday? I was greatly troubled when I heard of the accident.

I can imagine how tranquil and saintly you are with your leg in a trough! It is deuced awkward, to be sure, just as we had promised ourselves a glorious month together at the seaside; but we must make the best of it. It is unfortunate, too, that my father's health renders it impossible for me to leave him. I think he has much improved; the sea air is his native element; but he still needs my arm to lean upon in his walks, and requires someone more careful than a servant to look after him. I cannot come to you, dear Jack, but I have hours of unemployed time on hand, and I will write you a whole post-office full of letters, if that will divert you. Heaven knows, I haven't anything to write about. It isn't as if we were living at one of the beach houses; then I could do you some character studies, and fill your imagination with groups of sea-goddesses, with their (or somebody else's) raven and blonde manes hanging down their shoulders. You should have Aphrodite in morning wrapper, in evening costume, and in her prettiest bathing-suit. But we are far from all that here. We have rooms in a farmhouse, on a cross-road, two miles from the hotels, and lead the quietest of lives.

I wish I were a novelist. This old house, with its sanded floors and high wainscots, and its narrow windows looking out upon a cluster of pines that turn themselves into æolian harps every time the wind blows, would be the place in which to write a summer romance. It should be a story with the odours of the forest and the breath of the sea in it. It should be a novel like one of that Russian fellow's — what's his name? — Tourguénieff, Turguenef, Turgenif, Toorguniff, Turgénjew — nobody knows how to spell him. Yet I wonder if even a Liza or an Alexandra Paulovna could stir the heart of a man who has constant twinges in his leg. I wonder if one of our own Yankee girls of the best type, haughty and *spirituelle*, would be of any comfort to you in your present deplorable condition. If I thought so, I would hasten down to the Surf House and catch one for you; or, better still, I would find you one over the way.

Picture to yourself a large white house just across the road, nearly opposite our cottage. It is not a house, but a mansion, built, perhaps, in the colonial period, with rambling extensions, and gambrel roof, and a wide piazza on three sides—a self-possessed, high-bred piece of architecture, with its nose in the air. It stands back from the road, and has an obsequious retinue of fringed elms and oaks and weeping willows. Sometimes in the morning, and oftener in the afternoon, when the sun has withdrawn from that part of the mansion, a young woman appears on the piazza with some mysterious Penelope web of embroidery in her hand, or a book. There is a hammock over there—of pineapple fibre, it looks from here. A hammock is very becoming when one is eighteen, and has golden hair, and dark eyes, and an emerald-coloured illusion dress looped up after the fashion of a Dresden-china shepherdess, and is *chaussée* like a belle of the time of Louis Quatorze. All this splendour goes into that hammock, and sways there like a pond-lily in the golden afternoon. The window of my bedroom looks down on that piazza—and so do I.

But enough of this nonsense, which ill becomes a sedate young attorney taking his vacation with an invalid father. Drop me a line, dear Jack, and tell me how you really are. State your case. Write me a long, quiet letter. If you are violent or abusive, I'll take the law to you.

III. JOHN FLEMMING TO EDWARD DELANEY

11 August, 1872.

Your letter, dear Ned, was a godsend. Fancy what a fix I am in—I, who never had a day's sickness since I was born. My left leg weighs three tons. It is embalmed in spices and smothered in layers of fine linen, like a mummy. I can't move. I haven't moved for five thousand years. I'm of the time of Pharaoh.

I lie from morning till night on a lounge, staring into the hot street. Everybody is out of town enjoying himself. The brown-stone-front houses across the street resemble a row of particularly ugly coffins set up on end. A green mould is settling on the names of the deceased, carved on the silver door-plates. Sardonic spiders have sewed up the keyholes. All is silence and dust and desolation.—I interrupt this a moment, to take a shy at Watkins with the second volume of *César Birotteau*. Missed him! I think I could bring him down with a copy of *Sainte-Beuve* or the *Dictionnaire Universel*, if I had it. These small Balzac books somehow do not quite fit my hand; but I shall fetch him yet. I've an idea that Watkins is tapping the old gentleman's Château Yquem. Duplicate key of the wine-cellar. Hibernian swarries in the front basement. Young Cheops upstairs, snug in his cerements. Watkins glides into my chamber, with that colourless, hypocritical face of his drawn out long like an accordion; but I know he grins all the way downstairs, and is glad I have broken my leg. Was not my evil star in the very zenith when I ran up to town to attend that dinner at Delmonico's? I didn't come up altogether for that. It was partly to buy Frank Livingstone's roan mare Margot. And now I shall not be able to sit in the saddle these two months. I'll send the mare down to you at The Pines—is that the name of the place?

Old Dillon fancies that I have something on my mind. He drives me wild with lemons. Lemons for a mind diseased! Nonsense. I am only as restless as the devil under this confinement—a thing I'm not used to. Take a man who has never had so much as a headache or a toothache in his life, strap one of his legs in a section of water-spout, keep him in a room in the city for weeks, with the hot weather turned on, and then expect him to smile and purr and be happy! It is preposterous. I can't be cheerful or calm.

Your letter is the first consoling thing I have had

since my disaster, ten days ago. It really cheered me
up for half an hour. Send me a screed, Ned, as often
as you can, if you love me. Anything will do. Write
me more about that little girl in the hammock. That
was very pretty, all that about the Dresden-china
shepherdess and the pond-lily; the imagery a little
mixed, perhaps, but very pretty. I didn't suppose
you had so much sentimental furniture in your upper
story. It shows how one may be familiar for years
with the reception-room of his neighbour, and never
suspect what is directly under his mansard. I supposed
your loft stuffed with dry legal parchments, mortgages,
and affidavits; you take down a package of manu-
script, and lo! there are lyrics and sonnets and can-
zonettas. You really have a graphic descriptive touch,
Edward Delaney, and I suspect you of anonymous
love-tales in the magazines.

I shall be a bear until I hear from you again. Tell
me all about your pretty *inconnue* across the road.
What is her name? Who is she? Who's her father?
Where's her mother? Who's her lover? You cannot
imagine how this will occupy me. The more trifling,
the better. My imprisonment has weakened me in-
tellectually to such a degree that I find your epistolary
gifts quite considerable. I am passing into my second
childhood. In a week or two I shall take to india-
rubber rings and prongs of coral. A silver cup, with an
appropriate inscription, would be a delicate attention
on your part. In the meantime, write!

IV. EDWARD DELANEY TO JOHN FLEMMING

12 August, 1872.

The sick pasha shall be amused. *Bismillah!* he wills
it so. If the story-teller becomes prolix and tedious—
the bow-string and the sack, and two Nubians to drop
him into the Piscataqua! But truly, Jack, I have a
hard task. There is literally nothing here—except the
little girl over the way. She is swinging in the hammock at this moment. It is to me compensation for

many of the ills of life to see her now and then put out
a small kid boot, which fits like a glove, and set herself
going. Who is she, and what is her name? Her name
is Daw. Only daughter of Mr. Richard W. Daw,
ex-colonel and banker. Mother dead. One brother at
Harvard, elder brother killed at the battle of Fair Oaks,
ten years ago. Old, rich family, the Daws. This is
the homestead, where father and daughter pass eight
months of the twelve; the rest of the year in Baltimore
and Washington. The New England winter too many
for the old gentleman. The daughter is called Marjorie
—Marjorie Daw. Sounds odd at first, doesn't it?
But after you say it over to yourself half a dozen times,
you like it. There's a pleasing quaintness to it, something prim and pansy-like. Must be a nice sort of girl
to be called Marjorie Daw.

I had mine host of The Pines in the witness-box last
night, and drew the foregoing testimony from him. He
has charge of Mr. Daw's vegetable garden, and has
known the family these thirty years. Of course I shall
make the acquaintance of my neighbours before many
days. It will be next to impossible for me not to meet
Mr. Daw or Miss Daw in some of my walks. The young
lady has a favourite path to the sea-beach. I shall
intercept her some morning, and touch my hat to her.
Then the princess will bend her fair head to me with
courteous surprise not unmixed with haughtiness.
Will snub me, in fact. All this for thy sake, O Pasha of
the Snapt Axle-tree! . . . How oddly things fall out!
Ten minutes ago I was called down to the parlour—
you know the kind of parlours in farmhouses on the
coast, a sort of amphibious parlour, with sea-shells on
the mantelpiece and spruce branches in the chimney-
place—where I found my father and Mr. Daw doing the
antique polite to each other. He had come to pay
his respects to his new neighbours. Mr. Daw is a tall,
slim gentleman of about fifty-five, with a florid face and
snow-white moustache and side-whiskers. Looks like
Mr. Dombey, or as Mr. Dombey would have looked if
he had served a few years in the British Army. Mr.

Daw was a colonel in the late war, commanding the regiment in which his son was a lieutenant. Plucky old boy, backbone of New Hampshire granite. Before taking his leave, the colonel delivered himself of an invitation as if he were issuing a general order. Miss Daw has a few friends coming, at 4 p.m., to play croquet on the lawn (parade-ground) and have tea (cold rations) on the piazza. Will we honour them with our company? (or be sent to the guard-house.) My father declines on the plea of ill-health. My father's son bows with as much suavity as he knows, and accepts.

In my next I shall have something to tell you. I shall have seen the little beauty face to face. I have a presentiment, Jack, that this Daw is a *rara avis*! Keep up your spirits, my boy, until I write you another letter—and send me along word how's your leg.

V. EDWARD DELANEY TO JOHN FLEMMING

13 August, 1872.

The party, my dear Jack, was as dreary as possible. A lieutenant of the navy, the rector of the Episcopal church at Stillwater, and a society swell from Nahant. The lieutenant looked as if he had swallowed a couple of his buttons, and found the bullion rather indigestible; the rector was a pensive youth, of the daffydowndilly sort; and the swell from Nahant was a very weak tidal wave indeed. The women were much better, as they always are; the two Miss Kingsburys of Philadelphia, staying at the Sea-shell House, two bright and engaging girls. But Marjorie Daw!

The company broke up soon after tea, and I remained to smoke a cigar with the colonel on the piazza. It was like seeing a picture, to see Miss Marjorie hovering around the old soldier, and doing a hundred gracious little things for him. She brought the cigars and lighted the tapers with her own delicate fingers, in the most enchanting fashion. As we sat there, she came and went in the summer twilight, and seemed, with her white dress and pale gold hair, like some lovely phantom that had sprung into existence out of the smoke-wreaths. If she had melted into air, like the statue of Galatea in the play, I should have been more sorry than surprised.

It was easy to perceive that the old colonel worshipped her, and she him. I think the relation between an elderly father and a daughter just blooming into womanhood the most beautiful possible. There is in it a subtle sentiment that cannot exist in the case of mother and daughter, or that of son and mother. But this is getting into deep water.

I sat with the Daws until half-past ten, and saw the moon rise on the sea. The ocean, that had stretched motionless and black against the horizon, was changed by magic into a broken field of glittering ice, interspersed with marvellous silvery fiords. In the far distance the Isles of Shoals loomed up like a group of huge bergs drifting down on us. The Polar Regions in a June thaw! It was exceedingly fine. What did we talk about? We talked about the weather—and *you*! The weather has been disagreeable for several days past—and so have you. I glided from one topic to the other very naturally. I told my friends of your accident; how it had frustrated all our summer plans, and what our plans were. I played quite a spirited solo on the fibula. Then I described you; or, rather, I didn't. I spoke of your amiability, of your patience under this severe affliction; of your touching gratitude when Dillon brings you little presents of fruit; of your tenderness to your sister Fanny, whom you would not allow to stay in town to nurse you, and how you heroically sent her back to Newport, preferring to remain alone with Mary, the cook, and your man Watkins, to whom, by the way, you were devotedly attached. If you had been there, Jack, you wouldn't have known yourself. I should have excelled as a criminal lawyer, if I had not turned my attention to a different branch of jurisprudence.

Miss Marjorie asked all manner of leading questions concerning you. It did not occur to me then, but it struck me forcibly afterwards, that she evinced a singular interest in the conversation. When I got back to my room, I recalled how eagerly she leaned forward, with her full, snowy throat in strong moonlight, listening to what I said. Positively, I think I made her like you!

Miss Daw is a girl whom you would like immensely, I can tell you that. A beauty without affectation, a high and tender nature—if one can read the soul in the face. And the old colonel is a noble character, too.

I am glad that the Daws are such pleasant persons. The Pines is an isolated spot, and my resources are few. I fear I should have found life here somewhat monotonous before long, with no other society than that of my excellent sire. It is true, I might have made a target of the defenceless invalid; but I haven't a taste for artillery, *moi*.

VI. JOHN FLEMMING TO EDWARD DELANEY

17 August, 1872.

For a man who hasn't a taste for artillery, it occurs to me, my friend, you are keeping up a pretty lively fire on my inner works. But go on. Cynicism is a small brass field-piece that eventually bursts and kills the artilleryman.

You may abuse me as much as you like, and I'll not complain; for I don't know what I should do without your letters. They are curing me. I haven't hurled anything at Watkins since last Sunday, partly because I have grown more amiable under your teaching, and partly because Watkins captured my ammunition one night, and carried it off to the library. He is rapidly losing the habit he had acquired of dodging whenever I rub my ear, or make any slight motion with my right arm. He is still suggestive of the wine-cellar, however. You may break, you may shatter Watkins, if you will, but the scent of the Roederer will hang round him still.

Ned, that Miss Daw must be a charming person. I should certainly like her. I like her already. When you spoke in your first letter of seeing a young girl swinging in a hammock under your chamber window, I was somehow strangely drawn to her. I cannot account for it in the least. What you have subsequently written of Miss Daw has strengthened the impression. You seem to be describing a woman I have known in some previous state of existence, or dreamed of in this. Upon my word, if you were to send me her photograph, I believe I should recognise her at a glance. Her manner, that listening attitude, her traits of character, as you indicate them, the light hair and the dark eyes— they are all familiar things to me. Asked a lot of questions, did she? Curious about me? That is strange.

You would laugh in your sleeve, you wretched old cynic, if you knew how I lie awake nights, with my gas turned down to a star, thinking of The Pines and the house across the road. How cool it must be down there! I long for the salt smell in the air. I picture the colonel smoking his cheroot on the piazza. I send you and Miss Daw off on afternoon rambles along the beach. Sometimes I let you stroll with her under the elms in the moonlight, for you are great friends by this time, I take it, and see each other every day. I know your ways and your manners! Then I fall into a truculent mood, and would like to destroy somebody. Have you noticed anything in the shape of a lover hanging around the colonial Lares and Penates? Does that lieutenant of the horse-marines or that young Stillwater parson visit the house much? Not that I am pining for news of them, but any gossip of the kind would be in order. I wonder, Ned, you don't fall in love with Miss Daw. I am ripe to do it myself. Speaking of photographs, couldn't you manage to slip one of her *cartes de visite* from her album—she must have an album, you know— and send it to me? I will return it before it could be missed. That's a good fellow! Did the mare arrive safe and sound? It will be a capital animal this autumn for Central Park.

Oh—my leg? I forgot about my leg. It's better.

20 August, 1872.

You are correct in your surmises.   I am on the most friendly terms with our neighbours.   The colonel and my father smoke their afternoon cigar together in our sitting-room or on the piazza opposite, and I pass an hour or two of the day or the evening with the daughter. I am more and more struck by the beauty, modesty, and intelligence of Miss Daw.

You ask me why I do not fall in love with her.   I will be frank, Jack; I have thought of that.   She is young, rich, accomplished, uniting in herself more attractions, mental and personal, than I can recall in any girl of my acquaintance; but she lacks the something that would be necessary to inspire in me that kind of interest. Possessing this unnamed quantity, a woman neither beautiful nor wealthy nor very young could bring me to her feet.   But not Miss Daw.   If we were ship-wrecked together on an uninhabited island—let me suggest a tropical island, for it costs no more to be picturesque—I would build her a bamboo hut, I would fetch her bread-fruit and coconuts, I would fry yams for her, I would lure the ingenuous turtle and make her nourishing soups, but I wouldn't make love to her— not under eighteen months.   I would like to have her for a sister, that I might shield her and counsel her, and spend half my income on old thread-lace and camel's-hair shawls.   (We are off the island now.)   If such were not my feeling, there would still be an obstacle to my loving Miss Daw.   A greater misfortune could scarcely befall me than to love her.   Flemming, I am about to make a revelation that will astonish you.   I may be all wrong in my premises and consequently in my conclusions; but you shall judge.

That night when I returned to my room after the croquet party at the Daws', and was thinking over the trivial events of the evening, I was suddenly impressed by the air of eager attention with which Miss Daw had followed my account of your accident.   I think I mentioned this to you. Well, the next morning, as I went to mail my letter, I overtook Miss Daw on the road to Rye, where the post-office is, and accompanied her thither and back, an hour's walk. The conversation again turned on you, and again I remarked that inexplicable look of interest which had lighted up her face the previous evening. Since then, I have seen Miss Daw perhaps ten times, perhaps oftener, and on each occasion I found that when I was not speaking of you, or your sister, or some person or place associated with you, I was not holding her attention. She would be absent-minded, her eyes would wander away from me to the sea, or to some distant object in the landscape; her fingers would play with the leaves of a book in a way that convinced me she was not listening. At these moments if I abruptly changed the theme—I did it several times as an experiment—and dropped some remark about my friend Flemming, then the sombre blue eyes would come back to me instantly.

Now, is not this the oddest thing in the world? No, not the oddest. The effect which you tell me was produced on you by my casual mention of an unknown girl swinging in a hammock is certainly as strange. You can conjecture how that passage in your letter of Friday startled me. Is it possible, then, that two persons who have never met, and who are hundreds of miles apart, can exert a magnetic influence on each other? I have read of such psychological phenomena, but never credited them. I leave the solution of the problem to you. As for myself, all other things being favourable, it would be impossible for me to fall in love with a woman who listens to me only when I am talking of my friend!

I am not aware that anyone is paying marked attention to my fair neighbour. The lieutenant of the navy —he is stationed at Rivermouth—sometimes drops in of an evening, and sometimes the rector from Stillwater; the lieutenant the oftener. He was there last night. I should not be surprised if he had an eye to the heiress; but he is not formidable. Mistress Daw carries a neat little spear of irony, and the honest lieutenant seems to have a particular facility for impaling himself on the point of it. He is not dangerous, I should say; though I have known a woman to satirise a man for years, and marry him after all. Decidedly, the lowly rector is not dangerous; yet, again, who has not seen Cloth of Frieze victorious in the lists where Cloth of Gold went down?

As to the photograph. There is an exquisite ivory-type of Marjorie, in passe-partout, on the drawing-room mantelpiece. It would be missed at once if taken. I would do anything reasonable for you, Jack; but I've no burning desire to be hauled up before the local justice of the peace, on a charge of petty larceny.

P.S.—Enclosed is a spray of mignonette, which I advise you to treat tenderly. Yes, we talked of you again last night, as usual. It is becoming a little dreary for me.

VIII.   EDWARD DELANEY TO JOHN FLEMMING

22 August, 1872.

Your letter in reply to my last has occupied my thoughts all the morning. I do not know what to think. Do you mean to say that you are seriously half in love with a woman whom you have never seen—with a shadow, a chimera? for what else can Miss Daw be to you? I do not understand it at all. I understand neither you nor her. You are a couple of ethereal beings moving in finer air than I can breathe with my commonplace lungs. Such delicacy of sentiment is something that I admire without comprehending. I am bewildered. I am of the earth earthy, and I find myself in the incongruous position of having to do with mere souls, with natures so finely tempered that I run some risk of shattering them in my awkwardness. I am as Caliban among the spirits!

Reflecting on your letter, I am not sure that it is wise in me to continue this correspondence. But no, Jack; I do wrong to doubt the good sense that forms the basis of your character. You are deeply interested in Miss Daw; you feel that she is a person whom you may perhaps greatly admire when you know her: at the same time you bear in mind that the chances are ten to five that, when you do come to know her, she will fall far short of your ideal, and you will not care for her in the least. Look at it in this sensible light, and I will hold back nothing from you.

Yesterday afternoon my father and myself rode over to Rivermouth with the Daws. A heavy rain in the morning had cooled the atmosphere and laid the dust. To Rivermouth is a drive of eight miles, along a winding road lined all the way with wild barberry-bushes. I never saw anything more brilliant than these bushes, the green of the foliage and the faint blush of the berries intensified by the rain. The colonel drove, with my father in front, Miss Daw and I on the back seat. I resolved that for the first five miles your name should not pass my lips. I was amused by the artful attempts she made, at the start, to break through my reticence. Then a silence fell upon her; and then she became suddenly gay. That keenness which I enjoyed so much when it was exercised on the lieutenant was not so satisfactory directed against myself. Miss Daw has great sweetness of disposition, but she can be disagreeable. She is like the young lady in the rhyme, with the curl on her forehead:

> When she is good,
> She is very, very good,
> And when she is bad, she is horrid!

I kept to my resolution, however; but on the return home I relented, and talked of your mare! Miss Daw is going to try a side-saddle on Margot some morning. The animal is a trifle too light for my weight. By the by, I nearly forgot to say that Miss Daw sat for a picture yesterday to a Rivermouth artist. If the negative turns out well, I am to have a copy. So our ends will be accomplished without crime. I wish, though, I could send you the ivorytype in the drawing-room; it is cleverly coloured, and would give you an idea of her hair and eyes, which of course the other will not.

No, Jack, the spray of mignonette did not come from me. A man of twenty-eight doesn't enclose flowers in his letters—to another man. But don't attach too much significance to the circumstance. She gives sprays of mignonette to the rector, sprays to the lieutenant. She has even given a rose from her bosom to your slave. It is her jocund nature to scatter flowers, like Spring.

If my letters sometimes read disjointedly, you must understand that I never finish one at a sitting, but write at intervals, when the mood is on me.

The mood is not on me now.

IX. EDWARD DELANEY TO JOHN FLEMMING

23 August, 1872.

I have just returned from the strangest interview with Marjorie. She has all but confessed to me her interest in you. But with what modesty and dignity! Her words elude my pen as I attempt to put them on paper; and, indeed, it was not so much what she said as her manner; and that I cannot reproduce. Perhaps it was of a piece with the strangeness of this whole business, that she should tacitly acknowledge to a third party the love she feels for a man she has never beheld! But I have lost, through your aid, the faculty of being surprised. I accept things as persons do in dreams. Now that I am again in my room, it all appears like an illusion—the black masses of Rembrandtish shadow under the trees, the fireflies whirling in Pyrrhic dances among the shrubbery, the sea over there, Marjorie sitting in the hammock!

It is past midnight, and I am too sleepy to write more.

Thursday Morning.

My father has suddenly taken it into his head to spend a few days at the Shoals. In the meanwhile you will not hear from me. I see Marjorie walking in the garden with the colonel. I wish I could speak to her alone, but shall probably not have an opportunity before we leave.

X. EDWARD DELANEY TO JOHN FLEMMING

28 August, 1872.

You were passing into your second childhood, were you? Your intellect was so reduced that my epistolary gifts seemed quite considerable to you, did they? I rise superior to the sarcasm in your favour of the 11th instant, when I notice that five days' silence on my part is sufficient to throw you into the depths of despondency.

We returned only this morning from Appledore, that enchanted island—at four dollars per day. I find on my desk three letters from you! Evidently there is no lingering doubt in *your* mind as to the pleasure I derive from your correspondence. These letters are undated, but in what I take to be the latest are two passages that require my consideration. You will pardon my candour, dear Flemming, but the conviction forces itself upon me that as your leg grows stronger your head becomes weaker. You ask my advice on a certain point. I will give it. In my opinion you could do nothing more unwise than to address a note to Miss Daw, thanking her for the flower. It would, I am sure, offend her delicacy beyond pardon. She knows you only through me; you are to her an abstraction, a figure in a dream— a dream from which the faintest shock would awaken her. Of course, if you enclose a note to me and insist on its delivery, I shall deliver it; but I advise you not to do so.

You say you are able, with the aid of a cane, to walk about your chamber, and that you purpose to come to The Pines the instant Dillon thinks you strong enough to stand the journey. Again I advise you not to. Do you not see that, every hour you remain away, Marjorie's glamour deepens, and your influence over her increases? You will ruin everything by precipitancy.

Wait until you are entirely recovered; in any case, do not come without giving me warning. I fear the effect of your abrupt advent here—under the circumstances.

Miss Daw was evidently glad to see us back again, and gave me both hands in the frankest way. She stopped at the door a moment this afternoon in the carriage; she had been over to Rivermouth for her pictures. Unluckily the photographer had spilt some acid on the plate, and she was obliged to give him another sitting. I have an intuition that something is troubling Marjorie. She had an abstracted air not usual with her. However, it may be only my fancy. . . . I end this, leaving several things unsaid, to accompany my father on one of those long walks which are now his chief medicine—and mine!

XI.   EDWARD DELANEY TO JOHN FLEMMING

29 August, 1872.

I write in great haste to tell you what has taken place here since my letter of last night. I am in the utmost perplexity. Only one thing is plain—*you* must not dream of coming to The Pines. Marjorie has told her father everything! I saw her for a few minutes, an hour ago, in the garden; and, as near as I could gather from her confused statement, the facts are these: Lieutenant Bradley—that's the naval officer stationed at Rivermouth—has been paying court to Miss Daw for some time past, but not so much to her liking as to that of the colonel, who it seems is an old friend of the young gentleman's father. Yesterday (I knew she was in some trouble when she drove up to our gate) the colonel spoke to Marjorie of Bradley—urged his suit, I infer. Marjorie expressed her dislike for the lieutenant with characteristic frankness, and finally confessed to her father—well, I really do not know what she confessed. It must have been the vaguest of confessions, and must have sufficiently puzzled the colonel. At any rate, it exasperated him. I suppose I am implicated in the matter, and that the colonel feels bitterly towards me. I do not see why: I have carried no messages between you and Miss Daw; I have behaved with the greatest discretion. I can find no flaw anywhere in my proceeding. I do not see that anybody has done anything —except the colonel himself.

It is probable, nevertheless, that the friendly relations between the two houses will be broken off. "A plague o' both your houses," say you. I will keep you informed, as well as I can, of what occurs over the way. We shall remain here until the second week in September. Stay where you are, or, at all events, do not dream of joining me. . . . Colonel Daw is sitting on the piazza looking rather wicked. I have not seen Marjorie since I parted with her in the garden.

XII. EDWARD DELANEY TO THOMAS DILLON, M.D., MADISON SQUARE, NEW YORK

20 August, 1872.

MY DEAR DOCTOR,—If you have any influence over Flemming, I beg of you to exert it to prevent his coming to this place at present. There are circumstances, which I will explain to you before long, that make it of the first importance that he should not come into this neighbourhood. His appearance here, I speak advisedly, would be disastrous to him. In urging him to remain in New York, or to go to some inland resort, you will be doing him and me a real service. Of course you will not mention my name in this connection. You know me well enough, my dear doctor, to be assured that, in begging your secret co-operation, I have reasons that will meet your entire approval when they are made plain to you. We shall return to town on the 15th of next month, and my first duty will be to present myself at your hospitable door and satisfy your curiosity, if I have excited it. My father, I am glad to state, has so greatly improved that he can no longer be regarded as an invalid. With great esteem, I am, etc.

XIII.   EDWARD DELANEY TO JOHN FLEMMING

31 August, 1872.

Your letter, announcing your mad determination to
come here, has just reached me. I beseech you to
reflect a moment. The step would be fatal to your
interests and hers. You would furnish just cause for
irritation to R. W. D.; and, though he loves Marjorie
devotedly, he is capable of going to any lengths if
opposed. You would not like, I am convinced, to be
the means of causing him to treat *her* with severity.
That would be the result of your presence at The Pines
at this juncture. I am annoyed to be obliged to point
out these things to you. We are on very delicate ground,
Jack; the situation is critical, and the slightest mistake
in a move would cost us the game. If you consider it
worth the winning, be patient. Trust a little to my
sagacity. Wait and see what happens. Moreover, I
understand from Dillon that you are in no condition
to take so long a journey. He thinks the air of the
coast would be the worst thing possible for you; that
you ought to go inland, if anywhere. Be advised by
me. Be advised by Dillon.

XIV.   TELEGRAMS

1 September, 1872.

(1) *To Edward Delaney*

Letter received. Dillon be hanged. I think I ought
to be on the ground.   J. F.

(2) *To John Flemming*

Stay where you are. You would only complicate
matters. Do not move until you hear from me.

E. D.

(3) *To Edward Delaney*

My being at The Pines could be kept secret. I must
see her.   J. F.

(4) *To John Flemming*

Do not think of it.   It would be useless.   R. W. D. has locked M. in her room.   You would not be able to effect an interview.   E. D.

(5) *To Edward Delaney*

Locked her in her room.   Good God!   That settles the question.   I shall leave by the twelve-fifteen express.   J. F.

XV.   THE ARRIVAL

On the second day of September, 1872, as the down express, due at 3.40, left the station at Hampton, a young man, leaning on the shoulder of a servant, whom he addressed as Watkins, stepped from the platform into a hack, and requested to be driven to The Pines. On arriving at the gate of a modest farmhouse, a few miles from the station, the young man descended with difficulty from the carriage, and, casting a hasty glance across the road, seemed much impressed by some peculiarity in the landscape.   Again leaning on the shoulder of the person Watkins, he walked to the door of the farmhouse and inquired for Mr. Edward Delaney. He was informed by the aged man who answered his knock, that Mr. Edward Delaney had gone to Boston the day before, but that Mr. Jonas Delaney was within. This information did not appear satisfactory to the stranger, who inquired if Mr. Edward Delaney had left any message for Mr. John Flemming.   There *was* a letter for Mr. Flemming, if he were that person.   After a brief absence the aged man reappeared with a letter.

XVI.   EDWARD DELANEY TO JOHN FLEMMING

1 September, 1872.

I am horror-stricken at what I have done!   When I began this correspondence I had no other purpose than to relieve the tedium of your sick-chamber.   Dillon told me to cheer you up.   I tried to.   I thought that you entered into the spirit of the thing. I had no idea, until within a few days, that you were taking matters *au grand sérieux*.

What can I say? I am in sackcloth and ashes. I am a pariah, a dog of an outcast. I tried to make a little romance to interest you, something soothing and idyllic, and, by Jove! I have done it only too well! My father does not know a word of this, so don't jar the old gentleman any more than you can help. I fly from the wrath to come—when you arrive! For oh, dear Jack, there isn't any colonial mansion on the other side of the road, there isn't any piazza, there isn't any hammock—there isn't any Marjorie Daw!

THE CELEBRATED JUMPING FROG OF CALAVERAS COUNTY [1]

By MARK TWAIN (1835–1910)

IN compliance with the request of a friend of mine, who wrote me from the East, I called on good-natured, garrulous old Simon Wheeler, and inquired after my friend's friend, Leonidas W. Smiley, as requested to do, and I hereunto append the result. I have a lurking suspicion that *Leonidas W.* Smiley is a myth; that my friend never knew such a personage; and that he only conjectured that if I asked old Wheeler about him, it would remind him of his infamous *Jim* Smiley, and he would go to work and bore me to death with some exasperating reminiscence of him as long and as tedious as it should be useless to me. If that was the design, it succeeded.

I found Simon Wheeler dozing comfortably by the bar-room stove of the dilapidated tavern in the decayed mining camp of Angel's, and I noticed that he was fat and bald-headed, and had an expression of winning gentleness and simplicity upon his tranquil countenance. He roused up, and gave me good day. I told him a friend of mine had commissioned me to make some inquiries about a cherished companion of his boyhood named *Leonidas W.* Smiley — *Rev. Leonidas W.* Smiley, a young minister of the Gospel, who he had heard was at one time a resident of Angel's Camp. I added that if Mr. Wheeler could tell me anything about the Rev. Leonidas W. Smiley, I would feel under many obligations to him.

[1] From *The Saturday Press* (New York), 18 November, 1865, as "Jim Smiley and His Jumping Frog"; republished in *The Celebrated Jumping Frog of Calaveras County, and Other Sketches* (1867), by Mark Twain (Harper and Bros.).

Simon Wheeler backed me into a corner and blockaded me there with his chair, and then sat down and reeled off the monotonous narrative which follows this paragraph. He never smiled, he never frowned, he never changed his voice from the gentle-flowing key to which he tuned his initial sentence, he never betrayed the slightest suspicion of enthusiasm; but all through the interminable narrative there ran a vein of impressive earnestness and sincerity, which showed me plainly that, so far from his imagining that there was anything ridiculous or funny about his story, he regarded it as a really important matter, and admired its two heroes as men of transcendent genius in finesse. I let him go on in his own way, and never interrupted him once.

"Rev. Leonidas W. H'm, Reverend Le—— Well, there was a feller here once by the name of *Jim* Smiley, in the winter of '49—or may be it was the spring of '50— I don't recollect exactly, somehow, though what makes me think it was one or the other is because I remember the big flume warn't finished when he first came to the camp; but anyway, he was the curiousest man about always betting on anything that turned up you ever see, if he could get anybody to bet on the other side; and if he couldn't he'd change sides. Any way that suited the other man would suit *him*—any way just so's he got a bet, *he* was satisfied. But still he was lucky, uncommon lucky; he most always come out winner. He was always ready and laying for a chance; there couldn't be no solit'ry thing mentioned but that feller'd offer to bet on it, and take ary side you please, as I was just telling you. If there was a horse-race, you'd find him flush or you'd find him busted at the end of it; if there was a dog-fight, he'd bet on it; if there was a cat-fight, he'd bet on it; if there was a chicken-fight, he'd bet on it; why, if there was two birds setting on a fence, he would bet you which one would fly first; or if there was a camp-meeting, he would be there reg'lar to bet on Parson Walker, which he judged to be the best exhorter about here, and so he was too, and a good man. If he even see a straddle-bug start to go anywheres, he would bet you how long it would take him to get to—to wherever he was going to, and if you took him up, he would foller that straddle-bug to Mexico but what he would find out where he was bound for and how long he was on the road. Lots of the boys here has seen that Smiley and can tell you about him. Why, it never made no difference to *him*—he'd bet on *any* thing—the dangest feller. Parson Walker's wife laid very sick once, for a good while, and it seemed as if they warn't going to save her; but one morning he come in, and Smiley up and asked him how she was, and he said she was consid'rable better—thank the Lord for his inf'nit' mercy—and coming on so smart that with the blessing of Prov'dence she'd get well yet; and Smiley, before he thought, says, 'Well, I'll risk two-and-a-half she don't, anyway.'

"Thish-yer Smiley had a mare—the boys called her the fifteen-minute nag, but that was only in fun, you know, because of course she was faster than that—and he used to win money on that horse, for all she was so slow and always had the asthma, or the distemper, or the consumption, or something of that kind. They used to give her two or three hundred yards' start, and then pass her under way; but always at the fag-end of the race she'd get excited and desperate-like, and come cavorting and straddling up, and scattering her legs around limber, sometimes in the air, and sometimes out to one side amongst the fences, and kicking up m-o-r-e dust and raising m-o-r-e racket with her coughing and sneezing and blowing her nose—and *always* fetch up at the stand just about a neck ahead, as near as you could cipher it down.

"And he had a little small bull-pup, that to look at him you'd think he warn't worth a cent but to set around and look ornery and lay for a chance to steal something. But as soon as money was up on him he was a different dog; his under-jaw'd begin to stick out like the fo'-castle of a steamboat, and his teeth would uncover and shine like the furnaces. And a dog might tackle him and bully-rag him, and bite him, and throw him over his

shoulder two or three times, and Andrew Jackson—
which was the name of the pup—Andrew Jackson
would never let on but what *he* was satisfied, and hadn't
expected nothing else—and the bets being doubled and
doubled on the other side all the time, till the money was
all up; and then all of a sudden he would grab that other
dog jest by the j'int of his hind leg and freeze to it—
not chaw, you understand, but only jest grip and hang
on till they throwed up the sponge, if it was a year.
Smiley always come out winner on that pup, till he
harnessed a dog once that didn't have no hind legs,
because they'd been sawed off in a circular saw, and when
the thing had gone along far enough, and the money was
all up, and he come to make a snatch for his pet holt,
he see in a minute how he'd been imposed on, and how
the other dog had him in the door, so to speak, and he
'peared surprised, and then he looked sorter discouraged-
like, and didn't try no more to win the fight, and so he
got shucked out bad. He gave Smiley a look, as much
as to say his heart was broke, and it was *his* fault, for
putting up a dog that hadn't no hind legs for him to
take holt of, which was his main dependence in a fight,
and then he limped off a piece and laid down and died.
It was a good pup, was that Andrew Jackson, and would
have made a name for hisself if he'd lived, for the stuff
was in him and he had genius—I know it, because he
hadn't no opportunities to speak of, and it don't stand
to reason that a dog could make such a fight as he could
under the circumstances if he hadn't no talent. It
always makes me feel sorry when I think of that last
fight of hisn, and the way it turned out.

"Well, thish-yer Smiley had rat-tarriers, and chicken
cocks, and tom-cats and all of them kind of things, till
you couldn't rest, and you couldn't fetch nothing for
him to bet on but he'd match you. He ketched a frog
one day, and took him home, and said he cal'lated to
educate him; and so he never done nothing for three
months but set in his back-yard and learn that frog to
jump. And you bet you he *did* learn him, too. He'd
give him a little punch behind, and the next minute

you'd see that frog whirling in the air like a doughnut—
see him turn one summerset, or may be a couple, if he
got a good start, and come down flat-footed and all
right, like a cat. He got him up so in the matter of
ketching flies, and kep' him in practice so constant, that
he'd nail a fly every time as fur as he could see him.
Smiley said all a frog wanted was education, and he
could do 'most anything—and I believe him. Why, I've
seen him set Dan'l Webster down here on this floor—
Dan'l Webster was the name of the frog—and sing out,
'Flies, Dan'l, flies!' and quicker'n you could wink he'd
spring straight up and snake a fly off'n the counter
there, and flop down on the floor ag'in as solid as a gob
of mud, and fall to scratching the side of his head with
his hind foot as indifferent as if he hadn't no idea he'd
been doin' any more'n any frog might do. You never
see a frog so modest and straightfor'ard as he was, for
all he was so gifted. And when it come to fair and
square jumping on a dead level, he could get over more
ground at one straddle than any animal of his breed you
ever see. Jumping on a dead level was his strong suit,
you understand; and when it come to that, Smiley
would ante up money on him as long as he had a red.
Smiley was monstrous proud of his frog, and well he
might be, for fellers that had travelled and been every-
wheres all said he laid over any frog that ever *they* see.

"Well, Smiley kep' the beast in a little lattice box,
and he used to fetch him downtown sometimes and lay
for a bet. One day a feller—a stranger in the camp, he
was—come acrost him with his box, and says:

"'What might it be that you've got in the box?'

"And Smiley says, sorter indifferent-like, 'It might
be a parrot, or it might be a canary, maybe, but it
ain't—it's only just a frog.'

"And the feller took it, and looked at it careful, and
turned it round this way and that, and says, 'H'm—
so 'tis. Well, what's *he* good for?'

"'Well,' Smiley says, easy and careless, 'he's good
enough for *one* thing, I should judge—he can outjump
any frog in Calaveras County.'

"The feller took the box again, and took another long, particular look, and gave it back to Smiley, and says, very deliberate, 'Well,' he says, 'I don't see no p'ints about that frog that's any better'n any other frog.'

"'Maybe you don't,' Smiley says. 'Maybe you understand frogs and maybe you don't understand 'em; maybe you've had experience, and maybe you ain't only a amature, as it were. Anyways, I've got *my* opinion and I'll risk forty dollars that he can out-jump any frog in Calaveras County.'

"And the feller studied a minute, and then says, kinder sadlike, 'Well, I'm only a stranger here, and I ain't got no frog; but if I had a frog, I'd bet you.'

"And then Smiley says, 'That's all right—that's all right—if you'll hold my box a minute, I'll go and get you a frog.' And so the feller took the box, and put up his forty dollars along with Smiley's and set down to wait.

"So he set there a good while thinking and thinking to hisself, and then he got the frog out and prized his mouth open and took a teaspoon and filled him full of quail shot—filled him pretty near up to his chin—and set him on the floor. Smiley he went to the swamp and slopped around in the mud for a long time, and finally he ketched a frog, and fetched him in, and give him to this feller, and says:

"'Now, if you're ready, set him alongside of Dan'l, with his forepaws just even with Dan'l's, and I'll give the word.' Then he says, 'One—two—three—*git*!' and him and the feller touched up the frogs from behind, and the new frog hopped off lively, but Dan'l give a heave, and hysted up his shoulders—so—like a Frenchman, but it warn't no use—he couldn't budge; he was planted as solid as a church, and he couldn't no more stir than if he was anchored out. Smiley was a good deal surprised, and he was disgusted too, but he didn't have no idea what the matter was, of course.

"The feller took the money and started away; and when he was going out at the door, he sorter jerked his thumb over his shoulder—so—at Dan'l, and says again, very deliberate, 'Well,' he says, '*I* don't see no p'ints about that frog that's any better'n any other frog.'

"Smiley he stood scratching his head and looking down at Dan'l a long time, and at last he says, ' I do wonder what in the nation that frog throwed off for— I wonder if there ain't something the matter with him— he 'pears to look mighty baggy, somehow.' And he ketched Dan'l by the nap of the neck, and hefted him, and says, 'Why blame my cats if he don't weigh five pounds!' and turned him upside down and he belched out a double handful of shot. And then he see how it was, and he was the maddest man—he set the frog down and took out after that feller, but he never ketched him. And——"

[Here Simon Wheeler heard his name called from the front yard, and got up to see what was wanted.] And turning to me as he moved away, he said, "Just set where you are, stranger, and rest easy—I ain't going to be gone a second."

But, by your leave, I did not think that a continuation of the history of the enterprising vagabond *Jim* Smiley would be likely to afford me much information concerning the Rev. *Leonidas W.* Smiley, and so I started away.

At the door I met the sociable Wheeler returning, and he buttonholed me and recommenced:

"Well, thish-yer Smiley had a yaller one-eyed cow that didn't have no tail, only jest a short stump like a bannanner, and——"

However, lacking both time and inclination, I did not wait to hear about the afflicted cow, but took my leave.

THE GRIFFIN AND THE MINOR CANON[1]

By FRANK R. STOCKTON (1834–1902)

OVER the great door of an old, old church which stood in a quiet town of a far-away land there was carved in stone the figure of a large griffin. The old-time sculptor had done his work with great care, but the image he had made was not a pleasant one to look at. It had a large head, with enormous open mouth and savage teeth; from its back arose great wings, armed with sharp hooks and prongs; it had stout legs in front, with projecting claws; but there were no legs behind—the body running out into a long and powerful tail, finished off at the end with a barbed point. This tail was coiled up under him, the end sticking up just back of his wings.

The sculptor, or the people who had ordered this stone figure, had evidently been very much pleased with it, for little copies of it, also in stone, had been placed here and there along the sides of the church, not very far from the ground, so that people could easily look at them, and ponder on their curious forms. There were a great many other sculptures on the outside of this church—saints, martyrs, grotesque heads of men, beasts, and birds, as well as those of other creatures which cannot be named, because nobody knows exactly what they were; but none were so curious and interesting as the great griffin over the door, and the little griffins on the sides of the church.

A long, long distance from the town, in the midst of dreadful wilds scarcely known to man, there dwelt the Griffin whose image had been put up over the church door. In some way or other, the old-time sculptor had seen him, and afterward, to the best of his memory, had copied his figure in stone. The Griffin had never known this, until, hundreds of years afterward, he heard from a bird, from a wild animal, or in some manner which it is not now easy to find out, that there was a likeness of him on the old church in the distant town. Now, this Griffin had no idea how he looked. He had never seen a mirror, and the streams where he lived were so turbulent and violent that a quiet piece of water, which would reflect the image of anything looking into it, could not be found. Being, as far as could be ascertained, the very last of his race, he had never seen another griffin. Therefore it was, that, when he heard of this stone image of himself, he became very anxious to know what he looked like, and at last he determined to go to the old church, and see for himself what manner of being he was. So he started off from the dreadful wilds, and flew on and on until he came to the countries inhabited by men, where his appearance in the air created great consternation; but he alighted nowhere, keeping up a steady flight until he reached the suburbs of the town which had his image on its church. Here, late in the afternoon, he alighted in a green meadow by the side of a brook, and stretched himself on the grass to rest. His great wings were tired, for he had not made such a long flight in a century, or more.

The news of his coming spread quickly over the town, and the people, frightened nearly out of their wits by the arrival of so extraordinary a visitor, fled into their houses, and shut themselves up. The Griffin called loudly for someone to come to him, but the more he called, the more afraid the people were to show themselves. At length he saw two labourers hurrying to their homes through the fields, and in a terrible voice he commanded them to stop. Not daring to disobey, the men stood, trembling.

"What is the matter with you all?" cried the Griffin. "Is there not a man in your town who is brave enough to speak to me?"

"I think," said one of the labourers, his voice shaking so that his words could hardly be understood, "that—perhaps—the Minor Canon—would come."

"Go, call him, then!" said the Griffin; "I want to see him."

The Minor Canon, who filled a subordinate position in the old church, had just finished the afternoon services, and was coming out of a side door, with three aged women who had formed the week-day congregation. He was a young man of a kind disposition, and very anxious to do good to the people of the town. Apart from his duties in the church, where he conducted services every week-day, he visited the sick and the poor, counselled and assisted persons who were in trouble, and taught a school composed entirely of the bad children in the town with whom nobody else would have anything to do. Whenever the people wanted something difficult done for them, they always went to the Minor Canon. Thus it was that the labourer thought of the young priest when he found that someone must come and speak to the Griffin.

The Minor Canon had not heard of the strange event, which was known to the whole town except himself and the three old women, and when he was informed of it, and was told that the Griffin had asked to see him, he was greatly amazed, and frightened.

"Me!" he exclaimed. "He has never heard of me! What should he want with *me*?"

"Oh! you must go instantly!" cried the two men. "He is very angry now because he has been kept waiting so long; and nobody knows what may happen if you don't hurry to him."

The poor Minor Canon would rather have had his hand cut off than go out to meet an angry griffin; but he felt that it was his duty to go, for it would be a woeful thing if injury should come to the people of the town because he was not brave enough to obey the summons of the Griffin. So, pale and frightened, he started off.

"Well," said the Griffin, as soon as the young man

came near, "I am glad to see that there is someone who has the courage to come to me."

The Minor Canon did not feel very courageous, but he bowed his head.

"Is this the town," said the Griffin, "where there is a church with a likeness of myself over one of the doors?"

The Minor Canon looked at the frightful creature before him and saw that it was, without doubt, exactly like the stone image on the church. "Yes," he said, "you are right."

"Well, then," said the Griffin, "will you take me to it? I wish very much to see it."

The Minor Canon instantly thought that if the Griffin entered the town without the people knowing what he came for, some of them would probably be frightened to death, and so he sought to gain time to prepare their minds.

"It is growing dark, now," he said, very much afraid, as he spoke, that his words might enrage the Griffin, "and objects on the front of the church cannot be seen clearly. It will be better to wait until morning, if you wish to get a good view of the stone image of yourself."

"That will suit me very well," said the Griffin. "I see you are a man of good sense. I am tired, and I will take a nap here on this soft grass, while I cool my tail in the little stream that runs near me. The end of my tail gets red-hot when I am angry or excited, and it is quite warm now. So you may go, but be sure and come early to-morrow morning, and show me the way to the church."

The Minor Canon was glad enough to take his leave, and hurried into the town. In front of the church he found a great many people assembled to hear his report of his interview with the Griffin. When they found that he had not come to spread ruin and devastation, but simply to see his stony likeness on the church, they showed neither relief nor gratification, but began to upbraid the Minor Canon for consenting to conduct the creature into the town.

"What could I do?" cried the young man. "If I should not bring him he would come himself and, perhaps, end by setting fire to the town with his red-hot tail."

Still the people were not satisfied, and a great many plans were proposed to prevent the Griffin from coming into the town. Some elderly persons urged that the young men should go out and kill him; but the young men scoffed at such a ridiculous idea. Then someone said that it would be a good thing to destroy the stone image so that the Griffin would have no excuse for entering the town; and this proposal was received with such favour that many of the people ran for hammers, chisels, and crowbars, with which to tear down and break up the stone griffin. But the Minor Canon resisted this plan with all the strength of his mind and body. He assured the people that this action would enrage the Griffin beyond measure, for it would be impossible to conceal from him that his image had been destroyed during the night. But the people were so determined to break up the stone griffin that the Minor Canon saw that there was nothing for him to do but to stay there and protect it. All night he walked up and down in front of the church door, keeping away the men who brought ladders, by which they might mount to the great stone griffin, and knock it to pieces with their hammers and crowbars. After many hours the people were obliged to give up their attempts, and went home to sleep; but the Minor Canon remained at his post till early morning, and then he hurried away to the field where he had left the Griffin.

The monster had just awakened, and rising to his forelegs and shaking himself, he said that he was ready to go into the town. The Minor Canon, therefore, walked back, the Griffin flying slowly through the air, at a short distance above the head of his guide. Not a person was to be seen in the streets, and they proceeded directly to the front of the church, where the Minor Canon pointed out the stone griffin.

The real Griffin settled down in the little square

before the church and gazed earnestly at his sculptured likeness. For a long time he looked at it. First he put his head on one side, and then he put it on the other; then he shut his right eye and gazed with his left, after which he shut his left eye and gazed with his right. Then he moved a little to one side and looked at the image, then he moved the other way. After a while he said to the Minor Canon, who had been standing by all this time:

"It is, it must be, an excellent likeness! That breadth between the eyes, that expansive forehead, those massive jaws! I feel that it must resemble me. If there is any fault to find with it, it is that the neck seems a little stiff. But that is nothing. It is an admirable likeness—admirable!"

The Griffin sat looking at his image all the morning and all the afternoon. The Minor Canon had been afraid to go away and leave him, and had hoped all through the day that he would soon be satisfied with his inspection and fly away home. But by evening the poor young man was utterly exhausted, and felt that he must eat and sleep. He frankly admitted this fact to the Griffin, and asked him if he would not like something to eat. He said this because he felt obliged in politeness to do so, but as soon as he had spoken the words, he was seized with dread lest the monster should demand half a dozen babies, or some tempting repast of that kind.

"Oh, no," said the Griffin, "I never eat between the equinoxes. At the vernal and at the autumnal equinox I take a good meal, and that lasts me for half a year. I am extremely regular in my habits, and do not think it healthful to eat at odd times. But if you need food, go and get it, and I will return to the soft grass where I slept last night and take another nap."

The next day the Griffin came again to the little square before the church, and remained there until evening, steadfastly regarding the stone griffin over the door. The Minor Canon came once or twice to look at him, and the Griffin seemed very glad to see him; but the young clergyman could not stay as he had done before, for he had many duties to perform. Nobody went to the church, but the people came to the Minor Canon's house, and anxiously asked him how long the Griffin was going to stay.

"I do not know," he answered, "but I think he will soon be satisfied with regarding his stone likeness, and then he will go away."

But the Griffin did not go away. Morning after morning he came to the church, but after a time he did not stay there all day. He seemed to have taken a great fancy to the Minor Canon, and followed him about as he pursued his various avocations. He would wait for him at the side door of the church, for the Minor Canon held services every day, morning and evening, though nobody came now. "If anyone should come," he said to himself, "I must be found at my post." When the young man came out, the Griffin would accompany him in his visits to the sick and the poor, and would often look into the windows of the school-house where the Minor Canon was teaching his unruly scholars. All the other schools were closed, but the parents of the Minor Canon's scholars forced them to go to school, because they were so bad they could not endure them all day at home—griffin or no griffin. But it must be said they generally behaved very well when that great monster sat up on his tail and looked in at the schoolroom window.

When it was perceived that the Griffin showed no sign of going away, all the people who were able to do so left the town. The canons and the higher officers of the church had fled away during the first day of the Griffin's visit, leaving behind only the Minor Canon and some of the men who opened the doors and swept the church. All the citizens who could afford it shut up their houses and travelled to distant parts, and only the working people and the poor were left behind. After some days these ventured to go about and attend to their business, for if they did not work they would starve. They were getting a little used to seeing the

Griffin, and having been told that he did not eat between equinoxes, they did not feel so much afraid of him as before.

Day by day the Griffin became more and more attached to the Minor Canon. He kept near him a great part of the time, and often spent the night in front of the little house where the young clergyman lived alone. This strange companionship was often burdensome to the Minor Canon; but, on the other hand, he could not deny that he derived a great deal of benefit and instruction from it. The Griffin had lived for hundreds of years, and had seen much; and he told the Minor Canon many wonderful things.

"It is like reading an old book," said the young clergyman to himself; "but how many books I would have had to read before I would have found out what the Griffin has told me about the earth, the air, the water, about minerals, and metals, and growing things, and all the wonders of the world!"

Thus the summer went on, and drew toward its close. And now the people of the town began to be very much troubled again.

"It will not be long," they said, "before the autumnal equinox is here, and then that monster will want to eat. He will be dreadfully hungry, for he has taken so much exercise since his last meal. He will devour our children. Without doubt, he will eat them all. What is to be done?"

To this question no one could give an answer, but all agreed that the Griffin must not be allowed to remain until the approaching equinox. After talking over the matter a great deal, a crowd of the people went to the Minor Canon, at a time when the Griffin was not with him.

"It is all your fault," they said, "that that monster is among us. You brought him here, and you ought to see that he goes away. It is only on your account that he stays here at all, for, although he visits his image every day, he is with you the greater part of the time. If you were not here, he would not stay. It is your duty to go away and then he will follow you, and we shall be free from the dreadful danger which hangs over us."

"Go away!" cried the Minor Canon, greatly grieved at being spoken to in such a way. "Where shall I go? If I go to some other town, shall I not take this trouble there? Have I a right to do that?"

"No," said the people, "you must not go to any other town. There is no town far enough away. You must go to the dreadful wilds where the Griffin lives; and then he will follow you and stay there."

They did not say whether or not they expected the Minor Canon to stay there also, and he did not ask them anything about it. He bowed his head, and went into his house, to think. The more he thought, the more clear it became to his mind that it was his duty to go away, and thus free the town from the presence of the Griffin.

That evening he packed a leathern bag full of bread and meat, and early the next morning he set out on his journey to the dreadful wilds. It was a long, weary, and doleful journey, especially after he had gone beyond the habitations of men, but the Minor Canon kept on bravely, and never faltered. The way was longer than he had expected, and his provisions soon grew so scanty that he was obliged to eat but a little every day, but he kept up his courage, and pressed on, and, after many days of toilsome travel, he reached the dreadful wilds.

When the Griffin found that the Minor Canon had left the town he seemed sorry, but showed no disposition to go and look for him. After a few days had passed, he became much annoyed, and asked some of the people where the Minor Canon had gone. But, although the citizens had been so anxious that the young clergyman should go to the dreadful wilds, thinking that the Griffin would immediately follow him, they were now afraid to mention the Minor Canon's destination, for the monster seemed angry already, and, if he should suspect their trick, he would, doubtless, become very much enraged. So everyone said he did not know, and the Griffin wandered about disconsolate. One morning he looked into the Minor Canon's school-house, which was always empty now, and thought that it was a shame that everything should suffer on account of the young man's absence.

"It does not matter so much about the church," he said, "for nobody went there; but it is a pity about the school. I think I will teach it myself until he returns."

It was the hour for opening the school, and the Griffin went inside and pulled the rope which rang the school-bell. Some of the children who heard the bell ran in to see what was the matter, supposing it to be a joke of one of their companions; but when they saw the Griffin they stood astonished, and scared.

"Go tell the other scholars," said the monster, "that school is about to open, and that if they are not all here in ten minutes, I shall come after them."

In seven minutes every scholar was in place.

Never was seen such an orderly school. Not a boy or girl moved, or uttered a whisper. The Griffin climbed into the master's seat, his wide wings spread on each side of him, because he could not lean back in his chair while they stuck out behind, and his great tail coiled around, in front of the desk, the barbed end sticking up, ready to tap any boy or girl who might misbehave. The Griffin now addressed the scholars, telling them that he intended to teach them while their master was away. In speaking he endeavoured to imitate, as far as possible, the mild and gentle tones of the Minor Canon, but it must be admitted that in this he was not very successful. He had paid a good deal of attention to the studies of the school, and he determined not to attempt to teach them anything new, but to review them in what they had been studying; so he called up the various classes, and questioned them upon their previous lessons. The children racked their brains to remember what they had learned. They were so afraid of the Griffin's displeasure that they recited as they had never recited before. One of the boys, far down in his class, answered so well that the Griffin was astonished.

"I should think you would be at the head," said he. "I am sure you have never been in the habit of reciting so well. Why is this?"

"Because I did not choose to take the trouble," said the boy, trembling in his boots. He felt obliged to speak the truth, for all the children thought that the great eyes of the Griffin could see right through them, and that he would know when they told a falsehood.

"You ought to be ashamed of yourself," said the Griffin. "Go down to the very tail of the class, and if you are not at the head in two days, I shall know the reason why."

The next afternoon this boy was number one.

It was astonishing how much these children now learned of what they had been studying. It was as if they had been educated over again. The Griffin used no severity toward them, but there was a look about him which made them unwilling to go to bed until they were sure they knew their lessons for the next day.

The Griffin now thought that he ought to visit the sick and the poor; and he began to go about the town for this purpose. The effect upon the sick was miraculous. All, except those who were very ill indeed, jumped from their beds when they heard he was coming, and declared themselves quite well. To those who could not get up, he gave herbs and roots, which none of them had ever before thought of as medicines, but which the Griffin had seen used in various parts of the world; and most of them recovered. But, for all that, they afterward said that no matter what happened to them, they hoped that they should never again have such a doctor coming to their bedsides, feeling their pulses and looking at their tongues.

As for the poor, they seemed to have utterly disappeared. All those who had depended upon charity for their daily bread were now at work in some way or other; many of them offering to do odd jobs for their neighbours just for the sake of their meals—a thing which before had been seldom heard of in the town. The Griffin could find no one who needed his assistance.

The summer had now passed, and the autumnal equinox was rapidly approaching. The citizens were in a state of great alarm and anxiety. The Griffin showed no signs of going away, but seemed to have settled himself permanently among them. In a short time, the day for his semi-annual meal would arrive, and then what would happen? The monster would certainly be very hungry, and would devour all their children.

Now they greatly regretted and lamented that they had sent away the Minor Canon; he was the only one on whom they could have depended in this trouble, for he could talk freely with the Griffin, and so find out what could be done. But it would not do to be inactive. Some step must be taken immediately. A meeting of the citizens was called, and two old men were appointed to go and talk to the Griffin. They were instructed to offer to prepare a splendid dinner for him on equinox day—one which would entirely satisfy his hunger. They would offer him the fattest mutton, the most tender beef, fish, and game of various sorts, and anything of the kind that he might fancy. If none of these suited, they were to mention that there was an orphan asylum in the next town.

"Anything would be better," said the citizens, "than to have our dear children devoured."

The old men went to the Griffin, but their propositions were not received with favour.

"From what I have seen of the people of this town," said the monster, "I do not think I could relish anything which was prepared by them. They appear to be all cowards, and, therefore, mean and selfish. As for eating one of them, old or young, I could not think of it for a moment. In fact, there was only one creature in the whole place for whom I could have had any appetite, and that is the Minor Canon, who has gone away. He was brave, and good, and honest, and I think I should have relished him."

"Ah!" said one of the old men very politely, "in that case I wish we had not sent him to the dreadful wilds!"

"What!" cried the Griffin. "What do you mean? Explain instantly what you are talking about!"

The old man, terribly frightened at what he had said, was obliged to tell how the Minor Canon had been sent away by the people, in the hope that the Griffin might be induced to follow him.

When the monster heard this, he became furiously angry. He dashed away from the old men and, spreading his wings, flew backward and forward over the town. He was so much excited that his tail became red-hot, and glowed like a meteor against the evening sky. When at last he settled down in the little field where he usually rested, and thrust his tail into the brook, the steam arose like a cloud, and the water of the stream ran hot through the town. The citizens were greatly frightened, and bitterly blamed the old man for telling about the Minor Canon.

"It is plain," they said, "that the Griffin intended at last to go and look for him, and we should have been saved. Now who can tell what misery you have brought upon us!"

The Griffin did not remain long in the little field. As soon as his tail was cool he flew to the town-hall and rang the bell. The citizens knew that they were expected to come there, and although they were afraid to go, they were still more afraid to stay away; and they crowded into the hall. The Griffin was on the platform at one end, flapping his wings and walking up and down, and the end of his tail was still so warm that it slightly scorched the boards as he dragged it after him.

When everybody who was able to come was there, the Griffin stood still and addressed the meeting.

"I have had a contemptible opinion of you," he said, "ever since I discovered what cowards you are, but I had no idea that you were so ungrateful, selfish, and cruel as I now find you to be. Here was your

Minor Canon, who laboured day and night for your
good, and thought of nothing else but how he might
benefit you and make you happy; and as soon as you
imagine yourselves threatened with a danger—for well
I know you are dreadfully afraid of me—you send him
off, caring not whether he returns or perishes, hoping
thereby to save yourselves. Now, I had conceived a
great liking for that young man, and had intended, in
a day or two, to go and look him up. But I have
changed my mind about him, I shall go and find him,
but I shall send him back here to live among you, and
I intend that he shall enjoy the reward of his labour
and his sacrifices. Go, some of you, to the officers of
the church, who so cowardly ran away when I first
came here, and tell them never to return to this town
under penalty of death. And if, when your Minor
Canon comes back to you, you do not bow yourselves
before him, put him in the highest place among you,
and serve and honour him all his life, beware of my
terrible vengeance! There were only two good things
in this town: the Minor Canon and the stone image
of myself over your church door. One of these you
have sent away, and the other I shall carry away
myself."

With these words he dismissed the meeting, and it
was time, for the end of his tail had become so hot that
there was danger of its setting fire to the building.

The next morning, the Griffin came to the church,
and tearing the stone image of himself from its fastenings
over the great door, he grasped it with his powerful
forelegs and flew up into the air. Then, after hovering
over the town for a moment, he gave his tail an angry
shake and took up his flight to the dreadful wilds. When
he reached this desolate region, he set the stone griffin
upon a ledge of a rock which rose in front of the dismal
cave he called his home. There the image occupied a
position somewhat similar to that it had had over the
church door; and the Griffin, panting with the exertion
of carrying such an enormous load to so great a distance,
lay down upon the ground and regarded it with much

satisfaction. When he felt somewhat rested he went to look for the Minor Canon. He found the young man, weak and half-starved, lying under the shadow of a rock. After picking him up and carrying him to his cave, the Griffin flew away to a distant marsh, where he procured some roots and herbs which he well knew were strengthening and beneficial to man, though he had never tasted them himself. After eating these the Minor Canon was greatly revived, and sat up and listened while the Griffin told him what had happened in the town.

"Do you know," said the monster, when he had finished, "that I have had, and still have, a great liking for you?"

"I am very glad to hear it," said the Minor Canon, with his usual politeness.

"I am not at all sure that you would be," said the Griffin, "if you thoroughly understood the state of the case, but we will not consider that now. If some things were different, other things would be otherwise. I have been so enraged by discovering the manner in which you have been treated that I have determined that you shall at last enjoy the rewards and honours to which you are entitled. Lie down and have a good sleep, and then I will take you back to the town."

As he heard these words, a look of trouble came over the young man's face.

"You need not give yourself any anxiety," said the Griffin, "about my return to the town. I shall not remain there. Now that I have that admirable likeness of myself in front of my cave, where I can sit at my leisure, and gaze upon its noble features and magnificent proportions, I have no wish to see that abode of cowardly and selfish people."

The Minor Canon, relieved from his fears, lay back, and dropped into a doze; and when he was sound asleep the Griffin took him up and carried him back to the town. He arrived just before daybreak, and putting the young man gently on the grass in the little field where he himself used to rest, the monster, without having been seen by any of the people, flew back to his home.

When the Minor Canon made his appearance in the morning among the citizens, the enthusiasm and cordiality with which he was received were truly wonderful. He was taken to a house which had been occupied by one of the banished high officers of the place, and everyone was anxious to do all that could be done for his health and comfort. The people crowded into the church when he held services, so that the three old women who used to be his week-day congregation could not get to the best seats, which they had always been in the habit of taking; and the parents of the bad children determined to reform them at home, in order that he might be spared the trouble of keeping up his former school. The Minor Canon was appointed to the highest office of the old church, and before he died he became a bishop.

During the first years after his return from the dreadful wilds, the people of the town looked up to him as a man to whom they were bound to do honour and reverence; but they often, also, looked up to the sky, to see if there were any signs of the Griffin coming back. However, in the course of time, they learned to honour and reverence their former Minor Canon without the fear of being punished if they did not do so.

But they need never have been afraid of the Griffin. The autumnal equinox day came round, and the monster ate nothing. If he could not have the Minor Canon, he did not care for anything. So, lying down, with his eyes fixed upon the great stone griffin, he gradually declined, and died. It was a good thing for some of the people of the town that they did not know this.

If you should ever visit the old town, you would still see the little griffins on the sides of the church; but the great stone griffin that was over the door is gone.

A HORSEMAN IN THE SKY

By AMBROSE BIERCE (1842–1913?)

ONE sunny afternoon in the autumn of the year 1861, a soldier lay in a clump of laurel by the side of a road in Western Virginia. He lay at full length, upon his stomach, his feet resting upon the toes, his head upon the left forearm. His extended right hand loosely grasped his rifle. But for the somewhat methodical disposition of his limbs and a slight rhythmic movement of the cartridge-box at the back of his belt, he might have been thought to be dead. He was asleep at his post of duty. But if detected he would be dead shortly afterward, that being the just and legal penalty of his crime.

The clump of laurel in which the criminal lay was in the angle of a road which, after ascending, southward, a steep acclivity to that point, turned sharply to the west, running along the summit for perhaps one hundred yards. There it turned southward again and went zigzagging downward through the forest. At the salient of that second angle was a large flat rock, jutting out from the ridge to the northward, overlooking the deep valley from which the road ascended. The rock capped a high cliff; a stone dropped from its outer edge would have fallen sheer downward one thousand feet to the tops of the pines. The angle where the soldier lay was on another spur of the same cliff. Had he been awake he would have commanded a view, not only of the short arm of the road and the jutting rock but of the entire profile of the cliff below it. It might well have made him giddy to look.

The country was wooded everywhere except at the bottom of the valley to the northward, where there was a small natural meadow, through which flowed a stream scarcely visible from the valley's rim. This open ground looked hardly larger than an ordinary door-yard, but was really several acres in extent. Its green was more vivid than that of the enclosing forest. Away beyond it rose a line of giant cliffs similar to those upon which we are supposed to stand in our survey of the savage scene, and through which the road had somehow made its climb to the summit. The configuration of the valley, indeed, was such that from our point of observation it seemed entirely shut in, and one could not but have wondered how the road which found a way out of it had found a way into it, and whence came and whither went the waters of the stream that parted the meadow two thousand feet below.

No country is so wild and difficult but men will make it a theatre of war; concealed in the forest at the bottom of that military rat-trap, in which half a hundred men in possession of the exits might have starved an army to submission, lay five regiments of Federal infantry. They had marched all the previous day and night and were resting. At nightfall they would take to the road again, climb to the place where their unfaithful sentinel now slept, and, descending the other slope of the ridge, fall upon a camp of the enemy at about midnight. Their hope was to surprise it, for the road led to the rear of it. In case of failure their position would be perilous in the extreme; and fail they surely would should accident or vigilance apprise the enemy of the movement.

The sleeping sentinel in the clump of laurel was a young Virginian named Carter Druse. He was the son of wealthy parents, an only child, and had known such ease and cultivation and high living as wealth and taste were able to command in the mountain country of Western Virginia. His home was but a few miles from where he now lay. One morning he had risen from the breakfast table and said, quietly and gravely: "Father, a Union regiment has arrived at Grafton. I am going to join it."

The father lifted his leonine head, looked at the son a moment in silence, and replied: "Go, Carter, and, whatever may occur, do what you conceive to be your duty. Virginia, to which you are a traitor, must get on without you. Should we both live to the end of the war, we will speak further of the matter. Your mother, as the physician has informed you, is in a most critical condition; at the best she cannot be with us longer than a few weeks, but that time is precious. It would be better not to disturb her."

So Carter Druse, bowing reverently to his father, who returned the salute with a stately courtesy which masked a breaking heart, left the home of his childhood to go soldiering. By conscience and courage, by deeds of devotion and daring, he soon commended himself to his fellows and his officers; and it was to these qualities and to some knowledge of the country that he owed his selection for his present perilous duty at the extreme outpost. Nevertheless, fatigue had been stronger than resolution, and he had fallen asleep. What good or bad angel came in a dream to rouse him from his state of crime who shall say? Without a movement, without a sound, in the profound silence and the languor of the late afternoon, some invisible messenger of fate touched with unsealing finger the eyes of his consciousness—whispered into the ear of his spirit the mysterious awakening word which no human lips have ever spoken, no human memory ever has recalled. He quietly raised his forehead from his arm and looked between the masking stems of the laurels, instinctively closing his right hand about the stock of his rifle.

His first feeling was a keen artistic delight. On a colossal pedestal, the cliff, motionless at the extreme edge of the capping rock and sharply outlined against the sky, was an equestrian statue of impressive dignity. The figure of the man sat the figure of the horse, straight and soldierly, but with the repose of a Grecian god carved in the marble which limits the suggestion of activity. The grey costume harmonised with its aerial background; the metal of accoutrement and caparison was softened and subdued by the shadow; the animal's skin had no points of high light. A carbine, strikingly foreshortened, lay across the pommel of the saddle, kept in place by the right hand grasping it at the "grip"; the left hand, holding the bridle rein, was invisible. In silhouette against the sky, the profile of the horse was cut with the sharpness of a cameo; it looked across the heights of air to the confronting cliffs beyond. The face of the rider, turned slightly to the left, showed only an outline of temple and beard; he was looking downward to the bottom of the valley. Magnified by its lift against the sky and by the soldier's testifying sense of the formidableness of a near enemy, the group appeared of heroic, almost colossal, size.

For an instant Druse had a strange, half-defined feeling that he had slept to the end of the war and was looking upon a noble work of art reared upon that commanding eminence to commemorate the deeds of an heroic past of which he had been an inglorious part. The feeling was dispelled by a slight movement of the group; the horse, without moving its feet, had drawn its body slightly backward from the verge; the man remained immobile as before. Broad awake and keenly alive to the significance of the situation, Druse now brought the butt of his rifle against his cheek by cautiously pushing the barrel forward through the bushes, cocked the piece, and, glancing through the sights, covered a vital spot of the horseman's breast. A touch upon the trigger and all would have been well with Carter Druse. At that instant the horseman turned his head and looked in the direction of his concealed foeman—seemed to look into his very face, into his eyes, into his brave compassionate heart.

Is it, then, so terrible to kill an enemy in war—an enemy who has surprised a secret vital to the safety of oneself and comrades — an enemy more formidable for his knowledge than all his army for its numbers?

Carter Druse grew deathly pale; he shook in every limb, turned faint, and saw the statuesque group before him as black figures, rising, falling, moving unsteadily in arcs of circles in a fiery sky. His hand fell away from his weapon, his head slowly dropped until his face rested on the leaves in which he lay. This courageous gentleman and hardy soldier was near swooning from intensity of emotion.

It was not for long; in another moment his face was raised from earth, his hands resumed their places on the rifle, his forefinger sought the trigger; mind, heart, and eyes were clear, conscience and reason sound. He could not hope to capture that enemy; to alarm him would but send him dashing to his camp with his fatal news. The duty of the soldier was plain: the man must be shot dead from ambush—without warning, without a moment's spiritual preparation, with never so much as an unspoken prayer, he must be sent to his account. But no—there is a hope; he may have discovered nothing—perhaps he is but admiring the sublimity of the landscape. If permitted, he may turn and ride carelessly away in the direction whence he came. Surely it will be possible to judge at the instant of his withdrawing whether he knows. It may well be that his fixity of attention—Druse turned his head and looked below, through the deeps of air downward, as from the surface to the bottom of a translucent sea. He saw creeping across the green meadow a sinuous line of figures of men and horses—some foolish commander was permitting the soldiers of his escort to water their beasts in the open, in plain view from a hundred summits!

Druse withdrew his eyes from the valley and fixed them again upon the group of man and horse in the sky, and again it was through the sights of his rifle. But this time his aim was at the horse. In his memory, as if they were a divine mandate, rang the words of his father at their parting: "Whatever may occur, do what you conceive to be your duty." He was calm now. His teeth were firmly but not rigidly closed;

his nerves were as tranquil as a sleeping babe's—not a tremor affected any muscle of his body; his breathing, until suspended in the act of taking aim, was regular and slow. Duty had conquered; the spirit had said to the body: "Peace, be still." He fired.

At that moment an officer of the Federal force, who, in a spirit of adventure or in quest of knowledge, had left the hidden bivouac in the valley, and, with aimless feet, had made his way to the lower edge of a small open space near the foot of the cliff, was considering what he had to gain by pushing his exploration farther. At a distance of a quarter-mile before him, but apparently at a stone's-throw, rose from its fringe of pines the gigantic face of rock, towering to so great a height above him that it made him giddy to look up to where its edge cut a sharp, rugged line against the sky. At some distance away to his right it presented a clean, vertical profile against a background of blue sky to a point half of the way down, and of distant hills hardly less blue thence to the tops of the trees at its base. Lifting his eyes to the dizzy altitude of its summit, the officer saw an astonishing sight—a man on horseback riding down into the valley through the air!

Straight upright sat the rider, in military fashion, with a firm seat in the saddle, a strong clutch upon the rein to hold his charger from too impetuous a plunge. From his bare head his long hair streamed upward, waving like a plume. His right hand was concealed in the cloud of the horse's lifted mane. The animal's body was as level as if every hoof-stroke encountered the resistant earth. Its motions were those of a wild gallop, but even as the officer looked they ceased, with all the legs thrown sharply forward as in the act of alighting from a leap. But this was a flight!

Filled with amazement and terror by this apparition of a horseman in the sky—half believing himself the chosen scribe of some new Apocalypse, the officer was overcome by the intensity of his emotions; his legs failed him and he fell. Almost at the same instant he heard a crashing sound in the trees—a sound that died without an echo, and all was still.

The officer rose to his feet, trembling. The familiar sensation of an abraded shin recalled his dazed faculties. Pulling himself together, he ran rapidly obliquely away from the cliff to a point a half-mile from its foot; thereabout he expected to find his man; and thereabout he naturally failed. In the fleeting instant of his vision his imagination had been so wrought upon by the apparent grace and ease and intention of the marvellous performance that it did not occur to him that the line of march of aerial cavalry is directed downward, and that he could find the objects of his search at the very foot of the cliff. A half-hour later he returned to camp.

This officer was a wise man; he knew better than to tell an incredible truth. He said nothing of what he had seen. But when the commander asked him if in his scout he had learned anything of advantage to the expedition, he answered:

"Yes, sir; there is no road leading down into this valley from the southward."

The commander, knowing better, smiled.

After firing his shot Private Carter Druse reloaded his rifle and resumed his watch. Ten minutes had hardly passed when a Federal sergeant crept cautiously to him on hands and knees. Druse neither turned his head nor looked at him, but lay without motion or sign of recognition.

"Did you fire?" the sergeant whispered.

"Yes."

"At what?"

"A horse. It was standing on yonder rock—pretty far out. You see it is no longer there. It went over the cliff."

The man's face was white, but he showed no other sign of emotion. Having answered, he turned away his face and said no more. The sergeant did not understand.

"See here, Druse," he said, after a moment's silence,

"It's no use making a mystery.   I order you to report.
Was there anybody on the horse?"

"Yes."

"Who?"

"My father."

The sergeant rose to his feet and walked away.
"Good God!" he said.

A PASSIONATE PILGRIM [1]

By HENRY JAMES (1843–1916)

I

INTENDING to sail for America in the early part of
June, I determined to spend the interval of six weeks
in England, to which country my mind's eye only had
as yet been introduced. I had formed in Italy and
France a resolute preference for old inns, considering
that what they sometimes cost the ungratified body
they repay the delighted mind. On my arrival in
London, therefore, I lodged at a certain antique hostelry,
much to the east of Temple Bar, deep in the quarter
that I had inevitably figured as the Johnsonian. Here,
on the first evening of my stay, I descended to the
little coffee-room and bespoke my dinner of the genius
of "attendance" in the person of the solitary waiter.
No sooner had I crossed the threshold of this retreat
than I felt I had cut a golden-ripe crop of English
"impressions." The coffee-room of the Red Lion, like
so many other places and things I was destined to see
in the motherland, seemed to have been waiting for
long years, with just that sturdy sufferance of time
written on its visage, for me to come and extract the
romantic essence of it.

The latent preparedness of the American mind even
for the most characteristic features of English life was
a matter I meanwhile failed to get to the bottom of.
The roots of it are indeed so deeply buried in the soil
of our early culture that, without some great upheaval
of feeling, we are at a loss to say exactly when and
where and how it begins. It makes an American's

[1] From *The Reverberator* in the London Macmillan edition of
the "Novels and Stories." By permission of and by arrangement
with the Houghton Mifflin Co. and the Trustees of the Estate of
the author.

enjoyment of England an emotion more searching than anything continental. I had seen the coffee-room of the Red Lion years ago, at home—at Saragossa, Illinois—in books, in visions, in dreams, in Dickens, in Smollett, in Boswell. It was small and subdivided into six narrow compartments by a series of perpendicular screens of mahogany, something higher than a man's stature, furnished on either side with a meagre uncushioned ledge, denominated in ancient Britain a seat. In each of these rigid receptacles was a narrow table—a table expected under stress to accommodate no less than four pairs of active British elbows. High pressure indeed had passed away from the Red Lion for ever. It now knew only that of memories and ghosts and atmosphere. Round the room there marched, breast-high, a magnificent panelling of mahogany, so dark with time and so polished with unremitted friction that by gazing a while into its lucid blackness I made out the dim reflection of a party of wigged gentlemen in knee-breeches just arrived from York by the coach. On the dark yellow walls, coated by the fumes of English coal, of English mutton, of Scotch whisky, were a dozen melancholy prints, sallow-toned with age—the Derby favourite of the year 1807, the Bank of England, her Majesty the Queen. On the floor was a Turkey carpet—as old as the mahogany almost, as the Bank of England, as the Queen—into which the waiter had in his lonely revolutions trodden so many massive soot-flakes and drops of overflowing beer that the glowing looms of Smyrna would certainly not have recognised it. To say that I ordered my dinner of this archaic type would be altogether to misrepresent the process owing to which, having dreamed of lamb and spinach and a *salade de saison*, I sat down in penitence to a mutton-chop and a rice-pudding. Bracing my feet against the cross-beam of my little oaken table, I opposed to the mahogany partition behind me the vigorous dorsal resistance that must have expressed the old-English idea of repose. The sturdy screen refused even to creak, but my poor Yankee joints made up the deficiency.

While I was waiting there for my chop there came into
the room a person whom, after I had looked at him a
moment, I supposed to be a fellow-lodger and probably
the only one. He seemed, like myself, to have submitted to proposals for dinner; the table on the other
side of my partition had been prepared to receive him.
He walked up to the fire, exposed his back to it and,
after consulting his watch, looked directly out of the
window and indirectly at me. He was a man of something less than middle age and more than middle stature,
though indeed you would have called him neither
young nor tall. He was chiefly remarkable for his
emphasised leanness. His hair, very thin on the summit of his head, was dark, short and fine. His eye was
of a pale turbid grey, unsuited, perhaps, to his dark
hair and well-drawn brows, but not altogether out of
harmony with his colourless bilious complexion. His
nose was aquiline and delicate; beneath it his moustache
languished much rather than bristled. His mouth and
chin were negative, or at the most provisional; not
vulgar, doubtless, but ineffectually refined. A cold
fatal gentlemanly weakness was expressed indeed in
his attenuated person. His eye was restless and
deprecating; his whole physiognomy, his manner of
shifting his weight from foot to foot, the spiritless droop
of his head, told of exhausted intentions, of a will
relaxed. His dress was neat and "toned down"—he
might have been in mourning. I made up my mind
on three points: he was a bachelor, he was out of health,
he was not indigenous to the soil. The waiter approached
him, and they conversed in accents barely audible.
I heard the words "claret," "sherry" with a tentative
inflection, and finally "beer" with its last letter changed
to "ah." Perhaps he was a Russian in reduced circumstances; he reminded me slightly of certain sceptical
cosmopolite Russians whom I had met on the Continent.

While in my extravagant way I followed this train—
for you see I was interested—there appeared a short
brisk man with reddish-brown hair, with a vulgar nose,
a sharp blue eye, and a red beard confined to his lower

jaw and chin.   My putative Russian, still in possession
of the rug, let his mild gaze stray over the dingy ornaments of the room.   The other drew near, and his
umbrella dealt a playful poke at the concave melancholy
waistcoat.   "A penny ha'penny for your thoughts!"

My friend, as I call him, uttered an exclamation,
stared, then laid his two hands on the other's shoulders.
The latter looked round at me keenly, compassing me in
a momentary glance.   I read in its own vague light
that this was a transatlantic eyebeam; and with such
confidence that I hardly needed to see its owner, as he
prepared, with his companion, to seat himself at the
table adjoining my own, take from his overcoat-pocket
three New York newspapers and lay them beside his
plate.   As my neighbours proceeded to dine I felt
the crumbs of their conversation scattered pretty freely
abroad.   I could hear almost all they said, without
straining to catch it, over the top of the partition that
divided us.   Occasionally their voices dropped to
recovery of discretion, but the mystery pieced itself
together as if on purpose to entertain me.   Their speech
was pitched in the key that may in English air be called
alien in spite of a few coincidences.   The voices were
American, however, with a difference; and I had no
hesitation in assigning the softer and clearer sound to
the pale thin gentleman, whom I decidedly preferred
to his comrade.   The latter began to question him
about his voyage.

"Horrible, horrible!   I was deadly sick from the hour
we left New York."

"Well, you do look considerably reduced," said the
second-comer.

"Reduced!   I've been on the verge of the grave.
I haven't slept six hours for three weeks."   This was
said with great gravity.   "Well, I've made the voyage
for the last time."

"The plague you have!   You mean to locate here
permanently?"

"Oh, it won't be so very permanent!"

There was a pause; after which: "You're the same

merry old boy, Searle. Going to give up the ghost to-morrow, eh?"

"I almost wish I were."

"You're not so sweet on England then? I've heard people say at home that you dress and talk and act like an Englishman. But I know these people here and I know you. You're not one of this crowd, Clement Searle, not you. You'll go under here, sir; you'll go under as sure as my name's Simmons."

Following this I heard a sudden clatter as of the drop of a knife and fork. "Well, you're a delicate sort of creature, if it *is* your ugly name! I've been wandering about all day in this accursed city, ready to cry with homesickness and heartsickness and every possible sort of sickness, and thinking, in the absence of anything better, of meeting you here this evening and of your uttering some sound of cheer and comfort and giving me some glimmer of hope. Go under? Ain't I under now? I can't do more than get under the ground!"

Mr. Simmons's superior brightness appeared to flicker a moment in this gust of despair, but the next it was burning steady again. "*Don't* 'cry,' Searle," I heard him say. "Remember the waiter. I've grown Englishman enough for that. For heaven's sake don't let's have any nerves. Nerves won't do anything for you here. It's best to come to the point. Tell me in three words what you expect of me."

I heard another movement, as if poor Searle had collapsed in his chair. "Upon my word, sir, you're quite inconceivable. You never got my letter?"

"Yes, I got your letter. I was never sorrier to get anything in my life."

At this declaration Mr. Searle rattled out an oath, which it was well perhaps that I but partially heard. "Abijah Simmons," he then cried, "what demon of perversity possesses you? Are you going to betray me here in a foreign land, to turn out a false friend, a heartless rogue?"

"Go on, sir," said sturdy Simmons. "Pour it all out. I'll wait till you've done. Your beer's lovely."

he observed independently to the waiter. "I'll have some more."

"For God's sake explain yourself!" his companion appealed.

There was a pause, at the end of which I heard Mr. Simmons set down his empty tankard with emphasis. "You poor morbid mooning man," he resumed, "I don't want to say anything to make you feel sore. I regularly pity you. But you must allow that you've acted more like a confirmed crank than a member of our best society —in which everyone's so sensible."

Mr. Searle seemed to have made an effort to compose himself. "Be so good as to tell me then what was the meaning of your letter."

"Well, you had got on *my* nerves, if you want to know, when I wrote it. It came of my always wishing so to please folks. I had much better have let you alone. To tell you the plain truth, I never was so horrified in my life as when I found that on the strength of my few kind words you had come out here to seek your fortune."

"What then did you expect me to do?"

"I expected you to wait patiently till I had made further inquiries and had written you again."

"And you've made further inquiries now?"

"Inquiries! I've committed assaults."

"And you find I've no claim?"

"No claim that one of *these* big bugs will look at. It struck me at first that you had rather a neat little case. I confess the look of it took hold of me——"

"Thanks to your liking so to please folks!"

Mr. Simmons appeared for a moment at odds with something; it proved to be with his liquor. "I rather think your beer's too good to be true," he said to the waiter. "I guess I'll take water. Come, old man," he resumed, "don't challenge me to the arts of debate, or you'll have me right down on you, and then you *will* feel me. My native sweetness, as I say, was part of it. The idea that if I put the thing through it would be a very pretty feather in my cap and a very pretty

penny in my purse was part of it. And the satisfaction
of seeing a horrid low American walk right into an old
English estate was a good deal of it. Upon my word,
Searle, when I think of it I wish with all my heart that,
extravagant vain man as you are, I *could*, for the charm
of it, put you through! I should hardly care what you
did with the blamed place when you got it. I could
leave you alone to turn it into Yankee notions—into
ducks and drakes as they call 'em here. I should like
to see you tearing round over it and kicking up its
sacred dust in their very faces!"

"You don't know me one little bit," said Mr. Searle,
rather shirking, I thought, the burden of this tribute
and for all response to the ambiguity of the compliment.

"I should be very glad to think I didn't, sir. I've
been to no small amount of personal inconvenience for
you. I've pushed my way right up to the headspring.
I've got the best opinion that's to be had. The best
opinion that's to be had just gives you one leer over
its spectacles. I guess that look will fix you if you ever
get it straight. I've been able to tap, indirectly," Mr.
Simmons went on, "the solicitor of your usurping cousin,
and he evidently knows something to be in the wind.
It seems your elder brother twenty years ago put out
a feeler. So you're not to have the glory of even
making them sit up."

"I never made anyone sit up," I heard Mr. Searle
plead. "I shouldn't begin at this time of day. I
should approach the subject like a gentleman."

"Well, if you want very much to do something like
a gentleman you've got a capital chance. Take your
disappointment like a gentleman."

I had finished my dinner and had become keenly
interested in poor Mr. Searle's unencouraging—or un-
encouraged—claim; so interested that I at last hated
to hear his trouble reflected in his voice without being
able—all respectfully!—to follow it in his face. I left
my place, went over to the fire, took up the evening
paper and established a post of observation behind it.

His cold counsellor was in the act of choosing a soft

chop from the dish—an act accompanied by a great deal
of prying and poking with that gentleman's own fork.
My disillusioned compatriot had pushed away his plate;
he sat with his elbows on the table, gloomily nursing
his head with his hands. His companion watched him
and then seemed to wonder—to do Mr. Simmons justice
—how he could least ungracefully give him up. "I say,
Searle,"—and for my benefit, I think, taking me for a
native ingenuous enough to be dazzled by his wit, he
lifted his voice a little and gave it an ironical ring—
"in this country it's the inestimable privilege of a loyal
citizen, under whatsoever stress of pleasure or of pain,
to make a point of eating his dinner."

Mr. Searle gave his plate another push. "Anything
may happen now. I don't care a straw."

"You ought to care. Have another chop and you
will care. Have some better tipple. Take my advice!"
Mr. Simmons went on.

My friend—I adopt that name for him—gazed from
between his two hands coldly before him. "I've had
enough of your advice."

"A little more," said Simmons mildly; "I shan't
trouble you again. What do you mean to do?"

"Nothing."

"Oh, come!"

"Nothing, nothing, nothing!"

"Nothing but starve. How about meeting expenses?"

"Why do you ask?" said my friend. "You don't
care."

"My dear fellow, if you want to make me offer you
twenty pounds you set most clumsily about it. You
said just now I don't know you," Mr. Simmons went on.
"Possibly. Come back with me then," he said kindly
enough, "and let's improve our acquaintance."

"I won't go back. I shall never go back."

"Never?"

"Never."

Mr. Simmons thought it shrewdly over. "Well,
you *are* sick!" he exclaimed presently. "All I can
say is that if you're working out a plan for cold poison,

or for any other act of desperation, you had better give it right up. You can't get a dose of the commonest kind of cold poison for nothing, you know. Look here, Searle"—and the worthy man made what struck me as a very decent appeal. "If you'll consent to return home with me by the steamer of the twenty-third I'll pay your passage down. More than that, I'll pay for your beer."

My poor gentleman met it. "I believe I never made up my mind to anything before, but I think it's made up now. I shall stay here till I take my departure for a newer world than any patched-up newness of ours. It's an odd feeling—I rather like it! What should I do at home?"

"You said just now you were homesick."

"I meant I was sick for a home. Don't I belong here? Haven't I longed to get here all my life? Haven't I counted the months and the years till I should be able to 'go' as we say? And now that I've come, must I just back out? No, no, I'll move on. I'm much obliged to you for your offer. I've enough money for the present. I've about my person some forty pounds' worth of British gold, and the same amount, say, of the toughness of the heaven-sent idiot. They'll see me through together! After they're gone I shall lay my head in some English church-yard, beside some ivied tower, beneath an old gnarled black yew."

I had so far distinctly followed the dialogue; but at this point the landlord entered and, begging my pardon, would suggest that number 12, a most superior apart-ment, having now been vacated, it would give him pleasure if I would look in. I declined to look in, but agreed for number 12 at a venture and gave myself again, with dissimulation, to my friends. They had got up; Simmons had put on his overcoat; he stood polishing his rusty-black hat with his napkin. "Do you mean to go down to the place?" he asked.

"Possibly. I've thought of it so often that I should like to see it."

"Shall you call on Mr. Searle?"

"Heaven forbid!"

"Something has just occurred to me," Simmons pursued, with a grin that made his upper lip look more than ever denuded by the razor and jerked the ugly ornament of his chin into the air. "There's a certain Miss Searle, the old man's sister."

"Well?" my gentleman quavered.

"Well, sir!—you talk of moving on. You might move on the damsel."

Mr. Searle frowned in silence and his companion gave him a tap on the stomach. "Line those ribs a bit first!" He blushed crimson; his eyes filled with tears. "You *are* a coarse brute," he said. The scene quite harrowed me, but I was prevented from seeing it through by the reappearance of the landlord on behalf of number 12. He represented to me that I ought in justice to him to come and see how tidy they *had* made it. Half an hour afterwards I was rattling along in a hansom toward Covent Garden, where I heard Madame Bosio in *The Barber of Seville*. On my return from the opera I went into the coffee-room; it had occurred to me I might catch there another glimpse of Mr. Searle. I was not disappointed. I found him seated before the fire with his head sunk on his breast: he slept, dreaming perhaps of Abijah Simmons. I watched him for some moments. His closed eyes, in the dim lamplight, looked even more helpless and resigned, and I seemed to see the fine grain of his nature in his unconscious mask. They say fortune comes while we sleep, and, standing there, I felt really tender enough —though otherwise most unqualified—to be poor Mr. Searle's fortune. As I walked away I noted in one of the little prandial pews I have described the melancholy waiter, whose whiskered chin also reposed on the bulge of his shirt-front. I lingered a moment beside the old inn-yard in which, upon a time, the coaches and post-chaises found space to turn and disgorge. Above the dusky shaft of the enclosing galleries, where lounging lodgers and crumpled chambermaids and all the picturesque domesticity of a rattling tavern must have leaned on their elbows for many a year, I made out the far-off lurid twinkle of the London constellations. At the foot of the stairs, enshrined in the glittering niche of her well-appointed bar, the landlady sat napping like some solemn idol amid votive brass and plate.

The next morning, not finding the subject of my benevolent curiosity in the coffee-room, I learned from the waiter that he had ordered breakfast in bed. Into this asylum I was not yet prepared to pursue him. I spent the morning in the streets, partly under pressure of business, but catching all kinds of romantic impressions by the way. To the searching American eye there is no tint of association with which the great grimy face of London doesn't flush. As the afternoon approached, however, I began to yearn for some site more gracefully classic than what surrounded me, and, thinking over the excursions recommended to the ingenuous stranger, decided to take the train to Hampton Court. The day was the more propitious that it yielded just that dim subaqueous light which sleeps so fondly upon the English landscape.

At the end of an hour I found myself wandering through the apartments of the great palace. They follow each other in infinite succession, with no great variety of interest or aspect, but with persistent pomp and a fine specific effect. They are exactly of their various times. You pass from painted and panelled bedchambers and closets, anterooms, drawing-rooms, council-rooms, through king's suite, queen's suite, prince's suite, until you feel yourself move through the appointed hours and stages of some rigid monarchical day. On one side are the old monumental upholsteries, the big cold tarnished beds and canopies, with the circumference of disapparelled royalty symbolised by a gilded balustrade, and the great carved and yawning chimney - places where dukes - in - waiting may have warmed their weary heels; on the other, in deep recesses, rise the immense windows, the framed and draped embrasures where the sovereign whispered and favourites smiled, looking out on terraced gardens and misty park.

The brown walls are dimly illumined by innumerable
portraits of courtiers and captains, more especially with
various members of the Batavian entourage of William of
Orange, the restorer of the palace; with good store too
of the lily-bosomed models of Lely and Kneller. The
whole tone of this processional interior is singularly
stale and sad. The tints of all things have both faded
and darkened—you taste the chill of the place as you
walk from room to room. It was still early in the day
and in the season, and I flattered myself that I was
the only visitor. This complacency, however, dropped
at sight of a person standing motionless before a simper-
ing countess of Sir Peter Lely's creation. On hearing my
footstep this victim of an evaporated spell turned his
head and I recognised my fellow-lodger of the Red Lion.
I was apparently recognised as well; he looked as if he
could scarce wait for me to be kind to him, and in
fact didn't wait. Seeing I had a catalogue he asked
the name of the portrait. On my satisfying him he
appealed, rather timidly, as to my opinion of the lady.

"Well," said I, not quite timidly enough perhaps,
"I confess she strikes me as no great matter."

He remained silent and was evidently a little abashed.
As we strolled away he stole a sidelong glance of farewell at his leering shepherdess. To speak with him
face to face was to feel keenly that he was no less interesting than infirm. We talked of our inn, of London, of
the palace; he uttered his mind freely, but seemed to
struggle with a weight of depression. It was an honest
mind enough, with no great cultivation but with a certain
natural love of excellent things. I foresaw that I
should find him quite to the manner born—to ours;
full of glimpses and responses, of deserts and desolations.
His perceptions would be fine and his opinions pathetic;
I should moreover take refuge from his sense of proportion in his sense of humour, and then refuge from
that, ah me!—in what? On my telling him that I was
a fellow-citizen he stopped short, deeply touched, and,
silently passing his arm into my own, suffered me to
lead him through the other apartments and down

into the gardens. A large gravelled platform stretches itself before the basement of the palace, taking the afternoon sun. Parts of the great structure are reserved for private use and habitation, occupied by state-pensioners, reduced gentlewomen in receipt of the queen's bounty and other deserving persons. Many of the apartments have their dependent gardens, and here and there, between the verdure-coated walls, you catch a glimpse of these somewhat stuffy bowers. My companion and I measured more than once this long expanse, looking down on the floral figures of the rest of the affair and on the stoutly woven tapestry of creeping plants that muffle the foundations of the huge red pile. I thought of the various images of old-world gentility which, early and late, must have strolled in front of it and felt the protection and security of the place. We peeped through an antique grating into one of the mossy cages and saw an old lady with a black mantilla on her head, a decanter of water in one hand and a crutch in the other, come forth, followed by three little dogs and a cat, to sprinkle a plant. She would probably have had an opinion on the virtue of Queen Caroline. Feeling these things together made us quickly, made us extraordinarily, intimate. My companion seemed to ache with his impression; he scowled, all gently, as if it gave him pain. I proposed at last that we should dine somewhere on the spot and take a late train to town. We made our way out of the gardens into the adjoining village, where we entered an inn which I pronounced, very sincerely, exactly what we wanted. Mr. Searle had approached our board as shyly as if it had been a cold bath; but, gradually warming to his work, he declared at the end of half an hour that for the first time in a month he enjoyed his victuals.

"I'm afraid you're rather out of health," I risked.

"Yes, sir—I'm an incurable."

The little village of Hampton Court stands clustered about the entrance of Bushey Park, and after we had dined we lounged along into the celebrated avenue of horse-chestnuts. There is a rare emotion, familiar to every intelligent traveller, in which the mind seems to swallow the sum total of its impressions at a gulp. You take in the whole place, whatever it be. You feel England, you feel Italy, and the sensation involves for the moment a kind of thrill. I had known it from time to time in Italy and had opened my soul to it as to the spirit of the Lord. Since my landing in England I had been waiting for it to arrive. A bottle of tolerable Burgundy, at dinner, had perhaps unlocked to it the gates of sense; it arrived now with irresistible force. Just the scene around me was the England of one's early reveries. Over against us, amid the ripeness of its gardens, the dark red residence, with its formal facings and its vacant windows, seemed to make the past definite and massive; the little village, nestling between park and palace, around a patch of turfy common, with its taverns of figurative names, its ivy-towered church, its mossy roofs, looked like the property of a feudal lord. It was in this dark composite light that I had read the British classics; it was this mild moist air that had blown from the pages of the poets; while I seemed to feel the buried generations in the dense and elastic sod. And that I must have testified in some form or other to what I have called my thrill I gather, remembering it, from a remark of my companion's.

"You've the advantage over me in coming to all this with an educated eye. You already know what old things can be. I've never known it but by report. I've always fancied I should like it. In a small way at home, of course, I did try to stand by my idea of it. I must be a conservative by nature. People at home used to call me a cockney and a fribble. But it wasn't true," he went on; "if it had been I should have made my way over here long ago: before—before——" He paused, and his head dropped sadly on his breast.

The bottle of Burgundy had loosened his tongue; I had but to choose my time for learning his story. Something told me that I had gained his confidence and that, so far as attention and attitude might go, I was "in"

for responsibilities. But somehow I didn't dread them.
"Before you lost your health," I suggested.

"Before I lost my health," he answered. "And my
property—the little I had. And my ambition. And
any power to take myself seriously."

"Come!" I cried. "You shall recover everything.
This tonic English climate will wind you up in a month.
And *then* see how you'll take yourself—and how I shall
take you!"

"Oh," he gratefully smiled, "I may turn to dust in
your hands! I should like," he presently pursued, "to
be an old genteel pensioner, lodged over there in the
palace and spending my days in maundering about
these vistas. I should go every morning, at the hour
when it gets the sun, into that long gallery where all
those pretty women of Lely's are hung—I know you
despise them!—and stroll up and down and say something kind to them. Poor precious forsaken creatures!
So flattered and courted in their day, so neglected now!
Offering up their shoulders and ringlets and smiles to
that musty deadly silence!"

I laid my hand on my friend's shoulder. "Oh, sir,
you're all right!"

Just at this moment there came cantering down
the shallow glade of the avenue a young girl on a fine
black horse—one of those little budding gentlewomen,
perfectly mounted and equipped, who form to alien eyes
one of the prettiest incidents of English scenery. She
had distanced her servant and, as she came abreast of
us, turned slightly in her saddle and glanced back at
him. In the movement she dropped the hunting-crop
with which she was armed; whereupon she reined up
and looked shyly at us and at the implement. "This is
something better than a Lely," I said. Searle hastened
forward, picked up the crop and, with a particular
courtesy that became him, handed it back to the rider.
Fluttered and blushing she reached forward, took it
with a quick sweet sound, and the next moment was
bounding over the quiet turf. Searle stood watching her;
the servant, as he passed us, touched his hat. When

my friend turned toward me again I saw that he too
was blushing. "Oh, sir, you're all right," I repeated.

At a short distance from where we had stopped was
an old stone bench. We went and sat down on it and,
as the sun began to sink, watched the light mist powder
itself with gold. "We ought to be thinking of the train
back to London, I suppose," I at last said.

"Oh, hang the train!" sighed my companion.

"Willingly. There could be no better spot than this
to feel the English evening stand still." So we lingered,
and the twilight hung about us, strangely clear in spite
of the thickness of the air. As we sat there came into
view an apparition unmistakable from afar as an im-
memorial vagrant—the disowned, in his own rich way,
of all the English ages. As he approached us he
slackened pace and finally halted, touching his cap.
He was a man of middle age, clad in a greasy bonnet
with false-looking ear-locks depending from its sides.
Round his neck was a grimy red scarf, tucked into his
waistcoat; his coat and trousers had a remote affinity
with those of a reduced ostler. In one hand he had a
stick; on his arm he bore a tattered basket, with a handful
of withered vegetables at the bottom. His face was
pale, haggard, and degraded beyond description—as
base as a counterfeit coin, yet as modelled somehow as
a tragic mask. He too, like everything else, had a
history. From what height had he fallen, from what
depth had he risen? He was the perfect symbol of
generated constituted baseness; and I felt before him in
presence of a great artist or actor.

"For God's sake, gentlemen," he said in the raucous
tone of weather-beaten poverty, the tone of chronic
sore-throat exacerbated by perpetual gin, "for God's
sake, gentlemen, have pity on a poor fern-collector!"
turning up his stale daisies. "Food hasn't passed my
lips, gentlemen, for the last three days."

We gaped at him and at each other, and to our
imagination his appeal had almost the force of a command. "I wonder if half a crown would help?" I
privately wailed. And our fasting botanist went limp-

ing away through the park with the grace of controlled stupefaction still further enriching his outline.

"I feel as if I had seen my *Doppelgänger*," said Searle. "He reminds me of myself. What am I but a mere figure in the landscape, a wandering minstrel or picker of daisies?"

"What are you 'anyway,' my friend?" I thereupon took occasion to ask. "Who are you? kindly tell me."

The colour rose again to his pale face and I feared I had offended him. He poked a moment at the sod with the point of his umbrella before answering. "Who am I?" he said at last. "My name is Clement Searle. I was born in New York, and that's the beginning and the end of me."

"Ah, not the end!" I made bold to plead.

"Then it's because I *have* no end—any more than an ill-written book. I just stop anywhere; which means I'm a failure," the poor man all lucidly and unreservedly pursued: "a failure, as hopeless and helpless, sir, as any that ever swallowed up the slender investments of the widow and the orphan. I don't pay five cents on the dollar. What I might have been—once!—there's nothing left to show. I was rotten before I was ripe. To begin with, certainly, I wasn't a fountain of wisdom. All the more reason for a definite channel—for having a little character and purpose. But I hadn't even a little. I had nothing but nice tastes, as they call them, and fine sympathies and sentiments. Take a turn through New York to-day and you'll find the tattered remnants of these things dangling on every bush and fluttering in every breeze; the men to whom I lent money, the women to whom I made love, the friends I trusted, the follies I invented, the poisonous fumes of pleasure amid which nothing was worth a thought but the manhood they stifled! It was my fault that I believed in pleasure here below. I believe in it still, but as I believe in the immortality of the soul. The soul is immortal, certainly—if you've got one; but most people haven't. Pleasure would be right if it were pleasure straight through; but it never is. My taste was to be the best in the world; well, perhaps it was. I had a little money; it went the way of my little wit. Here in my pocket I have the scant dregs of it. I should tell you I was the biggest kind of ass. Just now that description would flatter me; it would assume there's something left of me. But the ghost of a donkey—what's that? I think," he went on with a charming turn and as if striking off his real explanation, "I should have been all right in a world arranged on different lines. Before heaven, sir— whoever you are—I'm in practice so absurdly tender- hearted that I can afford to say it: I entered upon life a perfect gentleman. I had the love of old forms and pleasant rites, and I found them nowhere—found a world all hard lines and harsh lights, without shade, without composition, as they say of pictures, without the lovely mystery of colour. To furnish colour I melted down the very substance of my own soul. I went about with my brush, touching up and toning down; a very pretty chiaroscuro you'll find in my track! Sitting here in this old park, in this old country, I feel that I hover on the misty verge of what might have been! I should have been born here and not there; here my makeshift distinctions would have found things they'd have been true of. How it was I never got free is more than I can say. I might have cut the knot, but the knot was too tight. I was always out of health or in debt or somehow desperately dangling. Besides, I had a horror of the great black sickening sea. A year ago I was reminded of the existence of an old claim to an English estate, which has danced before the eyes of my family, at odd moments, any time these eighty years. I confess it's a bit of a muddle and a tangle, and am by no means sure that to this hour I've got the hang of it. You look as if you had a clear head: some other time, if you consent, we'll have a go at it, such as it is, together. Poverty was staring me in the face; I sat down and tried to commit the 'points' of our case to memory, as I used to get nine-times-nine by heart as a boy. I dreamed of it for six months, half-expecting to wake up some fine morning and hear through a latticed casement the cawing of an English rookery. A couple of months ago there came out to England on business of his own a man who once got me out of a dreadful mess (not that I had hurt anyone but myself), a legal practitioner in our courts, a very rough diamond, but with a great deal of *flair*, as they say in New York. It was with him yesterday you saw me dining. He undertook, as he called it, to 'nose round' and see if anything could be made of our questionable but possible show. The matter had never seriously been taken up. A month later I got a letter from Simmons assuring me that it seemed a very good show indeed and that he should be greatly surprised if I were unable to do something. This was the greatest push I had ever got in my life; I took a deliberate step, for the first time; I sailed for England. I've been here three days: they've seemed three months. After keeping me waiting for thirty-six hours my legal adviser makes his appearance last night and states to me, with his mouth full of mutton, that I haven't a leg to stand on, that my claim is moonshine, and that I must do penance and take a ticket for six more days of purgatory with his presence thrown in. My friend, my friend—shall I say I was disappointed? I'm already resigned. I didn't really believe I had any case. I felt in my deeper consciousness that it was the crowning illusion of a life of illusions. Well, it was a pretty one. Poor legal adviser!—I forgive him with all my heart. But for him I shouldn't be sitting in this place, in this air, under these impressions. This is a world I could have got on with beautifully. There's an immense charm in its having been kept for the last. After it nothing else would have been tolerable. I shall now have a month of it, I hope, which won't be long enough for it to 'go back' on me. There's one thing!" —and here, pausing, he laid his hand on mine; I rose and stood before him—"I wish it were possible you should be with me to the end."

"I promise you to leave you only when you kick me downstairs." But I suggested my terms. "It must be on condition of your omitting from your conversation

this intolerable flavour of mortality. I know nothing
of 'ends.' I'm all for beginnings."

He kept on me his sad weak eyes. Then with a faint
smile: "Don't cut down a man you find hanging. He
has had a reason for it. I'm bankrupt."

"Oh, health's money!" I said. "Get well, and the
rest will take care of itself. I'm interested in your
questionable claim—it's the question that's the charm;
and pretenders, to anything big enough, have always
been, for me, an attractive class. Only their first
duty's to be gallant."

"Their first duty's to understand their own points
and to know their own mind," he returned with hopeless lucidity. "Don't ask me to climb our family tree
now," he added; "I fear I haven't the head for it. I'll
try some day—if it will bear my weight; or yours added
to mine. There's no doubt, however, that we, as they
say, go back. But I know nothing of business. If I
were to take the matter in hand I should break in two
the poor little silken thread from which everything hangs.
In a better world than this I think I should be listened
to. But the wind doesn't set to ideal justice. There's
no doubt that a hundred years ago we suffered a palpable
wrong. Yet we made no appeal at the time, and the dust of
a century now lies heaped upon our silence. Let it rest!"

"What then," I asked, "is the estimated value of
your interest?"

"We were instructed from the first to accept a
compromise. Compared with the whole property our
ideas have been small. We were once advised in the
sense of a hundred and thirty thousand dollars. Why
a hundred and thirty I'm sure I don't know. Don't
beguile me into figures."

"Allow me one more question," I said. "Who's
actually in possession?"

"A certain Mr. Richard Searle. I know nothing
about him."

"He's in some way related to you?"

"Our great-grandfathers were half-brothers. What
does that make us?"

"Twentieth cousins, say. And where does your twentieth cousin live?"

"At a place called Lackley—in Middleshire."

I thought it over. "Well, suppose we look up Lackley in Middleshire!"

He got straight up. "Go and see it?"

"Go and see it."

"Well," he said, "with you I'll go anywhere."

On our return to town we determined to spend three days there together and then proceed to our errand. We were as conscious one as the other of that deeper mystic appeal made by London to those superstitious pilgrims who feel it the mother-city of their race, the distributing heart of their traditional life. Certain characteristics of the dusky Babylon, certain aspects, phases, features, "say" more to the American spiritual ear than anything else in Europe. The influence of these things on Searle it charmed me to note. His observation I soon saw to be, as I pronounced it to him, searching and caressing. His almost morbid appetite for any over-scoring of time, well-nigh extinct from long inanition, threw the flush of its revival into his face and his talk.

II

We looked out the topography of Middleshire in a county guide, which spoke highly, as the phrase is, of Lackley Park, and took up our abode, our journey ended, at a wayside inn where, in the days of leisure, the coach must have stopped for luncheon and burnished pewters of rustic ale been handed up as straight as possible to outsiders athirst with the sense of speed. We stopped here for mere gaping joy of its steep-thatched roof, its latticed windows, its hospitable porch, and allowed a couple of days to elapse in vague undirected strolls and sweet sentimental observance of the land before approaching the particular business that had drawn us on. The region I allude to is a compendium of the general physiognomy of England. The noble friendliness of the scenery, its latent old-friendliness, the way we scarcely knew whether we were looking at it for the first or the last time, made it arrest us at every step. The countryside, in the full warm rains of the last of April, had burst into sudden perfect spring. The dark walls of the hedgerows had turned into blooming screens, the sodden verdure of lawn and meadow been washed over with a lighter brush. We went forth without loss of time for a long walk on the great grassy hills, smooth arrested central billows of some primitive upheaval, from the summits of which you find half England unrolled at your feet. A dozen broad counties, within the scope of your vision, commingle their green exhalations. Closely beneath us lay the dark rich hedgy flats and the copse-chequered slopes, white with the blossom of apples. At widely opposite points of the expanse two great towers of cathedrals rose sharply out of a reddish blur of habitation, taking the mild English light.

We gave an irrepressible attention to this same solar reserve, and found in it only a refinement of art. The sky never was empty and never idle; the clouds were continually at play for our benefit. Over against us, from our station on the hills, we saw them piled and dissolved, condensed and shifted, blotting the blue with sullen rain-spots, stretching, breeze-fretted, into dappled fields of grey, bursting into an explosion of light or melting into a drizzle of silver. We made our way along the rounded ridge of the downs and reached, by a descent, through slanting angular fields, green to cottage-doors, a russet village that beckoned us from the heart of the maze in which the hedges wrapped it up. Close beside it, I admit, the roaring train bounces out of a hole in the hills; yet there broods upon this charming hamlet an old-time quietude that makes a violation of confidence of naming it so far away. We struck through a narrow lane, a green lane, dim with its barriers of hawthorn; it led us to a superb old farm-house, now rather rudely jostled by the multiplied roads and by-ways that have reduced its ancient appanage.

It stands there in stubborn picturesqueness, doggedly submitting to be pointed out and sketched. It is a wonderful image of the domiciliary conditions of the past—cruelly complete; with bended beams and joists, beneath the burden of gables, that seem to ache and groan with memories and regrets. The short low windows, where lead and glass combine equally to create an inward gloom, retain their opacity as a part of the primitive idea of defence. Such an old house provokes on the part of an American a luxury of respect. So propped and patched, so tinkered with clumsy tenderness, clustered so richly about its central English sturdiness, its oaken vertebrations, so humanised with ages of use and touches of beneficent affection, it seemed to offer to our grateful eyes a small rude symbol of the great English social order. Passing out upon the high road, we came to the common browsing-patch, the "village-green" of the tales of our youth. Nothing was absent: the shaggy mouse-coloured donkey, nosing the turf with his mild and huge proboscis, the geese, the old woman—*the* old woman, in person, with her red cloak and her black bonnet, frilled about the face and double-frilled beside her decent placid cheeks—the towering ploughman with his white smock-frock puckered on chest and back, his short corduroys, his mighty calves, his big red rural face. We greeted these things as children greet the loved pictures in a story-book lost and mourned and found again. We recognised them as one recognises the handwriting on letter-backs. Beside the road we saw a ploughboy straddle whistling on a stile, and he had the merit of being not only a plough-boy but a Gainsborough. Beyond the stile, across the level velvet of a meadow, a footpath wandered like a streak drawn by a finger over a surface of fine plush. We followed it from field to field and from stile to stile; it was all adorably the way to church. At the church we finally arrived, lost in its rook-haunted churchyard, hidden from the work-day world by the broad stillness of pastures—a grey, grey tower, a huge black yew, a cluster of village-graves with crooked headstones and protrusions that had settled and sunk. The place seemed so to ache with consecration that my sensitive companion gave way to the force of it.

"You must bury me here, you know"—he caught at my arm. "It's the first place of worship I've seen in my life. How it makes a Sunday where it stands!"

It took the Church, we agreed, to make churches, but we had the sense the next day of seeing still better why. We walked over, some seven miles, to the nearer of the two neighbouring seats of that lesson; and all through such a mist of local colour that we felt ourselves a pair of Smollett's pedestrian heroes faring tavernward for a night of adventures. As we neared the provincial city we saw the steepled mass of the cathedral, long and high, rise far into the cloud-freckled blue; and as we got closer stopped on a bridge and looked down at the reflection of the solid minster in a yellow stream. Going farther yet we entered the russet town—where surely Miss Austen's heroines, in chariots and curricles, must often have come a-shopping for their sandals and mittens; we lounged in the grassed and gravelled precinct and gazed insatiably at that most soul-soothing sight, the waning wasting afternoon light, the visible ether that feels the voices of the chimes cling far aloft to the quiet sides of the cathedral-tower; saw it linger and nestle and abide, as it loves to do on all perpendicular spaces, converting them irresistibly into registers and dials; tasted too, as deeply, of the peculiar stillness of this place of priests; saw a rosy English lad come forth and lock the door of the old foundation-school that dovetailed with cloister and choir, and carry his big responsible key into one of the quiet canonical houses: and then stood musing together on the effect on one's mind of having in one's boyhood gone and come through cathedral-shades as a King's scholar, and yet kept ruddy with much cricket in misty river meadows. On the third morning we betook ourselves to Lackley, having learned that parts of the "grounds" were open to visitors, and that indeed on application the house was sometimes shown.

Within the range of these numerous acres the declining spurs of the hills continued to undulate and subside. A long avenue wound and circled from the outermost gate through an untrimmed woodland, whence you glanced at further slopes and glades and copses and bosky recesses—at everything except the limits of the place. It was as free and untended as I had found a few of the large loose villas of old Italy, and I was still never to see the angular fact of English landlordism muffle itself in so many concessions. The weather had just become perfect; it was one of the dozen exquisite days of the English year—days stamped with a purity unknown in climates where fine weather is cheap. It was as if the mellow brightness, as tender as that of the primroses which starred the dark waysides like petals wind-scattered over beds of moss, had been meted out to us by the cubic foot—distilled from an alchemist's crucible. From this pastoral abundance we moved upon the more composed scene, the park proper—passed through a second lodge-gate, with weather-worn gilding on its twisted bars, to the smooth slopes where the great trees stood singly and the tame deer browsed along the bed of a woodland stream. Here before us rose the gabled grey front of the Tudor-time, developed and terraced and gardened to some later loss, as we were afterwards to know, of type.

"Here you can wander all day," I said to Searle, "like an exiled prince who has come back on tiptoe and hovers about the dominion of the usurper."

"To think of 'others' having hugged this all these years!" he answered. "I know what I am, but what might I have been? What do such places make of a man?"

"I dare say he gets stupidly used to them," I said. "But I dare say too, even then, that when you scratch the mere owner you find the perfect lover."

"What a perfect scene and background it forms!" my friend, however, had meanwhile gone on. "What legends, what histories it knows! My heart really breaks with all I seem to guess. There's Tennyson's

Talking Oak! What summer days one could spend
here! How I could lounge the rest of my life away on
this turf of the middle ages! Haven't I some maiden
cousin in that old hall, or grange, or court—what in
the name of enchantment do you call the thing?—
who would give me kind leave?" And then he turned
almost fiercely upon me. "Why did you bring me
here? Why did you drag me into this distraction of
vain regrets?"

At this moment there passed within call a decent
lad who had emerged from the gardens and who might
have been an underling in the stables. I hailed him
and put the question of our possible admittance to
the house. He answered that the master was away
from home, but that he thought it probable the housekeeper would consent to do the honours. I passed
my arm into Searle's. "Come," I said; "drain the
cup, bitter-sweet though it be. We must go in." We
hastened slowly and approached the fine front. The
house was one of the happiest fruits of its freshly-
feeling era, a multitudinous cluster of fair gables and
intricate chimneys, brave projections and quiet recesses,
brown old surfaces weathered to silver and mottled
roofs that testified not to seasons but to centuries. Two
broad terraces commanded the wooded horizon. Our
appeal was answered by a butler, who condescended to
our weakness. He renewed the assertion that Mr.
Searle was away from home, but he would himself lay
our case before the housekeeper. We would be so good,
however, as to give him our cards. This request,
following so directly on the assertion that Mr. Searle
was absent, was rather resented by my companion.
"Surely not for the housekeeper."

The butler gave a diplomatic cough. "Miss Searle
is at home, sir."

"Yours alone will have to serve," said my friend.
I took out a card and pencil and wrote beneath my
name *New York*. As I stood with the pencil poised
a temptation entered into it. Without in the least
considering proprieties or results I let my implement

yield—I added above my name that of Mr. Clement Searle. What would come of it?

Before many minutes the housekeeper waited upon us—a fresh rosy little old woman in a clean dowdy cap and a scanty sprigged gown; a quaint careful person, but accessible to the tribute of our pleasure, to say nothing of any other. She had the accent of the country, but the manners of the house. Under her guidance we passed through a dozen apartments, duly stocked with old pictures, old tapestry, old carvings, old armour, with a hundred ornaments and treasures. The pictures were especially valuable. The two Vandykes, the trio of rosy Rubenses, the sole and sombre Rembrandt, glowed with conscious authenticity. A Claude, a Murillo, a Greuze, a couple of Gainsboroughs, hung there with high complacency. Searle strolled about, scarcely speaking, pale and grave, with bloodshot eyes and lips compressed. He uttered no comment on what we saw—he asked but a question or two. Missing him at last from my side I retraced my steps and found him in a room we had just left, on a faded old ottoman and with his elbows on his knees and his face buried in his hands. Before him, ranged on a great *crédence*, was a magnificent collection of old Italian majolica; plates of every shape, with their glaze of happy colour, jugs and vases nobly bellied and embossed. There seemed to rise before me, as I looked, a sudden vision of the young English gentleman who, eighty years ago, had travelled by slow stages to Italy and been waited on at his inn by persuasive toymen. "What is it, my dear man?" I asked. "Are you unwell?"

He uncovered his haggard face and showed me the flush of a consciousness sharper, I think, to myself than to him. "A memory of the past! There comes back to me a china vase that used to stand on the parlour mantel-shelf when I was a boy, with a portrait of General Jackson painted on one side and a bunch of flowers on the other. How long do you suppose that majolica has been in the family?"

"A long time probably. It was brought hither in

the last century, into old, old England, out of old, old
Italy, by some contemporary dandy with a taste for
foreign gimcracks. Here it has stood for a hundred
years, keeping its clear firm hues in this quiet light that
has never sought to advertise it."

Searle sprang to his feet. "I say, for mercy's sake,
take me away! I can't stand this sort of thing. Before
I know it I shall do something scandalous. I shall
steal some of their infernal crockery. I shall proclaim
my identity and assert my rights. I shall go blubbering
to Miss Searle and ask her in pity's name to 'put me up.'"

If he could ever have been said to threaten com-
plications he rather visibly did so now. I began to
regret my officious presentation of his name and prepared without delay to lead him out of the house. We
overtook the housekeeper in the last room of the series,
a small unused boudoir over whose chimney-piece
hung a portrait of a young man in a powdered wig and
a brocaded waistcoat. I was struck with his resemblance to my companion while our guide introduced
him. "This is Mr. Clement Searle, Mr. Searle's great-
uncle, by Sir Joshua Reynolds. He died young, poor
gentleman; he perished at sea, going to America."

"He was the young buck who brought the majolica
out of Italy," I supplemented.

"Indeed, sir, I believe he did," said the housekeeper
without wonder.

"He's the image of you, my dear Searle," I further
observed.

"He's remarkably like the gentleman, saving his
presence," said the housekeeper.

My friend stood staring. "Clement Searle—at sea—
going to America——?" he broke out. Then with some
sharpness to our old woman: "Why the devil did he go
to America?"

"Why indeed, sir? You may well ask. I believe he
had kinsfolk there. It was for them to come to him."

Searle broke into a laugh. "It was for them to come
to him! Well, well," he said, fixing his eyes on our
guide, "they've come to him at last!"

She blushed like a wrinkled rose-leaf. "Indeed, sir, I verily believe you're one of *us*!"

"My name's the name of that beautiful youth," Searle went on. "Dear kinsman, I'm happy to meet you! And what do you think of this?" he pursued as he grasped me by the arm. "I have an idea. He perished at sea. His spirit came ashore and wandered about in misery till it got another incarnation—in this poor trunk!" And he tapped his hollow chest. "Here it has rattled about these forty years, beating its wings against its rickety cage, begging to be taken home again. And I never knew what was the matter with me! Now at last the bruised spirit can escape!"

Our old lady gaped at a breadth of appreciation—if not at the disclosure of a connection — beyond her. The scene was really embarrassing, and my confusion increased as we became aware of another presence. A lady had appeared in the doorway and the housekeeper dropped just audibly: "Miss Searle!" My first impression of Miss Searle was that she was neither young nor beautiful. She stood without confidence on the threshold, pale, trying to smile and twirling my card in her fingers. I immediately bowed. Searle stared at her as if one of the pictures had stepped out of its frame.

"If I'm not mistaken, one of you gentlemen is Mr. Clement Searle," the lady adventured.

"My friend's Mr. Clement Searle," I took upon myself to reply. "Allow me to add that I alone am responsible for your having received his name."

"I should have been sorry not to—not to see him," said Miss Searle, beginning to blush. "Your being from America has led me—perhaps to intrude!"

"The intrusion, madam, has been on our part. And with just that excuse—that we come from so far away."

Miss Searle, while I spoke, had fixed her eyes on my friend as he stood silent beneath Sir Joshua's portrait. The housekeeper, agitated and mystified, fairly let herself go. "Heaven preserve us, Miss! It's your great-uncle's picture come to life."

"I'm not mistaken then," said Miss Searle—"we must be distantly related." She had the air of the shyest of women, for whom it was almost anguish to make an advance without help. Searle eyed her with gentle wonder from head to foot, and I could easily read his thoughts. This then was his maiden-cousin, prospective mistress of these hereditary treasures. She was of some thirty-five years of age, taller than was then common and perhaps stouter than is now enjoined. She had small kind grey eyes, a considerable quantity of very light-brown hair and a smiling well-formed mouth. She was dressed in a lustreless black satin gown with a short train. Disposed about her neck was a blue handkerchief, and over this handkerchief, in many convolutions, a string of amber beads. Her appearance was singular; she was large yet somehow vague, mature yet undeveloped. Her manner of addressing us spoke of all sorts of deep diffidences. Searle, I think, had prefigured to himself some proud cold beauty of five-and-twenty; he was relieved at finding the lady timid and not obtrusively fair. He at once had an excellent tone.

"We're distant cousins, I believe. I'm happy to claim a relationship which you're so good as to remember. I hadn't counted on your knowing anything about me."

"Perhaps I've done wrong." And Miss Searle blushed and smiled anew. "But I've always known of there being people of our blood in America, and have often wondered and asked about them—without ever learning much. To-day, when this card was brought me and I understood a Clement Searle to be under our roof as a stranger, I felt I ought to do something. But, you know, I hardly knew what. My brother's in London. I've done what I think he would have done. Welcome as a cousin." And with a resolution that ceased to be awkward she put out her hand.

"I'm welcome indeed if he would have done it half so graciously!" Again Searle, taking her hand, acquitted himself beautifully.

"You've seen what there is, I think," Miss Searle

went on. "Perhaps now you'll have luncheon." We followed her into a small breakfast-room where a deep bay window opened on the mossy flags of a terrace. Here, for some moments, she remained dumb and abashed, as if resting from a measurable effort. Searle too had ceased to overflow, so that I had to relieve the silence. It was of course easy to descant on the beauties of park and mansion, and as I did so I observed our hostess. She had no arts, no impulses nor graces— scarce even any manners; she was queerly, almost frowsily dressed; yet she pleased me well. She had an antique sweetness, a homely fragrance of old traditions. To be so simple, among those complicated treasures, so pampered and yet so fresh, so modest and yet so placid, told of just the spacious leisure in which Searle and I had imagined human life to be steeped in such places as that. This figure was to the Sleeping Beauty in the Wood what a fact is to a fairy-tale, an interpretation to a myth. We, on our side, were to our hostess subjects of a curiosity not cunningly veiled.

"I should like so to go abroad!" she exclaimed suddenly, as if she meant us to take the speech for an expression of interest in ourselves.

"Have you never been?" one of us asked.

"Only once. Three years ago my brother took me to Switzerland. We thought it extremely beautiful. Except for that journey I've always lived here. I was born in this house. It's a dear old place indeed, and I know it well. Sometimes one wants a change." And on my asking her how she spent her time and what society she saw, "Of course it's very quiet," she went on, proceeding by short steps and simple statements, in the manner of a person called upon for the first time to analyse to that extent her situation. "We see very few people. I don't think there are many nice ones hereabouts. At least we don't know them. Our own family's very small. My brother cares for nothing but riding and books. He had a great sorrow ten years ago. He lost his wife and his only son, a dear little boy, who of course would have had everything.

Do you know that that makes me the heir, as they've done something—I don't quite know what—to the entail? Poor old me! Since his loss my brother has preferred to be quite alone. I'm sorry he's away. But you must wait till he comes back. I expect him in a day or two." She talked more and more, as if our very strangeness led her on, about her circumstances, her solitude, her bad eyes, so that she couldn't read, her flowers, her ferns, her dogs, and the vicar, recently presented to the living by her brother and warranted quite safe, who had lately begun to light his altar candles; pausing every now and then to gasp in self-surprise, yet, in the quaintest way in the world, keeping up her story as if it were a slow rather awkward old-time dance, a difficult *pas seul* in which she would have been better with more practice, but of which she must complete the figure. Of all the old things I had seen in England this exhibited mind of Miss Searle's seemed to me the oldest, the most handed down and taken for granted; fenced and protected as it was by convention and precedent and usage, thoroughly acquainted with its subordinate place. I felt as if I were talking with the heroine of a last-century novel. As she talked she rested her dull eyes on her kinsman with wondering kindness. At last she put it to him: "Did you mean to go away without asking for us?"

"I had thought it over, Miss Searle, and had determined not to trouble you. You've shown me how unfriendly I should have been."

"But you knew of the place being ours, and of our relationship?"

"Just so. It was because of these things that I came down here—because of them almost that I came to England. I've always liked to think of them," said my companion.

"You merely wished to look, then? We don't pretend to be much to look at."

He waited; her words were too strange. "You don't know what you are, Miss Searle."

"You like the old place, then?"

Searle looked at her again in silence. "If I could only tell you!" he said at last.

"Do tell me. You must come and stay with us."

It moved him to an oddity of mirth. "Take care, take care—I should surprise you! I'm afraid I should bore you. I should never leave you."

"Oh you'd get homesick—for your real home!"

At this he was still more amused. "By the way, tell Miss Searle about our real home," he said to me. And he stepped, through the window, out upon the terrace, followed by two beautiful dogs, a setter and a young stag-hound who from the moment we came in had established the fondest relation with him. Miss Searle looked at him, while he went, as if she vaguely yearned over him; it began to be plain that she was interested in her exotic cousin. I suddenly recalled the last words I had heard spoken by my friend's adviser in London and which, in a very crude form, had reference to his making a match with this lady. If only Miss Searle could be induced to think of that, and if one had but the tact to put it in a light to her! Something assured me that her heart was virgin-soil, that the flower of romantic affection had never bloomed there. If I might just sow the seed! There seemed to shape itself within her the perfect image of one of the patient wives of old.

"He has lost his heart to England," I said. "He ought to have been born here."

"And yet he doesn't look in the least an Englishman," she still rather guardedly prosed.

"Oh it isn't his looks, poor fellow."

"Of course looks aren't everything. I never talked with a foreigner before; but he talks as I have fancied foreigners."

"Yes, he's foreign enough."

"Is he married?"

"His wife's dead and he's all alone in the world."

"Has he much property?"

"None to speak of."

'But he has means to travel."

I meditated. "He has not expected to travel far," I said at last. "You know, he's in very poor health."

"Poor gentleman! So I supposed."

"But there's more of him to go on with than he thinks. He came here because he wanted to see your place before he dies."

"Dear me—kind man!" And I imagined in the quiet eyes the hint of a possible tear. "And he was going away without my seeing him?"

"He's very modest, you see."

"He's very much the gentleman."

I couldn't but smile. "He's *all*——!"

At this moment we heard on the terrace a loud harsh cry. "It's the great peacock!" said Miss Searle, stepping to the window and passing out while I followed her. Below us, leaning on the parapet, stood our appreciative friend with his arm round the neck of the setter. Before him on the grand walk strutted the familiar fowl of gardens—a splendid specimen—with ruffled neck and expanded tail. The other dog had apparently indulged in a momentary attempt to abash the gorgeous biped, but at Searle's summons had bounded back to the terrace and leaped upon the ledge, where he now stood licking his new friend's face. The scene had a beautiful old-time air: the peacock flaunting in the foreground like the genius of stately places; the broad terrace, which flattered an innate taste of mine for all deserted walks where people may have sat after heavy dinners to drink coffee in old Sèvres and where the stiff brocade of women's dresses may have rustled over grass or gravel; and far around us, with one leafy circle melting into another, the timbered acres of the park. "The very beasts have made him welcome," I noted as we rejoined our companion.

"The peacock has done for you, Mr. Searle," said his cousin, "what he does only for very great people. A year ago there came here a great person—a grand old lady—to see my brother. I don't think that since then has he spread his tail as wide for anyone else—not by a dozen feathers."

"It's not alone the peacock," said Searle. "Just now there came slipping across my path a little green lizard, the first I ever saw, the lizard of literature! And if you've a ghost, broad daylight though it be, I expect to see him here. Do you know the annals of your house, Miss Searle?"

"Oh dear, no! You must ask my brother for all those things."

"You ought to have a collection of legends and traditions. You ought to have loves and murders and mysteries by the roomful. I shall be ashamed of you if you haven't."

"Oh Mr. Searle! We've always been a very well-behaved family," she quite seriously pleaded. "Nothing out of the way has ever happened, I think."

"Nothing out of the way? Oh that won't do! We've managed better than that in America. Why, I myself!"—and he looked at her ruefully enough, but enjoying too his idea that he might embody the social scandal or point to the darkest drama of the Searles. "Suppose I should turn out a better Searle than you— better than you nursed here in romance and extravagance? Come, don't disappoint me. You've some history among you all, you've some poetry, you've some accumulation of legend. I've been famished all my days for these things. Don't you understand? Ah, you can't understand! Tell me," he rambled on, "something tremendous. When I think of what must have happened here; of the lovers who must have strolled on this terrace and wandered under the beeches, of all the figures and passions and purposes that must have haunted these walls! When I think of the births and deaths, the joys and sufferings, the young hopes and the old regrets, the rich experience of life——!" He faltered a moment with the increase of his agitation. His humour of dismay at a threat of the commonplace in the history he felt about him had turned to a deeper reaction. I began to fear, however, that he was really losing his head. He went on with a wilder play. "To see it all called up there before me, if the Devil alone could do it I'd make a bargain with the Devil! Ah, Miss Searle," he cried, "I'm a most unhappy man!"

"Oh dear, oh dear!" she almost wailed while I turned half away.

"Look at that window, that dear little window!" I turned back to see him point to a small protruding oriel, above us, relieved against the purple brickwork, framed in chiselled stone and curtained with ivy.

"It's my little room," she said.

"Of course it's a woman's room. Think of all the dear faces—all of them so mild and yet so proud— that have looked out of that lattice, and of all the old-time women's lives whose principal view of the world has been this quiet park! Every one of them was a cousin of mine. And you, dear lady, you're one of them yet." With which he marched toward her and took her large white hand. She surrendered it, blushing to her eyes and pressing her other hand to her breast. "You're a woman of the past. You're nobly simple. It has been a romance to see you. It doesn't matter what I say to you. You didn't know me yesterday, you'll not know me to-morrow. Let me to-day do a mad sweet thing. Let me imagine in you the spirit of all the dead women who have trod the terrace-flags that lie here like sepulchral tablets in the pavement of a church. Let me say I delight in you!"—he raised her hand to his lips. She gently withdrew it and for a moment averted her face. Meeting her eyes the next instant I saw the tears had come. The Sleeping Beauty was awake.

There followed an embarrassed pause. An issue was suddenly presented by the appearance of the butler bearing a letter. "A telegram, Miss," he announced.

"Oh what shall I do?" cried Miss Searle. "I can't open a telegram. Cousin, help me."

Searle took the missive, opened it and read aloud: "*I shall be home to dinner. Keep the American.*"

III

"Keep the American!" Miss Searle, in compliance with the injunction conveyed in her brother's telegram (with something certainly of telegraphic curtness), lost no time in expressing the pleasure it would give her that our friend should remain. "Really you must," she said; and forthwith repaired to the housekeeper to give orders for the preparation of a room.

"But how in the world did he know of my being here?" my companion put to me.

I answered that he had probably heard from his solicitor of the other's visit. "Mr. Simmons and that gentleman must have had another interview since your arrival in England. Simmons, for reasons of his own, has made known to him your journey to this neighbourhood, and Mr. Searle, learning this, has immediately taken for granted that you've formally presented yourself to his sister. He's hospitably inclined and wishes her to do the proper thing by you. There may even," I went on, "be more in it than that. I've my little theory that he's the very phœnix of usurpers, that he has been very much struck with what the experts have had to say for you, and that he wishes to have the originality of making over to you your share—so limited, after all—of the estate."

"I give it up!" my friend mused. "Come what come will!"

"You, of course," said Miss Searle, reappearing and turning to me, "are included in my brother's invitation. I've told them to see about a room for you. Your luggage shall immediately be sent for."

It was arranged that I in person should be driven over to our little inn and that I should return with our effects in time to meet Mr. Searle at dinner. On my arrival several hours later I was immediately conducted to my room. The servant pointed out to me that it communicated by a door and a private passage with that of my fellow-visitor. I made my way along this passage—a low narrow corridor with a broad latticed casement through which there streamed upon a series of grotesquely sculptured oaken closets and cupboards the vivid animating glow of the western sun—knocked at his door and, getting no answer, opened it. In an armchair by the open window sat my friend asleep, his arms and legs relaxed and head dropped on his breast. It was a great relief to see him rest thus from his rhapsodies, and I watched him for some moments before waking him. There was a faint glow of colour in his cheek and a light expressive parting of his lips, something nearer to ease and peace than I had yet seen in him. It was almost happiness, it was almost health. I laid my hand on his arm and gently shook it. He opened his eyes, gazed at me a moment, vaguely recognised me, then closed them again. "Let me dream, let me dream!"

"What are you dreaming about?"

A moment passed before his answer came. "About a tall woman in a quaint black dress, with yellow hair and a sweet, sweet smile, and a soft low delicious voice! I'm in love with her."

"It's better to see her than to dream about her," I said. "Get up and dress; then we'll go down to dinner and meet her."

"Dinner—dinner——?" And he gradually opened his eyes again. "Yes, upon my word I shall dine!"

"Oh you're all right!" I declared for the twentieth time as he rose to his feet. "You'll live to bury Mr. Simmons." He told me he had spent the hours of my absence with Miss Searle—they had strolled together half over the place. "You must be very intimate," I smiled.

"She's intimate with *me*. Goodness knows what rigmarole I've treated her to!" They had parted an hour ago; since when, he believed, her brother had arrived.

The slow-fading twilight was still in the great drawing-room when we came down. The housekeeper had told us this apartment was rarely used, there being others, smaller and more convenient, for the same needs. It seemed now, however, to be occupied in my comrade's honour. At the farthest end, rising to the roof like a royal tomb in a cathedral, was a great chimney-piece of chiselled white marble, yellowed by time, in which a light fire was crackling. Before the fire stood a small short man, with his hands behind him; near him was Miss Searle, so transformed by her dress that at first I scarcely knew her. There was in our entrance and reception something remarkably chilling and solemn. We moved in silence up the long room; Mr. Searle advanced slowly, a dozen steps, to meet us; his sister stood motionless. I was conscious of her masking her visage with a large white tinselled fan, and that her eyes, grave and enlarged, watched us intently over the top of it. The master of Lackley grasped in silence the proffered hand of his kinsman and eyed him from head to foot, suppressing, I noted, a start of surprise at his resemblance to Sir Joshua's portrait. "This is a happy day." And then turning to me with an odd little sharp stare: "My cousin's friend is my friend." Miss Searle lowered her fan.

The first thing that struck me in Mr. Searle's appearance was his very limited stature, which was less by half a head than that of his sister. The second was the preternatural redness of his hair and beard. They intermingled over his ears and surrounded his head like a huge lurid nimbus. His face was pale and attenuated, the face of a scholar, a dilettante, a comparer of points and texts, a man who lives in a library bending over books and prints and medals. At a distance it might have passed for smooth and rather blankly composed; but on a nearer view it revealed a number of wrinkles, sharply etched and scratched, of a singularly aged and refined effect. It was the complexion of a man of sixty. His nose was arched and delicate, identical almost with the nose of my friend. His eyes, large and deep-set, had a kind of auburn glow, the suggestion of a keen metal red-hot—or, more plainly, were full of temper and spirit. Imagine this physiognomy—grave and solemn, grotesquely solemn, in spite of the bushy brightness which made a sort of frame for it—set in motion by a queer, quick, defiant, perfunctory, preoccupied smile, and you will have an imperfect notion of the remarkable presence of our host; something better worth seeing and knowing, I perceived as I quite breathlessly took him in, than anything we had yet encountered.   How thoroughly I had entered into sympathy with my poor picked-up friend, and how effectually I had associated my sensibilities with his own, I had not suspected till, within the short five minutes before the signal for dinner, I became aware, without his giving me the least hint, of his placing himself on the defensive.   To neither of us was Mr. Searle sympathetic.   I might have guessed from her attitude that his sister entered into our thoughts.   A marked change had been wrought in her since the morning; during the hour, indeed—as I read in the light of the wondering glance he cast at her—that had elasped since her parting with her cousin.   She had not yet recovered from some great agitation.   Her face was pale and she had clearly been crying.   These notes of trouble gave her a new and quite perverse dignity, which was further enhanced by something complimentary and commemorative in her dress.

Whether it was taste or whether it was accident I know not; but the amiable creature, as she stood there half in the cool twilight, half in the arrested glow of the fire as it spent itself in the vastness of its marble cave, was a figure for a painter.   She was habited in some faded splendour of sea-green crape and silk, a piece of millinery which, though it must have witnessed a number of dull dinners, preserved still a festive air.   Over her white shoulders she wore an ancient web of the most precious and venerable lace and about her rounded throat a single series of large pearls.   I went in with her to dinner, and Mr. Searle, following with my friend, took his arm, as the latter afterwards told me, and pretended jocosely to conduct him.   As dinner proceeded the feeling grew within me that a drama had begun to be played in which the three persons before me were

actors—each of a really arduous part. The character
allotted to my friend, however, was certainly the least
easy to represent with effect, though I overflowed with
the desire that he should acquit himself to his honour.
I seemed to see him urge his faded faculties to take
their cue and perform. The poor fellow tried to do
himself credit more seriously than ever in his old best
days. With Miss Searle, credulous, passive and pitying,
he had finally flung aside all vanity and propriety and
shown the bottom of his fantastic heart. But with our
host there might be no talking of nonsense nor taking
of liberties; there and then, if ever, sat a consummate
conservative, breathing the fumes of hereditary privilege
and security. For an hour, accordingly, I saw my poor
protégé attempt, all in pain, to meet a new decorum.
He set himself the task of appearing very American, in
order that his appreciation of everything Mr. Searle
represented might seem purely disinterested. What his
kinsman had expected him to be I know not; but
I made Mr. Searle out as annoyed, in spite of his
exaggerated urbanity, at finding him so harmless. Our
host was not the man to show his hand, but I think his
best card had been a certain implicit confidence that
so provincial a parasite would hardly have good manners.
He led the conversation to the country we had left;
rather as if a leash had been attached to the collar of
some lumpish and half-domesticated animal the tendency of whose movements had to be recognised. He
spoke of it indeed as of some fabled planet, alien to the
British orbit, lately proclaimed to have the admixture
of atmospheric gases required to support animal life,
but not, save under cover of a liberal afterthought, to
be admitted into one's regular conception of things.
I, for my part, felt nothing but regret that the spheric
smoothness of his universe should be disfigured by the
extrusion even of such inconsiderable particles as
ourselves.

"I knew in a general way of our having somehow
ramified over there," Mr. Searle mentioned; "but had
scarcely followed it more than you pretend to pick up

the fruit your long-armed pear-tree may drop, on the other side of your wall, in your neighbour's garden. There was a man I knew at Cambridge, a very odd fellow, a decent fellow too; he and I were rather cronies; I think he afterwards went to the Middle States. They'll be, I suppose, about the Mississippi? At all events, there was that great-uncle of mine whom Sir Joshua painted. He went to America, but he never got there. He was lost at sea. You look enough like him to make one fancy he *did* get there and that you've kept him alive by one of those beastly processes—I think you have 'em over there: what do you call it, 'putting up' things? If you're he you've not done a wise thing to show yourself here. He left a bad name behind him. There's a ghost who comes sobbing about the house every now and then, the ghost of one to whom he did a wrong."

"Oh mercy *on* us!" cried Miss Searle in simple horror.

"Of course *you* know nothing of such things," he rather dryly allowed. "You're too sound a sleeper to hear the sobbing of ghosts."

"I'm sure I should like immensely to hear the sobbing of a ghost," said my friend, the light of his previous eagerness playing up into his eyes. "Why does it sob? I feel as if that were what we've come above all to learn."

Mr. Searle eyed his audience a moment gaugingly; he held the balance as to measure his resources. He wished to do justice to his theme. With the long finger-nails of his left hand nervously playing against the tinkling crystal of his wine-glass and his conscious eyes betraying that, small and strange as he sat there, he knew himself, to his pleasure and advantage, remarkably impressive, he dropped into our untutored minds the sombre legend of his house. "Mr. Clement Searle, from all I gather, was a young man of great talents but a weak disposition. His mother was left a widow early in life, with two sons, of whom he was the elder and more promising. She educated him with the greatest affection and care. Of course when he came to manhood she wished him to marry well. His means

were quite sufficient to enable him to overlook the
want of money in his wife; and Mrs. Searle selected a
young lady who possessed, as she conceived, every good
gift save a fortune—a fine proud handsome girl, the
daughter of an old friend, an old lover I suspect, of her
own. Clement, however, as it appeared, had either
chosen otherwise or was as yet unprepared to choose.
The young lady opened upon him in vain the battery
of her attractions; in vain his mother urged her cause.
Clement remained cold, insensible, inflexible. Mrs.
Searle had a character which appears to have gone out
of fashion in my family nowadays; she was a great
manager, a *maîtresse-femme*. A proud passionate imperious woman, she had had immense cares and ever
so many law-suits; they had sharpened her temper
and her will. She suspected that her son's affections
had another object, and this object she began to hate.
Irritated by his stubborn defiance of her wishes she
persisted in her purpose. The more she watched him
the more she was convinced he loved in secret. If he
loved in secret of course he loved beneath him. He
went about the place all sombre and sullen and brooding.
At last, with the rashness of an angry woman, she
threatened to bring the young lady of her choice—who,
by the way, seems to have been no shrinking blossom—
to stay in the house. A stormy scene was the result.
He threatened that if she did so he would leave the
country and sail for America. She probably disbelieved
him; she knew him to be weak, but she overrated his
weakness. At all events the rejected one arrived and
Clement Searle departed. On a dark December day
he took ship at Southampton. The two women,
desperate with rage and sorrow, sat alone in this big
house, mingling their tears and imprecations. A fortnight later, on Christmas Eve, in the midst of a great
snowstorm long famous in the country, something
happened that quickened their bitterness. A young
woman, battered and chilled by the storm, gained
entrance to the house, and, making her way into the
presence of the mistress and her guest, poured out her

tale. She was a poor curate's daughter out of some little hole in Gloucestershire. Clement Searle had loved her—loved her all too well! She had been turned out in wrath from her father's house; his mother at least might pity her—if not for herself then for the child she was soon to bring forth. But the poor girl had been a second time too trustful. The women, in scorn, in horror, with blows possibly, drove her forth again into the storm. In the storm she wandered and in the deep snow she died. Her lover, as you know, perished in that hard winter weather at sea; the news came to his mother late, but soon enough. We're haunted by the curate's daughter!"

Mr. Searle retailed this anecdote with infinite taste and point, the happiest art; when he ceased there was a pause of some moments. "Ah, well we may be!" Miss Searle then mournfully murmured.

Searle blazed up into enthusiasm. "Of course, you know"—with which he began to blush violently—"I should be sorry to claim any identity with the poor devil my faithless namesake. But I should be immensely gratified if the young lady's spirit, deceived by my resemblance, were to mistake me for her cruel lover. She's welcome to the comfort of it. What one can do in the case I shall be glad to do. But can a ghost haunt a ghost? I *am* a ghost!"

Mr. Searle stared a moment and then had a subtle sneer. "I could almost believe you are!"

"Oh brother—and cousin!" cried Miss Searle with the gentlest yet most appealing dignity. "How can you talk so horribly?"

The horrible talk, however, evidently possessed a potent magic for my friend; and his imagination, checked a while by the influence of his kinsman, began again to lead him a dance. From this moment he ceased to steer his frail bark, to care what he said or how he said it, so long as he expressed his passionate appreciation of the scene around him. As he kept up this strain I ceased even secretly to wish he wouldn't. I have wondered since that I shouldn't have been annoyed by the way he reverted constantly to himself. But a great frankness, for the time, makes its own law and a great passion its own channel. There was, moreover, an irresponsible indescribable effect of beauty in everything his lips uttered. Free alike from adulation and from envy, the essence of his discourse was a divine apprehension, a romantic vision free as the flight of Ariel, of the poetry of his companions' situation and their contrasted general irresponsiveness.

"How does the look of age come?" he suddenly broke out at dessert. "Does it come of itself, unobserved, unrecorded, unmeasured? Or do you woo it and set baits and traps for it, and watch it like the dawning brownness of a meerschaum pipe, and make it fast, when it appears, just where it peeps out, and light a votive taper beneath it and give thanks to it daily? Or do you forbid it and fight it and resist it, and yet feel it settling and deepening about you as irresistible as fate?"

"What the deuce is the man talking about?" said the smile of our host.

"I found a little grey hair this morning," Miss Searle incoherently prosed.

"Well, then, I hope you paid it every respect!" cried her visitor.

"I looked at it for a long time in my hand-glass," she answered with more presence of mind.

"Miss Searle can for many years to come afford to be amused at grey hairs," I interposed in the hope of some greater ease.

It had its effect. "Ten years from last Thursday I shall be forty-four," she almost comfortably smiled.

"Well, that's just what I am," said Searle. "If I had only come here ten years ago! I should have had more time to enjoy the feast, but I should have had less appetite. I needed first to get famished."

"Oh why did you wait for that?" his entertainer asked. "To think of these ten years that we might have been enjoying you!" At the vision of which waste and loss Mr. Searle had a fine shrill laugh.

"Well," my friend explained, "I always had a notion
—a stupid vulgar notion if there ever was one—that to
come abroad properly one had to have a pot of money.
My pot was too nearly empty.   At last I came with
my empty pot!"

Mr. Searle had a wait for delicacy, but he proceeded.
"You're reduced, you're—a—straitened?"

Our companion's very breath blew away the veil.
"Reduced to nothing.   Straitened to the clothes on
my back!"

"You don't say so!" said Mr. Searle with a large
vague gasp.   "Well—well—well!" he added in a voice
which might have meant everything or nothing; and
then, in his whimsical way, went on to finish a glass
of wine.   His searching eye, as he drank, met mine, and
for a moment we each rather deeply sounded the other,
to the effect no doubt of a slight embarrassment.   "And
you," he said by way of carrying this off—"how about
your wardrobe?"

"Oh his!" cried my friend; "his wardrobe's immense.
He could dress up a regiment!"   He had drunk more
champagne—I admit that the champagne was good—
than was from any point of view to have been desired.
He was rapidly drifting beyond any tacit dissuasion of
mine.   He was feverish and rash, and all attempt to
direct would now simply irritate him.   As we rose from
the table he caught my troubled look.   Passing his
arm for a moment into mine, "This is the great night!"
he strangely and softly said; "the night and the crisis
that will settle me."

Mr. Searle had caused the whole lower portion of the
house to be thrown open and a multitude of lights to
be placed in convenient and effective positions.   Such
a marshalled wealth of ancient candlesticks and flam-
beaux I had never beheld.   Niched against the dusky
wainscots, casting great luminous circles upon the
pendent stiffness of sombre tapestries, enhancing and
completing with admirable effect the variety and mystery
of the great ancient house, they seemed to people the
wide rooms, as our little group passed slowly from one

to another, with a dim expectant presence. We had thus, in spite of everything, a wonderful hour of it. Mr. Searle at once assumed the part of cicerone, and—I had not hitherto done him justice—Mr. Searle became almost agreeable. While I lingered behind with his sister he walked in advance with his kinsman. It was as if he had said: "Well, if you want the old place you shall have it—so far as the impression goes!" He spared us no thrill—I had almost said no pang—of that experience. Carrying a tall silver candlestick in his left hand, he raised it and lowered it and cast the light hither and thither, upon pictures and hangings and carvings and cornices. He knew his house to perfection. He touched upon a hundred traditions and memories, he threw off a cloud of rich reference to its earlier occupants. He threw off again, in his easy elegant way, a dozen—happily lighter—anecdotes. His relative attended with a brooding deference. Miss Searle and I meanwhile were not wholly silent.

"I suppose that by this time you and your cousin are almost old friends," I remarked.

She trifled a moment with her fan and then raised her kind small eyes. "Old friends—yet at the same time strangely new! My cousin, my cousin"—and her voice lingered on the word—"it seems so strange to call him my cousin after thinking these many years that I've no one in the world but my brother. But he's really so very odd!"

"It's not so much he as—well, as his situation, that deserves that name," I tried to reason.

"I'm so sorry for his situation. I wish I could help it in some way. He interests me so much." She gave a sweet-sounding sigh. "I wish I could have known him sooner—and better. He tells me he's but the shadow of what he used to be."

I wondered if he had been consciously practising on the sensibilities of this gentle creature. If he had I believed he had gained his point. But his position had in fact become to my sense so precarious that I hardly ventured to be glad. "His better self just now seems again to be taking shape," I said. "It will have been a good deed on your part if you help to restore him to all he ought to be."

She met my idea blankly. "Dear me, what can I do?"

"Be a friend to him. Let him like you, let him love you. I dare say you see in him now much to pity and to wonder at. But let him simply enjoy a while the grateful sense of your nearness and dearness. He'll be a better and stronger man for it, and then you can love him, you can esteem him, without restriction."

She fairly frowned for helplessness. "It's a hard part for poor stupid me to play!"

Her almost infantine innocence left me no choice but to be absolutely frank. "Did you ever play any part at all?"

She blushed as if I had been reproaching her with her insignificance. "Never! I think I've hardly lived."

"You've begun to live now perhaps. You've begun to care for something else than your old-fashioned habits. Pardon me if I seem rather meddlesome; you know we Americans are very rough and ready. It's a great moment. I wish you joy!"

"I could almost believe you're laughing at me. I feel more trouble than joy."

"Why do you feel trouble?"

She paused with her eyes fixed on our companions. "My cousin's arrival's a great disturbance," she said at last.

"You mean you did wrong in coming to meet him? In that case the fault's mine. He had no intention of giving you the opportunity."

"I certainly took too much on myself. But I can't find it in my heart to regret it. I never shall regret it! I did the only thing I *could*, heaven forgive me!"

"Heaven bless you, Miss Searle! Is any harm to come of it? I did the evil: let me bear the brunt!"

She shook her head gravely. "You don't know my brother!"

"The sooner I master the subject the better then," I said. I couldn't help relieving myself—at least by the tone of my voice—of the antipathy with which, decidedly, this gentleman had inspired me. "Not perhaps that we should get on so well together!" After which, as she turned away, "Are you *very* much afraid of him?" I added.

She gave me a shuddering sidelong glance. "He's looking at me!"

He was placed with his back to us, holding a large Venetian hand-mirror, framed in chiselled silver, which he had taken from a shelf of antiquities, just at such an angle that he caught the reflection of his sister's person. It was evident that I too was under his attention, and I was resolved I wouldn't be suspected for nothing. "Miss Searle," I said with urgency, "promise me something."

She turned upon me with a start and a look that seemed to beg me to spare her. "Oh don't ask me—please don't!" It was as if she were standing on the edge of a place where the ground had suddenly fallen away, and had been called upon to make a leap. I felt retreat was impossible, however, and that it was the greater kindness to assist her to jump.

"Promise me," I repeated.

Still with her eyes she protested. "Oh what a dreadful day!" she cried at last.

"Promise me to let him speak to you alone if he should ask you—any wish you may suspect on your brother's part notwithstanding."

She coloured deeply. "You mean he has something so particular to say?"

"Something so particular!"

"Poor cousin!"

"Well, poor cousin! But promise me."

"I promise," she said, and moved away across the long room and out of the door.

"You're in time to hear the most delightful story," Searle began to me as I rejoined him and his host. They were standing before an old sombre portrait of a lady in the dress of Queen Anne's time, whose ill-painted flesh-tints showed livid, in the candle-light, against her dark drapery and background. "This is Mrs. Margaret Searle—a sort of Beatrix Esmond— *qui se passait ses fantaisies.* She married a paltry Frenchman, a penniless fiddler, in the teeth of her whole family. Pretty Mrs. Margaret, you must have been a woman of courage! Upon my word, she looks like Miss Searle! But pray go on. What came of it all?"

Our companion watched him with an air of distaste for his boisterous homage and of pity for his crude imagination. But he took up the tale with an effective dryness: "I found a year ago, in a box of very old papers, a letter from the lady in question to a certain Cynthia Searle, her elder sister. It was dated from Paris and dreadfully ill-spelled. It contained a most passionate appeal for pecuniary assistance. She had just had a baby, she was starving and dreadfully neglected by her husband—she cursed the day she had left England. It was a most dismal production. I never heard she found means to return."

"So much for marrying a Frenchman!" I said sententiously.

Our host had one of his waits. "This is the only lady of the family who ever was taken in by an adventurer."

"Does Miss Searle know her history?" asked my friend with a stare at the rounded whiteness of the heroine's cheek.

"Miss Searle knows nothing!" said our host with expression.

"She shall know at least the tale of Mrs. Margaret," their guest returned; and he walked rapidly away in search of her.

Mr. Searle and I pursued our march through the lighted rooms. "You've found a cousin with a vengeance," I doubtless awkwardly enough laughed.

"Ah a vengeance?" my entertainer stiffly repeated.

"I mean that he takes as keen an interest in your annals and possessions as yourself."

"Oh exactly so! He tells me he's a bad invalid," he added in a moment. "I should never have supposed it."

"Within the past few hours he's a changed man. Your beautiful house, your extreme kindness, have refreshed him immensely."

Mr. Searle uttered the vague ejaculation with which self-conscious Britons so often betray the concussion of any especial courtesy of speech. But he followed this by a sudden odd glare and the sharp declaration: "I'm an honest man!" I was quite prepared to assent; but he went on with a fury of frankness, as if it were the first time in his life he had opened himself to anyone, as if the process were highly disagreeable and he were hurrying through it as a task. "An honest man, mind you! I know nothing about Mr. Clement Searle! I never expected to see him. He has been to me a—a—!" And here he paused to select a word which should vividly enough express what, for good or for ill, his kinsman represented. "He has been to me an Amazement! I've no doubt he's a most amiable man. You'll not deny, however, that he's a very extraordinary sort of person. I'm sorry he's ill. I'm sorry he's poor. He's my fiftieth cousin. Well and good. I'm an honest man. He shall not have it to say that he wasn't received at my house."

"He too, thank heaven, is an honest man!" I smiled.

"Why the devil then," cried Mr. Searle, turning almost fiercely on me, "has he put forward this underhand claim to my property?"

The question, quite ringing out, flashed backward a gleam of light upon the demeanour of our host and the suppressed agitation of his sister. In an instant the jealous gentleman revealed itself. For a moment I was so surprised and scandalised at the directness of his attack that I lacked words to reply. As soon as he had spoken indeed Mr. Searle appeared to feel he had been wanting in form. "Pardon me," he began afresh, "if I speak of this matter with heat. But I've been more disgusted than I can say to hear, as I heard this morning from my solicitor, of the extraordinary proceedings of Mr. Clement Searle. Gracious goodness, sir, for what does the man take me? He pretends to the Lord knows what fantastic admiration for my place. Let him then show his respect for it by not taking too many liberties! Let him, with his high-flown parade of loyalty, imagine a tithe of what *I* feel! I love my estate; it's my passion, my conscience, my life! Am I to divide it up at this time of day with a beggarly foreigner—a man without means, without appearance, without proof, a pretender, an adventurer, a chattering mountebank? I thought America boasted having lands for all men! Upon my soul, sir, I've never been so shocked in my life."

I paused for some moments before speaking, to allow his passion fully to expend itself and to flicker up again if it chose; for so far as I was concerned in the whole awkward matter I but wanted to deal with him discreetly. "Your apprehensions, sir," I said at last, "your not unnatural surprise, perhaps, at the candour of our interest, have acted too much on your nerves. You're attacking a man of straw, a creature of unworthy illusion; though I'm sadly afraid you've wounded a man of spirit and conscience. Either my friend has no valid claim on your estate, in which case your agitation is superfluous; or he *has* a valid claim——"

Mr. Searle seized my arm and glared at me; his pale face paler still with the horror of my suggestion, his great eyes of alarm glowing and his strange red hair erect and quivering. "A valid claim!" he shouted. "Let him try it—let him bring it into court!"

We had emerged into the great hall and stood facing the main doorway. The door was open into the portico, through the stone archway of which I saw the garden glitter in the blue light of a full moon. As the master of the house uttered the words I have just repeated my companion came slowly up into the porch from without, bareheaded, bright in the outer moonlight, dark in the shadow of the archway, and bright again in the lamplight at the entrance of the hall. As he crossed the threshold the butler made an appearance at the head of the staircase on our left, faltering visibly a moment at sight of Mr. Searle; after which, noting my friend, he gravely descended. He bore in his hand a small silver tray. On the tray, gleaming in the light of the suspended lamp, lay a folded note. Clement Searle came forward, staring a little and startled, I think, by some quick nervous prevision of a catastrophe. The butler applied the match to the train. He advanced to my fellow-visitor, all solemnly, with the offer of his missive. Mr. Searle made a movement as if to spring forward, but controlled himself. "Tottenham!" he called in a strident voice.

"Yes, sir!" said Tottenham, halting.

"Stand where you are. For whom is that note?"

"For Mr. Clement Searle," said the butler, staring straight before him and dissociating himself from everything.

"Who gave it to you?"

"Mrs. Horridge, sir." This personage, I afterwards learned, was our friend the housekeeper.

"Who gave it Mrs. Horridge?"

There was on Tottenham's part just an infinitesimal pause before replying.

"My dear sir," broke in Searle, his equilibrium, his ancient ease, completely restored by the crisis, "isn't that rather my business?"

"What happens in my house is my business, and detestable things seem to be happening." Our host, it was clear, now so furiously detested them that I was afraid he would snatch the bone of contention without more ceremony. "Bring me that thing!" he cried; on which Tottenham stiffly moved to obey.

"Really this is too much!" broke out my companion, affronted and helpless.

So indeed it struck me, and before Mr. Searle had time to take the note I possessed myself of it. "If you've no consideration for your sister let a stranger at least act for her." And I tore the disputed object into a dozen pieces.

"In the name of decency, what does this horrid business mean?" my companion quavered.

Mr. Searle was about to open fire on him, but at

that moment our hostess appeared on the staircase, summoned evidently by our high-pitched contentious voices. She had exchanged her dinner-dress for a dark wrapper, removed her ornaments and begun to disarrange her hair, a thick tress of which escaped from the comb. She hurried down with a pale questioning face. Feeling distinctly that, for ourselves, immediate departure was in the air, and divining Mr. Tottenham to be a person of a few deep-seated instincts and of much latent energy, I seized the opportunity to request him, *sotto voce*, to send a carriage to the door without delay. "And put up our things," I added.

Our host rushed at his sister and grabbed the white wrist that escaped from the loose sleeve of her dress. "What was in that note?" he quite hissed at her.

Miss Searle looked first at its scattered fragments and then at her cousin. "Did you read it?"

"No, but I thank you for it!" said Searle.

Her eyes, for an instant, communicated with his own as I think they had never, never communicated with any other source of meaning; then she transferred them to her brother's face, where the sense went out of them, only to leave a dull sad patience. But there was something even in this flat humility that seemed to him to mock him, so that he flushed crimson with rage and spite and flung her away. "You always were an idiot! Go to bed."

In poor Searle's face as well the gathered serenity had been by this time all blighted and distorted and the reflected brightness of his happy day turned to blank confusion. "Have I been dealing these three hours with a madman?" he woefully cried.

"A madman, yes, if you will! A man mad with the love of his home and the sense of its stability. I've held my tongue till now, but you've been too much for me. Who the devil are you, and what and why and whence?" the terrible little man continued. "From what paradise of fools do you come that you fancy I shall make over to you, for the asking, a part of my property and my life? I'm forsooth, you ridiculous person, to go shares with you? Prove your preposterous claim! There isn't *that* in it!" And he kicked one of the bits of paper on the floor.

Searle received this broadside gaping. Then turning away he went and seated himself on a bench against the wall and rubbed his forehead amazedly. I looked at my watch and listened for the wheels of our carriage.

But his kinsman was too launched to pull himself up. "Wasn't it enough that you should have plotted against my rights? Need you have come into my very house to intrigue with my sister?"

My friend put his two hands to his face. "Oh, oh, oh!" he groaned while Miss Searle crossed rapidly and dropped on her knees at his side.

"Go to bed, you fool!" shrieked her brother.

"Dear cousin," she said, "it's cruel you're to have so to think of us!"

"Oh I shall think of *you* as you'd like!" He laid a hand on her head.

"I believe you've done nothing wrong," she brought bravely out.

"I've done what I could," Mr. Searle went on—"but it's arrant folly to pretend to friendship when this abomination lies between us. You were welcome to my meat and my wine, but I wonder you could swallow them. The sight spoiled *my* appetite!" cried the master of Lackley with a laugh. "Proceed with your trumpery case! My people in London are instructed and prepared."

"I shouldn't wonder if your case had improved a good deal since you gave it up," I was moved to observe to Searle.

"Oho! you don't feign ignorance then?" and our insane entertainer shook his shining head at me. "It's very kind of you to give it up! Perhaps you'll also give up my sister!"

Searle sat staring in distress at his adversary. "Ah miserable man—I thought we had become such beautiful friends."

"Boh, you hypocrite!" screamed our host.

Searle seemed not to hear him. "Am I seriously expected," he slowly and painfully pursued, "to defend myself against the accusation of any real indelicacy—to prove I've done nothing underhand or impudent? Think what you please!" And he rose, with an effort, to his feet. "I know what *you* think!" he added to Miss Searle.

The wheels of the carriage resounded on the gravel, and at the same moment a footman descended with our two portmanteaux. Mr. Tottenham followed him with our hats and coats.

"Good God," our host broke out again, "you're not going away?"—an ejaculation that, after all that had happened, had the grandest comicality. "Bless my soul," he then remarked as artlessly, "of course you're going!"

"It's perhaps well," said Miss Searle with a great effort, inexpressibly touching in one for whom great efforts were visibly new and strange, "that I should tell you what my poor little note contained."

"That matter of your note, madam," her brother interrupted, "you and I will settle together!"

"Let me imagine all sorts of kind things!" Searle beautifully pleaded.

"Ah too much has been imagined!" she answered simply. "It was only a word of warning. It was to tell you to go. I knew something painful was coming."

He took his hat. "The pains and the pleasures of this day," he said to his kinsman, "I shall equally never forget. Knowing you," and he offered his hand to Miss Searle, "has been the pleasure of pleasures. I hoped something more might have come of it."

"A monstrous deal too much has come of it!" Mr. Searle irrepressibly declared.

His departing guest looked at him mildly, almost benignantly, from head to foot, and then with closed eyes and some collapse of strength, "I'm afraid so, I can't stand more," he went on. I gave him my arm and we crossed the threshold. As we passed out I heard Miss Searle break into loud weeping.

"We shall hear from each other yet, I take it!" her brother pursued, harassing our retreat.

My friend stopped, turning round on him fiercely. "You very impossible man!" he cried in his face.

"Do you mean to say you'll not prosecute?"—Mr. Searle kept it up. "I shall force you to prosecute! I shall drag you into court, and you shall be beaten—beaten—beaten!" Which grim reiteration followed us on our course.

We drove of course to the little wayside inn from which we had departed in the morning so unencumbered in all broad England, either with enemies or friends. My companion, as the carriage rolled along, seemed overwhelmed and exhausted. "What a beautiful horrible dream!" he confusedly wailed. "What a strange awakening! What a long long day! What a hideous scene! Poor me! Poor woman!" When we had resumed possession of our two little neighbouring rooms I asked him whether Miss Searle's note had been the result of anything that had passed between them on his going to rejoin her. "I found her on the terrace," he said, "walking restlessly up and down in the moonlight. I was greatly excited—I hardly know what I said. I asked her, I think, if she knew the story of Margaret Searle. She seemed frightened and troubled, and she used just the words her brother had used—'I know nothing.' For the moment, somehow, I felt as a man drunk. I stood before her and told her, with great emphasis, how poor Margaret had married a beggarly foreigner—all in obedience to her heart and in defiance to her family. As I talked the sheeted moonlight seemed to close about us, so that we stood there in a dream, in a world quite detached. She grew younger, prettier, more attractive—I found myself talking all kinds of nonsense. Before I knew it I had gone very far. I was taking her hand and calling her 'Margaret, dear Margaret!' She had said it was impossible, that she could do nothing, that she was a fool, a child, a slave. Then with a sudden sense—it was odd how it came over me there—of the reality of my connection with the place, I spoke of my claim against the estate. 'It exists,' I declared, 'but I've given it up. Be generous! Pay me for my sacrifice.' For an instant her face was radiant. 'If I marry you,' she asked, 'will it make everything right?' Of that I at once assured her—in our marriage the whole difficulty would melt away like a rain drop in the great sea. 'Our marriage!' she repeated in wonder; and the deep ring of her voice seemed to wake us up and show us our folly. 'I love you, but I shall never see you again,' she cried; and she hurried away with her face in her hands. I walked up and down the terrace for some moments, and then came in and met you. That's the only witchcraft I've used!"

The poor man was at once so roused and so shaken by the day's events that I believed he would get little sleep. Conscious on my own part that I shouldn't close my eyes, I but partly undressed, stirred my fire and sat down to do some writing. I heard the great clock in the little parlour below strike twelve, one, half-past one. Just as the vibration of this last stroke was dying on the air the door of communication with Searle's room was flung open and my companion stood on the threshold, pale as a corpse, in his night-shirt, shining like a phantom against the darkness behind him. "Look well at me!" he intensely gasped; "touch me, embrace me, revere me! You see a man who has seen a ghost!"

"Gracious goodness, what do you mean?"

"Write it down!" he went on. "There, take your pen. Put it into dreadful words. How do I look? Am I human? Am I pale? Am I red? Am I speaking English? A ghost, sir! Do you understand?"

I confess there came upon me by contact a kind of supernatural shock. I shall always feel by the whole communication of it that I too have seen a ghost. My first movement—I can smile at it now—was to spring to the door, close it quickly and turn the key upon the gaping blackness from which Searle had emerged. I seized his two hands; they were wet with

perspiration. I pushed my chair to the fire and forced
him to sit down in it; then I got on my knees and held
his hands as firmly as possible. They trembled and
quivered; his eyes were fixed save that the pupil dilated
and contracted with extraordinary force. I asked no
questions, but waited there, very curious for what he
would say. At last he spoke. "I'm not frightened,
but I'm—oh excited! This is life! This is living!
My nerves—my heart—my brain! They're throbbing
—don't you feel it? Do you tingle? Are you hot?
Are you cold? Hold me tight—tight—tight! I shall
tremble away into waves—into surges—and know all
the secrets of things and all the reasons and all the
mysteries!" He paused a moment and then went on:
"A woman—as clear as that candle: no, far clearer!
In a blue dress, with a black mantle on her head and a
little black muff. Young and wonderfully pretty, pale
and ill; with the sadness of all the women who ever
loved and suffered pleading and accusing in her wet-
looking eyes. God knows I never did any such thing!
But she took me for my elder, for the other Clement.
She came to me here as she would have come to me
there. She wrung her hands and she spoke to me.
'Marry me!' she moaned; 'marry me and put an end to
my shame!' I sat up in bed, just as I sit here, looked at
her, heard her—heard her voice melt away, watched
her figure fade away. Bless us and save us! Here
I be!"

I made no attempt either to explain or to criticise
this extraordinary passage. It's enough that I yielded
for the hour to the strange force of my friend's emotion.
On the whole I think my own vision was the more
interesting of the two. He beheld but the transient
irresponsible spectre—I beheld the human subject hot
from the spectral presence. Yet I soon recovered my
judgment sufficiently to be moved again to try to guard
him against the results of excitement and exposure.
It was easily agreed that he was not for the night to
return to his room, and I made him fairly comfortable
in his place by my fire. Wishing above all to preserve

him from a chill I removed my bedding and wrapped him in the blankets and counterpane. I had no nerves either for writing or for sleep; so I put out my lights, renewed the fuel and sat down on the opposite side of the hearth. I found it a great and high solemnity just to watch my companion. Silent, swathed and muffled to his chin, he sat rigid and erect with the dignity of his adventure. For the most part his eyes were closed; though from time to time he would open them with a steady expansion and stare, never blinking, into the flame, as if he again beheld without terror the image of the little woman with the muff. His cadaverous emaciated face, his tragic wrinkles intensified by the upward glow from the hearth, his distorted moustache, his extraordinary gravity and a certain fantastical air as the red light flickered over him, all reinforced his fine likeness to the vision-haunted knight of La Mancha when laid up after some grand exploit. The night passed wholly without speech. Toward its close I slept for half an hour. When I awoke the awakened birds had begun to twitter and Searle, unperturbed, sat staring at me. We exchanged a long look, and I felt with a pang that his glittering eyes had tasted their last of natural sleep. "How is it? Are you comfortable?" I nevertheless asked.

He fixed me for a long time without replying and then spoke with a weak extravagance and with such pauses between his words as might have represented the slow prompting of an inner voice. "You asked me when you first knew me what I was. 'Nothing,' I said, 'nothing of any consequence.' Nothing I've always supposed myself to be. But I've wronged myself —I'm a great exception. I'm a haunted man!"

If sleep had passed out of his eyes I felt with even a deeper pang that sanity had abandoned his spirit. From this moment I was prepared for the worst. There were in my friend, however, such confirmed habits of mildness that I found myself not in the least fearing he would prove unmanageable. As morning began fully to dawn upon us I brought our curious vigil to a close.

Searle was so enfeebled that I gave him my hands to help him out of his chair, and he retained them for some moments after rising to his feet, unable as he seemed to keep his balance. "Well," he said, "I've been once favoured, but don't think I shall be favoured again. I shall soon be myself as fit to 'appear' as any of them. I shall haunt the master of Lackley! It can only mean one thing—that they're getting ready for me on the other side of the grave."

When I touched the question of breakfast he replied that he had his breakfast in his pocket; and he drew from his travelling-bag a phial of morphine. He took a strong dose and went to bed. At noon I found him on foot again, dressed, shaved, much refreshed. "Poor fellow," he said, "you've got more than you bargained for—not only a man with a grievance but a man with a ghost. Well, it won't be for long!" It had of course promptly become a question whither we should now direct our steps. "As I've so little time," he argued for this, "I should like to see the best, the best alone." I answered that either for time or eternity I had always supposed Oxford to represent the English maximum, and for Oxford in the course of an hour we accordingly departed.

IV

Of that extraordinary place I shall not attempt to speak with any order or indeed with any coherence. It must ever remain one of the supreme gratifications of travel for any American aware of the ancient pieties of race. The impression it produces, the emotions it kindles in the mind of such a visitor, are too rich and various to be expressed in the halting rhythm of prose. Passing through the small oblique streets in which the long grey battered public face of the colleges seems to watch jealously for sounds that may break upon the stillness of study, you feel it the most dignified and most educated of cities. Over and through it all the great corporate fact of the University slowly throbs after the

fashion of some steady bass in a concerted piece or that
of the medieval mystical presence of the Empire in the
old States of Germany. The plain perpendicular of
the so mildly conventual fronts, masking blest seraglios
of culture and leisure, irritates the imagination scarce
less than the harem-walls of Eastern towns. Within
their arching portals, however, you discover more sacred
and sunless courts, and the dark verdure soothing
and cooling to bookish eyes. The grey-green quad-
rangles stand for ever open with a trustful hospitality.
The seat of the humanities is stronger in her own good
manners than in a marshalled host of wardens and
beadles. Directly after our arrival my friend and I
wandered forth in the luminous early dusk. We reached
the bridge that underspans the walls of Magdalen and
saw the eight-spired tower, delicately fluted and embossed, rise in temperate beauty—the perfect prose of
Gothic—wooing the eyes to the sky that was slowly
drained of day. We entered the low monkish doorway
and stood in the dim little court that nestles beneath
the tower, where the swallows niche more lovingly in
the tangled ivy than elsewhere in Oxford, and passed
into the quiet cloister and studied the small sculptured
monsters on the entablature of the arcade. I rejoiced
in every one of my unhappy friend's responsive vibra-
tions, even while feeling that they might as direfully
multiply as those that had preceded them. I may say
that from this time forward I found it difficult to distinguish in his company between the riot of fancy and
the labour of thought, or to fix the balance between
what he saw and what he imagined. He had already
begun playfully to exchange his identity for that of the
earlier Clement Searle, and he now delivered himself
almost wholly in the character of his old-time kinsman.

"*This* was my college, you know," he would almost
anywhere break out, applying the words wherever we
stood—"the sweetest and noblest in the whole place.
How often have I strolled in this cloister with my
intimates of the other world! They are all dead and
buried, but many a young fellow as we meet him, dark

or fair, tall or short, reminds me of the past age and the
early attachment. Even as we stand here, they say,
the whole thing feels about its massive base the murmurs
of the tide of time; some of the foundation-stones are
loosened, some of the breaches will have to be repaired.
Mine was the old unregenerate Oxford, the home of rank
abuses, of distinctions and privileges the most delicious
and invidious. What cared I, who was a perfect
gentleman and with my pockets full of money? I had
an allowance of a thousand a year."

It was at once plain to me that he had lost the little
that remained of his direct grasp on life and was
unequal to any effort of seeing things in their order.
He read my apprehension in my eyes and took pains
to assure me I was right. "I'm going straight down
hill. Thank heaven it's an easy slope, coated with
English turf and with an English churchyard at the
foot." The hysterical emotion produced by our late
dire misadventure had given place to an unruffled
calm in which the scene about us was reflected as in
an old-fashioned mirror. We took an afternoon walk
through Christ-Church meadow and at the river-bank
procured a boat which I pulled down the stream to
Iffley and to the slanting woods of Nuneham—the
sweetest flattest reediest stream-side landscape that
could be desired. Here of course we encountered the
scattered phalanx of the young, the happy generation,
clad in white flannel and blue, muscular fair-haired
magnificent fresh, whether floated down the current
by idle punts and lounging in friendly couples when not
in a singleness that nursed ambitions, or straining
together in rhythmic crews and hoarsely exhorted
from the near bank. When to the exhibition of so
much of the clearest joy of wind and limb we added
the great sense of perfumed protection shed by all the
enclosed lawns and groves and bowers, we felt that to
be young in such scholastic shades must be a double,
an infinite blessing. As my companion found himself
less and less able to walk we repaired in turn to a series
of gardens and spent long hours sitting in their greenest

places. They struck us as the fairest things in England and the ripest and sweetest fruit of the English system. Locked in their antique verdure, guarded, as in the case of New College, by gentle battlements of silver-grey, outshouldering the matted leafage of undisseverable plants, filled with nightingales and memories, a sort of chorus of tradition; with vaguely-generous youths sprawling bookishly on the turf as if to spare it the injury of their boot-heels, and with the great conservative college countenance appealing gravely from the restless outer world, they seem places to lie down on the grass in for ever, in the happy faith that life is all a green old English garden and time an endless summer afternoon. This charmed seclusion was especially grateful to my friend, and his sense of it reached its climax, I remember, on one of the last of such occasions and while we sat in fascinated *flânerie* over against the sturdy back of Saint John's. The wide discreetly-windowed wall here perhaps broods upon the lawn with a more effective air of property than elsewhere. Searle dropped into fitful talk and spun his humour into golden figures. Any passing undergraduate was a peg to hang a fable, every feature of the place a pretext for more embroidery.

"Isn't it all a delightful lie?" he wanted to know. "Mightn't one fancy this the very central point of the world's heart, where all the echoes of the general life arrive but to falter and die? Doesn't one feel the air just thick with arrested voices? It's well there should be such places, shaped in the interest of factitious needs, invented to minister to the book-begotten longing for a medium in which one may dream unwaked and believe unconfuted; to foster the sweet illusion that all's well in a world where so much is so damnable, all right and rounded, smooth and fair, in this sphere of the rough and ragged, the pitiful unachieved especially, and the dreadful uncommenced. The world's made—work's over. Now for leisure! England's safe—now for Theocritus and Horace, for lawn and sky! What a sense it all gives one of the composite life of the country

and of the essential furniture of its luckier minds!
Thank heaven they had the wit to send me here in the
other time. I'm not much visibly the braver perhaps,
but think how I'm the happier! The misty spires and
towers, seen far off on the level, have been all these
years one of the constant things of memory. Seriously,
what do the spires and towers do for these people? Are
they wiser, gentler, finer, cleverer? My diminished dignity
reverts in any case at moments to the naked background
of our own education, the deadly dry air in which we
gasp for impressions and comparisons. I assent to it all
with a sort of desperate calmness; I accept it with a
dogged pride. We're nursed at the opposite pole.
Naked come we into a naked world. There's a certain
grandeur in the lack of decorations, a certain heroic
strain in that young imagination of ours which finds
nothing made to its hands, which has to invent its own
traditions and raise high into our morning-air, with a
ringing hammer and nails, the castles in which we dwell.
Noblesse oblige—Oxford must damnably do so. What
a horrible thing not to rise to such examples! If you
pay the pious debt to the last farthing of interest you
may go through life with her blessing; but if you let
it stand unhonoured you're a worse barbarian than we!
But for the better or worse, in a myriad private hearts,
think how she must be loved! How the youthful
sentiment of mankind seems visibly to brood upon
her! Think of the young lives now taking colour in
her cloisters and halls. Think of the centuries' tale of
dead lads—dead alike with the end of the young days
to which these haunts were a present world, and the
close of the larger lives which the general mother-scene
has dropped into less bottomless traps. What are those
two young fellows kicking their heels over on the grass
there? One of them has the *Saturday Review*; the
other—upon my word—the other has Artemus Ward!
Where do they live, how do they live, to what end
do they live? Miserable boys! How can they read
Artemus Ward under those windows of Elizabeth?
What do you think loveliest in all Oxford? The poetry

of certain windows. Do you see that one yonder, the second of those lesser bays, with the broken cornice and the lattice? That used to be the window of my bosom friend a hundred years ago. Remind me to tell you the story of that broken cornice. Don't pretend it's not a common thing to have one's bosom friend at another college. Pray was I committed to common things? He was a charming fellow. By the way he was a good deal like you. Of course his cocked hat, his long hair in a black ribbon, his cinnamon velvet suit and his flowered waistcoat made a difference. We gentlemen used to wear swords."

There was really the touch of grace in my poor friend's divagations—the disheartened dandy had so positively turned rhapsodist and seer. I was particularly struck with his having laid aside the diffidence and self-consciousness of the first days of our acquaintance. He had become by this time a disembodied observer and critic; the shell of sense, growing daily thinner and more transparent, transmitted the tremor of his quickened spirit. He seemed to pick up acquaintances, in the course of our contemplations, merely by putting out his hand. If I left him for ten minutes I was sure to find him on my return in earnest conversation with some affable wandering scholar. Several young men with whom he had thus established relations invited him to their rooms and entertained him, as I gathered, with rather rash hospitality. For myself, I chose not to be present at these symposia; I shrank partly from being held in any degree responsible for his extravagance, partly from the pang of seeing him yield to champagne and an admiring circle. He reported such adventures with less keen a complacency than I had supposed he might use, but a certain method in his madness, a certain dignity in his desire to fraternise, appeared to save him from mischance. If they didn't think him a harmless lunatic they certainly thought him a celebrity of the Occident. Two things, however, grew evident—that he drank deeper than was good for him and that the flagrant freshness of his young patrons rather interfered with his predetermined sense of the element of finer romance. At the same time it completed his knowledge of the place. Making the acquaintance of several tutors and fellows, he dined in hall in half a dozen colleges, alluding afterwards to these banquets with religious unction. One evening after a participation indiscreetly prolonged he came back to the hotel in a cab, accompanied by a friendly undergraduate and a physician and looking deadly pale. He had swooned away on leaving table and remained so rigidly unconscious as much to agitate his banqueters. The following twenty-four hours he of course spent in bed, but on the third day declared himself strong enough to begin afresh. On his reaching the street his strength once more forsook him, so that I insisted on his returning to his room. He besought me with tears in his eyes not to shut him up. "It's my last chance—I want to go back for an hour to that garden of Saint John's. Let me eat and drink—to-morrow I die." It seemed to me possible that with a Bath-chair the expedition might be accomplished. The hotel, it appeared, possessed such a convenience, which was immediately produced. It became necessary hereupon that we should have a person to propel the chair. As there was no one on the spot at liberty I was about to perform the office; but just as my patient had got seated and wrapped —he now had a perpetual chill—an elderly man emerged from a lurking-place near the door and, with a formal salute, offered to wait upon the gentleman. We assented, and he proceeded solemnly to trundle the chair before him. I recognised him as a vague personage whom I had observed to lounge shyly about the doors of the hotels, at intervals during our stay, with a depressed air of wanting employment and a poor semblance of finding it. He had once indeed in a half-hearted way proposed himself as an amateur cicerone for a tour through the colleges; and I now, as I looked at him, remembered with a pang that I had too curtly declined his ministrations. Since then his shyness, apparently, had grown less or his misery greater, for it was with a

strange grim avidity that he now attached himself to
our service. He was a pitiful image of shabby gentility
and the dinginess of "reduced circumstances." He
would have been, I suppose, some fifty years of age; but
his pale haggard unwholesome visage, his plaintive
drooping carriage and the irremediable disarray of his
apparel seemed to add to the burden of his days and
tribulations. His eyes were weak and bloodshot, his
bold nose was sadly compromised, and his reddish
beard, largely streaked with grey, bristled under a
month's neglect of the razor. In all this rusty forlorn-
ness lurked a visible assurance of our friend's having
known better days. Obviously he was the victim of
some fatal depreciation in the market value of pure
gentility. There had been something terribly affecting
in the way he substituted for the attempt to touch the
greasy rim of his antiquated hat some such bow as one
man of the world might make another. Exchanging
a few words with him as we went I was struck with the
decorum of his accent. His fine whole voice should
have been congruously cracked.

"Take me by some long roundabout way," said
Searle, "so that I may see as many college-walls as
possible."

"You know," I asked of our attendant, "all these
wonderful ins and outs?"

"I ought to, sir," he said, after a moment, with
pregnant gravity. And as we were passing one of the
colleges, "That used to be my place," he added.

At these words Searle desired him to stop and come
round within sight. "You say that's *your* college?"

"The place might deny me, sir; but heaven forbid
I should seem to take it ill of her. If you'll allow me
to wheel you into the quad I'll show you my windows
of thirty years ago."

Searle sat staring, his huge pale eyes, which now
left nothing else worth mentioning in his wasted face,
filled with wonder and pity. "If you'll be so kind,"
he said with great deference. But just as this per-
verted product of a liberal education was about to

propel him across the threshold of the court he turned about, disengaged the mercenary hands, with one of his own, from the back of the chair, drew their owner alongside and turned to me. "While we're here, my dear fellow," he said, "be so good as to perform this service. You understand?" I gave our companion a glance of intelligence and we resumed our way. The latter showed us his window of the better time, where a rosy youth in a scarlet smoking-fez now puffed a cigarette at the open casement. Thence we proceeded into the small garden, the smallest, I believe, and certainly the sweetest, of all the planted places of Oxford. I pushed the chair along to a bench on the lawn, turned it round toward the front of the college and sat down by it on the grass. Our attendant shifted mournfully from one foot to the other, his patron eyeing him open-mouthed. At length Searle broke out: "God bless my soul, sir, you don't suppose I expect you to stand! There's an empty bench."

"Thank you," said our friend, who bent his joints to sit.

"You English are really fabulous! I don't know whether I most admire or most abominate you! Now tell me: who are you? what are you? what brought you to this?"

The poor fellow blushed up to his eyes, took off his hat and wiped his forehead with an indescribable fabric drawn from his pocket. "My name's Rawson, sir. Beyond that it's a long story."

"I ask out of sympathy," said Searle. "I've a fellow-feeling. If you're a poor devil I'm a poor devil as well."

"I'm the poorer devil of the two," said the stranger with an assurance for once presumptuous.

"Possibly. I suppose an English poor devil's the poorest of all poor devils. And then you've fallen from a height. From a gentleman commoner—is that what they called you?—to a propeller of Bath-chairs. Good heavens, man, the fall's enough to kill you!"

"I didn't take it all at once, sir. I dropped a bit one time and a bit another."

"That's me, that's me!" cried Searle with all his seriousness.

"And now," said our friend, "I believe I can't drop any farther."

"My dear fellow"—and Searle clasped his hand and shook it—"I too am at the very bottom of the hole."

Mr. Rawson lifted his eyebrows. "Well, sir, there's a difference between sitting in such a pleasant convenience and just trudging behind it!"

"Yes—there's a shade. But I'm at my last gasp, Mr. Rawson."

"I'm at my last penny, sir."

"Literally, Mr. Rawson?"

Mr. Rawson shook his head with large loose bitterness. "I've almost come to the point of drinking my beer and buttoning my coat figuratively; but I don't talk in figures."

Fearing the conversation might appear to achieve something like gaiety at the expense of Mr. Rawson's troubles, I took the liberty of asking him, with all consideration, how he made a living.

"I don't make a living," he answered with tearful eyes; "I can't make a living. I've a wife and three children—and all starving, sir. You wouldn't believe what I've come to. I sent my wife to her mother's, who can ill afford to keep her, and came to Oxford a week ago, thinking I might pick up a few half-crowns by showing people about the colleges. But it's no use. I haven't the assurance. I don't look decent. They want a nice little old man with black gloves and a clean shirt and a silver-headed stick. What do I look as if I knew about Oxford, sir?"

"Mercy on us," cried Searle, "why didn't you speak to us before?"

"I wanted to; half a dozen times I've been on the point of it. I knew you were Americans."

"And Americans are rich!" cried Searle, laughing. "My dear Mr. Rawson, American as I am I'm living on charity."

"And I'm exactly not, sir! There it is. I'm dying

for the lack of that same. You say you're a pauper, but it takes an American pauper to go bowling about in a Bath-chair. America's an easy country."

"Ah me!" groaned Searle. "Have I come to the most delicious corner of the ancient world to hear the praise of Yankeeland?"

"Delicious corners are very well, and so is the ancient world," said Mr. Rawson; "but one may sit here hungry and shabby, so long as one isn't too shabby, as well as elsewhere. You'll not persuade me that it's not an easier thing to keep afloat yonder than here. I wish *I* were in Yankeeland, that's all!" he added with feeble force. Then brooding for a moment on his wrongs: "Have you a bloated brother? or you, sir? It matters little to you. But it has mattered to me with a vengeance! Shabby as I sit here I can boast that advantage—as he his five thousand a year. Being but a twelvemonth my elder he swaggers while I go thus. There's old England for you! A very pretty place for *him*!"

"Poor old England!" said Searle softly.

"Has your brother never helped you?" I asked.

"A five-pound note now and then! Oh I don't say there haven't been times when I haven't inspired an irresistible sympathy. I've not been what I should. I married dreadfully out of the way. But the devil of it is that he started fair and I started foul; with the tastes, the desires, the needs, the sensibilities of a gentleman—and not another blessed 'tip.' I can't afford to live in England."

"*This* poor gentleman fancied a couple of months ago that he couldn't afford to live in America," I fondly explained.

"I'd 'swap'—do you call it?—chances with him!" And Mr. Rawson looked quaintly rueful over his freedom of speech.

Searle sat supported there with his eyes closed and his face twitching for violent emotion, and then of a sudden had a glare of gravity. "My friend, you're a dead failure! Be judged! Don't talk about 'swapping.'"

Don't talk about chances. Don't talk about fair starts and false starts. I'm at that point myself that I've a right to speak. It lies neither in one's chance nor one's start to make one a success; nor in anything one's brother—however bloated—can do or can undo. It lies in one's character. You and I, sir, have *had* no character—that's very plain. We've been weak, sir; as weak as water. Here we are for it—sitting staring in each other's faces and reading our weakness in each other's eyes. We're of no importance whatever, Mr. Rawson!"

Mr. Rawson received this sally with a countenance in which abject submission to the particular affirmed truth struggled with the comparative propriety of his general rebellion against fate. In the course of a minute a due self-respect yielded to the warm comfortable sense of his being relieved of the cares of an attitude. "Go on, sir, go on," he said. "It's wholesome doctrine." And he wiped his eyes with what seemed his sole remnant of linen.

"Dear, dear," sighed Searle, "I've made you cry! Well, we speak as from man to man. I should be glad to think you had felt for a moment the sidelight of that great undarkening of the spirit which precedes —which precedes the grand illumination of death."

Mr. Rawson sat silent a little, his eyes fixed on the ground and his well-cut nose but the more deeply dyed by his agitation. Then at last looking up: "You're a very good-natured man, sir, and you'll never persuade me you don't come of a kindly race. Say what you please about a chance; when a man's fifty—degraded, penniless, a husband and father—a chance to get on his legs again is not to be despised. Something tells me that my luck may be in your country—which has brought luck to so many. I can come on the parish here of course, but I don't want to come on the parish. Hang it, sir, I want to hold up my head. I see thirty years of life before me yet. If only by God's help I could have a real change of air! It's a fixed idea of mine. I've had it for the last ten years. It's not that I'm a low radical.

Oh I've no vulgar opinions. Old England's good enough for me, but I'm not good enough for old England. I'm a shabby man that wants to get out of a room full of staring gentlefolk. I'm for ever put to the blush. It's a perfect agony of spirit; everything reminds me of my younger and better self. The thing for me would be a cooling cleansing plunge into the unknowing and the unknown! I lie awake thinking of it."

Searle closed his eyes, shivering with a long-drawn tremor which I hardly knew whether to take for an expression of physical or of mental pain. In a moment I saw it was neither. "Oh my country, my country, my country!" he murmured in a broken voice; and then sat for some time abstracted and lost. I signalled our companion that it was time we should bring our small session to a close, and he, without hesitating, possessed himself of the handle of the Bath-chair and pushed it before him. We had got half-way home before Searle spoke or moved. Suddenly in the High Street, as we passed a chop-house from whose open doors we caught a waft of old-fashioned cookery and other restorative elements, he motioned us to halt. "This is my last five pounds"—and he drew a note from his pocket-book. "Do me the favour, Mr. Rawson, to accept it. Go in there and order the best dinner they can give you. Call for a bottle of Burgundy and drink it to my eternal rest!"

Mr. Rawson stiffened himself up and received the gift with fingers momentarily irresponsive. But Mr. Rawson had the nerves of a gentleman. I measured the spasm with which his poor dispossessed hand closed upon the crisp paper, I observed his empurpled nostril convulsive under the other solicitation. He crushed the crackling note in his palm with a passionate pressure and jerked a spasmodic bow. "I shall not do you the wrong, sir, of anything but the best!" The next moment the door swung behind him.

Searle sank again into his apathy, and on reaching the hotel I helped him to get to bed. For the rest of the day he lay without motion or sound and beyond reach of any appeal. The doctor, whom I had constantly in attendance, was sure his end was near. He expressed great surprise that he should have lasted so long; he must have been living for a month on the very dregs of his strength. Toward evening, as I sat by his bedside in the deepening dusk, he roused himself with a purpose I had vaguely felt gathering beneath his stupor. "My cousin, my cousin," he said confusedly. "Is she here?" It was the first time he had spoken of Miss Searle since our retreat from her brother's house, and he continued to ramble. "I was to have married her. What a dream! That day was like a string of verses — rhymed hours. But the last verse is bad measure. What's the rhyme to 'love'? *Above!* Was she a simple woman, a kind sweet woman? Or have I only dreamed it? She had the healing gift; her touch would have cured my madness. I want you to do something. Write three lines, three words: 'Goodbye; remember me; be happy.'" And then after a long pause: "It's strange a person in my state should have a wish. Why should one eat one's breakfast the day one's hanged? What a creature is man! What a farce is life! Here I lie, worn down to a mere throbbing fever-point; I breathe and nothing more, and yet I *desire!* My desire lives. If I could see her! Help me out with it and let me die."

Half an hour later, at a venture, I dispatched by post a note to Miss Searle: "*Your cousin is rapidly sinking. He asks to see you.*" I was conscious of a certain want of consideration in this act, since it would bring her great trouble and yet no power to face the trouble; but out of her distress I fondly hoped a sufficient force might be born. On the following day my friend's exhaustion had become so great that I began to fear his intelligence altogether broken up. But toward evening he briefly rallied, to maunder about many things, confounding in a sinister jumble the memories of the past weeks and those of bygone years. "By the way," he said suddenly, "I've made no will. I haven't much to bequeath. Yet I have something." He had been playing listlessly with a large signet-ring on his left hand, which he now tried to draw off. "I leave you this"—working it round and round vainly—"if you can get it off. What enormous knuckles! There must be such knuckles in the mummies of the Pharaohs. Well, when I'm gone——! No, I leave you something more precious than gold—the sense of a great kindness. But I've a little gold left. Bring me those trinkets." I placed on the bed before him several articles of jewellery, relics of early foppery: his watch and chain, of great value, a locket and seal, some odds and ends of goldsmith's work. He trifled with them feebly for some moments, murmuring various names and dates associated with them. At last, looking up with clearer interest, "What has become," he asked, "of Mr. Rawson?"

"You want to see him?"

"How much are these things worth?" he went on without heeding me. "How much would they bring?" And he weighed them in his weak hands. "They're pretty heavy. Some hundred or so? Oh I'm richer than I thought! Rawson—Rawson—you want to get out of this awful England?"

I stepped to the door and requested the servant whom I kept in constant attendance in our adjacent sitting-room to send and ascertain if Mr. Rawson were on the premises. He returned in a few moments, introducing our dismal friend. Mr. Rawson was pale even to his nose and derived from his unaffectedly concerned state an air of some distinction. I led him up to the bed. In Searle's eyes, as they fell on him, there shone for a moment the light of a human message.

"Lord have mercy!" gasped Mr. Rawson.

"My friend," said Searle, "there's to be one American the less—so let there be at the same time one the more. At the worst you'll be as good a one as I. Foolish me! Take these battered relics; you can sell them; let them help you on your way. They're gifts and mementoes, but this is a better use. Heaven speed you! May America be kind to you. Be kind, at the last, to your own country!"

"Really this is too much; I can't," the poor man
protested, almost scared and with tears in his eyes.
"Do come round and get well and I'll stop here. I'll
stay with you and wait on you."

"No, I'm booked for my journey, you for yours. I
hope you don't mind the voyage."

Mr. Rawson exhaled a groan of helpless gratitude,
appealing piteously from so strange a windfall. "It's
like the angel of the Lord who bids people in the Bible
to rise and flee!"

Searle had sunk back upon his pillow, quite used up;
I led Mr. Rawson back into the sitting-room, where
in three words I proposed to him a rough valuation of
our friend's trinkets. He assented with perfect good-
breeding; they passed into my possession and a second
bank-note into his.

From the collapse into which this wondrous exercise
of his imagination had plunged him my charge then
gave few signs of being likely to emerge. He breathed,
as he had said, and nothing more. The twilight
deepened; I lighted the night-lamp. The doctor sat
silent and official at the foot of the bed; I resumed my
constant place near the head. Suddenly our patient
opened his eyes wide. "She'll not come," he murmured.
"Amen! she's an English sister." Five minutes passed;
he started forward. "She's come, she's here!" he
confidently quavered. His words conveyed to my mind
so absolute an assurance that I lightly rose and passed
into the sitting-room. At the same moment, through
the opposite door, the servant introduced a lady. A
lady, I say; for an instant she was simply such—tall,
pale, dressed in deep mourning. The next instant I
had uttered her name—"Miss Searle!" She looked
ten years older.

She met me with both hands extended and an
immense question in her face. "He has just announced
you," I said. And then with a fuller consciousness of
the change in her dress and countenance: "What has
happened?"

"Oh, death, death!" she wailed. "You and I are left."

There came to me with her words a sickening shock, the sense of poetic justice somehow cheated, defeated. "Your brother?" I panted.

She laid her hand on my arm and I felt its pressure deepen as she spoke. "He was thrown from his horse in the park. He died on the spot. Six days have passed. Six months!"

She accepted my support and a moment later we had entered the room and approached the bedside, from which the doctor withdrew. Searle opened his eyes and looked at her from head to foot. Suddenly he seemed to make out her mourning. "Already!" he cried audibly and with a smile, as I felt, of pleasure.

She dropped on her knees and took his hand. "Not for you, cousin," she whispered. "For my poor brother."

He started, in all his deathly longitude, as with a galvanic shock. "Dead! *He* dead! Life itself!" And then after a moment and with a slight rising inflection: "You're free?"

"Free, cousin. Too sadly free. And now—*now*—with what use for freedom?"

He looked steadily into her eyes, dark in the heavy shadow of her musty mourning-veil. "For me wear colours!"

In a moment more death had come, the doctor had silently attested it, and she had burst into sobs.

We buried him in the little churchyard in which he had expressed the wish to lie; beneath one of the blackest and widest of English yews and the little tower than which none in all England has a softer and hoarier grey. A year has passed; Miss Searle, I believe, has begun to wear colours.

THE HILTONS' HOLIDAY [1]

By SARAH ORNE JEWETT (1849–1909)

I

THERE was a bright, full moon in the clear sky, and the sunset was still shining faintly in the west. Dark woods stood all about the old Hilton farmhouse, save down the hill, westward, where lay the shadowy fields which John Hilton, and his father before him, had cleared and tilled with much toil—the small fields to which they had given the industry and even affection of their honest lives.

John Hilton was sitting on the doorstep of his house. As he moved his head in and out of the shadows, turning now and then to speak to his wife, who sat just within the doorway, one could see his good face, rough and somewhat unkempt, as if he were indeed a creature of the shady woods and brown earth, instead of the noisy town. It was late in the long spring evening, and he had just come from the lower field as cheerful as a boy, proud of having finished the planting of his potatoes.

"I had to do my last row mostly by feelin'," he said to his wife. "I'm proper glad I pushed through, an' went back an' ended off after supper. 'Twould have taken me a good part o' to-morrow mornin', an' broke my day."

"'Tain't no use for ye to work yourself all to pieces, John," answered the woman, quickly. "I declare it does seem harder than ever that we couldn't have kep' our boy; he'd been comin' fourteen years old this fall,

[1] From the *Century Magazine*, September 1893: copyright, 1893, by the Century Company. Copyright, 1895, by Houghton Mifflin Co., and republished by special arrangement and permission from their volume, *The Life of Nancy* (1895), by Sarah Orne Jewett.

most a grown man, and he'd work right 'longside of ye now the whole time.''

"'Twas hard to lose him; I do seem to miss little John,'' said the father, sadly. "I expect there was reasons why 'twas best. I feel able an' smart to work; my father was a girt strong man, an' a monstrous worker afore me. 'Tain't that; but I was thinkin' myself to-day what a sight o' company the boy would ha' been. You know, small's he was, how I could trust him to leave anywheres with the team, and how he'd beseech to go with me wherever I was goin'; always right in my tracks I used to tell 'em. Poor little John, for all he was so young he had a great deal o' judgment; he'd ha' made a likely man.''

The mother sighed heavily as she sat within the shadow.

"But then there's the little girls, a sight o' help an' company,'' urged the father, eagerly, as if it were wrong to dwell upon sorrow and loss. "Katy, she's most as good as a boy, except that she ain't very rugged. She's a real little farmer, she's helped me a sight this spring; an' you've got Susan Ellen, that makes a complete little housekeeper for ye as far as she's learnt. I don't see but we're better off than most folks, each on us having a workmate.''

"That's so, John,'' acknowledged Mrs. Hilton, wist-fully, beginning to rock steadily in her straight splint-bottom chair. It was always a good sign when she rocked.

"Where be the little girls so late?'' asked their father. "'Tis gettin' long past eight o'clock. I don't know when we've all set up so late, but it's so kind o' summer-like an' pleasant. Why, where be they gone?''

"I've told ye; only over to Becker's folks,'' answered the mother. "I don't see myself what keeps 'em so late; they beseeched me after supper till I let 'em go. They're all in a dazzle with the new teacher; she asked 'em to come over. They say she's unusual smart with 'rethmetic, but she has a kind of gorpen look to me. She's goin' to give Katy some pieces for her doll, but

I told Katy she ought to be ashamed wantin' dolls' pieces, big as she's gittin' to be. I don't know's she ought, though; she ain't but nine this summer."

"Let her take her comfort," said the kind-hearted man. "Them things draws her to the teacher, an' makes them acquainted. Katy's shy with new folks, more so'n Susan Ellen, who's of the business kind. Katy's shy-feelin' and wishful."

"I don't know but she is," agreed the mother slowly. "Ain't it sing'lar how well acquainted you be with that one, an' I with Susan Ellen? 'Twas always so from the first. I'm doubtful sometimes our Katy ain't one that'll be like to get married—anyways not about here. She lives right with herself, but Susan Ellen ain't nothin' when she's alone, she's always after company; all the boys is waitin' on her a'ready. I ain't afraid but she'll take her pick when the time comes. I expect to see Susan Ellen well settled—she feels grown up now—but Katy don't care one mite 'bout none o' them things. She wants to be rovin' out o' doors. I do believe she'd stand an' hark to a bird the whole forenoon."

"Perhaps she'll grow up to be a teacher," suggested John Hilton. "She takes to her books more'n the other one. I should like one on 'em to be a teacher same's my mother was. They're good girls as anybody's got."

"So they be," said the mother, with unusual gentleness, and the creak of her rocking-chair was heard, regular as the ticking of a clock. The night breeze stirred in the great woods, and the sound of a brook that went falling down the hillside grew louder and louder. Now and then one could hear the plaintive chirp of a bird. The moon glittered with whiteness like a winter moon, and shone upon the low-roofed house until its small window-panes gleamed like silver, and one could almost see the colours of a blooming bush of lilac that grew in a sheltered angle by the kitchen door. There was an incessant sound of frogs in the lowlands.

"Be you sound asleep, John?" asked the wife presently.

"I don't know but what I was a'most," said the tired

man, starting a little. "I should laugh if I was to fall sound asleep right here on the step; 'tis the bright night, I expect, makes my eyes feel heavy, an' 'tis so peaceful. I was up an' dressed a little past four an' out to work. Well, well!" and he laughed sleepily and rubbed his eyes. "Where's the little girls? I'd better step along an' meet 'em."

"I wouldn't just yet; they'll get home all right, but 'tis late for 'em certain. I don't want 'em keepin' Mis' Becker's folks up neither. There, le's wait a few minutes," urged Mrs. Hilton.

"I've be'n a-thinkin' all day I'd like to give the child'n some kind of a treat," said the father, wide awake now. "I hurried up my work 'cause I had it so in mind. They don't have the opportunities some do, an' I want 'em to know the world, an' not stay right here on the farm like a couple o' bushes."

"They're a sight better off not to be so full o' notions as some is," protested the mother, suspiciously.

"Certain," answered the farmer; "but they're good, bright child'n, an' commencin' to take a sight o' notice. I want 'em to have all we can give 'em. I want 'em to see how other folks does things."

"Why, so do I"—here the rocking-chair stopped ominously—"but so long's they're contented——"

"Contented ain't all in this world; hopper-toads may have that quality an' spend all their time a-blinkin'. I don't know's bein' contented is all there is to look for in a child. Ambition's somethin' to me."

"Now you've got your mind on to some plot or other." (The rocking-chair began to move again.) "Why can't you talk right out?"

"'Tain't nothin' special," answered the good man, a little ruffled; he was never prepared for his wife's mysterious powers of divination. "Well there, you do find things out the master! I only thought perhaps I'd take 'em to-morrow, an' go off somewhere if 'twas a good day. I've been promisin' for a good while I'd take 'em to Topham Corners; they've never been there since they was very small."

"I believe you want a good time yourself. You ain't never got over bein' a boy." Mrs. Hilton seemed much amused. "There, go if you want to an' take 'em; they've got their summer hats an' new dresses. I don't know o' nothin' that stands in the way. I should sense it better if there was a circus or anythin' to go to. Why don't you wait an' let the girls pick 'em some strawberries or nice ros'berries, and then they could take an' sell 'em to the stores?"

John Hilton reflected deeply. "I should like to get me some good yellow-turnip seed to plant late. I ain't more'n satisfied with what I've been gettin' o' late years o' Ira Speed. An' I'm goin' to provide me with a good hoe; mine's gettin' wore out an' all shackly. I can't seem to fix it good."

"Them's excuses," observed Mrs. Hilton, with friendly tolerance. "You just cover up the hoe with somethin', if you get it—I would. Ira Speed's so jealous he'll remember it of you this twenty year, your goin' an' buyin' a new hoe o' anybody but him."

"I've always thought 'twas a free country," said John Hilton, soberly. "I don't want to vex Ira neither; he favours us all he can in trade. 'Tis difficult for him to spare a cent, but he's as honest as daylight."

At this moment there was a sudden sound of young voices, and a pair of young figures came out from the shadow of the woods into the moon-lighted open space. An old cock crowed loudly from his perch in the shed, as if he were a herald of royalty. The little girls were hand in hand, and a brisk young dog capered about them as they came.

"Wa'n't it dark gittin' home through the woods this time o' night?" asked the mother, hastily, and not without reproach.

"I don't love to have you gone so late; mother an' me was timid about ye, and you've kep' Mis' Becker's folks up, I expect," said their father, regretfully. "I don't want to have it said that my little girls ain't got good manners."

"The teacher had a party," chirped Susan Ellen, the

elder of the two children. "Goin' home from school she asked the Grover boys, an' Mary an' Sarah Speed. An' Mis' Becker was real pleasant to us: she passed round some cake, an' handed us sap sugar on one of her best plates, an' we played games an' sung some pieces too. Mis' Becker thought we did real well. I can pick out most of a tune on the cabinet organ; teacher says she'll give me lessons."

"I want to know, dear!" exclaimed John Hilton.

"Yes, an' we played Copenhagen, an' took sides spellin', an' Katy beat everybody spellin' there was there."

Katy had not spoken, she was not so strong as her sister, and while Susan Ellen stood a step or two away addressing her eager little audience, Katy had seated herself close to her father on the doorstep. He put his arm around her shoulder, and drew her close to his side, where she stayed.

"Ain't you got nothin' to tell, daughter?" he asked, looking down fondly, and Katy gave a pleased little sigh for answer.

"Tell 'em what's goin' to be the last day o' school, and about our trimmin' the schoolhouse," she said, and Susan Ellen gave the programme in most spirited fashion.

"'Twill be a great time," said the mother, when she had finished. "I don't see why folks want to go trapesin' off to strange places when such things is happenin' right about 'em." But the children did not observe her mysterious air. "Come, you must step yourselves right to bed."

They all went into the dark, warm house, the bright moon shone upon it steadily all night, and the lilac flowers were shaken by no breath of wind until the early dawn.

II

The Hiltons always waked early. So did their neighbours, the crows and song-sparrows and robins, the light-footed foxes and squirrels in the woods.

When John Hilton waked, before five o'clock, an hour later than usual because he had sat up so late, he opened the house door and came out into the yard, crossing the short green turf hurriedly as if the day were too far spent for any loitering. The magnitude of the plan for taking a whole day of pleasure confronted him seriously, but the weather was fair, and his wife, whose disapproval could not have been set aside, had accepted and even smiled upon the great project. It was inevitable now that he and the children should go to Topham Corners. Mrs. Hilton had the pleasure of waking them, and telling the news.

In a few minutes they came frisking out to talk over the great plans. The cattle were already fed, and their father was milking. The only sign of high festivity was the wagon pulled out into the yard, with both seats put in as if it were Sunday; but Mr. Hilton still wore his everyday clothes, and Susan Ellen suffered instantly from disappointment.

"Ain't we goin', father?" she asked, complainingly, but he nodded and smiled at her, even though the cow, impatient to get to pasture, kept whisking her rough tail across his face. He held his head down and spoke cheerfully, in spite of this vexation.

"Yes, sister, we're goin' certain, an' goin' to have a great time, too." Susan Ellen thought that he seemed like a boy at that delightful moment, and felt new sympathy and pleasure at once. "You go an' help mother about breakfast an' them things; we want to get off quick's we can. You coax mother now, both on ye, an' see if she won't go with us."

"She said she wouldn't be hired to," responded Susan Ellen. "She says it's goin' to be hot, an' she's laid out to go over an' see how her aunt Tamsen Brooks is this afternoon."

The father gave a little sigh; then he took heart again. The truth was that his wife made light of the contemplated pleasure, and, much as he usually valued her companionship and approval, it was sure that they should have a better time without her. It was impossible, however, not to feel guilty of disloyalty at the thought. Even though she might be completely unconscious of his best ideals, he only loved her and the ideals the more, and bent his energies to satisfying her indefinite expectations. His wife still kept much of that youthful beauty which Susan Ellen seemed likely to reproduce.

An hour later the best wagon was ready, and the great expedition set forth. The little dog sat apart, and barked as if it fell entirely upon him to voice the general excitement. Both seats were in the wagon, but the empty place testified to Mrs. Hilton's unyielding disposition. She had wondered why one broad seat would not do, but John Hilton meekly suggested that the wagon looked better. The little girls sat on the back seat dressed alike in their Sunday hats of straw with blue ribbons, and their little plaid shawls pinned neatly about their small shoulders. They wore grey thread gloves, and sat very straight. Susan Ellen was half a head the taller, but otherwise, from behind, they looked much alike. As for their father, he was in his Sunday best—a plain black coat, and a winter hat of felt, which was heavy and rusty-looking for that warm early-summer day. He had it in mind to buy a new straw hat at Topham, so that this with the turnip-seed and the hoe made three important reasons for going.

"Remember an' lay off your shawls when you get there, an' carry them over your arms," said the mother, clucking like an excited hen to her chickens. "They'll do to keep the dust off your new dresses goin' and comin'. An' when you eat your dinners don't get spots on you, an' don't point at folks as you ride by, an' stare, or they'll know you came from the country. An' John, you call into Cousin Ad'line Marlow's an' see how they all be, an' tell her I expect her over certain to stop a while before hayin'. It always eases her phthisic to git up here on the highland, an' I've got a new notion about doin' over her best-room carpet sence I see her that'll save rippin' one breadth. An' don't come home all wore out; an', John, don't you go an' buy

me no kickshaws to fetch home. I ain't a child, an'
you ain't got no money to waste. I expect you'll go,
like's not, an' buy you some kind of a foolish boy's hat;
do look an' see if it's reasonable good straw, an' won't
splinter all off round the edge. An' you mind, John—"

"Yes, yes, hold on!" cried John, impatiently; then he
cast a last affectionate, reassuring look at her face,
flushed with the hurry and responsibility of starting
them off in proper shape. "I wish you was goin' too,"
he said, smiling. "I do so!" Then the old horse
started, and they went out at the bars, and began the
careful long descent of the hill. The young dog, tethered
to the lilac bush, was frantic with piteous appeals; the
little girls piped their eager good-byes again and again,
and their father turned many times to look back and
wave his hand. As for their mother, she stood alone
and watched them out of sight.

There was one place far out on the high road where
she could catch a last glimpse of the wagon, and she
waited what seemed a very long time until it appeared
and then was lost to sight again behind a low hill.
"They're nothin' but a pack o' child'n together," she
said aloud, and then felt lonelier than she expected.
She even stooped and patted the unresigned little dog
as she passed him, going into the house.

The occasion was so much more important than anyone had foreseen that both the little girls were speechless. It seemed at first like going to church in new
clothes, or to a funeral; they hardly knew how to behave
at the beginning of a whole day of pleasure. They
made grave bows at such persons of their acquaintance
as happened to be straying in the road. Once or twice
they stopped before a farmhouse, while their father
talked an inconsiderately long time with someone about
the crops and the weather and even dwelt upon town
business and the doings of the selectmen, which might
be talked of at any time. The explanations that he
gave of their excursion seemed quite unnecessary. It
was made entirely clear that he had a little business to
do at Topham Corners, and thought he had better

give the little girls a ride; they had been very steady at school, and he had finished planting, and could take the day as well as not. Soon, however, they all felt as if such an excursion were an everyday affair, and Susan Ellen began to ask eager questions, while Katy silently sat apart enjoying herself as she never had done before. She liked to see the strange houses, and the children who belonged to them; it was delightful to find flowers that she knew growing all along the road, no matter how far she went from home. Each small homestead looked its best and pleasantest, and shared the exquisite beauty that early summer made, shared the luxury of greenness and floweriness that decked the rural world. There was an early peony or a late lilac in almost every dooryard.

It was seventeen miles to Topham. After a while they seemed very far from home, having left the hills far behind, and descended to a great level country with fewer tracts of woodland, and wider fields where the crops were much more forward. The houses were all painted, and the roads were smoother and wider. It had been so pleasant driving along that Katy dreaded going into the strange town when she first caught sight of it, though Susan Ellen kept asking with bold fretfulness if they were not almost there. They counted the steeples of four churches, and their father presently showed them the Topham Academy, where their grandmother once went to school, and told them that perhaps some day they would go there too. Katy's heart gave a strange leap; it was such a tremendous thing to think of, but instantly the suggestion was transformed for her into one of the certainties of life. She looked with solemn awe at the tall belfry, and the long rows of windows in the front of the academy, there where it stood high and white among the clustering trees. She hoped that they were going to drive by, but something forbade her taking the responsibility of saying so.

Soon the children found themselves among the crowded village houses. Their father turned to look at them with affectionate solicitude.

"Now sit up straight and appear pretty," he whispered to them. "We're among the best people now, an' I want folks to think well of you."

"I guess we're just as good as they be," remarked Susan Ellen, looking at some innocent passers-by with dark suspicion, but Katy tried indeed to sit straight, and folded her hands prettily in her lap, and wished with all her heart to be pleasing for her father's sake. Just then an elderly woman saw the wagon and the sedate party it carried, and smiled so kindly that it seemed to Katy as if Topham Corners had welcomed and received them. She smiled back again as if this hospitable person were an old friend, and entirely forgot that the eyes of all Topham had been upon her.

"There, now we're coming to an elegant house that I want you to see; you'll never forget it," said John Hilton. "It's where Judge Masterson lives, the great lawyer; the handsomest house in the county, everybody says."

"Do you know him, father?" asked Susan Ellen.

"I do," answered John Hilton, proudly. "Him and my mother went to school together in their young days, and were always called the two best scholars of their time. The judge called to see her once; he stopped to our house to see her when I was a boy. An' then, some years ago—you've heard me tell how I was on the jury, an' when he heard my name spoken he looked at me sharp, and asked if I wa'n't the son of Catharine Winn, an' spoke most beautiful of your grandmother, an' how well he remembered their young days together."

"I like to hear about that," said Katy.

"She had it pretty hard, I'm afraid, up on the old farm. She was keepin' school in our district when father married her—that's the main reason I backed 'em down when they wanted to tear the old school-house all to pieces," confided John Hilton, turning eagerly. "They all say she lived longer up here on the hill than she could anywhere, but she never had her health. I wa'n't but a boy when she died. Father an' me lived alone afterward till the time your mother come; 'twas a good while, too; I wa'n't married so young as some. 'Twas lonesome, I tell you; father was plumb discouraged losin' of his wife, an' her long sickness an' all set him back, an' we'd work all day on the land an' never say a word. I s'pose 'tis bein' so lonesome early in life that makes me so pleased to have some nice girls growin' up around me now."

There was a tone in her father's voice that drew Katy's heart toward him with new affection. She dimly understood, but Susan Ellen was less interested. They had often heard this story before, but to one child it was always new and to the other old. Susan Ellen was apt to think it tiresome to hear about her grandmother, who, being dead, was hardly worth talking about.

"There's Judge Masterson's place," said their father in an everyday manner, as they turned a corner, and came into full view of the beautiful old white house standing behind its green trees and terraces and lawns. The children had never imagined anything so stately and fine, and even Susan Ellen exclaimed with pleasure. At that moment they saw an old gentleman, who carried himself with great dignity, coming slowly down the wide, box-bordered path toward the gate.

"There he is now, there's the judge!" whispered John Hilton, excitedly, reining his horse quickly to the green roadside. "He's goin' downtown to his office; we can wait right here an' see him. I can't expect him to remember me; it's been a good many years. Now you are goin' to see the great Judge Masterson!"

There was a quiver of expectation in their hearts. The judge stopped at his gate, hesitating a moment before he lifted the latch, and glanced up the street at the country wagon with its two prim little girls on the back seat, and the eager man who drove. They seemed to be waiting for something; the old horse was nibbling at the fresh roadside grass. The judge was used to being looked at with interest, and responded now with a smile as he came out to the sidewalk, and unexpectedly turned their way. Then he suddenly lifted his hat with grave politeness, and came directly toward them.

"Good morning, Mr. Hilton," he said. "I am very glad to see you, sir," and Mr. Hilton, the little girls' own father, took off his hat with equal courtesy, and bent forward to shake hands.

Susan Ellen cowered and wished herself away, but little Katy sat straighter than ever, with joy in her father's pride and pleasure shining in her pale, flower-like little face.

"These are your daughters, I am sure," said the old gentleman, kindly, taking Susan Ellen's limp and reluctant hand; but when he looked at Katy, his face brightened. "How she recalls your mother!" he said with great feeling. "I am glad to see this dear child. You must come to see me with your father, my dear," he added, still looking at her. "Bring both little girls, and let them run about the old garden; the cherries will soon be getting ripe," said Judge Masterson, hospitably. "Perhaps you will have time to stop this afternoon as you go home?"

"I should call it a great pleasure if you would come and see us again some time. You may be driving our way, sir," said John Hilton.

"Not very often in these days," answered the old judge. "I thank you for the kind invitation. I should like to see the fine view again from your hill westward. Can I serve you in any way while you are in town? Good-bye, my little friends!"

Then they parted, but not before Katy, the shy Katy, whose hand the judge still held unconsciously while he spoke, had reached forward as he said good-bye, and lifted her face to kiss him. She could not have told why, except that she felt drawn to something in the serious, worn face. For the first time in her life the child had felt the charm of manners; perhaps she owned a kinship between that which made him what he was, and the spark of nobleness and purity in her own simple soul. She turned again and again to look back at him as they drove away.

"Now you have seen one of the first gentlemen in the country," said their father. "It was worth comin'

twice as far——" But he did not say any more, nor
turn as usual to look in the children's faces.

In the chief business street of Topham a great many
country wagons like the Hiltons' were fastened to the
posts, and there seemed to our holiday-makers to be a
great deal of noise and excitement.

"Now I've got to do my errands, and we can let the
horse rest and feed," said John Hilton. "I'll slip his
headstall right off, an' put on his halter. I'm goin' to
buy him a real good treat o' oats. First we'll go an'
buy me my straw hat; I feel as if this one looked a little
past to wear in Topham. We'll buy the things we
want, an' then we'll walk all along the street, so you
can look in the windows an' see the han'some things,
same's your mother likes to. What was it mother told
you about your shawls?"

"To take 'em off an' carry 'em over our arms," piped
Susan Ellen, without comment, but in the interest of
alighting and finding themselves afoot upon the pavement the shawls were forgotten. The children stood
at the doorway of a shop while their father went inside,
and they tried to see what the Topham shapes of bonnets
were like, as their mother had advised them; but everything was exciting and confusing, and they could arrive
at no decision. When Mr. Hilton came out with a hat
in his hand to be seen in a better light, Katy whispered
that she wished he would buy a shiny one like Judge
Masterson's; but her father only smiled and shook his
head, and said that they were plain folks, he and Katy.
There were dry-goods for sale in the same shop, and a
young clerk who was measuring linen kindly pulled off
some pretty labels with gilded edges and gay pictures,
and gave them to the little girls, to their exceeding joy.
He may have had small sisters at home, this friendly
lad, for he took pains to find two pretty blue boxes
besides, and was rewarded by their beaming gratitude.

It was a famous day; they even became used to seeing
so many people pass. The village was full of its morning
activity, and Susan Ellen gained a new respect for her

father, and an increased sense of her own consequence, because even in Topham several persons knew him and called him familiarly by name. The meeting with an old man who had once been a neighbour seemed to give Mr. Hilton the greatest pleasure. The old man called to them from a house doorway as they were passing, and they all went in. The children seated themselves wearily on the wooden step, but their father shook his old friend eagerly by the hand, and declared that he was delighted to see him so well and enjoying the fine weather.

"Oh, yes," said the old man, in a feeble, quavering voice, "I'm astonishin' well for my age. I don't complain, John, I don't complain."

They talked long together of people whom they had known in the past, and Katy, being a little tired, was glad to rest, and sat still with her hands folded, looking about the front yard. There were some kinds of flowers that she never had seen before.

"This is the one that looks like my mother," her father said, and touched Katy's shoulder to remind her to stand up and let herself be seen. "Judge Masterson saw the resemblance; we met him at his gate this morning."

"Yes, she certain does look like your mother, John," said the old man, looking pleasantly at Katy, who found that she liked him better than at first. "She does, certain; the best of young folks is, they remind us of the old ones. 'Tis nateral to cling to life, folks say, but for me, I git impatient at times. Most everybody's gone now, an' I want to be goin'. 'Tis somethin' before me, an' I want to have it over with. I want to be there 'long o' the rest o' the folks. I expect to last quite a while though; I may see ye couple o' times more, John."

John Hilton responded cheerfully, and the children were urged to pick some flowers. The old man awed them with his impatience to be gone. There was such a townful of people about him and he seemed as lonely as if he were the last survivor of a former world. Until that moment they had felt as if everything was just beginning.

"Now I want to buy somethin' pretty for your mother," said Mr. Hilton, as they went soberly away down the street, the children keeping fast hold of his hands. "By now the old horse will have eat his dinner and had a good rest, so pretty soon we can jog along home. I'm goin' to take you round by the academy, and the old North meeting-house where Dr. Barstow used to preach. Can't you think o' somethin' that your mother 'd want?" he asked suddenly, confronted by a man's difficulty of choice.

"She was talkin' about wantin' a new pepper-box, one day; the top o' the old one won't stay on," suggested Susan Ellen, with delightful readiness. "Can't we have some candy, father?"

"Yes, ma'am," said John Hilton, smiling and swinging her hand to and fro as they walked. "I feel as if some would be good myself. What's all this?" They were passing a photographer's doorway with its enticing array of portraits. "I do declare!" he exclaimed, excitedly, "I'm goin' to have our pictures taken; 'twill please your mother more'n a little."

This was, perhaps, the greatest triumph of the day, except the delightful meeting with the judge; they sat in a row, with the father in the middle, and there was no doubt as to the excellence of the likeness. The best hats had to be taken off because they cast a shadow, but they were not missed, as their owners had feared. Both Susan Ellen and Katy looked their brightest and best; their eager young faces would forever shine there; the joy of the holiday was mirrored in the little picture. They did not know why their father was so pleased with it; they would not know until age had dowered them with the riches of association and remembrance.

Just at nightfall the Hiltons reached home again, tired out and happy. Katy had climbed over into the front seat beside her father, because that was always her place when they went to church on Sundays. It was a cool evening, there was a fresh sea wind that brought a light mist with it, and the sky was fast growing cloudy. Somehow the children looked different; it seemed to their mother as if they had grown older and taller since they went away in the morning, and as if they belonged to the town now as much as to the country. The greatness of their day's experience had left her far behind, the day had been silent and lonely without them, and she had had their supper ready, and been watching anxiously, ever since five o'clock. As for the children themselves they had little to say at first —they had eaten their luncheon early on the way to Topham. Susan Ellen was childishly cross, but Katy was pathetic and wan. They could hardly wait to show the picture, and their mother was as much pleased as everybody had expected.

"There, what did make you wear your shawls?" she exclaimed a moment afterward, reproachfully. "You ain't been an' wore 'em all day long? I wanted folks to see how pretty your new dresses was, if I did make 'em. Well, well! I wish more'n ever now I'd gone an' seen to ye!"

"An' here's the pepper-box!" said Katy, in a pleased, unconscious tone.

"That really is what I call beautiful," said Mrs. Hilton, after a long and doubtful look. "Our other one was only tin. I never did look so high as a chiny one with flowers, but I can get us another any time for every day. That's a proper hat, as good as you could have got, John. Where's your new hoe?" she asked, as he came toward her from the barn, smiling with satisfaction.

"I declare to Moses if I didn't forget all about it," meekly acknowledged the leader of the great excursion. "That an' my yellow-turnip seed, too; they went clean out o' my head, there was so many other things to think of. But 'tain't no sort o' matter; I can get a hoe just as well to Ira Speed's."

His wife could not help laughing. "You an' the little girls have had a great time. They was full o' wonder to me about everythin', and I expect they'll talk about it for a week. I guess we was right about havin' 'em see somethin' more o' the world."

"Yes," answered John Hilton, with humility, "yes, we did have a beautiful day. I didn't expect so much. They looked as nice as anybody, and appeared so modest an' pretty. The little girls will remember it perhaps by an' by. I guess they won't never forget this day they had 'long o' father."

It was evening again, the frogs were piping in the lower meadows, and in the woods, higher up the great hill, a little owl began to hoot. The sea air, salt and heavy, was blowing in over the country at the end of the hot, bright day. A lamp was lighted in the house, the happy children were chatting together, and supper was waiting. The father and mother lingered for a moment outside and looked down over the shadowy fields; then they went in, without speaking. The great day was over, and they shut the door.

'SIEUR GEORGE [1]

By George W. Cable (1844–1925)

In the heart of New Orleans stands a large four-story brick building, that has so stood for about three-quarters of a century. Its rooms are rented to a class of persons occupying them simply for lack of activity to find better and cheaper quarters elsewhere. With its grey stucco peeling off in broad patches, it has a solemn look of gentility in rags, and stands, or, as it were, hangs, about the corner of two ancient streets, like a faded fop who pretends to be looking for employment.

Under its main archway is a dingy apothecary-shop. On one street is the bazaar of a *modiste en robes et chapeaux* and other humble shops; on the other, the immense batten doors with gratings over the lintels, barred and bolted with masses of cobwebbed iron, like the door of a donjon, are overhung by a creaking sign (left by the sheriff), on which is faintly discernible the mention of wines and liquors. A peep through one of the shops reveals a square court within, hung with many lines of wet clothes, its sides hugged by rotten staircases that seem vainly trying to clamber out of the rubbish.

The neighbourhood is one long since given up to fifth-rate shops, whose masters and mistresses display such enticing mottoes as *"Au gagne petit"*! Innumerable children swarm about, and, by some charm of the place, are not run over, but obstruct the sidewalks playing their clamorous games.

The building is a thing of many windows, where passably good-looking women appear and disappear, clad in cotton gowns, watering little outside shelves of

[1] From *Old Creole Days*. Copyright, 1879, 1897, by Charles Scribner's Sons. By permission of the publishers.

flowers and cacti, or hanging canaries' cages. Their husbands are keepers in wine warehouses, rent-collectors for the agents of old Frenchmen who have been laid up to dry in Paris, custom-house supernumeraries and court-clerks' deputies (for your second-rate Creole is a great seeker for little offices). A decaying cornice hangs over, dropping bits of mortar on passers below, like a boy at a boarding-house.

The landlord is one Kookoo, an ancient Creole of doubtful purity of blood, who in his landlordly old age takes all suggestions of repairs as personal insults. He was but a stripling when his father left him this inheritance, and has grown old and wrinkled and brown, a sort of periodically animate mummy, in the business. He smokes cascarilla, wears velveteen, and is as punctual as an executioner.

To Kookoo's venerable property a certain old man used for many years to come every evening, stumbling through the groups of prattling children who frolicked about in the early moonlight—whose name no one knew, but whom all the neighbours designated by the title of 'Sieur George. It was his wont to be seen taking a straight—too straight—course toward his home, never careening to right or left, but now forcing himself slowly forward, as though there were a high gale in front, and now scudding briskly ahead at a ridiculous little dog-trot, as if there were a tornado behind. He would go up the main staircase very carefully, sometimes stopping half-way up for thirty or forty minutes' doze, but getting to the landing eventually, and tramping into his room in the second story, with no little elation to find it still there. Were it not for these slight symptoms of potations, he was such a one as you would pick out of a thousand for a miser. A year or two ago he suddenly disappeared.

A great many years ago, when the old house was still new, a young man with no baggage save a small hair-trunk came and took the room I have mentioned and another adjoining. He supposed he might stay fifty days—and he stayed fifty years and over. This was a very fashionable neighbourhood, and he kept the rooms on that account month after month.

But when he had been here about a year something happened to him, so it was rumoured, that greatly changed the tenor of his life; and from that time on there began to appear in him and to accumulate upon each other in a manner which became the profound study of Kookoo, the symptoms of a decay, whose cause baffled the landlord's limited powers of conjecture for well-nigh half a century. Hints of a duel, of a reason warped, of disinheritance, and many other unauthorised rumours, fluttered up and floated off, while he became recluse, and, some say, began incidentally to betray the unmanly habit which we have already noticed. His neighbours would have continued neighbourly had he allowed them, but he never let himself be understood, and *les Américains* are very droll anyhow; so, as they could do nothing else, they cut him.

So exclusive he became that (though it may have been for economy) he never admitted even a housemaid, but kept his apartments himself. Only the merry serenaders, who in those times used to sing under the balconies, would now and then give him a crumb of their feast for pure fun's sake; and after a while, because they could not find out his full name, called him, at hazard, George—but always prefixing Monsieur. Afterward, when he began to be careless in his dress, and the fashion of serenading had passed away, the commoner people dared to shorten the title to "'Sieur George."

Many seasons came and went. The city changed like a growing boy; gentility and fashion went uptown, but 'Sieur George still retained his rooms. Everyone knew him slightly, and bowed, but no one seemed to know him well, unless it were a brace or so of those convivial fellows in regulation-blue at little Fort St. Charles. He often came home late, with one of these on either arm, all singing different tunes and stopping at every twenty steps to tell secrets. But by and by the fort was demolished, church and government property melted down under the warm demand for building-lots, the city spread like a ringworm—and one day 'Sieur George steps out of the old house in full regimentals!

The Creole neighbours rush bareheaded into the middle of the street, as though there were an earthquake or a chimney on fire. What to do or say or think they do not know; they are at their wits' ends, therefore well-nigh happy. However, there is a German blacksmith's shop near by, and they watch to see what *Jacob* will do. Jacob steps into the street with every eye upon him; he approaches Monsieur—he addresses to him a few remarks—they shake hands—they engage in some conversation—Monsieur places his hand on his sword!—now Monsieur passes.

The populace crowd around the blacksmith, children clap their hands softly and jump up and down on tiptoes of expectation—'Sieur George is going to the war in Mexico!

"Ah!" says a little girl in the throng, "'Sieur George's two rooms will be empty; I find that very droll."

The landlord—this same Kookoo—is in the group. He hurls himself into the house and up the stairs. "Fifteen years pass since he have been in those room!" He arrives at the door—it is shut—"It is lock!"

In short, further investigation revealed that a youngish lady in black, who had been seen by several neighbours to enter the house, but had not, of course, been suspected of such remarkable intentions, had, in company with a middle-aged slave-woman, taken these two rooms, and now, at the slightly-opened door, proffered a month's rent in advance. What could a landlord do but smile? Yet there was a pretext left: "The rooms must need repairs?" "No, sir; he could look in and see." Joy! he looked in. All was neatness. The floor unbroken, the walls cracked but a little, and the cracks closed with new plaster, no doubt by the jealous hand of 'Sieur George himself. Kookoo's eyes swept sharply round the two apartments. The furniture was all there. Moreover, there was Monsieur's little hair-trunk. He should not soon forget that trunk. One day, fifteen years or more before, he had taken hold of that trunk to assist Monsieur to arrange his apartment, and Monsieur had drawn his fist back and cried to him to "drop it!" *Mais!* there it was, looking very suspicious in Kookoo's eyes, and the lady's domestic, as tidy as a yellow-bird, went and sat on it. Could that trunk contain treasure? It might, for Madame wanted to shut the door, and, in fact, did so.

The lady was quite handsome—had been more so, but was still young—spoke the beautiful language, and kept, in the inner room, her discreet and taciturn mulattress, a tall, straight woman, with a fierce eye, but called by the young Creoles of the neighbourhood "confound' good-lookin'."

Among *les Américaines*, where the new neighbour always expects to be called upon by the older residents, this lady might have made friends in spite of being as reserved as 'Sieur George; but the reverse being the Creole custom, and she being well pleased to keep her own company, chose mystery rather than society.

The poor landlord was sorely troubled; it must not that anything *de trop* take place in his house. He watched the two rooms narrowly, but without result, save to find that Madame plied her needle for pay, spent her money for little else besides harpstrings, and took good care of the little trunk of Monsieur. This espionage was a good turn to the mistress and maid, for when Kookoo announced that all was proper, no more was said by outsiders. Their landlord never got but one question answered by the middle-aged maid:

"Madame, he feared, was a litt' bit embarrass' *pour* money, eh?"

"*Non;* Mademoiselle [Mademoiselle, you notice!] had some property, but did not want to eat it up."

Sometimes lady friends came, in very elegant private carriages, to see her, and one or two seemed to beg her—but in vain—to go away with them; but these gradually dropped off, until lady and servant were alone in the world. And so years, and the Mexican war, went by.

The volunteers came home; peace reigned, and the city went on spreading up and down the land; but 'Sieur George did not return. It overran the country like cocoa-grass. Fields, roads, woodlands, that were once 'Sieur George's places of retreat from mankind, were covered all over with little one-story houses in the "Old Third," and fine residences and gardens up in "Lafayette." Streets went slicing like a butcher's knife through old colonial estates, whose first masters never dreamed of the city reaching them — and 'Sieur George was still away. The four-story brick got old and ugly, and the surroundings dim and dreamy. Theatres, processions, dry-goods stores, government establishments, banks, hotels, and all spirit of enterprise were gone to Canal Street and beyond, and the very beggars were gone with them. The little trunk got very old and bald, and still its owner lingered; still the lady, somewhat the worse for lapse of time, looked from the balcony-window in the brief southern twilights, and the maid every morning shook a worn rug or two over the dangerous-looking railing; and yet neither had made friends or enemies.

The two rooms, from having been stingily kept at first, were needing repairs half the time, and the occupants were often moving, now into one, now back into the other; yet the hair-trunk was seen only by glimpses, the landlord, to his infinite chagrin, always being a little too late in offering his services, the women, whether it was light or heavy, having already moved it. He thought it significant.

Late one day of a most bitter winter—that season when, to the ecstatic amazement of a whole cityful of children, snow covered the streets ankle-deep—there came a soft tap on the corridor-door of this pair of rooms. The lady opened it, and beheld a tall, lank, iron-grey man, a total stranger, standing behind— Monsieur George! Both men were weather-beaten, scarred, and tattered. Across 'Sieur George's crown, leaving a long, bare streak through his white hair, was the souvenir of a Mexican sabre.

The landlord had accompanied them to the door; it was a magnificent opportunity. Mademoiselle asked them all in, and tried to furnish a seat to each; but failing, 'Sieur George went straight across the room and *sat on the hair-trunk*. The action was so conspicuous, the landlord laid it up in his penetrative mind.

'Sieur George was quiet, or, as it appeared, quieted. The mulattress stood near him, and to her he addressed, in an undertone, most of the little he said, leaving Mademoiselle to his companion. The stranger was a warm talker, and seemed to please the lady from the first; but if he pleased, nothing else did. Kookoo, intensely curious, sought some pretext for staying, but found none. They were, altogether, an uncongenial company. The lady seemed to think Kookoo had no business there; 'Sieur George seemed to think the same concerning his companion; and the few words between Mademoiselle and 'Sieur George were cool enough. The maid appeared nearly satisfied, but could not avoid casting an anxious eye at times upon her mistress. Naturally the visit was short.

The next day but one the two gentlemen came again in better attire. 'Sieur George evidently disliked his companion, yet would not rid himself of him. The stranger was a gesticulating, stagy fellow, much Monsieur's junior, an incessant talker in Creole-French, always excited on small matters and unable to appreciate a great one. Once, as they were leaving, Kookoo— accidents will happen—was under the stairs. As they began to descend the tall man was speaking: "—better to bury it"—the startled landlord heard him say, and held his breath, thinking of the trunk; but no more was uttered.

A week later they came again.

A week later they came again.

A week later they came yet again!

The landlord's eyes began to open. There must be a courtship in progress. It was very plain now why 'Sieur George had wished not to be accompanied by the tall gentleman; but since his visits had become

regular and frequent, it was equally plain why he did
not get rid of him—because it would not look well to
be going and coming too often alone. Maybe it was
only this tender passion that the tall man had thought
"better to bury." Lately there often came sounds of
gay conversation from the first of the two rooms,
which had been turned into a parlour; and as, week after
week, the friends came downstairs, the tall man was
always in high spirits and anxious to embrace 'Sieur
George, who—"sly dog," thought the landlord—would
try to look grave, and only smiled in an embarrassed
way. "Ah! Monsieur, you tink to be varry conning;
mais you not so conning as Kookoo, no"; and the
inquisitive little man would shake his head and smile,
and shake his head again, as a man has a perfect right
to do under the conviction that he has been for twenty
years baffled by a riddle and is learning to read it at
last; he had guessed what was in 'Sieur George's head,
he would by and by guess what was in the trunk.

A few months passed quickly away, and it became
apparent to every eye in or about the ancient mansion
that the landlord's guess was not so bad; in fact, that
Mademoiselle was to be married.

On a certain rainy spring afternoon, a single hired
hack drove up to the main entrance of the old house,
and after some little bustle and the gathering of a crowd
of damp children about the big doorway, 'Sieur George,
muffled in a newly-repaired overcoat, jumped out and
went upstairs. A moment later he reappeared, leading
Mademoiselle, wreathed and veiled, down the stairway.
Very fair was Mademoiselle still. Her beauty was
mature—fully ripe—maybe a little too much so, but
only a little; and as she came down with the rav-
ishing odour of bridal flowers floating about her, she
seemed the garlanded victim of a pagan sacrifice. The
mulattress in holiday gear followed behind.

The landlord owed a duty to the community. He
arrested the maid on the last step: "Your mistress,
she goin' *pour marier* 'Sieur George? It make me glad,
glad, glad!"

"Marry 'Sieur George? *Non*, Monsieur."

"*Non?* Not marrie 'Sieur George? *Mais comment?*"

"She's going to marry the tall gentleman."

"*Diable!* ze long gentyman!"—With his hands upon his forehead, he watched the carriage trundle away. It passed out of sight through the rain; he turned to enter the house, and all at once tottered under the weight of a tremendous thought—they had left the trunk! He hurled himself upstairs as he had done seven years before, but again—"Ah, bah!"—the door was locked, and not a picayune of rent due.

Late that night a small square man, in a wet overcoat, fumbled his way into the damp entrance of the house, stumbled up the cracking stairs, unlocked, after many languid efforts, the door of the two rooms, and falling over the hair-trunk, slept until the morning sunbeams climbed over the balcony and in at the window, and shone full on the back of his head. Old Kookoo, passing the door just then, was surprised to find it slightly ajar—pushed it open silently, and saw, within, 'Sieur George in the act of rising from his knees beside the mysterious trunk! He had come back to be once more the tenant of the two rooms.

'Sieur George, for the second time, was a changed man—changed from bad to worse; from being retired and reticent, he had come, by reason of advancing years, or mayhap that which had left the terrible scar on his face, to be garrulous. When, once in a while, employment sought him (for he never sought employment), whatever remuneration he received went its way for something that left him dingy and threadbare. He now made a lively acquaintance with his landlord, as, indeed, with every soul in the neighbourhood, and told all his adventures in Mexican prisons and Cuban cities; including full details of the hardships and perils experienced jointly with the "long gentleman" who had married Mademoiselle, and who was no Mexican or Cuban, but a genuine Louisianian.

"It was he that fancied me," he said, "not I him; but once he had fallen in love with me I hadn't the force to cast him off. How Madame ever should have liked him was one of those woman's freaks that a man mustn't expect to understand. He was no more fit for her than rags are fit for a queen; and I could have choked his head off the night he hugged me round the neck and told me what a suicide she had committed. But other fine women are committing that same folly every day, only they don't wait until they're thirty-four or five to do it.—'Why don't I like him?' Well, for one reason, he's a drunkard!" Here Kookoo, whose imperfect knowledge of English prevented his intelligent reception of the story, would laugh as if the joke came in just at this point.

However, with all Monsieur's prattle, he never dropped a word about the man he had been before he went away; and the great hair-trunk puzzle was still the same puzzle, growing greater every day.

Thus the two rooms had been the scene of some events quite queer, if not really strange; but the queerest that ever they presented, I guess, was 'Sieur George coming in there one day, crying like a little child, and bearing in his arms an infant—a girl—the lovely off-spring of the drunkard whom he so detested, and poor, robbed, spirit-broken and now dead Madame. He took good care of the orphan, for orphan she was very soon. The long gentleman was pulled out of the Old Basin one morning, and 'Sieur George identified the body at the Trémé station. He never hired a nurse— the father had sold the lady's maid quite out of sight; so he brought her through all the little ills and around all the sharp corners of baby-life and childhood, without a human hand to help him, until one evening, having persistently shut his eyes for weeks and months, like one trying to sleep in the sunshine, he awoke to the realisation that she was a woman. It was a smoky one in November, the first cool day of autumn. The sunset was dimmed by the smoke of burning prairies, the air was full of the ashes of grass and reeds, ragged urchins were lugging home sticks of cordwood, and when a bit of coal fell from a cart in front of Kookoo's old house, a child was boxed half across the street and robbed of the booty by a *blanchisseuse de fin* from over the way.

The old man came home quite steady. He mounted the stairs smartly without stopping to rest, went with a step unusually light and quiet to his chamber and sat by the window opening upon the rusty balcony.

It was a small room, sadly changed from what it had been in old times; but then so was 'Sieur George. Close and dark it was, the walls stained with dampness and the ceiling full of bald places that showed the lathing. The furniture was cheap and meagre, including conspicuously the small, curious-looking hair-trunk. The floor was of wide slabs fastened down with spikes, and sloping up and down in one or two broad undulations, as if they had drifted far enough down the current of time to feel the tide-swell.

However, the floor was clean, the bed well made, the cypress table in place, and the musty smell of the walls partly neutralised by a geranium on the window-sill.

He so coming in and sitting down, an unseen person called from the room adjoining (of which, also, he was still the rentee) to know if he were he, and being answered in the affirmative, said, "Papa George, guess who was here to-day?"

"Kookoo, for the rent?"

"Yes, but he will not come back."

"No? why not?"

"Because you will not pay him."

"No? and why not?"

"Because I have paid him."

"Impossible! where did you get the money?"

"Cannot guess?—Mother Nativity."

"What, not for embroidery?"

"No? and why not? *Mais oui!*" saying which, and with a pleasant laugh, the speaker entered the room. She was a girl of sixteen or thereabout, very beautiful, with very black hair and eyes. A face and form more entirely out of place you could not have found in the whole city. She sat herself at his feet,

and, with her interlocked hands upon his knee, and her
face, full of childish innocence mingled with womanly
wisdom, turned to his, appeared for a time to take
principal part in a conversation which, of course,
could not be overheard in the corridor outside.

Whatever was said, she presently rose, he opened
his arms, and she sat on his knee and kissed him. This
done, there was a silence, both smiling pensively and
gazing out over the rotten balcony into the street.
After a while she started up, saying something about
the change of weather, and, slipping away, thrust a
match between the bars of the grate. The old man
turned about to the fire, and she from her little room
brought a low sewing-chair and sat beside him, laying
her head on his knee, and he stroking her brow with
his brown palm.

And then, in an altered—a low, sad tone—he began
a monotonous recital.

Thus they sat, he talking very steadily and she
listening, until all the neighbourhood was wrapped in
slumber—all the neighbours, but not Kookoo.

Kookoo in his old age had become a great eaves-
dropper; his ear and eye took turns at the keyhole
that night, for he tells things that were not intended
for outside hearers. He heard the girl sobbing, and
the old man saying, "But you must go now. You
cannot stay with me safely or decently, much as I wish
it. The Lord only knows how I'm to bear it, or where
you're to go; but He's your Lord, child, and He'll
make a place for you. I was your grandfather's death·
I frittered your poor, dead mother's fortune away
let that be the last damage I do.

"I have always meant everything for the best," he
added half in soliloquy.

From all Kookoo could gather, he must have been
telling her the very story just recounted. She had
dropped quite to the floor, hiding her face in her hands,
and was saying between her sobs, "I cannot go, Papa
George; oh, Papa George, I cannot go!"

Just then 'Sieur George, having kept a good resolution

all day, was encouraged by the orphan's pitiful tones to contemplate the most senseless act he ever attempted to commit. He said to the sobbing girl that she was not of his blood; that she was nothing to him by natural ties; that his covenant was with her grandsire to care for his offspring; and though it had been poorly kept, it might be breaking it worse than ever to turn her out upon ever so kind a world.

"I have tried to be good to you all these years. When I took you, a wee little baby, I took you for better or worse. I intended to do well by you all your childhood-days, and to do best at last. I thought surely we should be living well by this time, and you could choose from a world full of homes and a world full of friends.

"I don't see how I missed it!" Here he paused a moment in meditation, and presently resumed with some suddenness:

"I thought that education, far better than Mother Nativity has given you, should have afforded your sweet charms a noble setting; that good mothers and sisters would be wanting to count you into their families, and that the blossom of a happy womanhood would open perfect and full of sweetness.

"I would have given my life for it. I did give it, such as it was; but it was a very poor concern, I know —my life—and not enough to buy any good thing.

"I have had a thought of something, but I'm afraid to tell it. It didn't come to me to-day or yesterday; it has beset me a long time—for months."

The girl gazed into the embers, listening intensely.

"And oh! dearie, if I could only get you to think the same way, you might stay with me then."

"How long?" she asked, without stirring.

"Oh, as long as heaven should let us. But there is only one chance," he said, as it were feeling his way, "only one way for us to stay together. Do you understand me?"

She looked up at the old man with a glance of painful inquiry.

"If you could be—my wife, dearie?"

She uttered a low, distressful cry, and, gliding swiftly into her room, for the first time in her young life turned the key between them.

And the old man sat and wept.

Then Kookoo, peering through the keyhole, saw that they had been looking into the little trunk. The lid was up, but the back was toward the door, and he could see no more than if it had been closed.

He stooped and stared into the aperture until his dry old knees were ready to crack. It seemed as if 'Sieur George was stone, only stone couldn't weep like that.

Every separate bone in his neck was hot with pain. He would have given ten dollars—ten sweet dollars! —to have seen 'Sieur George get up and turn that trunk around.

There! 'Sieur George rose up—what a face!

He started toward the bed, and as he came to the trunk he paused, looked at it, muttered something about "ruin," and something about "fortune," kicked the lid down and threw himself across the bed.

Small profit to old Kookoo that he went to his own couch; sleep was not for the little landlord. For well-nigh half a century he had suspected his tenant of having a treasure hidden in his house, and to-night he had heard his own admission that in the little trunk was a fortune. Kookoo had never felt so poor in all his days before. He felt a Creole's anger, too, that a tenant should be the holder of wealth while his landlord suffered poverty.

And he knew very well, too, did Kookoo, what the tenant would do. If he did not know what he kept in the trunk, he knew what he kept behind it, and he knew he would take enough of it to-night to make him sleep soundly.

No one would ever have supposed Kookoo capable of a crime. He was too fearfully impressed with the extra-hazardous risks of dishonesty; he was old, too, and weak, and, besides all, intensely a coward. Nevertheless, while it was yet two or three hours before day-break, the sleep-forsaken little man arose, shuffled into his garments, and in his stocking-feet sought the corridor leading to 'Sieur George's apartment. The November night, as it often does in that region, had grown warm and clear; the stars were sparkling like diamonds pendent in the deep blue heavens, and at every window and lattice and cranny the broad, bright moon poured down its glittering beams upon the hoary-headed thief, as he crept along the mouldering galleries and down the ancient corridor that led to 'Sieur George's chamber.

'Sieur George's door, though ever so slowly opened, protested with a loud creak. The landlord, wet with cold sweat from head to foot, and shaking till the floor trembled, paused for several minutes, and then entered the moonlit apartment. The tenant, lying as if he had not moved, was sleeping heavily. And now the poor coward trembled so, that to kneel before the trunk, without falling, he did not know how. Twice, thrice, he was near tumbling headlong. He became as cold as ice. But the sleeper stirred, and the thought of losing his opportunity strung his nerves up in an instant. He went softly down upon his knees, laid his hands upon the lid, lifted it, and let in the intense moonlight. The trunk was full, full, crowded down and running over full, of the tickets of the Havana Lottery!

A little after daybreak, Kookoo from his window saw the orphan, pausing on the corner. She stood for a moment, and then dived into the dense fog which had floated in from the river, and disappeared. He never saw her again.

But her Lord is taking care of her. Once only she has seen 'Sieur George. She had been in the belvedere of the house which she now calls home, looking down upon the outspread city. Far away southward and westward the great river glistened in the sunset. Along its sweeping bends the chimneys of a smoking commerce, the magazines of surplus wealth, the gardens of the opulent, the steeples of a hundred sanctuaries and thousands on thousands of mansions and hovels covered the fertile birthright arpents which 'Sieur George, in his fifty years' stay, had seen tricked away from dull colonial Esaus by their blue-eyed brethren of the North. Nearer by she looked upon the forlornly silent region of lowly dwellings, neglected by legislation and shunned by all lovers of comfort, that once had been the smiling fields of her own grandsire's broad plantation; and but a little way off, trudging across the marshy commons, her eye caught sight of 'Sieur George following the sunset out upon the prairies to find a night's rest in the high grass.

She turned at once, gathered the skirt of her pink calico uniform, and, watching her steps through her tears, descended the steep winding stair to her frequent kneeling-place under the fragrant candles of the chapel altar in Mother Nativity's asylum.

'Sieur George is houseless. He cannot find the orphan. Mother Nativity seems to know nothing of her. If he could find her now, and could get from her the use of ten dollars for but three days, he knows a combination which would repair all the past; it could not fail, he— thinks. But he cannot find her, and the letters he writes—all containing the one scheme—disappear in the mail-box, and there's an end.

MADAME CÉLESTIN'S DIVORCE [1]

By KATE CHOPIN (1851–1904)

MADAME CÉLESTIN always wore a neat and snugly-fitting calico wrapper when she went out in the morning to sweep her small gallery. Lawyer Paxton thought she looked very pretty in the grey one that was made with a graceful Watteau fold at the back, and with which she invariably wore a bow of pink ribbon at the throat. She was always sweeping her gallery when Lawyer Paxton passed by in the morning on his way to his office at St. Denis Street.

Sometimes he stopped and leaned over the fence to say good morning at his ease; to criticise or admire her rose bushes; or, when he had time enough, to hear what she had to say. Madame Célestin usually had a good deal to say. She would gather up the train of her calico wrapper in one hand, and balancing the broom gracefully in the other, would go tripping down to where the lawyer leaned, as comfortably as he could, over her picket fence.

Of course she had talked to him of her troubles. Everyone knew of Madame Célestin's troubles.

"Really, Madame," he told her once, in his deliberate, calculating, lawyer-tone, "it's more than human nature — woman's nature — should be called upon to endure. Here you are, working your fingers off" — she glanced down at two rosy finger-tips that showed through the rents of her baggy doeskin gloves—"taking in sewing; giving music lessons; doing God knows what in the way of manual labour to support yourself and those two little ones"—Madame Célestin's pretty face beamed with satisfaction at this enumeration of her trials.

[1] From *Braon Folk*, 1894. By courtesy of Houghton Mifflin Co. and Dr. C. F. Chopin.

"You right, Judge. Not a picayune, not one, not one, have I lay my eyes on in the pas' fo' months that I can say Célestin give it to me or sen' it to me."

"The scoundrel!" muttered Lawyer Paxton in his beard.

"An' *pourtant*," she resumed, "they say he is making money down round Alexandria w'en he wants to work."

"I dare say you haven't seen him for months?" suggested the lawyer.

"It's good six month' since I see a sight of Célestin," she admitted.

"That's it, that's what I say; he has practically deserted you; fails to support you. It wouldn't surprise me a bit to learn that he has ill-treated you."

"Well, you know, Judge," with an evasive cough, "a man that drinks—w'at can you expec'? An' if you would know the promises he has made me! Ah, if I had as many dolla' as I had promise from Célestin, I wouldn' have to work, *je vous garantis*."

"And in my opinion, Madame, you would be a foolish woman to endure it longer, when the divorce court is there to offer you redress."

"You spoke about that befo', Judge; I'm goin' think about that divo'ce. I believe you right."

Madame Célestin thought about the divorce and talked about it, too; and Lawyer Paxton grew deeply interested in the theme.

"You know, about that divo'ce, Judge,"—Madame Célestin was waiting for him that morning—"I been talking to my family an' my frien's, an' it's me that tell you, they all plumb agains' that divo'ce."

"Certainly, to be sure; that's to be expected, Madame, in this community of Creoles. I warned you that you would meet with opposition, and would have to face it and brave it."

"Oh, don't fear, I'm going to face it! Maman says it's a disgrace like it's neva been in the family. But it's good for Maman to talk, her. W'at trouble she ever had? She says I mus' go by all means consult with Père Duchéron — it's my confessor, you undastan.'

Well, I'll go, Judge, to please Maman. But all the confessor' in the world en't goin' make me put up with that conduc' of Célestin any longa."

A day or two later, she was there waiting for him again. "You know, Judge, about that divo'ce."

"Yes, yes," responded the lawyer, well pleased to trace a new determination in her brown eyes and in the curves of her pretty mouth. "I suppose you saw Père Duchéron and had to brave it out with him, too."

"Oh, fo' that, a perfec' sermon, I assho you. A talk of giving scandal an' bad example that I thought would neva en'! He says, fo' him, he wash' his hands; I mus' go see the bishop."

"You won't let the bishop dissuade you, I trust," stammered the lawyer more anxiously than he could well understand.

"You don't know me yet, Judge," laughed Madame Célestin with a turn of the head and a flirt of the broom which indicated that the interview was at an end.

"Well, Madame Célestin! And the bishop!" Lawyer Paxton was standing there holding to a couple of shaky pickets. She had not seen him. "Oh, it's you, Judge?" and she hastened towards him with an *empressement* that could not but have been flattering.

"Yes, I saw Monseigneur," she began. The lawyer had already gathered from her expressive countenance that she had not wavered in her determination. "Ah, he's a eloquent man. It's not a mo' eloquent man in Natchitoches parish. I was fo'ced to cry, the way he talked to me about my troubles; how he undastan's them, an' feels for me. It would move even you, Judge, to hear how he talk' about that step I want to take; its danga, its temptation. Now it is the duty of a Catholic to stan' everything till the las' extreme. An' that life of retirement an' self-denial I would have to lead—he tole me all that."

"But he hasn't turned you from your resolve, I see," laughed the lawyer complacently.

"For that, no," she returned emphatically. "The bishop don't know w'at it is to be married to a man like

Célestin, an' have to endu' that conduc' like I have to endu' it. The Pope himse'f can't make me stan' that any longer, if you say I got the right in the law to sen' Célestin sailing."

A noticeable change had come over Lawyer Paxton. He discarded his work-day coat and began to wear his Sunday one to the office. He grew solicitous as to the shine of his boots, his collar, and the set of his tie. He brushed and trimmed his whiskers with a care that had not before been apparent. Then he fell into a stupid habit of dreaming as he walked the streets of the old town. It would be good to take unto himself a wife, he dreamed. And he could dream of no other than pretty Madame Célestin filling that sweet and sacred office as she filled his thoughts now. Old Natchitoches would not hold them comfortably, perhaps; but the world was surely wide enough to live in, outside of Natchitoches town.

His heart beat in a strangely irregular manner as he neared Madame Célestin's house one morning, and discovered her behind the rose bushes, as usual plying her broom. She had finished the gallery and steps and was sweeping the little brick walk along the edge of the violet border.

"Good morning, Madame Célestin."

"Ah, it's you, Judge? Good morning." He waited. She seemed to be doing the same. Then she ventured, with some hesitancy. "You know, Judge, about that divo'ce. I been thinking—I reckon you betta neva mine about that divo'ce." She was making deep rings in the palm of her gloved hand with the end of her broom-handle, and looking at them critically. Her face seemed to the lawyer to be unusually rosy; but maybe it was only the reflection of the pink bow at the throat. "Yes, I reckon you needn' mine. You see, Judge, Célestin came home las' night. An' he's promise' me on his word an' honour he's going to turn ova a new leaf."

THE LITTLE ROOM [1]

By MADELENE YALE WYNNE (1847-1918)

"How would it do for a smoking-room?"

"Just the very place! Only, you know, Roger, you must not think of smoking in the house. I am almost afraid that having just a plain, common man around, let alone a smoking man, will upset Aunt Hannah. She is New England — Vermont, New England — boiled down."

"You leave Aunt Hannah to me; I'll find her tender side. I'm going to ask her about the old sea-captain and the yellow calico."

"Not yellow calico—blue chintz."

"Well, yellow *shell* then."

"No, no! don't mix it up so; you won't know yourself what to expect, and that's half the fun."

"Now you tell me again exactly what to expect; to tell the truth, I didn't half hear about it the other day; I was wool-gathering. It was something queer that happened when you were a child, wasn't it?"

"Something that began to happen long before that, and kept happening, and may happen again—but I hope not."

"What was it?"

"I wonder if the other people in the car can hear us?"

"I fancy not; we don't hear them—not consecutively, at least."

"Well, mother was born in Vermont, you know; she was the only child by a second marriage. Aunt Hannah and Aunt Maria are only half-aunts to me, you know."

"I hope they are half as nice as you are."

"Roger, be still—they certainly will hear us."

"Well, don't you want them to know we are married?"

[1] From *The Little Room and Other Stories*, Way and Williams, 1895. By special arrangement.

"Yes, but not just married.   There's all the difference
in the world."

"You are afraid we look too happy!"

"No, only I want my happiness all to myself."

"Well, the little room?"

"My aunts brought mother up; they were nearly
twenty years older than she.   I might say Hiram and
they brought her up.   You see, Hiram was bound
out to my grandfather when he was a boy, and when
grandfather died Hiram said he 's'posed he went with
the farm, 'long o' the critters,' and he has been there
ever since.   He was my mother's only refuge from the
decorum of my aunts.   They are simply workers.   They
make me think of the Maine woman who wanted her
epitaph to be: 'She was a *hard*-working woman.'"

"They must be almost beyond their working-days.
How old are they"?

"Seventy, or thereabouts; but they will die standing;
or, at least, on a Saturday night, after all the house-
work is done up.   They were rather strict with mother,
and I think she had a lonely childhood.   The house is
almost a mile away from any neighbours, and off on top
of what they call Stony Hill.   It is bleak enough up
there, even in summer.

"When mamma was about ten years old they sent
her to cousins in Brooklyn, who had children of their
own, and knew more about bringing them up.   She
stayed there till she was married; she didn't go to
Vermont in all that time, and of course hadn't seen her
sisters, for they never would leave home for a day.   They
couldn't even be induced to go to Brooklyn for her
wedding, so she and father took their wedding trip up
there."

"And that's why we are going up there on our own?"

"Don't, Roger; you have no idea how loud you speak."

"You never say so except when I am going to say
that one little word."

"Well, don't say it, then, or say it very, very quietly."

"Well, what was the queer thing?"

"When they got to the house, mother wanted to take

father right off into the little room; she had been telling
him about it, just as I am going to tell you, and she had
said that of all the rooms, that one was the only one
that seemed pleasant to her.   She described the furniture
and the books and paper and everything, and said it
was on the north side, between the front and back rooms.
Well, when they went to look for it, there was no little
room there; there was only a shallow china-closet.   She
asked her sisters when the house had been altered and
a closet made of the room that used to be there.   They
both said the house was exactly as it had been built
—that they had never made any changes, except to
tear down the old wood-shed and build a smaller one.

"Father and mother laughed a good deal over it, and
when anything was lost they would always say it must
be in the little room, and any exaggerated statement
was called 'little-roomy.'   When I was a child I
thought that was a regular English phrase, I heard it
so often.

"Well, they talked it over, and finally they concluded
that my mother had been a very imaginative sort of a
child, and had read in some book about such a little
room, or perhaps even dreamed it, and then had 'made
believe,' as children do, till she herself had really thought
the room was there."

"Why, of course, that might easily happen."

"Yes, but you haven't heard the queer part yet; you
wait and see if you can explain the rest as easily.

"They stayed at the farm two weeks, and then went
to New York to live.   When I was eight years old my
father was killed in the war, and mother was broken-
hearted.   She never was quite strong afterwards, and
that summer we decided to go up to the farm for three
months.

"I was a restless sort of a child, and the journey seemed
very long to me; and finally, to pass the time, mamma
told me the story of the little room, and how it was all
in her own imagination, and how there really was only
a china-closet there.

"She told it with all the particulars; and even to me,

who knew beforehand that the room wasn't there, it seemed just as real as could be. She said it was on the north side, between the front and back rooms; that it was very small, and they sometimes called it an entry. There was a door also that opened out-of-doors, and that one was painted green, and was cut in the middle like the old Dutch doors, so that it could be used for a window by opening the top part only. Directly opposite the door was a lounge or couch; it was covered with blue chintz—India chintz—some that had been brought over by an old Salem sea-captain as a 'venture.' He had given it to Hannah when she was a young girl. She was sent to Salem for two years to school. Grandfather originally came from Salem."

"I thought there wasn't any room or chintz."

"*That is just it*. They had decided that mother had imagined it all, and yet you see how exactly everything was painted in her mind, for she had even remembered that Hiram had told her that Hannah could have married the sea-captain if she had wanted to!

"The India cotton was the regular blue stamped chintz, with the peacock figure on it. The head and body of the bird were in profile, while the tail was full front view behind it. It had seemed to take mamma's fancy, and she drew it for me on a piece of paper as she talked. Doesn't it seem strange to you that she could have made all that up, or even dreamed it?

"At the foot of the lounge were some hanging shelves with some old books on them. All the books were leather-coloured except one; that was bright red, and was called the *Ladies' Album*. It made a bright break between the other thicker books.

"On the lower shelf was a beautiful pink sea-shell, lying on a mat made of balls of red shaded worsted. This shell was greatly coveted by mother, but she was only allowed to play with it when she had been particularly good. Hiram had shown her how to hold it close to her ear and hear the roar of the sea in it.

"I know you will like Hiram, Roger; he is quite a character in his way.

"Mamma said she remembered, or *thought* she remembered, having been sick once, and she had to lie quietly for some days on the lounge; then was the time she had become so familiar with everything in the room, and she had been allowed to have the shell to play with all the time. She had had her toast brought to her in there, with make-believe tea. It was one of her pleasant memories of her childhood; it was the first time she had been of any importance to anybody, even herself.

"Right at the head of the lounge was a light-stand, as they called it, and on it was a very brightly-polished brass candlestick and a brass tray with snuffers. That is all I remember of her describing, except that there was a braided rag rug on the floor, and on the wall was a beautiful flowered paper—roses and morning-glories in a wreath on a light blue ground. The same paper was in the front room."

"And all this never existed except in her imagination?"

"She said that when she and father went up there, there wasn't any little room at all like it anywhere in the house; there was a china-closet where she had believed the room to be."

"And your aunts said there had never been any such room?"

"That is what they said."

"Wasn't there any blue chintz in the house with a peacock figure?"

"Not a scrap, and Aunt Hannah said there had never been any that she could remember; and Aunt Maria just echoed her—she always does that. You see, Aunt Hannah is an up-and-down New England woman. She looks just like herself; I mean, just like her character. Her joints move up and down or backward and forward in a plain square fashion. I don't believe she ever leaned on anything in her life, or sat in an easy chair. But Maria is different; she is rounder and softer —she hasn't any ideas of her own, she never had any. I don't believe she would think it right or becoming to have one that differed from Aunt Hannah's, so what would be the use of having any? She is an echo, that's all.

"When mamma and I got there, of course I was all excitement to see the china-closet, and I had a sort of feeling that it would be the little room after all. So I ran ahead and threw open the door, crying, 'Come and see the little room.'

"And, Roger," said Mrs. Grant, laying her hand in his, "there really was a little room there, exactly as mother had remembered it. There was the lounge, the peacock chintz, the green door, the shell, the morning-glory, and the rose paper, *everything exactly as she had described it to me.*"

"What in the world did the sisters say about it?"

"Wait a minute and I will tell you. My mother was in the front hall still talking with Aunt Hannah. She didn't hear me at first, but I ran out there and dragged her through the front room, saying, 'The room *is* here —it is all right.'

"It seemed for a minute as if my mother would faint. She clung to me in terror. I can remember now how strained her eyes looked and how pale she was.

"I called out to Aunt Hannah and asked her when they had had the closet taken away and the little room built; for in my excitement I thought that was what had been done.

"'That little room has always been there,' said Aunt Hannah, 'ever since the house was built.'

"'But mamma said there wasn't any little room here, only a china-closet, when she was here with papa,' said I.

"'No, there has never been any china-closet there; it has always been just as it is now,' said Aunt Hannah.

"Then mother spoke; her voice sounded weak and far off. She said, slowly, and with an effort, 'Maria, don't you remember that you told me that there had *never been any little room here*, and Hannah said so too, and then I said I must have dreamed it?'

"'No, I don't remember anything of the kind,' said Maria, without the slightest emotion. 'I don't remember you ever said anything about any china-closet. The house has never been altered; you used to play in this room when you were a child, don't you remember?'

"'I know it,' said mother, in that queer slow voice that made me feel frightened. 'Hannah, don't you remember my finding the china-closet here, with the gilt-edged china on the shelves, and then you said the *china-closet* had always been here?'

"'No,' said Hannah, pleasantly but unemotionally, 'no, I don't think you ever asked me about any china-closet, and we haven't any gilt-edged china that I know of.'

"And that was the strangest thing about it. We never could make them remember that there had ever been any question about it. You would think they could remember how surprised mother had been before, unless she had imagined the whole thing. Oh, it was so queer! They were always pleasant about it, but they didn't seem to feel any interest or curiosity. It was always this answer: 'The house is just as it was built; there have never been any changes, so far as we know.'

"And my mother was in an agony of perplexity. How cold their grey eyes looked to me! There was no reading anything in them. It just seemed to break my mother down, this queer thing. Many times that summer, in the middle of the night, I have seen her get up and take a candle and creep softly downstairs. I could hear the steps creak under her weight. Then she would go through the front room and peer into the darkness, holding her thin hand between the candle and her eyes. She seemed to think the little room might vanish. Then she would come back to bed and toss about all night, or lie still and shiver; it used to frighten me.

"She grew pale and thin, and she had a little cough; then she did not like to be left alone. Sometimes she would make errands in order to send me to the little room for something—a book, or her fan, or her handkerchief; but she would never sit there or let me stay in there long, and sometimes she wouldn't let me go in there for days together. Oh, it was pitiful!"

"Well, don't talk any more about it, Margaret, if it makes you feel so," said Mr. Grant.

"Oh yes, I want you to know all about it, and there isn't much more—no more about the room.

"Mother never got well, and she died that autumn. She used often to sigh, and say, with a wan little laugh, 'There is one thing I am glad of, Margaret; your father knows now all about the little room.' I think she was afraid I distrusted her. Of course, in a child's way, I thought there was something queer about it, but I did not brood over it. I was too young then, and took it as a part of her illness. But, Roger, do you know, it really did affect me. I almost hate to go there after talking about it; I somehow feel as if it might, you know, be a china-closet again."

"That's an absurd idea."

"I know it; of course it can't be. I saw the room, and there isn't any china-closet there, and no gilt-edged china in the house, either."

And then she whispered: "But, Roger, you may hold my hand as you do now, if you will, when we go to look for the little room."

"And you won't mind Aunt Hannah's grey eyes?"

"I won't mind *anything*."

It was dusk when Mr. and Mrs. Grant went into the gate under the two old Lombardy poplars and walked up the narrow path to the door, where they were met by the two aunts.

Hannah gave Mrs. Grant a frigid but not unfriendly kiss; and Maria seemed for a moment to tremble on the verge of an emotion, but she glanced at Hannah, and then gave her greeting in exactly the same repressed and non-committal way.

Supper was waiting for them. On the table was the *gilt-edged* china. Mrs. Grant didn't notice it immediately, till she saw her husband smiling at her over his teacup; then she felt fidgety, and couldn't eat. She was nervous, and kept wondering what was behind her, whether it would be a little room or a closet.

After supper she offered to help about the dishes, but,

mercy! she might as well have offered to help bring the seasons round; Maria and Hannah couldn't be helped.

So she and her husband went to find the little room, or closet, or whatever was to be there.

Aunt Maria followed them, carrying the lamp, which she set down, and then went back to the dish-washing.

Margaret looked at her husband. He kissed her, for she seemed troubled; and then, hand in hand, they opened the door. It opened into a *china-closet*. The shelves were neatly draped with scalloped paper; on them was the gilt-edged china, with the dishes missing that had been used at the supper, and which at that moment were being carefully washed and wiped by the two aunts.

Margaret's husband dropped her hand and looked at her. She was trembling a little, and turned to him for help, for some explanation, but in an instant she knew that something was wrong. A cloud had come between them; he was hurt, he was antagonised.

He paused for an appreciable instant, and then said, kindly enough, but in a voice that cut her deeply:

"I am glad this ridiculous thing is ended; don't let us speak of it again."

"Ended!" said she. "How ended?" And somehow her voice sounded to her as her mother's voice had when she stood there and questioned her sisters about the little room. She seemed to have to drag her words out. She spoke slowly: "It seems to me to have only begun in my case. It was just so with mother when she——"

"I really wish, Margaret, you would let it drop. I don't like to hear you speak of your mother in connection with it. It——" He hesitated, for was not this their wedding-day? "It doesn't seem quite the thing, quite delicate, you know, to use her name in the matter."

She saw it all now; *he didn't believe her*. She felt a chill sense of withering under his glance.

"Come," he added, "let us go out, or into the dining-room, somewhere, anywhere, only drop this nonsense."

He went out; he did not take her hand now—he was vexed, baffled, hurt. Had he not given her his sym-

pathy, his attention, his belief—and his hand?—and she
was fooling him. What did it mean? She so truthful,
so free from morbidness—a thing he hated. He walked
up and down under the poplars, trying to get into the
mood to go and join her in the house.

Margaret heard him go out; then she turned and shook
the shelves; she reached her hand behind them and
tried to push the boards away; she ran out of the house
on to the north side and tried to find in the darkness,
with her hands, a door, or some steps leading to one.
She tore her dress on the old rose-trees, she fell and rose
and stumbled, then she sat down on the ground and
tried to think. What could she think — was she
dreaming?

She went into the house and out into the kitchen, and
begged Aunt Maria to tell her about the little room—
what had become of it, when they had built the closet,
when they had bought the gilt-edged china?

They went on washing dishes and drying them on the
spotless towels with methodical exactness; and as they
worked they said that there had never been any little
room, so far as they knew; the china-closet had always
been there, and the gilt-edged china had belonged to
their mother, it had always been in the house.

"No, I don't remember that your mother ever asked
about any little room," said Hannah. "She didn't
seem very well that summer, but she never asked about
any changes in the house; there hadn't ever been any
changes."

There it was again: not a sign of interest, curiosity,
or annoyance, not a spark of memory.

She went out to Hiram. He was telling Mr. Grant
about the farm. She had meant to ask him about the
room, but her lips were sealed before her husband.

Months afterwards, when time had lessened the sharpness of their feelings, they learned to speculate reason-
ably about the phenomenon, which Mr. Grant had
accepted as something not to be scoffed away, not to
be treated as a poor joke, but to be put aside as something inexplicable on any ordinary theory.

Margaret alone in her heart knew that her mother's words carried a deeper significance than she had dreamed of at that time. "One thing I am glad of, your father knows now," and she wondered if Roger or she would ever know.

Five years later they were going to Europe. The packing was done; the children were lying asleep, with their travelling things ready to be slipped on for an early start.

Roger had a foreign appointment. They were not to be back in America for some years. She had meant to go up to say good-bye to her aunts; but a mother of three children intends to do a great many things that never get done. One thing she had done that very day, and as she paused for a moment between the writing of two notes that must be posted before she went to bed, she said:

"Roger, you remember Rita Lash? Well, she and Cousin Nan go up to the Adirondacks every autumn. They are clever girls, and I have entrusted to them something I want done very much."

"They are the girls to do it, then, every inch of them."

"I know it, and they are going to."

"Well?"

"Why, you see, Roger, that little room——"

"Oh——"

"Yes, I was a coward not to go myself, but I didn't find time, because I hadn't the courage."

"Oh! *that* was it, was it?"

"Yes, just that. They are going, and they will write us about it."

"Want to get——?"

"No; I only want to know."

Rita Lash and Cousin Nan planned to go to Vermont on their way to the Adirondacks. They found they would have three hours between trains, which would give them time to drive up to the Keys farm, and they could still get to the camp that night. But, at the last minute, Rita was prevented from going. Nan had to go to meet the Adirondack party, and she promised to telegraph Rita when she arrived at the camp. Imagine Rita's amusement when she received this message: "Safely arrived; went to Keys farm; it is a little room."

Rita was amused, because she did not in the least think Nan had been there. She thought it was a hoax; but it put it into her mind to carry the joke further by really stopping herself when she went up, as she meant to do the next week. She did stop over. She introduced herself to the two maiden ladies, who seemed familiar, as they had been described by Mrs. Grant.

They were, if not cordial, at least not disconcerted at her visit, and willingly showed her over the house. As they did not speak of any other stranger's having been to see them lately, she became confirmed in her belief that Nan had not been there.

In the north room she saw the roses and morning-glory paper on the wall, and also the door that should open into—what?

She asked if she might open it.

"Certainly," said Hannah; and Maria echoed, "Certainly."

She opened it, and found the china-closet. She experienced a certain relief; she at least was not under any spell. Mrs. Grant left it a china-closet; she found it the same. Good.

But she tried to induce the old sisters to remember that there had at various times been certain questions relating to a confusion as to whether the closet had always been a closet. It was no use: their stony eyes gave no sign.

Then she thought of the story of the sea-captain, and said, "Miss Keys, did you ever have a lounge covered with India chintz, with a figure of a peacock on it, given to you in Salem by a sea-captain, who brought it from India?"

"I dunno as I ever did," said Hannah. That was all. She thought Maria's cheeks were a little flushed, but her eyes were like a stone wall.

She went on that night to the Adirondacks. When

Nan and she were alone in their room, she said: "By the way, Nan, what did you see at the farmhouse, and how did you like Maria and Hannah?"

Nan didn't mistrust that Rita had been there, and she began excitedly to tell her all about her visit. Rita could almost have believed Nan had been there if she hadn't known it was not so. She let her go on for some time, enjoying her enthusiasm, and the impressive way in which she described her opening the door and finding the "little room." Then Rita said: "Now, Nan, that is enough fibbing. I went to the farm myself on my way up yesterday, and there is *no* little room, and there *never* has been any; it is a china-closet, just as Mrs. Grant saw it last."

She was pretending to be busy unpacking her trunk, and did not look up for a moment; but as Nan did not say anything, she glanced at her over her shoulder. Nan was actually pale, and it was hard to say whether she was more angry or frightened. There was something of both in her look. And then Rita began to explain how her telegram had put her in the spirit of going up there alone. She hadn't meant to cut Nan out. She only thought—— Then Nan broke in: "It isn't that; I am sure you can't think it is that. But I went myself, and you did not go; you can't have been there, for *it is a little room.*"

Oh, what a night they had! They couldn't sleep. They talked and argued, and then kept still for a while, only to break out again, it was so absurd. They both maintained that they had been there, but both sure the other one was either crazy or obstinate beyond reason. They were wretched; it was perfectly ridiculous, two friends at odds over such a thing; but there it was— "little room," "china-closet," "china-closet," "little room."

The next morning Nan was tacking up some tarlatan at a window to keep the midges out. Rita offered to help her, as she had done for the past ten years. Nan's "No, thanks," cut her to the heart.

"Nan," said she, "come right down from that step-ladder and pack your satchel. The stage leaves in just twenty minutes. We can catch the afternoon express train, and we will go together to the farm. I am either going there or going home. You had better go with me."

Nan didn't say a word. She gathered up the hammer and tacks, and was ready to start when the stage came round.

It meant for them thirty miles of staging and six hours of train, besides crossing the lake; but what of that, compared to having a lie lying round loose between them! Europe would have seemed easy to accomplish, if it would settle the question.

At the little junction in Vermont they found a farmer with a wagon full of meal-bags. They asked him if he could not take them up to the old Keys farm and bring them back in time for the return train, due in two hours.

They had planned to call it a sketching trip, so they said: "We have been there before, we are artists, and we might find some views worth taking; and we want also to make a short call upon the Misses Keys."

"Did ye calculate to paint the old *house* in the picture?"

They said it was possible they might do so. They wanted to see it, anyway.

"Waal, I guess you are too late. The *house* burnt down last night, and everything in it."

A VILLAGE LEAR [1]

By MARY E. WILKINS (1862)

"JEST wait a minute, Sary." The old man made a
sly, backward motion of his hand; his voice was a
cautious whisper.

Sarah Arnold stood back and waited. She was a
large, fair young woman in a brown calico dress. She
held a plate of tapioca pudding that she had brought
for the old man's dinner, and she was impatient to give
it to him and be off; but she said nothing. The old man
stood in the shop door; he had in one hand a stick of
red-and-white peppermint candy, and he held it out
enticingly towards a little boy in a white frock. The
little boy had a sweet, rosy face, and his glossy, fair
hair was carefully curled. He stood out in the green
yard, and there were dandelions blooming around his
feet. It was May, and the air was sweet and warm;
over on one side of the yard there was some linen laid
out to bleach in the sun.

The little boy looked at the old man and frowned,
yet he seemed fascinated.

The old man held out the stick of candy, and coaxed,
in his soft, cracked voice. "Jest look a-here, Willy!"
said he; "jest look a-here! See what gran'pa's got:
a whole stick of candy! He bought it down to the
store on purpose for Willy, an' he can have it if he'll
jest come here an' give gran'pa a kiss. Does Willy
want it, hey?—Willy want it?" The old man took a
step forward.

But the child drew back, and shook his head violently,
while the frown deepened. "No, no," said he, with
baby vehemence.

[1] From *A New England Nun*, etc. Copyright, 1891, by Harper
& Brothers. By permission of Author and Publishers.

The old man stepped back and began again. It was as if he were enticing a bird. "Now, Willy," said he, "jest look a-here! Don't Willy like candy?"

The child did not nod, but his blue, solemn eyes were riveted on the candy.

"Well," the grandfather went on, "here's a whole stick of candy come from the store, real nice pep'mint candy, an' Willy shall have it if he'll jest come here an' give gran'pa a kiss."

The child reached out a desperate hand. "Gimme!" he cried, imperatively.

"Yes, Willy shall have it jest as soon as he gives gran'pa a kiss." The old man waved the stick of candy; his sunken mouth was curved in a sly smile. "Jest look at it! Willy, see it! Red-an'-white candy, real sweet an' nice, with pep'mint in it. An' it's all twisted! Willy want it?"

The child began to take almost imperceptible steps forward, his eyes still fixed on the candy. His grandfather stood motionless, while his smile deepened. Once he rolled his eyes delightedly around at Sarah. The child advanced with frequent halts.

Suddenly the old man made a spring forward. "Now I've got ye!" he cried. He threw his arms around the boy and hugged him tight.

The child struggled. "Lemme go!—lemme go!" he half sobbed.

"Yes, Willy shall go jest as soon as he gives gran'pa the kiss," said the old man. "Give gran'pa the kiss, and then he shall have the candy an' go."

The child put up his pretty, rosy face and pursed his lips sulkily. The grandfather bent down and gave him an ecstatic kiss.

"There! Now Willy shall have the candy, 'cause he's kissed gran'pa. He's a good boy, an' gran'pa 'll let him have the candy right off. He shan't wait no longer."

The child snatched the candy and fled across the yard.

The old man laughed, and his laugh was a shrill, rapturous cackle, like the high notes of an old parrot. He turned to the young woman. "I knowed I could toll him in," he said; "I knowed I could. The little fellar likes candy, I tell you."

Sarah smiled sympathetically and extended the plate of pudding. "I brought you over a little of our pudding," said she. "Mother thought you might relish it."

The old man took it quite eagerly. "Brought a spoon in't, didn't ye?"

"Yes; I thought maybe you'd like to eat it out here."

"Well, I guess I may jest as well eat it out here, an' not carry it into the house. Viny might kinder git the notion that it would clutter up some. I'll jest set down here an' eat this, an' then I won't want no dinner in the house. I guess they're goin' to have beef, an' I don't relish beef much lately. I'd ruther have soft victuals; but Viny she don't cook much soft victuals; the folks in the house don't care much about 'em."

The old man held the plate of pudding, but did not at once begin to eat; his eyes still followed the little boy, who stood aloof under a blooming apple-tree and sucked his candy.

"Jest look at him," he said, admiringly. "I tell ye what 'tis, Sary, that little fellar does like candy. I can allers toll him in with a stick of candy. He's dreadful kind o' bashful. I s'pose Ellen she don't jest like to have him round in the shop here much. She dresses him up real nice an' clean in them little white frocks, an' she's afeard he'll get somethin' on 'em; so I guess she tells him he must keep away, an' it makes him kind of afeard. I s'pose she thinks I ain't none too clean nuther to be a-handlin' of him, an' I dun know as I be, but I allers wash my hands real perticker afore I tech him. I've got my tin wash-dish there on the bench, an' I'm real perticker 'bout it."

The old man waved his hand towards a rusty tin wash-basin on the old shoemaker's bench under the window. There was a smoky curtain over the window; the plastered walls and the ceiling were dark with smoke; the place was full of brown lights. Sarah, in her brown dress, with her fair, rosy face, stood waiting until the old man should finish talking.

"Well, I must go now," said she. "I haven't been to dinner myself."

"You jest wait a minute," whispered the old man, with a mysterious air. In the little shop, beside the old shoe-maker's bench, was a table that was brown and dark with age and dirt, and it was heaped with litter. There was a drawer in it, and this the old man opened with an effort; it stuck a little. "Look a-here," he whispered —"look a-here, Sary."

Sarah came close, and peered around his elbow.

The old man took a little parcel from the midst of the leather chips and waxed threads and pegs that half filled the drawer. He unrolled it carefully. "Look a-here," he said again, with a chuckle. He held up a stick of pink candy. "There," he went on, winking an old blue eye at Sarah, "I ain't goin' to give that to him till to-morrer. To-morrer I'll jest toll him in with that, don't ye see? Hey?"

"That's checkerberry, ain't it?"

"Yes, that's checkerberry, an' t'other was pep'mint. I got two sticks of candy down to the store this mornin', one checkerberry an' t'other pep'mint. Ye see, I put a patch on a shoe for the Briggs boy last week, an' he give me ten cents for't. I'd kinder calkilated to lay it out in terbacker—I ain't had none lately—but the more I thought 'bout it the more I thought I'd git a leetle candy. Ye never see sech a chap fer candy as he is; he'll hang off, an' hang off, but he can't stan' it to lose the candy nohow. I dun know but the Old Nick could toll him in with a stick of candy, he's in such a takin' for't; never see sech a fellar fer candy." The old man raised his cackling laugh again, and Sarah laughed too, going out the back door of the shop. "I'm real obleeged to your mother, Sary; you tell her," he called after her.

He replaced the candy in the drawer, still chuckling to himself; then he sat down to his pudding. He sat on his shoemaker's bench, well back from the door, and ate. He smacked his lips loudly; he liked this soft, sweet food.

Barney Swan was a small, frail, old man; he stooped

weakly, and did not look much larger than a child, sitting there on his bench. His face, too, was like a child's; his sunken mouth had an innocent, infantile expression, and his eyes had that blank, fixed gaze, with an occasional twinkle of shrewdness, that babies' eyes have. His thin, white hair hung to his shoulders, and he had no beard. He owned only one decent coat, and that he kept for Sundays: he always went to meeting. On weekdays he wore his brown calico shirt-sleeves and his old sagging vest. His bagging, brownish-black trousers were hauled high around his waist, and his ankles showed like a little boy's.

Old Barney Swan had sat upon that shoemaker's bench the greater part of his time for sixty years. His father before him had been a shoemaker and cobbler; he had learned the trade when a child, and been faithful to it all his life. Now not only his own powers had failed, but hand shoe-making and cobbling were at a discount. There were two thriving boot and shoe factories in the town, and the new boots and shoes were finer to see than the old coarsely cobbled ones. Old Barney was too old to go to work in the shoe factory, but it is doubtful if he would have done so in any case. He had always had a vein of childish obstinacy in spite of his mildness, and it had not decreased with age. "If folks want to wear them manufactured shoes, they can," he would say, with a sudden stiffening of his bent back; "old shackly things! You'd orter seen them shoes the Briggs boy brought in here t'other day; they wa'n't wuth treein' up, an' they never had been."

Although now old Barney's revenue was derived from the Briggs boy and sundry other sturdy, stubbed urchins, whose shoe-leather demanded the cheapest and most thorough repairs to be had, he had accumulated quite a little property through his faithful toil on that leathern seat on the end of that old bench. But it had seemed easier for him to accumulate property than to care for it. His greatest talent was for patient, unremitting labour and economy; his financial conceptions were limited to them. Ten years before, he had made a misadventure and lost a few hundred dollars, and was so humbled and dejected over it that he had made his property over to his daughters on consideration of a life support. They had long been urging him to make such an arrangement. He had two daughters, Malvina and Ellen. His wife had died when they were about twenty. The wife had been a delicate, feeble woman, yet with a certain spirit of her own. In her day the daughters had struggled hard for the mastery of the little household, but with only partial success; after her death they were entirely victorious. Barney had always thought his daughters perfect; they had their own way in everything, with the exception of the money. He clung to that for a while. He was childishly fond of the few dollars he had earned all by himself and stowed away in his house and acres of green meadow-land and the village savings-bank. He was fond of the dollars for themselves; the sense of treasure pleased him. He did not care to spend for himself; there were few things that he wished for except a decent meeting-coat and a little tobacco. The tobacco was one point upon which he displayed his obstinacy; his daughters had never been able entirely to do away with that, although they waged constant war upon it. He would still occasionally have his little comforting pipe, and chew in spite of all berating and disgust. But the tobacco was sadly curtailed since the property had changed hands; he had only his little earnings with which to purchase it. The daughters gave him no money to spend. They argued that "father ain't fit to spend money." So his most urgent necessities were doled out to him.

When the property was divided, Malvina, the elder daughter, had for her share the homestead and a part of the money in the bank; Ellen, the younger, had the larger portion of the bank money and some wooded property. Malvina stipulated to furnish a home and care for the old man as long as he lived, and Ellen was to pay her sister a certain sum towards his support. Both daughters were married at the time; Malvina had one daughter of her own. Malvina had remained at her old home after her marriage, but Ellen had removed to a town some twenty miles away. Her father had visited there several times, but he never liked to remain long. He would never have gone had not Malvina insisted upon it. She considered that her sister ought to share her burden, and sometimes give her a relief. So Barney would go, although with reluctance; in fact, his little shoe-shop was to him his beloved home, his small solitary nest, where he could fold his old wings in peace. Nobody knew how regretfully he thought of it during his visits at Ellen's. While there he sat mostly in her kitchen, by the cooking-stove, and miserably pored over the almanac or the religious paper. Occasionally he would steal out behind the barn and smoke a pipe, but there was always a hard reckoning with Ellen afterwards, and it was a dearly-purchased pleasure. Ellen was a small, fair woman; she was delicate, much as her mother had been, and her weakness and nervousness made her imperious will less evident but more potent. Old Barney stood more in awe of her than of Malvina. He was anxiously respectful towards her husband, who was a stout, silent man, covering his own projects and his own defeats with taciturnity. He was a steady grubber on a farm, and very close with old Barney's money, of which, however, his wife understood that she had full control. She had had out of it a set of red plush parlour furniture and a new silk dress. Once in a while old Barney, while on a visit, would stand on the parlour threshold, and gaze admiringly in at the furniture; but did he venture to step over, his daughter would check him. "Now don't go in there, father," she would cry out; "you'll track in somethin'."

"No, I ain't a-goin' in, Ellen," Barney would reply, and meekly shuffle back.

Old Barney was intensely loyal towards both of his daughters; not even to himself would he admit anything to their disadvantage. He always spoke admiringly of them, and would acknowledge no preference for one above the other. Still he undoubtedly preferred Malvina. She was a large, stout woman, but some people thought that she looked like her father. When the property was divided, Malvina had had every room in the house newly painted and papered; then she stood before them like a vigilant watch-dog. She had been neat before, but with her new paint and paper and a few new carpets her neatness became almost a mono-mania. She was fairly fierce, and her voice sounded like a bark sometimes when old Barney, with shoes heavy with loam and clothes stained with tobacco juice, shuffled into her spotless house. However, in a certain harsh way she did her duty by her simple old father. She saw to it that his clothes were comfortably warm and mended, and he had enough to eat, although his own individual tastes were never consulted. Still, he was scrupulously bidden to meals, and his plate was well filled. She did not like to have him in the house, and showed that she did not, but she had no com-punctions upon that point, for he preferred the shop. She never gave him spending-money, for she did not consider that he was capable of spending money judiciously. She bought all that he had herself. She was a good financier, and made a little go a long way.

Malvina's husband was dead, and her daughter was now eighteen years old. Her name was Annie. She was a pretty girl, and had a lover. She was to be married soon. They had not told old Barney about it, but he found it out two weeks before the wedding. He stood in his shop door one morning and called cautiously to Sarah Arnold. (The Arnolds lived in the next house, and Sarah was out in the yard picking some roses.) "Sary, come here a minute," he called. And Sarah came, with her roses in her hand. The old man beckoned her mysteriously into the shop. He drew well back from the door, after having peered sharply at the house windows. Then he began: "Ye heard on't, Sary," whispered he—"what's goin' on in there? Hey?" He gave his hand a backward jerk towards the house.

Sarah laughed. "I suppose so," said she.

"How long ye known it? Hey?"

"Well, I've heard 'twas coming off before long."

"The weddin's goin' to be in two weeks. Did ye know that? Hey?"

"I heard so."

"Well, it's the first I've heard on't. I knew that young fellar'd been shinin' round there consider'ble, an' I s'pos'd 'twas comin' off some time or other, but I didn't have no idee 'twas goin' to be so soon. Look a-here, Sary"—Sarah, placid and fair and pleasant, holding her roses, gazed attentively at him—"*I'm—a-goin' to— give her somethin' !*"

"What are you going to give her?"

"Ye'll see. I've got some money laid up, an' I know a way to raise a leetle more. Ye'll see when the time comes—ye'll see." The old man raised his pleasant cackle, then he hushed it suddenly, with a wary glance towards the house. "You mind you don't say nothin' about it, Sary," said he.

"No, I won't say a word about it," returned Sarah. Then she went home with her roses and her own thoughts. She herself was to be married soon, but there would be no such commotion over her wedding as over Annie's. The Arnolds were very humble folk, according to the social status of the village, and were not on very intimate terms with their neighbours. Old Mr. Arnold took care of people's gardens and sawed wood for a living, and Mrs. Arnold and Sarah sewed, and even went out for extra work when some of the more prosperous village people had company. However, Sarah was going to marry a young man who had saved quite a sum of money. He was building a new house on a cross-street at the foot of a meadow that lay behind Barney Swan's shop. Sarah had told Barney all about it, and he often strolled down the meadow and watched the workmen on the new house with a wise and interested air. He was very fond of Sarah. Sarah had her own opinion about Annie and the old man's daughters, but she was calm about expressing it even to her mother. She was a womanly young girl. However, once in a while her indignation grew warm.

"I think it's a shame," she told her mother, when she carried her roses into the house, "that they haven't told Grandpa Swan about Annie's going to be married, and the poor old man's planning to give her a present." The tears stood in Sarah's blue eyes. She crowded the roses into a tumbler.

It was only the next day that old Barney called her into the shop to display the present. He had been so eager about it that he was not able to wait. However, the idea that the gift must not be presented to his grand-daughter until her wedding day was firmly fixed in his mind. He had obtained in some way this notion of etiquette, and he was resolved to abide by it, no matter how impatient he might be. "I've got it here all ready, but I ain't a-goin' to give it to her till the day she's married, ye know," he told Sarah while he was fumbling in the table-drawer (that was his poor little treasure-box). There he kept his surreptitious quids of tobacco and his pipe and his small hoards of pennies. His hands trembled as he drew out a little square parcel. He undid it with slow pains. "Look a-here!" In a little jeweller's box, on a bed of pink cotton, lay a gold-plated brooch with a red stone in the centre. The old man stood holding it, and looking at Sarah with a speechless appeal for admiration.

"Why, ain't it handsome!" said she; "it's just as pretty as it can be!"

Old Barney still did not speak; he stood holding the box, as silent as a statue whose sole purpose is to pose for admiration.

"Where did you get it?" asked Sarah.

The old man ushered in his words with an exultant chuckle. "Down to Bixby's; an' 'twas jest about the pertiest thing he had in his hull store. It cost consider'ble; I ain't a-goin' to tell ye how much, but I didn't pay no ninepence for't, I can tell ye. But I had a leetle somethin' laid up, an' there was some truck I traded off. I was bound I'd git somethin' wuth somethin' whilst I was about it."

As Barney spoke, Sarah noticed that his old silver

watch-chain was gone, and a suspicion as to the "truck" seized her, but she did not speak of it. She admired the brooch to Barney's full content, and he stowed it away in the drawer with pride and triumph. He was true to his resolution not to mention the present to his grand-daughter, but he could not help throwing out sundry sly hints to the effect that one was forthcoming. However, no one paid any attention to them; they knew too well the state of Barney's exchequer to have any great expectations, and all the family were in the habit of disregarding the old man's chatter. He always talked a great deal, and asked many questions; and they seemed to look upon him much in the light of a vener-able cricket, constantly chirping upon their hearth, which for some obscure religious reasons they were bound to harbour.

The question of old Barney's appearance at the marriage was quite a serious one. The wedding was to be a brilliant affair for the village, and the old man was not to be considered in the light of an ornament. Still the idea of not allowing him to be present could not decently be entertained, and Malvina began training him to make the best appearance possible. She in-structed him as to his deportment, and had even made a new black silk stock for him to wear at the wedding. He was so delighted that he wanted to take possession at once, and hide it away in his table-drawer, but she would not allow it. She had planned how he should be well shaven and thoroughly brushed, and his pockets searched for tobacco, on the wedding morning. "I should feel like goin' through the floor if your grandfather should come in lookin' the way he does sometimes," she told her daughter Annie.

Annie concerned herself very little about it. She was a young girl of a sweet, docile temperament. She was somewhat delicate physically, and was indolent, partly from that, partly from her nature. Now her mother was making her work so hard over her wedding clothes that she was half ill; her little forefinger was all covered with needle-pricks, and there were hollows under her

eyes. Malvina had always been a veritable queen-
mother to Annie.

Ellen and her little boy visited Malvina for several
weeks before the wedding. Ellen assisted about the
sewing; she was a fine sewer.

Old Barney did not dare stay much in the house, but
he wandered about the yard, and absurdly peeped in
at the doors and windows. Back in his second childhood, he had all the delighted excitement of a child
over a great occasion. It was perhaps a poor and pitiful
happiness, but he was as happy in his own way as
Annie was over her coming marriage, and, after all,
happiness is only one's own heartful.

But three days before the wedding old Barney was
attacked with a severe cold, and all his anticipations
came to naught. The cold grew worse, and his daughters
promptly decided that he could not be present at the
wedding. "There ain't no use talkin' 'bout it, father,"
said Malvina; "you can't go. You'd jest cough an'
sneeze right through it, an' we can't have such work."

The old man pleaded, even with tears, but with no
avail; on the wedding day he was almost forcibly exiled
to his little shop in the yard. The excitement in the
house reached a wild height, and he was not allowed to
enter after breakfast; his dinner of bread and butter
and tea was brought down to the shop. He sat in the
door and watched the house and the hurrying people.
He called Sarah Arnold over many times; he was in
a panic over his present. "How am I goin' to give her
that breastpin, if they don't let me go to the weddin'?"
he queried, with sharp anxiety. "There shan't nobody
else give her that pin nohow."

"I guess you'll have a chance," Sarah said, com-
fortingly.

When it was time for the people to come to
the wedding, Ellen, in her silk dress, with her hair
finely crimped, came rustling out to the shop, and
ordered old Barney away from the door.

"Do keep away from the door, father," said she, "for
mercy sakes. Such a spectacle as you are, an' the folks

beginnin' to come! I should think you'd know better."
Ellen's forehead was all corrugated with anxious lines;
she was nervous and fretful. She even pushed her father
away from the door with one long, veiny hand; then
she shut the door with a clash.

Then Barney stood at the window and watched. He
held the little jewellery-box tightly clutched in his hand.
The window-panes were all clouded and cobwebbed;
it was hard for his dim old eyes to see through them,
but he held back the stained curtain and peered as
sharply as he could.

He saw the neighbours come to the wedding. Several
covered wagons were hitched out in the yard. When
the minister came into the yard he could scarcely keep
himself from rushing to the door.

"There he is!" he said out loud to himself. "There
he is! He's come to marry 'em!"

The hubbub of voices in the house reached old Barney's
ears. A little after the minister arrived there was a
hush. "He's marryin' of 'em!" ejaculated Barney.
He danced up and down before the window.

After the hush the voices swelled out louder than
before. Barney kept his eyes riveted upon the house.
It was some two hours before people began to issue
from the doors.

"The weddin's over!" shouted Barney. He looked
quite wild; he gave himself a little shake, and opened
the shop door and took up his stand there. Everybody
could see him in his brown calico shirt-sleeves, and his
slouching, untidy vest and trousers. His white locks
straggled over his shoulders; his face was not very clean.
Suddenly, Ellen, standing and smirking in the house
door, spied him. Presently she came across the yard,
swaying her rattling skirts with a genteel air. She
smiled all the way, and old Barney innocently smiled
back at her when she reached him. But he jumped,
her voice was so fierce.

"You go right in there this minute, father, an' keep
that door *shut*," she said between her smiling lips.

She shut the door upon Barney, but she had no sooner

reached the house than he opened it again and stood there. He still held the box.

The bridal pair were to set up housekeeping in a village ten miles away. They were to drive over that night. When at last the bridegroom and the bride appeared in the door, old Barney leaned forward, breathless. The bridegroom's glossy buggy and bay horse stood in the yard; the horse was restive, and a young man was holding him by the bridle.

Old Barney did not venture to step outside his shop door. Malvina and Ellen were both in the yard, but it was as if his soul were feeling for ways to approach the young couple. He leaned forward, his eyes were intent and prominent, the hand that held the jewellery-box shook with long, rigid motions.

The bride, at her husband's side, stepped across the green yard to the buggy. This was a simple country wedding, and Annie rode in her wedding dress to her new home. The wedding dress was white muslin, full of delicate frills and loops of ribbons that the wind caught. Annie, coming across the yard, was blown to one side like a white flower. Her slender neck and arms showed pink through the muslin, and she wore her wedding bonnet, which was all white, with bows of ribbon and plumes. Her cheeks were very red.

Old Barney opened his mouth wide. "Good Lord!" said he, with one great gasp of admiration. He laughed in a kind of rapture; he forgot for a minute his wedding present. "Look at 'em!—jest look at 'em!" he repeated. Suddenly he called out, "Annie! Annie! jest look a-here! See what gran'pa's got for ye."

Annie stopped and looked. She hesitated, and seemed about to approach Barney, when the horse started; the young man had hard work to hold him. The bridegroom lifted the bride into the carriage as soon as the horse was quiet enough, sprang in after her, and they flew out of the yard, with everybody shouting merrily after them. Old Barney's piteous cry of "Annie! Annie! jest come here a minute!" was quite lost.

The old man went into the shop and closed the door

of his own accord. Then he replaced the little box in the table-drawer. Then he settled down on his old shoe-bench, and dropped his head on his hands. Soon he had a severe coughing-spell. Nobody came near him until it was quite dark; then Malvina came and asked him, in a hard, absent way, if he were not coming into the house to have any supper that night.

Old Barney arose and shuffled after her into the house; he ate the supper that she gave him; then he went to bed. He never took Annie's gold brooch out of the drawer again. He never spoke of it to Sarah Arnold nor anyone else. He had the grieved dignity that pertains to the donor of a scorned gift. As the weeks went on, his cold grew no better; he coughed harder and harder. Once Malvina bought some cough medicine for him, but it did no good. The old man grew thinner and weaker, but she did not realise that; the cough arrested her attention; it tired her to hear it so constantly. She told him that there was no need of his coughing so much.

Sarah Arnold was married in August. She and her husband went to live in their new house across the meadow from old Barney's shop.

Sarah had been married a few weeks when one night old Barney came toddling down the meadow to her house. He was so weak that he tottered, but he almost ran. The short growth of golden-rod brushing his ankles seemed enough to throw him over. He waded through it as through a golden sea that would soon throw him from his footing and roll him over, but he never slackened his pace until he reached Sarah's door. She had seen him coming, and ran to meet him.

"Why, what is the matter?" she cried. Old Barney's face was pale and wild. He looked at her and gasped. She caught him by the arm and dragged him into the house, and set him in a chair. "What *is* the matter?" she asked again. She looked white and frightened herself.

Old Barney did not reply for a minute; he seemed to be collecting breath. Then he burst out in a great sobbing cry: "My shop! my shop! She's goin' to have my shop tore down! They're goin' to begin to-morrer. They're movin' my bench. Oh! oh!"

Sarah stood close to him and patted his head. "Who's goin' to have it torn down?"

"Mal—viny."

"When did she say so?"

"Jest—now—come out an' told me. Says the—old—thing looks dreadful bad out—in the yard, an' she wants it—tore down. She's goin' to have me—go to Ellen's an' stay—all winter. Puttin' my bench up—in the garret. I ain't—a-goin' to have the—bench to set on—no longer, I ain't. Oh, hum!"

Sarah's pleasant mouth was set hard. She made old Barney lie down on her sitting-room lounge, and got him a cup of tea. It was evident that the old man was completely exhausted; he could not have walked home had he tried. Sarah sat down beside him and heard his complaint, and tried to comfort him. When her husband came home to tea she told him the story, and he went up across the meadow to the shop before he took off his coat.

"It's so," he growled, when he returned. "They're lugging the things out. It's a blasted shame. Poor old man!"

Sarah's husband had a brown, boyish face and a set chin; he took off his coat and began washing his hands at the kitchen sink with such energy that the leather stains might have been the ingratitude of the world.

"Did you say anything about his being down here?" asked Sarah.

"No, I didn't. Let 'em hunt."

About nine o'clock that evening Malvina, holding her skirts up well, came striding over the meadow. She had missed her father, and traced him to Sarah's. Sarah and her husband had put him to bed in their pretty little spare chamber when Malvina came in. It was evident that the old man was very ill; he was wandering a little, and he had terrible paroxysms of coughing; his breath was laboured. Malvina stood looking at him; Sarah's husband kept opening his mouth to speak, and his wife kept nudging him to be silent. Finally he spoke:

"He's all upset because his shop's going to be torn down," said he; but his voice was not as bold as his intentions.

"Tain't that," replied Malvina. "He's dretful careless; he's been goin' round in his stockin'-feet, an' he's got more cold. I dun know what's goin' to be done. I don't see how I can get him home to-night."

"He can stay here just as well as not," said Sarah, nudging her husband again.

"Well, I'll come over an' git him home in the mornin'," Malvina said.

But she could not get him home when she came over in the morning. Old Barney never went home again. He died the second day after he came to Sarah's. Both of his daughters came to see him, and did what they could, but he did not seem to notice them much. An hour before he died he called Sarah. She ran into the room. Just then there was nobody else in the house. Old Barney sat up in bed, and he was pointing out of the window over the meadow. His pointing forefinger shook, his face was ghastly, but there was a strange childish delight in it.

"Look a-there, Sary—jest look a-there," said old Barney. "Over in the meader—look. There's Ellen a-comin', an' Viny, an' they look jest as they did when they was young; an' Ellen she's a-bringin' me some tea, an' Viny she's a-bringin' me some custard puddin'. An' there's Willy a-dancin' along. Jest see the leetle fellar a-comin' to see gran'pa all of his own accord. An' there's Annie all in her white dress, jest as pretty as a pictur', a-comin' arter her breastpin. Jest see 'em, Sary." The old man laughed. Out of his ghastly, death-stricken features shone the expression of a happy child. "Jest look at 'em, Sary," he repeated.

Sarah looked, and she saw only the meadow covered with a short waving crop of golden-rod, and over it the September sky.

VAN BIBBER'S BURGLAR [1]

By RICHARD HARDING DAVIS (1864–1916)

THERE had been a dance up-town, but as Van Bibber could not find Her there, he accepted young Travers's suggestion to go over to Jersey City and see a "go" between "Dutchy" Mack and a coloured person professionally known as the Black Diamond. They covered up all signs of their evening dress with their great-coats, and filled their pockets with cigars, for the smoke which surrounds a "go" is trying to sensitive nostrils, and they also fastened their watches to both key-chains. Alf Alpin, who was acting as master of ceremonies, was greatly pleased and flattered at their coming, and boisterously insisted on their sitting on the platform. The fact was generally circulated among the spectators that the "two gents in high hats" had come in a carriage, and this and their patent-leather boots made them objects of keen interest. It was even whispered that they were the "parties" who were putting up the money to back the Black Diamond against the "Hester Street Jackson." This in itself entitled them to respect. Van Bibber was asked to hold the watch, but he wisely declined the honour, which was given to Andy Spielman, the sporting reporter of the *Track and Ring*, whose watch-case was covered with diamonds, and was just the sort of a watch a timekeeper should hold.

It was two o'clock before "Dutchy" Mack's backer threw the sponge into the air, and three before they reached the city. They had another reporter in the cab with them besides the gentleman who had bravely held the watch in the face of several offers to "do for" him; and as Van Bibber was ravenously hungry, and as

[1] From *Gallegher and Other Stories*. Copyright, 1891, by Charles Scribner's Sons. By permission of the publishers.

he doubted that he could get anything at that hour at the club, they accepted Spielman's invitation and went for a porterhouse steak and onions at the Owl's Nest, Gus McGowan's all-night restaurant on Third Avenue.

It was a very dingy, dirty place, but it was as warm as the engine-room of a steamboat, and the steak was perfectly done and tender. It was too late to go to bed, so they sat around the table, with their chairs tipped back and their knees against its edge. The two club men had thrown off their great-coats, and their wide shirt fronts and silk facings shone grandly in the smoky light of the oil lamps and the red glow from the grill in the corner. They talked about the life the reporters led, and the Philistines asked foolish questions, which the gentlemen of the press answered without showing them how foolish they were.

"And I suppose you have all sorts of curious adventures," said Van Bibber, tentatively.

"Well, no, not what I would call adventures," said one of the reporters. "I have never seen anything that could not be explained or attributed directly to some known cause, such as crime or poverty or drink. You may think at first that you have stumbled on something strange and romantic, but it comes to nothing. You would suppose that in a great city like this one would come across something that could not be explained away—something mysterious or out of the common, like Stevenson's Suicide Club. But I have not found it so. Dickens once told James Payn that the most curious thing he ever saw in his rambles around London was a ragged man who stood crouching under the window of a great house where the owner was giving a ball. While the man hid beneath a window on the ground floor, a woman, wonderfully dressed and very beautiful, raised the sash from the inside and dropped her bouquet down into the man's hand, and he nodded and stuck it under his coat and ran off with it.

"I call that, now, a really curious thing to see. But I have never come across anything like it, and I have been in every part of this big city, and at every hour of the night and morning, and I am not lacking in imagination either, but no captured maidens have ever beckoned to me from barred windows nor 'white hands waved from a passing hansom.' Balzac and De Musset and Stevenson suggest that they have had such adventures, but they never come to me. It is all commonplace and vulgar, and always ends in a police court or with a 'found drowned' in the North River."

McGowan, who had fallen into a doze behind the bar, woke suddenly and shivered and rubbed his shirt-sleeves briskly. A woman knocked at the side door and begged for a drink "for the love of heaven," and the man who tended the grill told her to be off. They could hear her feeling her way against the wall and cursing as she staggered out of the alley. Three men came in with a hack driver and wanted everybody to drink with them, and became insolent when the gentlemen declined, and were in consequence hustled out one at a time by McGowan, who went to sleep again immediately, with his head resting among the cigar-boxes and pyramids of glasses at the back of the bar, and snored.

"You see," said the reporter, "it is all like this. Night in a great city is not picturesque and it is not theatrical. It is sodden, sometimes brutal, exciting enough until you get used to it, but it runs in a groove. It is dramatic, but the plot is old and the motives and characters always the same."

The rumble of heavy market wagons and the rattle of milk carts told them that it was morning, and as they opened the door the cold fresh air swept into the place and made them wrap their collars around their throats and stamp their feet. The morning wind swept down the cross-street from the East River and the lights of the street lamps and of the saloon looked old and tawdry. Travers and the reporter went off to a Turkish bath, and the gentleman who held the watch, and who had been asleep for the last hour, dropped into a night-hawk and told the man to drive home. It was almost clear now and very cold, and Van Bibber determined to walk. He had the strange feeling one gets when one stays up until the sun rises, of having lost a day somewhere, and the dance he had attended a few hours before seemed to have come off long ago, and the fight in Jersey City was far back in the past.

The houses along the cross-street through which he walked were as dead as so many blank walls, and only here and there a lace curtain waved out of the open window where some honest citizen was sleeping. The street was quite deserted; not even a cat or a policeman moved on it and Van Bibber's footsteps sounded brisk on the sidewalk. There was a great house at the corner of the avenue and the cross-street on which he was walking. The house faced the avenue and a stone wall ran back to the brown stone stable which opened on the side street. There was a door in this wall, and as Van Bibber approached it on his solitary walk it opened cautiously, and a man's head appeared in it for an instant and was withdrawn again like a flash, and the door snapped to. Van Bibber stopped and looked at the door and at the house and up and down the street. The house was tightly closed, as though someone was lying inside dead, and the streets were still empty.

Van Bibber could think of nothing in his appearance so dreadful as to frighten an honest man, so he decided the face he had had a glimpse of must belong to a dishonest one. It was none of his business, he assured himself, but it was curious, and he liked adventure, and he would have liked to prove his friend the reporter, who did not believe in adventure, in the wrong. So he approached the door silently, and jumped and caught at the top of the wall and stuck one foot on the handle of the door, and, with the other on the knocker, drew himself up and looked cautiously down on the other side. He had done this so lightly that the only noise he made was the rattle of the door-knob on which his foot had rested, and the man inside thought that the one outside was trying to open the door, and placed his shoulder to it and pressed against it heavily. Van Bibber, from his perch on the top of the wall, looked down directly on the other's head and shoulders. He could see the top of the man's head only two feet below, and he also saw that in one hand he held a revolver and that two bags filled with projecting articles of different sizes lay at his feet.

It did not need explanatory notes to tell Van Bibber that the man below had robbed the big house on the corner, and that if it had not been for his having passed when he did the burglar would have escaped with his treasure. His first thought was that he was not a policeman, and that a fight with a burglar was not in his line of life; and this was followed by the thought that though the gentleman who owned the property in the two bags was of no interest to him, he was, as a respectable member of society, more entitled to consideration than the man with the revolver.

The fact that he was now, whether he liked it or not, perched on the top of the wall like Humpty Dumpty, and that the burglar might see him and shoot him the next minute, had also an immediate influence on his movements. So he balanced himself cautiously and noiselessly and dropped upon the man's head and shoulders, bringing him down to the flagged walk with him and under him. The revolver went off once in the struggle, but before the burglar could know how or from where his assailant had come, Van Bibber was standing up over him and had driven his heel down on his hand and kicked the pistol out of his fingers. Then he stepped quickly to where it lay and picked it up and said, "Now, if you try to get up I'll shoot at you." He felt an unwarranted and ill-timedly humorous inclination to add, "and I'll probably miss you," but subdued it. The burglar, much to Van Bibber's astonishment, did not attempt to rise, but sat up with his hands locked across his knees and said: "Shoot ahead. I'd a damned sight rather you would."

His teeth were set and his face desperate and bitter, and hopeless to a degree of utter hopelessness that Van Bibber had never imagined.

"Go ahead," reiterated the man, doggedly, "I won't move. Shoot me."

It was a most unpleasant situation. Van Bibber felt the pistol loosening in his hand, and he was conscious of a strong inclination to lay it down and ask the burglar to tell him all about it.

"You haven't got much heart," said Van Bibber, finally. "You're a pretty poor sort of a burglar, I should say."

"What's the use?" said the man, fiercely. "I won't go back—I won't go back there alive. I've served my time forever in that hole. If I have to go back again—s'help me if I don't do for a keeper and die for it. But I won't serve there no more."

"Go back where?" asked Van Bibber, gently, and greatly interested; "to prison?"

"To prison, yes!" cried the man, hoarsely: "to a grave. That's where. Look at my face," he said, "and look at my hair. That ought to tell you where I've been. With all the colour gone out of my skin, and all the life out of my legs. You needn't be afraid of me. I couldn't hurt you if I wanted to. I'm a skeleton and a baby, I am. I couldn't kill a cat. And now you're going to send me back again for another lifetime. For twenty years, this time, into that cold, forsaken hole, and after I done my time so well and worked so hard." Van Bibber shifted the pistol from one hand to the other and eyed his prisoner doubtfully.

"How long have you been out?" he asked, seating himself on the steps of the kitchen and holding the revolver between his knees. The sun was driving the morning mist away, and he had forgotten the cold.

"I got out yesterday," said the man.

Van Bibber glanced at the bags and lifted the revolver. "You didn't waste much time," he said.

"No," answered the man, sullenly, "no, I didn't. I knew this place and I wanted money to get West to my folks, and the Society said I'd have to wait until I earned it, and I couldn't wait. I haven't seen my wife for seven years, nor my daughter. Seven years, young man; think of that—seven years. Do you know how long that is? Seven years without seeing your wife or your child! And they're straight people, they are," he added, hastily. "My wife moved West after I was put away and took another name, and my girl never knew nothing about me. She thinks I'm away at sea. I was to join 'em. That was the plan. I was to join 'em, and I thought I could lift enough here to get the fare, and now," he added, dropping his face in his hands, "I've got to go back. And I had meant to live straight after I got West—God help me, but I did! Not that it makes much difference now. An' I don't care whether you believe it or not neither," he added, fiercely.

"I didn't say whether I believed it or not," answered Van Bibber, with grave consideration.

He eyed the man for a brief space without speaking, and the burglar looked back at him, doggedly and defiantly, and with not the faintest suggestion of hope in his eyes, or of appeal for mercy. Perhaps it was because of this fact, or perhaps it was the wife and child that moved Van Bibber, but whatever his motives were, he acted on them promptly. "I suppose, though," he said, as though speaking to himself, "that I ought to give you up."

"I'll never go back alive," said the burglar, quietly.

"Well, that's bad, too," said Van Bibber. "Of course I don't know whether you're lying or not, and as to your meaning to live honestly, I very much doubt it; but I'll give you a ticket to wherever your wife is, and I'll see you on the train. And you can get off at the next station and rob my house to-morrow night, if you feel that way about it. Throw those bags inside that door where the servant will see them before the milkman does, and walk on out ahead of me, and keep your hands in your pockets, and don't try to run. I have your pistol, you know."

The man placed the bags inside the kitchen door; and, with a doubtful look at his custodian, stepped out into the street, and walked, as he was directed to do, toward the Grand Central station. Van Bibber kept just behind him, and kept turning the question over in his mind as to what he ought to do. He felt very guilty as he passed each policeman, but he recovered himself when he thought of the wife and child who lived in the West, and who were "straight."

"Where to?" asked Van Bibber, as he stood at the ticket-office window. "Helena, Montana," answered the man with, for the first time, a look of relief. Van Bibber bought the ticket and handed it to the burglar. "I suppose you know," he said, "that you can sell that at a place down-town for half the money." "Yes, I know that," said the burglar. There was a half-hour before the train left, and Van Bibber took his charge into the restaurant and watched him eat everything placed before him, with his eyes glancing all the while to the right or left. Then Van Bibber gave him some money and told him to write to him, and shook hands with him. The man nodded eagerly and pulled off his hat as the car drew out of the station; and Van Bibber came downtown again with the shop-girls and clerks going to work still wondering if he had done the right thing.

He went to his rooms and changed his clothes, took a cold bath, and crossed over to Delmonico's for his breakfast, and, while the waiter laid the cloth in the café, glanced at the headings in one of the papers. He scanned first with polite interest the account of the dance on the night previous and noticed his name among those present. With greater interest he read of the fight between "Dutchy" Mack and the "Black Diamond," and then he read carefully how "Abe" Hubbard, alias "Jimmie the Gent," a burglar, had broken jail in New Jersey, and had been traced to New York. There was a description of the man, and Van Bibber breathed quickly as he read it. "The detectives have a clue to his whereabouts," the account said; "if he is still in the city they are confident of recapturing him. But they fear that the same friends who helped him to break jail will probably assist him from the country or to get out West."

"They may do that," murmured Van Bibber to himself, with a smile of grim contentment; "they probably will."

Then he said to the waiter, "Oh, I don't know. Some bacon and eggs and green things and coffee."

THE GOD OF HIS FATHERS [1]

By JACK LONDON (1876–1910)

I

On every hand stretched the forest primeval—the home of noisy comedy and silent tragedy. Here the struggle for survival continued to wage with all its ancient brutality. Briton and Russian were still to overlap in the land of the Rainbow's End—and this was the very heart of it—nor had Yankee gold yet purchased its vast domain. The wolf pack still clung to the flank of the cariboo herd, singling out the weak and the big with calf, and pulling them down as remorselessly as it were a thousand, thousand generations into the past. The sparse aborigines still acknowledged the rule of their chiefs and medicine men, drove out bad spirits, burned their witches, fought their neighbours, and ate their enemies with a relish which spoke well of their bellies. But it was at the moment when the stone age was drawing to a close. Already, over unknown trails and chartless wildernesses, were the harbingers of the steel arriving—fair-faced, blue-eyed, indomitable men, incarnations of the unrest of their race. By accident or design, single-handed and in twos and threes, they came from no one knew whither, and fought, or died, or passed on, no one knew whence. The priests raged against them, the chiefs called forth their fighting men, and stone clashed with steel; but to little purpose. Like water seeping from some mighty reservoir they trickled through the dark forests and mountain passes, treading the highways in bark canoes, or with their moccasined feet breaking trail for the wolf-dogs.

[1] From *The God of His Fathers* by Jack London, copyright 1901 by Charmean Kittredge, London, and reprinted by permission of Doubleday, Doran & Co. Inc., publishers, and Hughes, Massie & Co.

They came of a great breed, and their mothers were many; but the fur-clad denizens of the Northland had this yet to learn. So many an unsung wanderer fought his last and died under the cold fire of the aurora, as did his brothers in burning sands and reeking jungles, and as they shall continue to do till in the fullness of time the destiny of their race be achieved.

It was near twelve. Along the northern horizon a rosy glow, fading to the west and deepening to the east, marked the unseen dip of the midnight sun. The gloaming and the dawn were so commingled that there was no night—simply a wedding of day with day, a scarcely perceptible blending of two circles of the sun. A kildee timidly chirped good-night; the full, rich throat of a robin proclaimed good-morrow. From an island on the breast of the Yukon a colony of wild fowl voiced its interminable wrongs, while a loon laughed mockingly back across a still stretch of river.

In the foreground, against the bank of a lazy eddy, birch-bark canoes were lined two and three deep. Ivory-bladed spears, bone-barbed arrows, buckskin-thonged bows, and simple basket-woven traps bespoke the fact that in the muddy current of the river the salmon-run was on. In the background, from the tangle of skin tents and drying frames, rose the voices of the fisher-folk. Bucks skylarked with bucks or flirted with the maidens, while the older squaws, shut out from this by virtue of having fulfilled the end of their existence in reproduction, gossiped as they braided rope from the green roots of trailing vines. At their feet their naked progeny played and squabbled, or rolled in the muck with the tawny wolf-dogs.

To one side of the encampment, and conspicuously apart from it, stood a second camp of two tents. But it was a white man's camp. If nothing else, the choice of position at least bore convincing evidence of this. In case of offence, it commanded the Indian quarters a hundred yards away; of defence, a rise to the ground and the cleared intervening space; and last, of defeat, the swift slope of a score of yards to the canoes below.

From one of the tents came the petulant cry of a sick child and the crooning song of a mother. In the open, over the smouldering embers of a fire, two men held talk.

"Eh! I love the church like a good son. *Bien !* So great a love that my days have been spent in fleeing away from her, and my nights in dreaming dreams of reckoning. Look you!" The half-breed's voice rose to an angry snarl. "I am Red River born. My father was white—as white as you. But you are Yankee, and he was British bred, and a gentleman's son. And my mother was the daughter of a chief, and I was a man. Ay, and one had to look the second time to see what manner of blood ran in my veins; for I lived with the whites, and was one of them, and my father's heart beat in me. It happened there was a maiden—white—who looked on me with kind eyes. Her father had much land and many horses; also he was a big man among his people, and his blood was the blood of the French. He said the girl knew not her own mind, and talked over-much with her, and became wroth that such things should be.

"But she knew her mind, for we came quick before the priest. And quicker had come her father, with lying words, false promises, I know not what; so that the priest stiffened his neck and would not make us that we might live one with the other. As at the beginning it was the church which would not bless my birth, so now it was the church which refused me marriage and put the blood of men upon my hands. *Bien !* Thus have I cause to love the church. So I struck the priest on his woman's mouth, and we took swift horses, the girl and I, to Fort Pierre, where was a minister of good heart. But hot on our trail was her father, and brothers, and other men he had gathered to him. And we fought, our horses on the run, till I emptied three saddles and the rest drew off, and went on to Fort Pierre. Then we took east, the girl and I, to the hills and forests, and we lived one with the other, and we were not married—the work of the good church which I love like a son.

"But mark you, for this is the strangeness of woman, the way of which no man may understand. One of the saddles I emptied was that of her father, and the hoofs of those who came behind had pounded him into the earth. This we saw, the girl and I, and this I had forgot had she not remembered. And in the quiet of the evening, after the day's hunt were done, it came between us, and in the silence of the night when we lay beneath the stars and should have been one. It was there always. She never spoke, but it sat by our fire and held us ever apart. She tried to put it aside; but at such times it would rise up till I could read it in the look of her eyes, in the very intake of her breath.

"So in the end she bore me a child, a woman-child, and died. Then I went among my mother's people, that it might nurse at a warm breast and live. But my hands were wet with the blood of men, look you, because of the church, wet with the blood of men. And the riders of the North came for me, but my mother's brother, who was then chief in his own right, hid me and gave me horses and food. And we went away, my woman-child and I, even to the Hudson Bay Country, where white men were few and the questions they asked not many. And I worked for the company as a hunter, as a guide, as a driver of dogs, till my woman-child was become a woman, tall and slender, and fair to the eye.

"You know the winter, long and lonely, breeding evil thoughts and bad deeds. The chief factor was a hard man, and bold. And he was not such that a woman would delight in looking upon. But he cast eyes upon my woman-child who was become a woman. Mother of God! he sent me away on a long trip with the dogs, that he might—you understand, he was a hard man and without heart. She was most white, and her soul was white, and a good woman, and—well, she died.

"It was bitter cold the night of my return and I had been away months, and the dogs were limping sore when

I came to the fort. The Indians and breeds looked on me in silence, and I felt the fear of I knew not what, but I said nothing till the dogs were fed and I had eaten as a man with work before him should. Then I spoke up, demanding the word, and they shrank from me, afraid of my anger and what I should do; but the story came out, the pitiful story, word for word and act for act, and they marvelled that I should be so quiet.

"When they had done I went to the factor's house, calmer than now in the telling of it. He had been afraid, and called upon the breeds to help him; but they were not pleased with the deed, and had left him to lie on the bed he had made. So he had fled to the house of the priest. Thither I followed. But when I was come to that place, the priest stood in my way, and spoke soft words, and said a man in anger should go neither to the right nor left, but straight to God. I asked by the right of a father's wrath that he give me past, but he said only over his body, and besought with me to pray. Look you, it was the church, always the church; for I passed over his body and sent the factor to meet my woman-child before his god, which is a bad god, and the god of the white men.

"Then was there hue and cry, for word was sent to the station below, and I came away. Through the Land of the Great Slave, down the Valley of the Mackenzie to the never-opening ice, over the White Rockies, past the Great Curve of the Yukon, even to this place did I come. And from that day to this, yours is the first face of my father's people I have looked upon. May it be the last! These people, which are my people, are a simple folk, and I have been raised to honour among them. My word is their law, and their priests but do my bidding, else would I not suffer them. When I speak for them I speak for myself. We ask to be let alone. We do not want your kind. If we permit you to sit by our fires, after you will come your church, your priests, and your gods. And know this, for each white man who comes to my village, him will I make deny his god. You are the first, and I give you grace. So it were well you go, and go quickly."

"I am not responsible for my brothers," the second man spoke up, filling his pipe in a meditative manner. Hay Stockard was at times as thoughtful of speech as he was wanton of action; but only at times.

"But I know your breed," responded the other. "Your brothers are many, and it is you and yours who break the trail for them to follow. In time they shall come to possess the land, but not in my time. Already, have I heard, are they on the head-reaches of the Great River, and far away below are the Russians."

Hay Stockard lifted his head with a quick start. This was startling geographical information. The Hudson Bay post at Fort Yukon had other notions concerning the course of the river, believing it to flow into the Arctic.

"Then the Yukon empties into Bering Sea?" he asked.

"I do not know, but below there are Russians, many Russians. Which is neither here nor there. You may go on and see for yourself; you may go back to your brothers; but up the Koyukuk you shall not go while the priests and fighting men do my bidding. Thus do I command, I, Baptiste the Red, whose word is law and who am head man over this people."

"And should I not go down to the Russians, or back to my brothers?"

"Then shall you go swift-footed before your god, which is a bad god, and the god of the white men."

The red sun shot up above the northern skyline, dripping and bloody. Baptiste the Red came to his feet, nodded curtly, and went back to his camp amid the crimson shadows and the singing of the robins.

Hay Stockard finished his pipe by the fire, picturing in smoke and coal the unknown upper reaches of the Koyukuk, the strange stream which ended here its arctic travels and merged its waters with the muddy Yukon flood. Somewhere up there, if the dying words of a shipwrecked sailorman, who had made the fearful overland journey, were to be believed, and if the vial of golden grains in his pouch attested anything—somewhere up there, in that home of winter, stood the Treasure House of the North. And as keeper of the gate, Baptiste the Red, English half-breed and renegade, barred the way.

"Bah!" He kicked the embers apart and rose to his full height, arms lazily outstretched, facing the flushing north with careless soul.

II

Hay Stockard swore, harshly, in the rugged monosyllables of his mother tongue. His wife lifted her gaze from the pots and pins, and followed his in a keen scrutiny of the river. She was a woman of the Teslin Country, wise in the ways of her husband's vernacular when it grew intensive. From the slipping of a snow-shoe thong to the forefront of sudden death, she could gauge occasion by the pitch and volume of his blasphemy. So she knew the present occasion merited attention. A long canoe, with paddles flashing back the rays of the westering sun, was crossing the current from above and urging in for the eddy. Hay Stockard watched it intently. Three men rose and dipped, rose and dipped, in rhythmical precision; but a red bandanna, wrapped about the head of one, caught and held his eye.

"Bill!" he called. "Oh, Bill!"

A shambling, loose-jointed giant rolled out of one of the tents, yawning and rubbing the sleep from his eyes. Then he sighted the strange canoe and was wide awake on the instant.

"By the jumping Methuselah! That damned sky-pilot!"

Hay Stockard nodded his head bitterly, half-reached for his rifle, then shrugged his shoulders.

"Pot-shot him," Bill suggested, "and settle the thing out of hand. He'll spoil us sure if we don't."

But the other declined this drastic measure and turned away, at the same time bidding the woman return to her work, and calling Bill back from the bank. The two Indians in the canoe moored it on the edge of the eddy, while its white occupant, conspicuous by his gorgeous headgear, came up the bank.

"Like Paul of Tarsus, I give you greeting. Peace be unto you and grace before the Lord."

His advances were met sullenly, and without speech.

"To you, Hay Stockard, blasphemer and Philistine, greeting. In your heart is the lust of Mammon, in your mind cunning devils, in your tent this woman whom you live with in adultery; yet of these divers sins, even here in the wilderness, I, Sturges Owen, apostle to the Lord, bid you to repent and cast from you your iniquities."

"Save your cant! Save your cant!" Hay Stockard broke in testily. "You'll need all you've got, and more, for the Red Baptiste over yonder."

He waved his hand toward the Indian camp, where the half-breed was looking steadily across, striving to make out the new-comers. Sturges Owen, disseminator of light and apostle to the Lord, stepped to the edge of the steep and commanded his men to bring up the camp outfit. Stockard followed him.

"Look here," he demanded, plucking the missionary by the shoulder and twirling him about. "Do you value your hide?"

"My life is in the Lord's keeping, and I do but work in His vineyard," he replied solemnly.

"Oh, stow that! Are you looking for a job of martyrship?"

"If He so wills."

"Well, you'll find it right here, but I'm going to give you some advice first. Take it or leave it. If you stop here, you'll be cut off in the midst of your labours. And not you alone, but your men, Bill, my wife——"

"Who is a daughter of Belial and hearkeneth not to the true Gospel."

"And myself. Not only do you bring trouble upon yourself, but upon us. I was frozen in with you last winter, as you will well recollect, and I know you for a good man and a fool. If you think it your duty to strive with the heathen, well and good; but do exercise some wit in the way you go about it. This man, Red Baptiste, is no Indian. He comes of our common stock, is as bull-necked as I ever dared be, and as wild a fanatic the one way as you are the other. When you two come together, hell'll be to pay, and I don't care to be mixed up in it. Understand? So take my advice and go away. If you go down-stream, you'll fall in with the Russians. There's bound to be Greek priests among them, and they'll see you safe through to Bering Sea—that's where the Yukon empties—and from there it won't be hard to get back to civilisation. Take my word for it, and get out of here as fast as God'll let you."

"He who carries the Lord in his heart and the Gospel in his hand hath no fear of the machinations of man or devil," the missionary answered stoutly. "I will see this man and wrestle with him. One backslider returned to the fold is a greater victory than a thousand heathen. He who is strong for evil can be as mighty for good, witness Saul when he journeyed up to Damascus to bring Christian captives to Jerusalem. And the voice of the Saviour came to him, crying, 'Saul, Saul, why persecutest thou Me?' And therewith Paul arrayed himself on the side of the Lord, and thereafter was most mighty in the saving of souls. And even as thou, Paul of Tarsus, even so do I work in the vineyard of the Lord, bearing trials and tribulations, scoffs and sneers, stripes and punishments, for His dear sake."

"Bring up the little bag with the tea and a kettle of water," he called the next instant to his boatmen; "not forgetting the haunch of cariboo and the mixing-pan."

When his men, converts by his own hand, had gained the bank, the trio fell to their knees, hands and backs burdened with camp equipage, and offered up thanks for their passage through the wilderness and their safe arrival. Hay Stockard looked upon the function with sneering disapproval, the romance and solemnity of it lost to his matter-of-fact soul. Baptiste the Red, still gazing across, recognised the familiar postures, and remembered the girl who had shared his star-roofed couch in the hills and forests, and the woman-child who lay somewhere by bleak Hudson's Bay.

III

"Confound it, Baptiste, couldn't think of it. Not for a moment. Grant that this man is a fool and of small use in the nature of things; but still, you know, I can't give him up."

Hay Stockard paused, striving to put into speech the rude ethics of his heart.

"He's worried me, Baptiste, in the past and now, and caused me all manner of troubles; but can't you see, he's my own breed—white—and—and—why, I couldn't buy my life with his, not if he was a nigger."

"So be it," Baptiste the Red made answer. "I have given you grace and choice. I shall come presently, with my priests and fighting men, and either shall I kill you, or you deny your god. Give up the priest to my pleasure, and you shall depart in peace. Otherwise your trail ends here. My people are against you to the babies. Even now have the children stolen away your canoes."

He pointed down to the river. Naked boys had slipped down the water from the point above, cast loose the canoes, and by then had worked them into the current. When they had drifted out of rifle-shot they clambered over the sides and paddled ashore.

"Give me the priest, and you may have them back again. Come! Speak your mind, but without haste."

Stockard shook his head. His glance dropped to the woman of the Teslin Country with his boy at her breast, and he would have wavered had he not lifted his eyes to the men before him.

"I am not afraid," Sturges Owen spoke up. "The Lord bears me in His right hand, and alone am I ready to go into the camp of the unbeliever. It is not too late.

Faith may move mountains. Even in the eleventh hour may I win his soul to the true righteousness."

"No," Stockard answered. "I gave him my word that he could speak with us unmolested. Rules of warfare, Bill; rules of warfare. He's been on the square, given us warning, and all that, and—why, damn it, man, I can't break my word."

"He'll keep his, never fear."

"Don't doubt it, but I won't let a half-breed outdo me in fair dealing. Why not do what he wants,—give him the missionary and be done with it?"

"N-no," Bill hesitated doubtfully.

"Shoe pinches, eh?"

Bill flushed a little and dropped the discussion. Baptiste the Red was still waiting the final decision. Stockard went up to him.

"It's this way, Baptiste. I came to your village minded to go up the Koyukuk. I intended no wrong. My heart was clean of evil. It is still clean. Along comes this priest, as you call him. I didn't bring him here. He'd have come whether I was here or not. But now that he is here, being of my people, I've got to stand by him. And I'm going to. Further, it will be no child's play. When you have done, your village will be silent and empty, your people wasted as after a famine. True, we will be gone; likewise the pick of your fighting men——"

"But those who remain shall be in peace, nor shall the word of strange gods and the tongue of strange priests be buzzing in their ears."

Both men shrugged their shoulders and turned away, the half-breed going back to his own camp. The missionary called his two men to him, and they fell into prayer. Stockard and Bill attacked the few standing pines with their axes, felling them into convenient breastworks. The child had fallen asleep, so the woman placed it on a heap of furs and lent a hand in fortifying the camp. Three sides were thus defended, the steep declivity at the rear precluding attack from that direction. When these arrangements had been completed, the two men stalked into the open, clearing away, here and there, the scattered under-brush. From the opposing camp came the booming of war-drums and the voices of the priests stirring the people to anger.

"Worst of it is they'll come in rushes," Bill complained, as they walked back with shouldered axes.

"And wait till midnight, when the light gets dim for shooting."

"Can't start the ball a-rolling too early, then." Bill exchanged the axe for a rifle, and took a careful rest. One of the medicine-men, towering above his tribesmen, stood out distinctly. Bill drew a bead on him.

"All ready?" he asked.

Stockard opened the ammunition box, placed the woman where she could reload in safety, and gave the word. The medicine-man dropped. For a moment there was silence, then a wild howl went up and a flight of bone arrows fell short.

"I'd like to take a look at the beggar," Bill remarked throwing a fresh shell into place. "I'll swear I drilled him clean between the eyes."

"Didn't work." Stockard shook his head gloomily. Baptiste had evidently quelled the more warlike of his followers, and instead of precipitating an attack in the bright light of day, the shot had caused a hasty exodus, the Indians drawing out of the village beyond the zone of fire.

In the full tide of his proselytising fervour, borne along by the hand of God, Sturges Owen would have ventured alone into the camp of the unbeliever, equally prepared for miracle or martyrdom; but in the waiting which ensued, the fever of conviction died away gradually, as the natural man asserted itself. Physical fear replaced spiritual hope; the love of life, the love of God. It was no new experience. He could feel his weakness coming on, and knew it of old time. He had struggled against it and been overcome by it before. He remembered when the other men had driven their paddles like mad in the van of a roaring ice-flood, how, at the critical moment, in a panic of worldly terror, he had dropped his paddle and besought wildly with his

God for pity. And there were other times. The recollection was not pleasant. It brought shame to him that his spirit should be so weak and his flesh so strong. But the love of life! the love of life! He could not strip it from him. Because of it had his dim ancestors perpetuated their line; because of it was he destined to perpetuate his. His courage, if courage it might be called, was bred of fanaticism. The courage of Stockard and Bill was the adherence to deep-rooted ideals. Not that the love of life was less, but the love of race tradition more! not that they were unafraid to die, but that they were brave enough not to live at the price of shame.

The missionary rose, for the moment swayed by the mood of sacrifice. He half crawled over the barricade to proceed to the other camp, but sank back, a trembling mass, wailing. "As the spirit moves! As the spirit moves! Who am I that I should set aside the judgments of God? Before the foundations of the world were all things written in the book of life. Worm that I am, shall I erase the page or any portion thereof? As God wills, so shall the spirit move!"

Bill reached over, plucked him to his feet, and shook him, fiercely, silently. Then he dropped the bundle of quivering nerves and turned his attention to the two converts. But they showed little fright and a cheerful alacrity in preparing for the coming passage at arms.

Stockard, who had been talking in undertones with the Teslin woman, now turned to the missionary.

"Fetch him over here," he commanded of Bill.

"Now," he ordered, when Sturges Owen had been duly deposited before him, "make us man and wife, and be lively about it." Then he added apologetically to Bill: "No telling how it's to end, so I just thought I'd get my affairs straightened up."

The woman obeyed the behest of her white lord. To her the ceremony was meaningless. By her lights she was his wife, and had been from the day they first foregathered. The converts served as witnesses. Bill stood over the missionary, prompting him when he stumbled. Stockard put the responses in the woman's mouth, and when the time came, for want of better, ringed her finger with thumb and forefinger of his own.

"Kiss the bride!" thundered Bill, and Sturges Owen was too weak to disobey.

"Now baptise the child!"

"Neat and tidy," Bill commented.

"Gathering the proper outfit for a new trail," the father explained, taking the boy from the mother's arms. "I was grub-staked, once, into the Cascades, and had everything in the kit except salt. Never shall forget it. And if the woman and the kid cross the divide to-night they might as well be prepared for pot-luck. A long shot, Bill, between ourselves, but nothing lost if it misses."

A cup of water served the purpose, and the child was laid away in a secure corner of the barricade. The men built the fire, and the evening meal was cooked.

The sun hurried round to the north, sinking closer to the horizon. The heavens in that quarter grew red and bloody. The shadows lengthened, the light dimmed, and in the sombre recesses of the forest, life slowly died away. Even the wild fowl in the river softened their raucous chatter and feigned the nightly farce of going to bed. Only the tribesmen increased their clamour, war-drums booming and voices raised in savage folk-songs. But as the sun dipped they ceased their tumult. The rounded hush of midnight was complete. Stockard rose to his knees and peered over the logs. Once the child wailed in pain and disconcerted him. The mother bent over it, but it slept again. The silence was interminable, profound. Then, of a sudden, the robins burst into full-throated song. The night had passed.

A flood of dark figures boiled across the open. Arrows whistled and bow-thongs sang. The shrill-tongued rifles answered back. A spear, and a mighty cast, transfixed the Teslin woman as she hovered above the child. A spent arrow, diving between the logs, lodged in the missionary's arm.

There was no stopping the rush. The middle distance was cumbered with bodies, but the rest surged on, breaking against and over the barricade like an ocean wave. Sturges Owen fled to the tent, while the men were swept from their feet, buried beneath the human tide. Hay Stockard alone regained the surface, flinging the tribesmen aside like yelping curs. He had managed to seize an axe. A dark hand grasped the child by a naked foot, and drew it from beneath its mother. At arm's length its puny body circled through the air, dashing to death against the logs. Stockard clove the man to the chin and fell to clearing space. The ring of savage faces closed in, raining upon him spear-thrusts and bone-barbed arrows. The sun shot up, and they swayed back and forth in the crimson shadows. Twice, with his axe blocked by too deep a blow, they rushed him; but each time he flung them clear. They fell under foot and he trampled dead and dying, the way slippery with blood. And still the day brightened and the robins sang. Then they drew back from him in awe, and he leaned breathless upon his axe.

"Blood of my soul!" cried Baptiste the Red. "But thou art a man. Deny thy god, and thou shalt yet live."

Stockard swore his refusal, feebly but with grace.

"Behold! A woman!" Sturges Owen had been brought before the half-breed.

Beyond a scratch on the arm, he was uninjured, but his eyes roved about him in an ecstasy of fear. The heroic figure of the blasphemer, bristling with wounds and arrows, leaning defiantly upon his axe, indifferent, indomitable, superb, caught his wavering vision. And he felt a great envy of the man who could go down serenely to the dark gates of death. Surely Christ, and not he, Sturges Owen, had been moulded in such manner. And why not he? He felt dimly the curse of ancestry, the feebleness of spirit which had come down to him out of the past, and he felt an anger at the creative force, symbolise it as he would, which had formed him, its servant, so weakly. For even a stronger man, this anger and the stress of circumstance were sufficient to breed apostasy, and for Sturges Owen it was inevitable. In the fear of man's anger he would dare the wrath of God. He had been raised up to serve the Lord only that he might be cast down. He had been given faith without the strength of faith; he had been given spirit without the power of spirit. It was unjust.

"Where now is thy god?" the half-breed demanded.

"I do not know." He stood straight and rigid, like a child, repeating a catechism.

"Hast thou then a god at all?"

"I had."

"And now?"

"No."

Hay Stockard swept the blood from his eyes and laughed. The missionary looked at him curiously, as in a dream. A feeling of infinite distance came over him, as though of a great remove. In that which had transpired, and which was to transpire, he had no part. He was a spectator—at a distance, yes, at a distance. The words of Baptiste came to him faintly:

"Very good. See that this man go free, and that no harm befall him. Let him depart in peace. Give him a canoe and food. Set his face toward the Russians, that he may tell their priests of Baptiste the Red, in whose country there is no god."

They led him to the edge of the steep, where they paused to witness the final tragedy. The half-breed turned to Hay Stockard.

"There is no god," he prompted.

The man laughed in reply. One of the young men poised a war-spear for the cast.

"Hast thou a god?"

"Ay, the God of my fathers."

He shifted the axe for a better grip. Baptiste the Red gave the sign, and the spear hurtled full against his breast. Sturges Owen saw the ivory head stand out beyond his back, saw the man sway, laughing, and snap the shaft short as he fell upon it. Then he went down to the river, that he might carry to the Russians the message of Baptiste the Red, in whose country there was no god.

THE FURNISHED ROOM [1]

By O. HENRY (1867–1910)

RESTLESS, shifting, fugacious as time itself is a certain vast bulk of the population of the red brick district of the lower West Side. Homeless, they have a hundred homes. They flit from furnished room to furnished room, transients for ever—transients in abode, transients in heart and mind. They sing "Home Sweet Home" in ragtime; they carry their *lares et penates* in a bandbox; their vine is entwined about a picture hat; a rubber plant is their fig tree.

Hence the houses of this district, having had a thousand dwellers, should have a thousand tales to tell, mostly dull ones, no doubt; but it would be strange if there could not be found a ghost or two in the wake of all these vagrant ghosts.

One evening after dark a young man prowled among these crumbling red mansions, ringing their bells. At the twelfth he rested his lean hand-baggage upon the step and wiped the dust from his hat-band and forehead. The bell sounded faint and far away in some remote, hollow depths.

To the door of this, the twelfth house whose bell he had rung, came a housekeeper who made him think of an unwholesome, surfeited worm that had eaten its nut to a hollow shell and now sought to fill the vacancy with edible lodgers.

He asked if there was a room to let.

"Come in," said the housekeeper. Her voice came from her throat; her throat seemed lined with fur. "I have the third floor back, vacant since a week back. Should you wish to look at it?"

[1] From *The Four Million*. Copyright, 1904, by Doubleday, Doran & Co. Published in England by Hodder & Stoughton.

The young man followed her up the stairs. A faint light from no particular source mitigated the shadows of the halls. They trod noiselessly upon a stair carpet that its own loom would have forsworn. It seemed to have become vegetable; to have degenerated in that rank, sunless air to lush lichen or spreading moss that grew in patches to the staircase and was viscid under the foot like organic matter. At each turn of the stairs were vacant niches in the wall. Perhaps plants had once been set within them. If so, they had died in that foul and tainted air. It may be that statues of the saints had stood there; but it was not difficult to conceive that imps and devils had dragged them forth in the darkness and down to the unholy depths of some furnished pit below.

"This is the room," said the housekeeper, from her furry throat. "It's a nice room. It ain't often vacant. I had some most elegant people in it last summer—no trouble at all, and paid in advance to the minute. The water's at the end of the hall. Sprowls and Mooney kept it three months. They done a vaudeville sketch. Miss B'retta Sprowls—you may have heard of her—Oh, that was just the stage names—right there over the dresser is where the marriage certificate hung, framed. The gas is here, and you see there is plenty of closet room. It's a room everybody likes. It never stays idle long."

"Do you have many theatrical people rooming here?" asked the young man.

"They comes and goes. A good proportion of my lodgers is connected with the theatres. Yes, sir, this is the theatrical district. Actor people never stays long anywhere. I get my share. Yes, they comes and they goes."

He engaged the room, paying for a week in advance. He was tired, he said, and would take possession at once. He counted out the money. The room had been made ready, she said, even to towels and water. As the housekeeper moved away he put, for the thousandth time, the question that he carried at the end of his tongue.

"A young girl—Miss Vashner—Miss Eloise Vashner
—do you remember such a one among your lodgers?
She would be singing on the stage, most likely. A fair
girl, of medium height and slender, with reddish, gold
hair and a dark mole near her left eyebrow."

"No, I don't remember the name. Them stage people
has names they change as often as their rooms. They
comes and they goes. No, I don't call that one to mind."

No. Always no. Five months of ceaseless interro-
gation and the inevitable negative. So much time spent
by day in questioning managers, agents, schools, and
choruses; by night among the audiences of theatres
from all-star casts down to music halls so low that he
dreaded to find what he most hoped for. He who had
loved her best had tried to find her. He was sure that
since her disappearance from home this great water-
girt city held her somewhere, but it was like a monstrous
quicksand, shifting its particles constantly, with no
foundation, its upper granules of to-day buried to-
morrow in ooze and slime.

The furnished room received its latest guest with a
first glow of pseudo-hospitality, a hectic, haggard,
perfunctory welcome like the specious smile of a
demi-rep. The sophistical comfort came in reflected
gleams from the decayed furniture, the ragged brocade
upholstery of a couch and two chairs, a foot-wide cheap
pier glass between the two windows; from one or two
gilt picture frames, and a brass bedstead in a corner.

The guest reclined, inert, upon a chair, while the
room, confused in speech as though it were an apartment in Babel, tried to discourse to him of its divers
tenantry.

A polychromatic rug like some brilliant-flowered
rectangular tropical islet lay surrounded by a billowy
sea of soiled matting. Upon the gay-papered wall
were those pictures that pursue the homeless one from
house to house—The Huguenot Lovers, The First
Quarrel, The Wedding Breakfast, Psyche at the Fountain. The mantel's chastely severe outline was in-
gloriously veiled behind some pert drapery drawn

rakishly askew like the sashes of the Amazonian ballet.
Upon it was some desolate flotsam cast aside by the
room's marooned when a lucky sail had borne them to
a fresh port—a trifling vase or two, pictures of actresses,
a medicine bottle, some stray cards out of a deck.

One by one, as the characters of a cryptograph become
explicit, the little signs left by the furnished room's
procession of guests developed a significance. The
threadbare space in the rug in front of the dresser told
that lovely woman had marched in the throng. Tiny
finger prints on the wall spoke of little prisoners trying
to feel their way to sun and air. A splattered stain,
raying like the shadow of a bursting bomb, witnessed
where a hurled glass or bottle had splintered with its
contents against the wall. Across the pier glass had
been scrawled with a diamond in staggering letters the
name "Marie." It seemed that the succession of
dwellers in the furnished room had turned in fury—
perhaps tempted beyond forbearance by its garish
coldness—and wreaked upon it their passions. The
furniture was chipped and bruised; the couch, distorted
by bursting springs, seemed a horrible monster that
had been slain during the stress of some grotesque
convulsion. Some more potent upheaval had cloven
a great slice from the marble mantel. Each plank
in the floor owned its particular cant and shriek as
from a separate and individual agony. It seemed
incredible that all this malice and injury had been
wrought upon the room by those who had called it for
a time their home; and yet it may have been the cheated
home instinct surviving blindly, the resentful rage at
false household gods that had kindled their wrath. A
hut that is our own we can sweep and adorn and cherish.

The young tenant in the chair allowed these thoughts
to file, soft-shod, through his mind, while there drifted
into the room furnished sounds and furnished scents.
He heard in one room a tittering and incontinent, slack
laughter; in others the monologue of a scold, the rattling
of a dice, a lullaby, and one crying dully; above him a
banjo tinkled with spirit. Doors banged somewhere;

the elevated trains roared intermittently; a cat yowled
miserably upon a back fence. And he breathed the
breath of the house—a dank savour rather than a
smell—a cold, musty effluvium as from underground
vaults mingled with the reeking exhalations of linoleum
and mildewed and rotten woodwork.

Then, suddenly, as he rested there, the room was
filled with the strong, sweet odour of mignonette. It
came as upon a single buffet of wind with such sureness
and fragrance and emphasis that it almost seemed a
living visitant. And the man cried aloud: "What,
dear?" as if he had been called, and sprang up and
faced about. The rich odour clung to him and wrapped
him about. He reached out his arms for it, all his
senses for the time confused and commingled. How
could one be peremptorily called by an odour? Surely
it must have been a sound. But, was it not the sound
that had touched, that had caressed him?

"She has been in this room," he cried; and he sprang
to wrest from it a token, for he knew he would recognise
the smallest thing that had belonged to her or that she
had touched. This enveloping scent of mignonette,
the odour that she had loved and made her own—
whence came it?

The room had been but carelessly set in order.
Scattered upon the flimsy dresser scarf were half a
dozen hairpins—those discreet, indistinguishable friends
of womankind, feminine of gender, infinite of mood and
uncommunicative of tense. These he ignored, conscious
of their triumphant lack of identity. Ransacking the
drawers of the dresser he came upon a discarded, tiny,
ragged handkerchief. He pressed it to his face. It
was racy and insolent with heliotrope; he hurled it to
the floor. In another drawer he found odd buttons, a
theatre programme, a pawnbroker's card, two lost
marsh-mallows, a book on the divination of dreams.
In the last was a woman's black satin hair-bow, which
halted him, poised between ice and fire. But the black
satin hair-bow also is femininity's demure, impersonal,
common ornament, and tells no tales.

And then he traversed the room like a hound on the scent, skimming the walls, considering the corners of the bulging matting on his hands and knees, rummaging mantel and tables, the curtains and hangings, the drunken cabinet in the corner, for a visible sign unable to perceive that she was there beside, around, against, within, above him, clinging to him, wooing him, calling him so poignantly through the finer senses that even his grosser ones became cognisant of the call. Once again he answered loudly: "Yes, dear!" and turned, wild-eyed, to gaze on vacancy, for he could not yet discern form and colour and love and outstretched arms in the odour of mignonette. Oh, God! whence that odour, and since when have odours had a voice to call? Thus he groped.

He burrowed in crevices and corners, and found corks and cigarettes. These he passed in passive contempt. But once he found in a fold of the matting a half-smoked cigar, and this he ground beneath his heel with a green and trenchant oath. He sifted the room from end to end. He found dreary and ignoble small records of many a peripatetic tenant; but of her whom he sought, and who may have lodged there, and whose spirit seemed to hover there, he found no trace.

And then he thought of the housekeeper.

He ran from the haunted room downstairs and to a door that showed a crack of light. She came out to his knock. He smothered his excitement as best he could.

"Will you tell me, madam," he besought her, "who occupied the room I have before I came?"

"Yes, sir. I can tell you again. 'Twas Sprowls and Mooney, as I said. Miss B'retta Sprowls it was in the theatres, but Missis Mooney she was. My house is well known for respectability. The marriage certificate hung, framed, on a nail over——"

"What kind of a lady was Miss Sprowls—in looks, I mean?"

"Why, black-haired, sir, short and stout, with a comical face. They left a week ago Tuesday."

"And before they occupied it?"

"Why, there was a single gentleman connected with the draying business. He left owing me a week. Before him was Missis Crowder and her two children, that stayed four months; and back of them was old Mr. Doyle, whose sons paid for him. He kept the room six months. That goes back a year, sir, and further I do not remember."

He thanked her and crept back to his room. The room was dead. The essence that had vivified it was gone. The perfume of mignonette had departed. In its place was the old, stale odour of mouldy house furniture, of atmosphere in storage.

The ebbing of his hope drained his faith. He sat staring at the yellow, singing gaslight. Soon he walked to the bed and began to tear the sheets into strips. With the blade of his knife he drove them tightly into every crevice around windows and door. When all was snug and taut he turned out the light, turned the gas full on again and laid himself gratefully upon the bed.

.   .   .   .

It was Mrs. McCool's night to go with the can for beer. So she fetched it and sat with Mrs. Purdy in one of those subterranean retreats where housekeepers foregather and the worm dieth seldom.

"I rented out my third floor back, this evening," said Mrs. Purdy, across a fine circle of foam. "A young man took it. He went up to bed two hours ago."

"Now did ye, Mrs. Purdy, ma'am?" said Mrs. McCool, with intense admiration. "You do be a wonder for rentin' rooms of that kind. And did ye tell him, then?" she concluded in a husky whisper, laden with mystery.

"Rooms," said Mrs. Purdy, in her furriest tones, "are furnished for to rent. I did not tell him, Mrs. McCool."

"'Tis right ye are, ma'am; 'tis by renting rooms we kape alive. Ye have the rale sense for business, ma'am. There be many people will rayjict the rentin' of a room if they be tould a suicide has been after dyin' in the bed of it."

"As you say, we has our living to be making," remarked Mrs. Purdy.

"Yis, ma'am; 'tis true. 'Tis just one wake ago this day I helped ye lay out the third floor back. A pretty slip of a colleen she was to be killin' herself wid the gas —a swate little face she had, Mrs. Purdy, ma'am."

"She'd a-been called handsome, as you say," said Mrs. Purdy, assenting but critical, "but for that mole she had a-growin' by her left eyebrow. Do fill up your glass again, Mrs. McCool."